About the Authors

Yahrah St. John is the author of forty-four published books and won an award from *RT* Book Reviews in 2013 for *A Chance with You*. She earned a Bachelor of Arts degree in English from Northwestern University. A member of Romance Writers of America, St. John is an avid reader, enjoys cooking, travelling and adventure sports, but her true passion is writing. Visit: yahrahstjohn.com

USA Today bestselling author **Heidi Betts** writes sexy, sassy, sensational romance. The recipient of several awards and stellar reviews, Heidi's books combine believable characters with compelling plotlines, and are consistently described as 'delightful,' 'sizzling,' and 'wonderfully witty.'

Cathy Williams is a great believer in the power of perseverance as she had never written anything before her writing career. From the starting point of zero, she has now fulfilled her ambition to pursue this most enjoyable of careers. She would encourage any would-be writer to have faith and go for it! She derives inspiration from the tropical island of Trinidad and from the peaceful countryside of middle England. Cathy lives in Warwickshire with her family.

Sinfully Yours

Sinfully Yours:
The Boss

YAHRAH ST. JOHN

HEIDI BETTS

CATHY WILLIAMS

MILLS & BOON

First Published in Great Britain 2023
by Mills & Boon, an imprint of HarperCollins*Publishers* Ltd,
1 London Bridge Street, London, SE1 9GF

www.harpercollins.co.uk

HarperCollins*Publishers*
Macken House, 39/40 Mayor Street Upper,
Dublin 1, D01 C9W8, Ireland

Sinfully Yours: The Boss © 2023 Harlequin Enterprises ULC.

At the CEO's Pleasure © 2018 Yahrah Yisrael
Secrets, Lies & Lullabies © 2012 Heidi Betts
Her Impossible Boss © 2011 Cathy Williams

ISBN: 978-0-263-31963-7

This book is produced from independently certified FSC™ paper
to ensure responsible forest management.

For more information visit: www.harpercollins.co.uk/green

Printed and Bound in the UK using 100% Renewable Electricity
at CPI Group (UK) Ltd, Croydon, CR0 4YY

AT THE CEO'S PLEASURE

YAHRAH ST. JOHN

To my agent, Christine Witthohn, for her hard work in
helping me move to the Desire line.

One

Ayden Stewart stared out at the Austin city skyline from the fiftieth floor of Stewart Investments. It had taken him fifteen years since graduating from Harvard to build his company, but at thirty-six, he'd finally achieved his goal. And he'd done it all on his own. Without the help of his father, Henry Stewart, a rich man who'd never bothered to acknowledge his eldest son's existence, not after his second wife had given him two heirs for his own company, Stewart Technologies. It was just as well. He'd long ago stopped looking for love and acceptance from his old man.

Knock. Knock. Knock.

"Come in." His office door opened and his assistant, Carolyn Foster, walked in. The statuesque blonde wore pregnancy well; barely a baby bump could be seen in the smart attire she wore.

"Do you have a minute?"

"Of course," Ayden responded, moving away from the window. "What can I do for you?"

"I have some not so pleasant news to deliver," Carolyn said.

"Oh, yeah? Whatever it is, just give it to me straight, no chaser."

"Very well…" She paused for several beats. "I won't be coming back after my maternity leave in a few months."

"Excuse me?" This couldn't be happening to him *again*.

"I'm sorry, Ayden—really, I am—but my husband and I have been trying for some time to start a family. And, well, I just want to enjoy the time with our first child because I'm not sure when we might have another."

Carolyn would make a fantastic mother because she was already putting her child first. It made Ayden think of the only person who'd ever cared one iota about him, who was gone, taken away too soon. His mother Lillian Stewart-Johnson, God rest her soul, had passed away several years ago from a heart attack. He suspected his mother's illness had been caused by years of stress and abuse at the hands of his stepfather Jack Johnson. Jack was a habitual smoker and a mean drunk.

Ayden had focused hard on his studies, so he could get the hell out of the house. And he'd been lucky. In junior high, his teachers recognized his high IQ and had helped Ayden receive a scholarship to a prestigious boarding school in the East. From there, his grades helped him get into Harvard and he'd never looked back.

Growing up, Ayden had developed a thick skin. He'd had to in order to live in the Johnson household, and not just because of the bruises, but because of the lack of love or affection. He'd learned he didn't need either. If he hadn't met his roommate, Luke Williams, in boarding school in the ninth grade, who knows how long Ayden would have gone without any real feelings. Ayden's goal had been to save his mama from working two jobs to support Jack's pack-and-bottle-a-day habit, but it had been useless. By the time he'd finally started making enough money, his mother was gone and he was all alone in the world except for Luke, his closest friend. Why had his mother let men bully her all her life? First, Henry had intimidated her into a small settlement, cutting her out of her rightful shares in Stewart Technologies. Then, Jack spent the little money she had received. Why hadn't she fought for the child support she was entitled to?

"I imagine there's nothing I could do to change your mind?" Ayden inquired. He knew it was a long shot, but he couldn't understand why anyone would throw away a good-paying job in order to stay home and change poopy diapers. Carolyn's departure was going to leave him in quite a pickle. One he hadn't been in since a certain uptight but beautiful assistant had left him five years ago.

"No, there isn't," Carolyn said, "but we can find a replacement. You always said you never thought you'd find someone as good as Maya and look what happened—you hired me."

He would never forget the day, ten years ago, when Maya Richardson had walked through his door looking for a job. She'd been a godsend, helping Ayden grow Stewart Investments into the company it was today. Thinking of her brought a smile to Ayden's face. How could it not? Not only was she the best assistant he'd ever had, Maya had fascinated him. Utterly and completely. Maya had hidden an exceptional figure beneath professional clothing and kept her hair in a tight bun. But Ayden had often wondered what it would be like to throw her over his desk and muss her up. Five years ago, he hadn't gone quite that far, but he had crossed a boundary.

Maya had been devastated over her breakup with her boyfriend. She'd come to him for comfort, and, instead, Ayden had made love to her. Years of wondering what it would be like to be with Maya had erupted into a passionate encounter. Their one night together had been so explosive the next morning Ayden had needed to take a step back to regain his perspective. He'd had to put up his guard; otherwise, he would have hurt her badly. He thought he'd been doing the right thing, but Maya hadn't thought so. In retrospect, Ayden wished he'd never given in to temptation. But he had, and he'd lost a damn good assistant. Maya had quit, and Ayden hadn't seen or heard from her since.

Shaking his head, Ayden strode to his desk and picked up the phone, dialing the recruiter who'd helped him find Carolyn. He wasn't looking forward to this process. It had taken a long time to find and train Carolyn. Before her, Ayden had dealt with several candidates walking into his office thinking they could ensnare him.

No, he had someone else in mind. A hardworking, dedicated professional who could read his mind without him saying a word and who knew how to handle a situation in his absence. Someone who knew about the big client he'd always wanted to capture but never could attain. She also had a penchant for numbers and research like no one he'd ever seen, not even Carolyn.

Ayden knew exactly who he wanted. He just needed to find out where she'd escaped to.

"Aren't you tired yet?" Callie Lewis asked Maya Richardson after they'd jogged nearly five miles in the muggy San Antonio weather. They'd met up at 6:00 a.m. after Maya had stumbled out of bed, placed her shoulder-length black hair in a ponytail, and put on her favorite sports tank with built-in bra and running shorts.

"No. Not yet." Maya hazarded a glance at Callie. Her friend was five foot two and nearly two hundred pounds, and had been following an intense exercise routine to lose weight. She'd already lost fifty pounds and Maya was trying to encourage her. They'd been best friends ever since Callie had defended Maya from bullies in the fifth grade, so Callie's well-being was important to her.

"Well, I need to stop a sec," Callie paused midstride. She limped over to a nearby bench and began a series of stretches.

"Okay, no problem." Maya jogged in place while she stretched.

"What's got you all riled up?" Callie asked. "You've been on edge for a couple of days."

Maya stopped jogging and stood still. She'd been trying to outrun the past, which was impossible, but she was giving it the old college try. "I received an invitation from Raven and Thomas for Nysha's baptism."

"You received what?" Callie's brown eyes grew large with amazement.

"You heard me."

"I just can't believe your sister and that sleazy husband of hers had the nerve to send it. Not after what they did to you."

Maya shrugged. It had been five long years since she'd felt the sting of Raven's betrayal with her boyfriend, Thomas. If anyone had told her that her baby sister would steal her man and marry him, she would have called them a liar. Maya and Raven had always been so close. When their father had left their mother, it had broken up their family, leaving her mom Sophia alone to support them. It hadn't been easy especially because her mother favored Raven.

"How can you be silent about this?"

"Because… I've made my peace, Callie," Maya replied. "I had to. They got *married*, for Christ's sake. I didn't have much choice."

"You didn't go to their wedding."

"How could I? Back then it was all too fresh."

"Including what happened between you and Ayden?"

Maya rolled her eyes. "Let's not talk about him, okay?"

"Why not? If I recall what you said back then, it was the best sex you'd ever had in your life," Callie said, making air quotes. "Yet after your night with him and his failure to acknowledge what happened, you quit your dream job."

Maya sighed heavily. She wished she'd kept that secret to herself. Five years ago, for better or for worse, her life had changed. She'd accepted it and moved on.

She began running in place again. "C'mon, my muscles are starting to tense up. We have to finish our run."

"You go on ahead," Callie stated. "I'm going to sit this one out. I'll call you later."

"Sure thing." Maya jogged off in the opposite direction. As she did, she thought back to that horrible night.

She'd been working late because Ayden needed a presentation for the following day. She'd picked up takeout to bring to her boyfriend, Thomas. Using the key he'd given her, she'd opened the door to his town house and found it dark. It was surprising, given his car was sitting in the driveway. After placing the bags on the kitchen counter, she'd heard voices.

Who was visiting Thomas? It was well after eight o'clock, so Maya had walked upstairs to investigate. She'd never forget the sight that greeted her: her baby sister, Raven, on top of Thomas as they writhed on the bed. Maya had screamed bloody murder. Raven had rushed off the bed to the bathroom while Thomas tried to cover himself with a sheet as he'd attempted to explain. What was there to discuss? She'd caught him banging her sister. Maya had rushed out of the room, damn near falling down the stairs and losing a great shoe in the process to make it to her car. Fumbling with the key, she'd eventually started it up and was pulling off when Raven came running out the door in Thomas's shirt calling after her. The whole incident had been humiliating.

How long had their affair been going on?

How long had both of them been laughing behind her back?

Maya ran harder. Faster. But she couldn't outrun the memories. They must have really thought she was a fool for believing his lies that she was the kind of girl he wanted to marry. Her mother was right. Raven was the beauty in the family.

That was the state she'd been in when she'd arrived on Ayden's doorstep. Maya hadn't known where else to go. Callie lived in San Antonio and Maya had just lost her sister to a man she thought she loved. Over the five years of their working relationship, she and Ayden had shared some personal stories, especially when he'd told her about his past; she'd hoped he could lend her an ear now when she needed someone to listen.

Ah, Ayden. He'd been her secret crush for years before she'd met Thomas. When she'd started working for him, Maya had thought the sun and moon hung on the green-eyed devil, but Ayden hadn't seen her like that, like a woman. All he saw was a smart, efficient PA who did his bidding—which included making reservations for his dates with beautiful women, and sending them expensive flowers or trinkets as a parting gift when he was done with them. And yet, she'd chosen to go to Ayden, the man who didn't believe in love and thought it was a hoax meant to sell greeting cards.

That night, he'd offered her comfort. A shoulder to cry on. Comfort in ways she'd never been able to forget. Initially, he'd been shocked by her disheveled presence on his doorstep, but as soon as he'd seen her puffy, red-rimmed eyes, Ayden had immediately taken her into his embrace and closed the door behind him. He'd sat her down on the couch and listened as she'd told him of Raven and Tom's betrayal, of her failure. No one was ever going to love her, *want* her. She was a nothing. A nobody. A plain Jane that no man would ever be compelled to marry. Ayden had refused to hear of it. Had told her she was wrong. He'd stroked her hair and told her everything was going to be all right. With tears in her eyes, she'd glanced up at him, and then she'd done something desperate. She'd kissed him.

The surprising thing was he hadn't pushed her away. Instead, he'd kissed her back. One thing had led to another and the next moment, she and Ayden were making love on his bear skin rug on the floor of his living room. To this day, Maya had never been able to fully understand what had happened. One minute, he'd been consoling her and telling her she was beautiful and worthy of love, and the next, she'd been wrapped in his arms having wild, passionate sex.

It had literally been the most exciting sexual encounter of her life. Maya had experienced true bliss and one hell of an orgasm, but as soon as it was over, Ayden had pulled away. What she'd thought was heaven on earth had soon turned into a nightmare. Ayden told her he hadn't meant for it to happen. Maya had been crushed for the second time in one night. She'd dressed as fast as she could and had left to lick her wounds in private.

She'd relived that moment many nights since, wondering how their relationship had taken such a turn. Maya had always harbored feelings for Ayden in the past, but she'd never thought for a second that they were reciprocated. She'd eventually come to the conclusion that he'd made love to her out of pity because she'd been so pathetic. Knowing how he felt, Maya couldn't face Ayden again and had tendered her resignation.

Looking back, Maya realized that she'd been more upset over Ayden's rejection than Thomas's. Sure, she'd been hurt by Thomas because she'd loved him, but it had been her sister stealing her man that hurt the most. She'd never forgiven Raven, and they hadn't spoken in five years. It was Ayden who'd really broken her heart.

Once Maya had pushed herself to the limit with ten miles, she stopped running. It was time she faced the past with her sister so she could move forward with her life. And there was no better time than the present.

"Do you think she'll come back?" Ayden asked his best friend on a transatlantic call later that evening. It was before 7:00 a.m. in London, but he knew Luke Williams would already be up. How did he know? Because they were alike—notorious workaholics and driven to succeed. Luke was a financial analyst making millions.

"After the way you treated her when she left?" Luke said. "I wouldn't."

Ayden frowned. "Was I really that bad?"

"Hmm, I don't know, let me think," Luke paused for dramatic effect. "You were a slave driver at the office, rarely giving the poor girl a day off. And at a moment of weakness, you shag her and then tell her to kick rocks. I dunno, I might have a problem with that."

"Thanks a lot, Luke."

"You did call me, you know," Luke responded. "If you

didn't want me to keep it one hundred with you then you should have called another mate."

"You're my only *mate*." Ayden replied. He didn't have many friends. He'd never had the time to make any because he was too busy pushing himself to excel, to make something of himself despite Henry Stewart turning his back and leaving him and his mom with an abusive stepfather.

"Yeah, that's true. No one else can tolerate you. Except maybe Maya, and you made a royal mess of that relationship."

"I know I messed up, but I can fix it."

Luke snorted. "By offering Maya her job back? Why on earth would she ever agree? What does she get out of it?"

"I'm prepared to offer her a generous salary."

"And if she wants more?"

"What do you mean?"

"C'mon, man, don't be an idiot. Maya left because you two slept together. If you offer her a job, she might be thinking there's more on the table."

Ayden had never thought Maya might want more. "I'm not prepared to give her anything else. You know how I feel about love, marriage, the whole white-picket-fence thing."

"Yeah, yeah, sing to the choir. I've already heard this bit before," Luke stated. "Poor you, your dad left your mom to marry a hot tart, leaving you and your mom with nothing."

"That's right. Love is for other poor dumb schmucks."

"Like me, you mean," Luke countered.

Darn. He'd stuck his foot in his mouth. Luke had just married a beautiful redhead named Helena and they were head over heels in love. But if anyone could make a go of marriage, it was Luke. "Present company excluded," Ayden stated.

Luke chuckled. "You've never minced words before, Ayden, so don't start now."

"Helena is lovely," Ayden replied. "And she's madly in love with you. She can't wait to have a mess of babies with you."

"That's right, my friend. I'll have Helena knocked up before the year is out," Luke said, laughing. "That way she can't leave me for another man when she realizes she married a dumb schmuck like me."

Ayden laughed. That's what he loved about Luke. He could be self-deprecating and still be the life of the party. "So let's return to my original point for this call."

"What was that again?"

"Maya. And what it would take for her to agree to come back to me, I mean, the position of executive assistant at Stewart Investments."

"You would have to find the right incentive that doesn't include becoming a notch on your bedpost."

"That's not going to happen again," Ayden said. "Bedding Maya was a one-time thing. Plus, I doubt she's been carrying a torch for me. For Christ's sake, it was only one night!"

"If you say so, my friend. I've given my advice, for what it's worth. Good luck, and let me know how it turns out."

"Will do." Ayden ended the call and stared down at the folder in his lap. It held the address of where Maya was staying in Austin. He'd hired a private investigator to research her whereabouts. His timing was perfect because she was back in town for her niece's baptism and staying at a downtown hotel.

Ayden had to admit he was shocked by what he'd read in the file. He recalled how devastated Maya had been the night she'd come to him after discovering her sister in bed with her boyfriend. If she was returning, it had to mean she'd forgiven them. Surely that meant good news for him? He could ask her to come back to Stewart Investments, and things would be different between them now. After all, it had been years since Ayden had seen her. Although he might have had the odd fantasy about her, on his part, any residual feelings from their night together five years ago were long gone. Ayden had been with many women since Maya. More beautiful. More stunning.

He and Maya had always enjoyed an excellent working relationship. He was certain they could get past this if she was willing to forgive him for his lack of sensitivity and give them another chance. He knew it was a long shot, but there was only one way to find out. He had to go to her, and he wasn't leaving until her answer was yes.

From the bathroom of the Baptist church, Maya fretted as she smoothed down the dress she'd chosen to wear to Nysha's baptism. Should she have come?

Throughout the years, Raven had tried to extend an olive branch, but Maya had rebuffed each and every effort. Why? Because Maya was jealous. Raven was living the life that should have been hers. If she was honest, Maya would have loved that life with Ayden, but he hadn't wanted her five years ago. Or not in the way she'd hoped.

So why come back?

Because she couldn't go on living this way, holding on to past hurts and hiding away from the world. It was time to move on with her life. She'd come to make peace with her sister.

She glanced at herself in the mirror. The sleeveless plum dress had a deep V showing a swell of cleavage, thanks to the push-up bra she'd spent a fortune on in the hopes it would give her a bosom. Her long black hair, her best feature, was coiffed and hung in big curls down her back. She'd even allowed her hair stylist, who doubled as a makeup artist, to do her face. After all these years, she had to look her best because, Lord knows, her mother would be in full diva mode. Raven, of course, wouldn't have to try hard because she was naturally beautiful.

And now it was time to face the music. She couldn't very well hang out in the church bathroom forever. Grabbing her clutch purse, she made for the door. Sophia Richardson was greeting guests at the church entrance. From where Maya stood, she noted her mother's stylish salt-and-pepper updo and what looked like her Sunday-best suit, complete with pumps. But rather than looking the picture of a radiant grandma, her mother had lost weight and appeared a bit gaunt with sunken cheeks. Her normal caramel skin looked sallow.

Maya braced herself as she walked toward her. "Mother."

"Maya?" On cue, Sophia looked her over from head to toe—from the designer sandals to the simple Marc Jacobs sheath to the designer handbag. Apparently she passed muster, because her mother said, "I'm happy you've finally chosen to put the past behind you and return to the fold."

She held open her arms and Maya reluctantly walked into them. As expected, the embrace was brief. Maya suspected she'd received it because several guests had walked in and her mother wouldn't dare make a scene.

"Raven and Thomas will be so happy to see you," Sophia whispered in her ear. "Please go in." She motioned Maya toward the pews.

Would they be happy to see her? Or would her presence be a reminder of their past transgressions? Maya forced herself to put one foot in front of the other and enter the hall. Raven and Thomas were at the end of the aisle talking with the pastor. Her sister looked as stunning as ever even though she'd just had the baby two months ago. She was wearing a cream suit and had her hair in a French roll. Raven was already back to her svelte size-six figure. Thomas wore a suit and striped tie and beamed by her side, holding the baby.

Maya walked toward them. When Raven turned around and saw Maya, Maya felt her heart constrict. It had hurt being estranged from her baby sister.

"Maya?" Raven said as she drew near.

Maya glanced at Thomas and gave him a nod, stepping toward Raven. "Yes, I'm here."

Tears welled in her sister's eyes. "Oh, thank God, our prayers were answered. I've asked God for forgiveness every day for what we—" she glanced at her husband "—did to you. And now, I'm blessed to have you back in my life, in our daughter's life."

"Don't get carried away, Raven," Maya responded. "All is not swept under the rug."

"Of course not," Raven said. "I owe you a long overdue apology." She reached for Maya's hands and grasped them in her own. "I'm so sorry for hurting you, Maya. Can you please find it in your heart to forgive me?"

Maya stared at her in stunned disbelief. She had never expected an apology. Least of all, from Raven, who'd always been self-centered. But then again she'd never given her the chance.

"We're both sorry," Thomas said from Raven's side. "You deserved better than how we treated you. You deserved the truth. We should never have sneaked behind your back. It was wrong and I'm sorry."

Maya swallowed and nodded. She was too overcome to speak. She didn't know what she'd thought would happen during the visit, but clearly Raven and Thomas had matured enough to admit their mistakes.

"Would you like to meet your niece?" Raven asked, tears brimming in her eyes.

"Y-yes, I'd like that very much."

Raven walked over to Thomas, took their daughter out of his arms and placed the sleeping baby in Maya's. Her niece was the most beautiful little girl Maya had ever seen, with her smooth brown skin and shock of hair surrounded by a white headband with a bow. She was outfitted in the cutest white lace baptism dress. "She's beautiful." Maya grasped her niece's little finger in her hand.

"Can you believe I'm a mom?" Raven asked in wonder.

"Actually, I can't," Maya said, glancing her way, "but you are."

Raven gave a halfhearted smile. "You were always supposed to be the stay-at-home wife while I was supposed to be the career girl. It's funny how the tide changes."

"Yes, it's funny." Maya leaned over and returned Nysha into her sister's arms. "She's really beautiful. Congratulations to you both."

Maya stepped away as fast as humanly possible. It didn't hurt that guests were already headed toward them to greet the happy family. She needed some air. She couldn't breathe; it felt like she was suffocating. Maya sidestepped several guests entering the church and rushed outside.

Leaning against the building, she took in large gulps of air and forced the rising tide of emotions overwhelming her to calm. Had she honestly thought it would be easy seeing Raven and Thomas with their daughter? Maya glanced at the door. It should have been her. She should be the one who was a wife and mother; it's what she'd always wanted. Maya had always known she would make a good mom because she'd cared for Raven her entire life. Sophia Richardson had been too busy working two or, sometimes, three jobs to be there for them. Maya had been left to care for Raven, make her dinner, help with her homework and pick out her school clothes. So much so that Raven once

had called her Mommy. Sophia had been livid and had
yelled at Raven that *she* was her mommy.

Maternal instinct ran through Maya's veins, while
Raven had never cared for another human being beside
herself until now. But it was clear to Maya that Raven
loved her daughter and was happy. Maya didn't begrudge
her sister happiness, but did it have to come at her expense? Perhaps she'd made a mistake in attending? She
could sneak off with no one being the wiser. She'd made
an appearance. Surely that had to count for something?

Maya was just about to head down the church steps
when her mother's voice rang out. "Maya, dear, we're about
to begin."

Darn. She'd missed her chance to use her get-out-of-
jail-free card.

Inhaling, Maya spun around to face her mother and
walked inside the church.

Hours later, Maya was looking for her handbag in one
of the many bedrooms of Nysha's godparents' home. She
was ready to leave. After the baptism ceremony, the entire
group had adjourned here for a light meal. True to form,
Sophia had gushed over their home, how beautiful it was
and what great godparents they would make. It made Maya
ill to see that nothing had changed; her mother was just as
superficial as she'd been before.

Maya had done her part by showing up and making polite pleasantries. It was time for her to leave.

"Ah, there it is," she said aloud when she discovered
her purse.

"Do you have a minute?" a male voice said from behind her.

Maya didn't need to turn around to know who it belonged to. They'd once been lovers. She whirled on her heel

to face Thomas. If looks could kill, he would have been struck down on the spot. "What do you want?"

Thomas held up his hands in a defensive posture. "I'm sorry. I didn't mean to scare you."

"You didn't."

"I was hoping I could speak to you for a few minutes."

"I don't wish to discuss the past," Maya responded. Just being with her family had conjured enough of her old insecurities.

Thomas lowered his eyes. "Quite frankly, neither do I. It wasn't my finest moment."

"Then what is it that you want? I don't have all day."

Thomas glanced up and Maya hated to see the regret in his eyes. But she wasn't prepared for his next words. "It's about Sophia."

Maya's ears perked up. "What about my mother?"

"You may have noticed she's lost some weight?"

"Yes, I did, but I figured maybe she was dieting for the big event," Maya offered. It wasn't completely out of the realm of possibility. Her mother believed in looking her best, especially when the spotlight was on her.

"She's not dieting, Maya. Your mother is sick."

"Sick?" Maya clutched her purse to her chest. "How sick?"

"She has pancreatic cancer."

"Cancer?" The words felt like an anchor around her heart, but she managed to ask, "What stage?"

"Stage three. Sophia has been undergoing treatments the last month and, needless to say, it's taken its toll."

"Months? How long have you known about her condition?"

"Maya…"

"How long?" How long had her family had been keeping her in the dark? Why they hadn't told her Sophia was dying?

"Two months."

"And you didn't think to inform me sooner? She's my mother."

"Whom you've been estranged from for five years," Thomas retorted with a huff, "along with the rest of this family."

"You're *not* my family."

"I may not be a blood relation, but I care about Sophia. Raven and I have been carrying the load because her treatments are expensive even with insurance, not to mention the laboratory visits, PET scans and medications. And besides, it's been tearing Raven up seeing Sophia like this and not having anyone to talk to beside me. She needs you."

"She's always *needed* me," Maya responded tightly, "and I've always been there, but what do I get out of it? The short end of the stick."

"I—I thought you were going to let go of the past, Maya. You came today."

Guilt surged through her. Her mother was sick and this wasn't the time or place to take score on who'd harmed who. "Thank you for telling me." She started toward the door.

"What are you going to do?" Thomas inquired.

Maya had no idea. Today had been hard enough as it was. She needed a few minutes to digest everything he'd told her and come up with a plan. "I don't know, but I'll be in touch."

When Maya finally made it back to her hotel room, she was mentally and emotionally exhausted. Confronting the members of her family who'd hurt her and feigning to be the happy aunt had been hard enough. But finding out her mother had cancer was the straw that broke the camel's back. Not only did she have a splitting headache, but her feet were aching from the new designer sandals she'd bought to ensure she measured up to her mother's scrutiny. All she wanted to do was run a hot bath, take some ibuprofen and go to bed. In that exact order.

Maya had kicked off her shoes and was unzipping her dress when there was a knock on her door. She glanced down at her watch. It was seven o'clock. She was in no mood for company after the bomb Thomas dropped on her. And who knew she was in town anyway?

Padding to the door in her bare feet, Maya swung it open in frustration. The person on the other side was someone she never thought she'd see again, not after the one night they'd shared.

"Ayden?"

"Hello, Maya."

Two

At six foot three, weighing about 210 pounds of solid muscle, Ayden looked as yummy as he ever had. Maya was dumbfounded to see the man she'd once adored standing in the flesh in front of her. How could she not be enthralled by those hazel eyes, his strong nose and the light stubble surrounding the best mouth and cleft chin in Texas? He was impeccably dressed in a dark suit with a purple-and-white-striped tie.

"Wh-what are you doing here?" She pulled back her shoulder blades to project that she wasn't taken aback by seeing him after all this time, when she definitely was.

"I came to see you." He rewarded her with one of his sexy smiles. "May I come in?"

"I don't think so…" Maya responded, and began to close the door. What did you say to the man you'd once slept with, but hadn't seen in five years?

"Maya, please." Ayden stuck a foot in the door to prevent her from shutting it. "I wouldn't have come if it wasn't important."

"All right, but only for a few minutes. It's late and I've had a trying day."

"Thank you." Ayden brushed past Maya, and she caught a hint of his cologne that was so uniquely him. Her stomach clenched in knots like it always did whenever she was around him. And her nipples puckered to attention underneath her dress.

Maya closed the door and turned around to face him. "I repeat, what are you doing here?"

"Is that any way to greet an old friend?" Ayden teased.

Maya folded her arms across her chest because, with Ayden's radar, he might see he'd aroused her, and she'd be mortified if he knew she was still attracted to him. "We were never friends, Ayden."

"Weren't we?" he asked, stepping toward her. "You knew all my secrets. I told you everything."

"And you knew nothing about me."

"That's not true," Ayden said. "I know your favorite color is green. I know *Pretty Woman* is your favorite movie because you're a closet romantic. I know you write in a journal when you think no one is looking. I know you run when you need an outlet to ease tension."

Maya chuckled inwardly. She was surprised he knew that much, but she supposed he would have had to pick up on something. She'd been his executive assistant for half a decade. "All right, you know a few things about me."

Ayden raised a brow. "A few? I think I know a lot more than that."

His implication was clear. He'd known her in the biblical sense and there was no getting around that. But why bring it up? It was over and done with. Finito. He'd made sure of that.

"Why are you here? Clearly, you sought me out. How else would you know I'm back in Austin?"

"I admit I had an investigator try to find you. They informed me you were back for your niece's baptism," Ayden replied. "How did that go? Have you ever been back since..."

He stopped. *Have you ever been back since the night we slept together?* That was the question he couldn't bring himself to finish. At least he had the grace to stop before he embarrassed them both.

"Why would you have an investigator look for me? I don't appreciate you treating me like one of your females," Maya stated.

Ayden was notorious for having the women in his love life investigated to be sure they had no ulterior motives. But Maya, why her? It wasn't like she was one of them. All she'd wanted out of today was to make peace with her family and move on with her life, but now that wasn't possible. First, because of her mother's illness and now Ayden's surprise visit. He wanted something, and despite her anger at his invasion of her privacy she was curious to find out what it was.

"I'm sorry about that, but I didn't know where you were or how to find you. When you left five years ago, you disappeared without a trace."

"Yet, you didn't come looking for me."

"No, I didn't, and I think we both know why. I'm here now and we can talk about that. But first, you mentioned having a bad day. I can't imagine seeing your sister and your ex-boyfriend, now married with a child, was easy, especially when you thought you were headed down the aisle to matrimonial bliss with him yourself."

Maya laughed bitterly to avoid the pain of hearing him say out loud what she'd already thought so many times today. "Apparently, he didn't get the memo, so no, today wasn't a pleasant experience."

Ayden began removing the jacket he was wearing.

"What are you doing?" she asked with a frown. "I didn't ask you to stay. I only agreed to talk for a few minutes." He had no right to make himself comfortable in her hotel room. Not after the way he'd dismissed her so long ago.

Ayden paused. "I'm sorry yet again. I keep apologizing to you tonight." He held up his jacket. "May I?"

"I suppose you can stay a few minutes longer." Ayden draped the jacket across the sofa and sank down into its plushness.

He sat forward on the couch and rested his very large forearms on those powerfully muscled thighs of his. *Jesus!* Why couldn't she think straight when she was around him? Sure, he'd always had this effect on her, but she would have thought his treatment of her five years ago would have cooled any physical response she might have to him now. Apparently, she'd been wrong.

"I'm sorry for what you went through with your sister. It's truly a shame because you're worth a thousand Ravens."

Maya couldn't resist a small smile forming on her lips. Ayden didn't compliment people often. "You don't have to say that."

"You don't think I mean it?"

She spun away and shrugged. It didn't matter. None of it mattered. Ayden, Raven, Thomas—they were all in her rearview. She'd only come back to Austin to get closure and move on with her life. She'd done that. Her mother having cancer had certainly put a wrinkle in her plans to go back to San Antonio and her new life.

When she didn't answer him, Ayden must have risen

from the sofa, because Maya felt rather than saw him behind her. "What? What is it that you want from me?"

His large hands grasped her shoulders and guided her around to look at him. "Don't hide from me, Maya. Aren't you tired of it?"

Maya jerked out of his hands. "Don't presume to think you know me, Ayden, just because you can spit out a few obvious facts about me."

"All right. Then how about this. I want you back."

Maya sucked in a deep breath and reminded herself that Ayden was a master at getting his way, especially with women. Over the years, she'd seen him bring the most intelligent and independent women to their knees and have them beg him to take them back. He never did. Instead, he'd have Maya send a farewell gift with his regards. *His regards!*

It must have crushed his ego when she'd chosen not to stay working for him after he bid her adieu after their night together. She wasn't about to go backward even though her heart yearned for more. Still, she was curious and found herself asking, "Why do you want me back?"

"You're the best assistant I ever had. You know how Stewart Investments is run. Hell, how I work. I can count on you to make decisions whether I'm there or not. I trust you implicitly. And remember the Kincaid Corporation deal that I've always wanted a crack at?"

She nodded.

"I have the opportunity to pitch Stewart Investments to them again. You remember how important it was for me to land that account. He's one of my father's largest suppliers. You remember how hard we worked on that first pitch only for him to go to a larger firm. Times have changed and Stewart Investments is in better shape than ever to compete with the big boys."

Ayden didn't want *her* back. He wanted his trusty workaholic assistant back under his grip. "I see."

"You see what?"

"You want me back so I can be your shadow, following you around, being at your beck and call. Well, I'm not your pet, Ayden."

"I never thought you were." He sounded offended. "And I've never treated you like one. You were always a valuable employee."

Maya shook her head. So he was just going to act like it never happened. That they'd never seen each other naked? That they'd hadn't slept together on the bear skin rug in front of his fireplace? "You should go, Ayden." She pushed at his rock-hard chest, which was darn near impenetrable, and walked to the door.

"Why?" He grasped her wrist. His eyes were fire when he said, "You haven't even heard me out."

"Why should I, Ayden, when you refuse to even acknowledge the elephant in the room? I left for a reason and you damn well know why."

Ayden sighed heavily and slowly released her as if she'd struck him. He leaned backward against the door and his intense gaze rested on her. "I'd hoped we wouldn't have to discuss it."

Maya rolled her eyes upward, not wanting him to know how hurt she was by his words. Yet again, Ayden was bruising her already fragile ego. But try as she might, she couldn't ignore the tears that trickled down her cheeks. She wiped at them with the back of her hands.

Ayden swore when he saw her tears. "Christ! I'm sorry, Maya. I didn't mean to hurt you. Not again."

"But yet you continue to do it."

"Not on purpose," Ayden said. "Never on purpose. I care for you, Maya. I always have. I suppose that's why I allowed our relationship to become—" he paused for the right word "—*complicated*. And I take all the blame for what happened. You were destroyed when you came to me, but rather than comforting you, I took advantage of you, and for that I'm terribly sorry. I should never have let things go as far as they did."

Maya glanced up at him through her tears. He was apologizing for making love to her? Was he mad? He was making the situation so much worse, because to her that night had been one of the most sensual encounters she'd ever experienced. But why should she be surprised? He'd only been with her out of pity. He could never find her, Maya Richardson, attractive like he did the many beautiful women he frequently bedded.

Much to her chagrin, Ayden kept going. "The next morning I was so mortified by my actions that I sought to sweep it under the rug like it never happened, which I know wasn't fair to you. But I didn't know what else to do, Maya. Clearly, I'd compromised our working relationship so much that you couldn't come back to work for me. It's why I gave you such a generous termination package. I was sorry for taking advantage of you. I'm still sorry, but I promise, should you choose to work for me again, I will never cross that line and take advantage of you again. I promise I will respect you and your right to have a life of your own without me taking up every minute of your free time."

"Why are you saying all of this?"

"Because I *need* you, Maya. My assistant, Carolyn, is leaving in a couple of months to be a stay-at-home wife and mother, and I need you back."

The desperation in Ayden's tone stunned Maya. She

watched him reach into the jacket pocket of his suit and pull out a thin envelope. He handed it to her. "Read it. I'm offering you an extremely generous salary and benefit package to return to Stewart Investments."

Slowly Maya ripped open the envelope and pulled out the single sheet of paper. The offer letter was nothing short of impressive. The salary was more than generous, it was astronomical. And the benefits of increased 401(k), profit sharing and an abundance of time off was staggering. "Ayden…"

"Listen, I'll make this worth your while. I'm willing to offer you a signing bonus of twenty-five thousand dollars if you'll agree to come back *right now*."

She looked in his direction and saw the worry that she would say no etched all over his face. And she should. She had every right to turn him down. He wasn't good for her. And she'd made a good life in San Antonio. She should go back where it was safe, but when had she ever used her head when it came to this man? The bonus he was offering her was too great a sum to turn down, not when the funds could help her ailing mother. When he looked at her with those puppy-dog eyes, she was a goner.

"Please, don't say no. Think it over."

"I don't need to think it over," she answered impulsively. "My answer is no. I have a life in San Antonio, Ayden. I can't just drop everything because you need me." She had a home, a job she enjoyed and her best friend, Callie. Why would she uproot her life?

"You haven't even thought about it," Ayden said. "Isn't there anything I can do to entice you? There has to be something."

The thought continued to nag at her that if she accepted Ayden's offer, she could help out with her mother's cancer treatments. Even though they were estranged, Maya couldn't imagine letting her mother suffer when she could have the potential means to help. What kind of person would she be if she did that? But could she go back to working for Ayden knowing her feelings for him weren't truly resolved? "I don't know."

"Maya, we can make this work," Ayden murmured. "With you by my side, we can not only win over Kincaid, but take Stewart Investments to new heights. And with that offer, you would get a share in the earnings. It's a win-win. Please say yes."

"All right, all right, I'll come back."

Ayden couldn't believe the joy that surged through him at Maya's response. Without thinking, he stepped closer. He called himself all kinds of foolish for torturing himself with her familiar sweet aroma, but he couldn't resist. Ayden pulled her into his embrace, squeezing her tightly to him. He felt her breasts pebble against his chest and his groin tightened.

Maya stiffened and Ayden knew he'd done the wrong thing. She didn't welcome his advances. The one night they'd shared had been her attempt to feel loved, coddled, but that was in the past. He mustn't forget that. Still, being in her hotel room was doing funny things to his anatomy again; he pulled away. "I'm sorry. I was just so overjoyed. Won't happen again." He couldn't touch her again. Otherwise, he might lose his head and start to remember what it was like to feel that soft skin of hers as she melted underneath him. He blinked rapidly.

"It's all right," Maya finally said, letting him off the hook. "I guess you were right. It's time I finally stop hiding and return to the life I once loved."

"Do you really mean that?" Ayden quirked a brow. He knew it wasn't entirely true. The report he'd received had told him of Sophia Richardson's health. He knew that the signing bonus was the reason Maya was coming back—she needed it for Sophia Richardson's health costs. He would have given her the money even if she hadn't agreed to come back. Maya was someone he cared about, and if it was in his power to help her mother, he would. He wouldn't want her to experience the guilt he'd felt at not being able to help his mother during her illness. It was guilt he still carried to this day.

"Not the long nights," she added with a smile, "but I did enjoy working with you. We were a good team."

"And we will be again." Once they got back into their work groove, the past would be left behind and they could make a new beginning. He offered Maya his hand. She glanced down at it and Ayden wondered if she was going to renege, but instead her soft fingers clasped his in a firm shake.

"It's a deal."

Ayden grinned. "You don't know how much this means to me."

"Oh, I can guess," Maya laughed. "I suppose there's lots of work piled up?"

Ayden grinned unabashedly. "No. Carolyn is still here for a few weeks, but I wasn't relishing working with someone new. Plus I already had my mind made up that no one but you would do."

Maya Richardson was one of a kind. And although Carolyn had done an acceptable job in her place, Maya was irreplaceable. He'd discovered that when he'd made the mistake of mixing business with pleasure. And speaking of that, it was late. He needed to get out of her room before he did something he couldn't take back. He moved toward the door, but stopped midstep. "How much time do you need to get your affairs in order?"

"A couple of weeks to give notice at my current job. And when I get back to Austin, I'll need some time with Carolyn to get up to speed before she leaves."

He pointed his index finger at her. "I'm holding you to it."

"I've never gone back on my word."

"Very true." She never had and never would, because Maya was a woman he could count on. "I'll see you soon." Ayden left swiftly and closed the door behind him, then leaned up against it.

Closing his eyes, he sucked in a deep breath. It had been dicey in there for a minute. He hadn't realized just how much of a physical tug he'd feel being with Maya again. It had been five years, but the moment she'd opened the door to her hotel room, he'd been transported to that night at his apartment when she'd exploded in his arms and kissed him with a passion unlike anything he'd ever known. Maya had kissed him as if he were a man and not the boss she'd worked with for years. She had aroused him to the point that he'd acted rather than thought about his actions.

For a split second when he'd held her in his arms and their bodies collided, he'd felt compelled to act as he had back then, but in the nick of time he'd managed to do the right thing and move away. He'd just convinced Maya to come back to him and Ayden wasn't about to mess it up because he couldn't keep it in his trousers. He was already the worst kind of scoundrel, having played on feelings he suspected she might still harbor for him.

How did he know?

There had a moment when she thought she'd disguised her true emotions that he had caught a glimpse of something in her eyes. He wasn't positive of how deep her feelings went after all these years, but at the very least, Maya still cared for him, and Ayden had used it to get what he wanted. Which was why he would ensure he kept their relationship platonic going forward—he refused to lose her a second time.

"Are you insane?" Callie stared at Maya in disbelief from across the table of the Starbucks where they'd met the following afternoon when she returned to San Antonio.

"No, I'm not."

"Clearly, you must have lost your mind." Callie reached across the short distance to place the back of her hand on Maya's forehead. "Why else would you agree to go back and work for Ayden?"

"He made me an attractive offer."

"This isn't about money, Maya," Callie responded hotly, "and you know it. You're going because you're still hung up on the man."

"That's not true."

Callie raised a brow.

"It's not. Listen, Callie, I got over Ayden a long time ago, when he nearly kicked me out of his place the morning after we had sex. It made me wise up real quick."

"Well, if that's the case, why go back for more? Why put yourself in harm's way? You know you're not immune to his charms. And I suspect he knows. How else would he have lured you back into his web?"

"I'm not his prey."

"Are you sure about that?" Callie inquired, sipping on her Frappuccino. "Because I suspect you have no idea what you're in for. Five years ago, you opened Pandora's box and found out what it was like to *be* with the man. Do you honestly think you can act as if those feelings never existed?"

"He's offering me enough money to ensure I ignore them."

"I still don't understand, after the way he treated you."

Maya leaned back in her chair and regarded her best friend. She hadn't yet divulged her mother's condition. "Mama is ill."

"Excuse me?"

"Thomas shared with me that she has pancreatic cancer."

"Omigod!" Callie jerked back in her seat. Then she immediately reached across the table and clutched Maya's hand. "What's the diagnosis?"

"They are hoping that, after chemo and radiation, she will go into remission, but the treatments are expensive. Thomas and Raven have been helping out, but with the baby, they are stretched thin."

Callie nodded. "Now I understand why you accepted Ayden's offer."

"The influx of cash will help Mama. Without worrying about finances, she can focus on getting better." Although she and her mother had never seen eye to eye, she was *her mother*. How could she not help out?

"Oh, Maya." Callie's eyes filled with tears. "You are so selfless. Does your mother have any idea of your plans?"

"I called her earlier and told her I was moving back to Austin," Maya replied. "She was pleased that I would be closer, but I didn't tell her about the money. She knows Raven and Thomas have been covering the out-of-pocket expenses, but I don't want her to know that I'll take up the slack going forward. "And promise me you won't tell her."

"Of course not. I would never betray your confidence. But where are you going to live? With your mother? I can't imagine you staying with your sister."

"That's completely out of the question. Although I'm willing to get to know my niece and I accepted Raven's apology, it's going to be a long time, if ever, before we can get back to the sister relationship we once shared. And as for my mother, we're like oil and water. We don't mix. If I stayed with her, all she would do is criticize and compare me to Raven like she did when we were children. It is best if I find my own place, but I'll visit Mom." She'd contacted a property management company who'd forwarded some listings for sublets and short-term rentals until she could find a place she liked.

"All right. I just worry about you, and not only with where you lay your head. I'm talking about Ayden. You're walking into the lion's den with no protection for your heart."

"My heart has nothing to do with the situation. What I felt for Ayden is in the past."

"That's easy to say when you're not seeing the man day and night. I remember the hours you kept before."

"It won't be like that now. He promised. Plus, he didn't want me five years ago, so nothing has really changed."

"Maya…you were intimate with Ayden. Trust me, he *wanted* you."

"For all of five seconds. Anyway, have a little faith in me, Callie. I can do this. I *have* to. Not for myself, but for Mama."

Three

Two weeks later, Maya sat outside her mother's house with the engine of her Honda running. She'd arrived in Austin the day before. Ayden had ensured her sign-on bonus check had arrived within days of accepting his offer, so she'd been able to secure her short-term rental for next six months. She'd put most of her belongings in storage until she was sure returning to Stewart Investments would work out. In the meantime, she'd kept the news of her return to Austin a secret from her family, but now it was time to face the music. Since her relationship with her sister was strained, she'd informed Raven via text of her plans a few days ago. Raven was happy she was coming back home if the emoji that accompanied her texts were anything to go by, but Maya hadn't yet told her mother.

After turning off the ignition, Maya exited the car and climbed the porch steps. The neighborhood looked much the same as it had when she'd left some ten-odd years ago except now the homes appeared older and more worn. Her mother's could use a coat of paint and the lawn needed mowing. Maya was just about to ring the doorbell when the door swung wide.

"Maya?" her mother said incredulously.

"Yes, it's me. Can I come in?" Maya was startled by how thin her mother was. Although it had only been a little over two weeks since she'd last seen her, Sophia had lost another five pounds. Her normally dark hair lay limp on her shoulders and the simple print house shift she was wearing hung off her slender frame. Meanwhile her skin seemed sallow and her eyes had sunk even deeper into her face.

"Of course." Sophia stood back and motioned her into the formal living room. "Would you like anything to drink? I think I have some sweet tea in the fridge."

Maya shook her head. "Nothing for me." She didn't plan on staying long.

Her mother took a seat on the sofa and Maya did the same. "What are you doing here? I thought you went back to San Antonio."

"I did, but I came back."

"So you could start to mend fences with your sister?" her mother offered, folding one leg over the other.

One day, yes, but not now." Although she'd accepted Raven's marriage and her baby niece, Maya wasn't ready to tackle more than that. She had Ayden to deal with.

"Oh, Maya. That's water under the bridge now. You have to let it go and move on."

"I have let it go, Mother," Maya responded. "I came to the baptism."

"Yes, you did. And that was a start."

"Listen, Mama. I didn't come here to talk about Raven.

I came to let you know that I'm moving back home. I've gotten my old position back at Stewart Investments."

"With that good-looking fella you used to work for?" Sophia touched her chest. "Now there was a sight for sore eyes if ever I saw one. That man is gorgeous. Why couldn't you ever snag him?"

Of course her mother would think along those lines. But finding a man wasn't a number-one priority for Maya. She was an independent woman who used her brains to get ahead. "Ayden is my boss, nothing more." And there could never been anything ever again.

"That's too bad. With his looks and all that money, you'd never have to worry a day in your life about how to pay the next bill."

"That's the thing, Mama. I make good money and I can more than help out with whatever it is that you need around the house." Maya looked about the room and noted the peeling wallpaper and loose wood flooring.

Her mother rose to her feet and began pacing the room. "I don't need your handouts, Maya Richardson. I've been doing just fine without you. Raven and Thomas have seen to that."

"I'm sure they have. I just thought—" Her mother might want her help? It was clear Sophia didn't want Maya to know about her cancer.

"That you could come in on your white horse and save the day?" Sophia interrupted. "Well, that's not necessary. We've got it covered."

Maya sighed. "Very well, then." She would just have to tackle her mother's financial woes a different way. She pulled out a slip of paper. "Here's my new address and phone number if you need to reach me since it's clear you're doing just fine without me."

She rose to her feet to depart, but her mother touched her arm softly.

"I'm sorry, Maya. That came out all wrong. I'm glad you're back in town and that you took the time to come see me," she said. "I just don't want to be anyone's charity case, ya hear?"

"Yes, ma'am." Maya nodded and allowed Sophia to walk her to the front door. "I'll stop by again real soon."

"I'd like that."

Maya let out a deep breath once the door closed behind her. What had she expected, that her mother would welcome her with open arms? She and Sophia had never had that kind of mother-daughter relationship. Raven was her favorite child and that hadn't changed. Thanks to her therapy, Maya had learned to accept it and to understand her mother loved her in her own way even though she had a funny way of showing it. But it didn't matter. Maya would figure out a way to help with Sophia's medical bills despite her stubbornness. If there was a will, there was a way.

The next morning, Maya wasn't nervous as she walked through the revolving doors of Stewart Investments' offices. She strutted toward the elevator bank feeling great. She was returning to her old stomping grounds and it felt like home.

She planned on spending the next week gathering as much information from Carolyn as possible. She was so busy running through a mental checklist that she didn't notice Ayden until he was standing beside her.

"Good morning, Maya."

Maya popped her head up and looked at him. "Good morning." She glanced down at her watch. "You're here a bit early, aren't you?" It was a little after seven, and typically Ayden came in around eight. First, he hit the gym for a morning workout before having two cups of strong black coffee for breakfast. Sometimes with fruit and dry toast, other times with an egg-white omelet. She still knew his schedule like the back of her hand.

A chime echoed in the lobby and the elevator doors opened. "Times have changed," Ayden said as they entered. "Since I didn't have you, I've had to adjust."

"And you will need to adjust again because I like having the morning to myself."

Ayden chuckled. "And now so do I."

Maya wondered if she would have time to mentally prepare for working with him again? Apparently not, because here she was being thrown into the deep end of the ocean without a life vest.

They were both silent on the ride to the fiftieth floor. When they reached the top, Maya exited the elevator first. Ayden fell into step beside her as they walked toward the executive offices.

"Not much has changed," Ayden said, "except some of the decor."

The interior offices that were once browns and beige had been replaced with an open concept done in whites and primary colors. The new atmosphere was bright and airy. "I like it."

"I'm glad. I want you to love your working environment since you'll be spending a great deal of time here."

"You promised me that would change," Maya responded.

"I did," Ayden said, glancing down at her. "And I will hold up my end of the bargain."

Despite what she'd told Callie, Maya doubted he would be able to help himself. Some days there would be long hours, but she wouldn't let it consume her life as it once had.

When they made it to the area outside Ayden's office, she placed her purse on what was once her desk and studied her surroundings. It felt surreal being back after all this time.

"Everything all right?" Ayden inquired from behind her.

Maya whirled around. "Yes, of course."

"You can change anything you like."

"Wow! I'm not even out the door and you're ready to replace all semblance of me?" a beautiful blonde said as she walked toward them. She wore a chic knee-length black sheath and to-die-for designer pumps. She was nearly as tall as Ayden. "Hey, it's not my fault you want to leave the best job in town to go off and play wife and mom," Ayden said.

Maya could only assume the stunning Scandinavian beauty was none other than Carolyn, Ayden's current assistant. She stepped forward and held out her hand. "Maya. Maya Richardson."

Carolyn shook her hand. "Ah, Maya. I've heard a lot of great things about you. It's a pleasure to finally meet you."

"Congratulations on your pregnancy." Maya tried not to let the envy show on her face that yet another woman was living the life she'd always wanted while she was destined to remain alone.

"It doesn't mean I'm not here for both of you," she said, looking at Maya. "I'm just a phone call away if you need me."

"Hopefully, that won't be necessary if you get me up to speed this week."

"Let's get started." Carolyn made for her desk.

"I'll leave you to it." Ayden disappeared into his office and closed the door.

Carolyn chuckled to herself. "He's not much of talker, is he?"

"Nope. Never has been and never will be."

"I hear you." Carolyn stashed her purse in her drawer and locked it before taking a seat at her desk. "When I first started working here, it took him months to learn my name. I guess he'd gone through so many assistants he couldn't keep up. Eventually, I put my foot down and forced him to acknowledge me. We've gotten along marvelously ever since."

"That's great."

"It wasn't easy filling your shoes," Carolyn continued as she turned on her laptop and punched in the appropriate password. "Ayden thought the world of you and made sure everyone knew it."

"Did he really?" Maya was surprised.

Years ago, she'd learned there were only two avenues a girl could go. The pretty route or the smart route. Her mother had always told Maya her looks were unremarkable, so she'd become a bookworm and excelled in her studies. After college, she'd had options, but had been afraid to branch out. Needing work, she'd become a temporary admin and found she was skilled at multitasking for successful men. That was how she'd come to work for Ayden. Her reputation as the miracle worker had wowed him. It was good to know that her unwavering work ethic had garnered his respect.

Maya spent the duration of the morning going through the dozens of active client files to help her become familiar with all the players. It was well past noon when she looked up from the table in the small breakout conference room she'd relegated herself to and found Carolyn at the doorway.

"You hungry yet?" Carolyn asked. "Because I'm starved. Eating for two has me ravenous all the time." She patted her small baby bump.

"You go ahead. I'm just finishing up and will grab a quick bite later."

Finally she stopped long enough to grab a salad from the building's café only to return to the mountain of paper. Hours later, Carolyn stopped by to tell her she was leaving for the day. Maya hadn't realized it was so late, but she waved goodbye.

She was reading her last file when she felt Ayden's presence. Heat washed over Maya at seeing him again. He'd abandoned his jacket and tie, and had rolled up his sleeves to reveal enormous biceps. Ayden came closer and Maya could swear she felt a light spark inside her when he looked at her so intently.

"Burning the midnight oil?"

"Excuse me?"

He tapped his watch. "It's after six. I thought we agreed that you would have a life outside of this office."

Maya pinched the bridge of her nose. "Well, I intend to. I just finished the last file." She closed the folder and placed it on the table. "Guess I should get on home, or should I say to my short-term rental." She wasn't ready to sign a long-term lease just yet; the rental was affordable and allowed her the flexibility to move quickly if working with Ayden again didn't pan out.

"How about dinner?" Ayden asked, jamming his hands into his trouser pockets. How was it he could look so amazingly good with several days' worth of stubble on his jaw?

"Not necessary. I can pick up some takeout on the way home."

He studied her through hooded eyes. "I wasn't trying anything, Maya. I just thought after a long first day, it might be nice to catch up. And it's not like we haven't shared a meal together before."

He was right, of course. They'd worked late and eaten together on many occasions, though usually it had been takeout, not a formal dinner. But how bad could it be? "All right, I'd like that."

"Let me grab my jacket and I'll be right with you." He was gone for several seconds, giving Maya enough time to regret accepting the invitation. Why was she doing this to herself? Was she so determined to prove that he had no power over her that she would agree to be alone with him? Maybe she was. If they were going to work together, Maya would have to be comfortable spending time in his company. *Alone.*

Dinner on the terrace at the quaint Italian restaurant was exactly that. Ayden didn't make any untoward moves. Instead, he was nothing short of hospitable and caring, holding out her chair, making sure he selected her favorite wine and generally steering the conversation to lighter topics such as movies, books and his favorite sports team. Maya began to relax.

Ayden could be great company. She found herself laughing at his anecdotes and funny jokes. She recalled how he had a sense of humor, but it had taken time to manifest itself. Back in the day, he'd close his door for hours, shutting himself off from the world, only calling Maya on the intercom to do his bidding. In time, Ayden had learned to open up to her and share some of his past, his struggles and his hopes for Stewart Investments. It's why she knew how important securing Kincaid's business was to him. He was more approachable than he'd ever been, and Maya had to admit she liked this new version of Ayden. Perhaps she'd had something to do with him learning to be more open.

When the dessert menu came along, Maya patted her full stomach. "I don't think so."

"C'mon, don't be a spoilsport. Their cannoli is the best."

"Sounds like you know from personal experience?"

"I do." Ayden turned to the waitress, who was still standing near their table. "We'll have the cannoli and coffee."

"Sure thing, Mr. Stewart," the waitress replied, and scurried away.

"This was really nice, Ayden. Thank you."

"You're welcome. I told you things were going to be different this time."

"Yes, you did," Maya replied, "but I wasn't sure."

"I've learned from the past and generally don't make the same mistakes over again."

Maya wondered if that meant becoming intimate with her. She would never know because the waitress returned with their dessert and coffee. Maya watched Ayden pour them each a cup and was surprised when he put three cubes of sugar and a splash of milk in hers. "Thanks." When had he learned how she liked her coffee? Probably the same time he'd discovered she liked to run and kept a journal.

"No problem."

Soon dessert was over and Ayden was walking Maya to her Honda. "Thank you for dinner."

"You're welcome. It's the least I could do since you're working so hard."

"I worked late so I could get up to speed."

"Well, I want you to know I appreciate it. It's good to have you back, Maya. I missed you."

He missed her.

"I missed you, too." Maya didn't wait for his response, and wasted no time hopping into her car and speeding away. She needed distance.

Once she had made it to her apartment, Maya tried not to think about Ayden. She had to focus on something else, anything else, so she called Raven. After her mother's refusal of her help, Maya was going to have to find another approach.

Raven answered on the second ring. "Maya, it's so good to hear from you. Have you made it safely to Austin from San Antonio?"

"I have," Maya replied, "but this really isn't a social call."

"Oh, all right. What's going on?"

Maya heard the disappointment in her sister's voice, but she pressed on. The familial relationship they'd once shared had been shattered. "Thomas told me about Mama's medical bills."

"Really? When did you speak with him?"

"After the baptism, but that's beside the point. I want to help out with the house bills and Mama doesn't want me to. When I mentioned it, she told me you and Thomas had it under control."

"I wish that were true, but with a new baby, it's gotten tight paying for her medications, plus the balance the insurance doesn't cover. Any help you could give would be greatly appreciated."

"Well, I'm here now. Tell me what I can do."

Their call ended soon after, with Raven promising to email Maya with the details of what was outstanding and any upcoming payments. Maya had set aside a good portion of her $25,000 bonus for her mother's care. Feeling accomplished, she retired to bed, but when she did, her mind wandered to Ayden's words. He missed her. She told herself he missed the dependable, efficient assistant who could keep him on task. She knew her job and how to effectively implement the decisions he made. Ayden was no more interested in her than he'd been five years ago. At least now he valued her and liked her well enough to offer friendship. And that was sufficient, because quite frankly she had as much as she could handle on her plate. She was trying to reconnect with her mother while she still had the chance. And maybe she'd even try her hand at dating again. Maya was determined to take back her life, starting now.

Four

The next morning, Maya arrived at the office around the same time as she had the previous day. Neither Ayden nor Carolyn were in sight this time. Maya set about turning on the Keurig machine and making herself a cup of coffee. Although she'd slept through the night, she still felt tired. Probably because it wasn't her own bed in San Antonio.

Wouldn't it be nice if she were sharing it with a certain CEO?

Maya tried to shake the cobwebs from her brain. Why were thoughts of Ayden popping into her head? She'd stopped fantasizing about him years ago. Why was this happening again? Was her subconscious trying to tell her that she wasn't as over him as she thought?

She was heading back to her desk when Carolyn's phone rang. She glanced at her watch. It was early for the phones to start ringing. Maya picked up the receiver. "Stewart Investments."

"Maya, it's Carolyn."

"Carolyn? Is everything okay?" Her voice sounded weak, as if she'd been crying.

"N-no, it's not. I woke up this morning and I was spotting. My husband took me the hospital and we are waiting to see the doctor. Oh, Maya, I don't want to lose this baby."

"And you won't." Maya tried to sound encouraging. "You're a strong, healthy woman, Carolyn. You can do this."

"I hope so, but Ayden…"

"I'll take care of him, don't you worry. You just take care of yourself and that baby."

"Thank you, I appreciate it. But you should know he has a big meeting coming up tonight with a high-profile client. I finished the presentation yesterday. It will just need to be printed out and bound."

"I'm on it. Don't worry. I've got this. If you can, call me later and let me know you're okay?"

"I will. And Maya?"

"Yes?"

"Thank you."

The line went dead and Maya stared at the receiver in her hand. That was how Ayden found her as he approached. "Maya?" He dropped his briefcase and rushed toward her. "Is everything okay?"

She nodded. "Yes, yes, I'm fine. It's not me. It's Carolyn. She's in the hospital. Could be something wrong with the baby."

"Oh, Lord!"

"I know, right?" Tears formed in the corners of Maya's eyes at the thought that Carolyn could lose the baby. Although she'd only just met her, it was obvious how much she wanted to be a mother.

Ayden crouched by the desk and reached for Maya's

hands. "We have to believe that she and the baby will be all right."

Maya nodded and slowly Ayden released her hands to stand up straight. "She told me about a dinner meeting you have tonight with the Kincaid's. That's great. I know how much you've wanted their business."

"Yes, Carolyn was working up a prospectus."

"I'll have it ready for you."

"You mean, ready for us."

Maya stared back in confusion. "I don't understand."

"Carolyn was accompanying me to this dinner tonight. Kincaid is big on family. Although I don't have one to speak of, Carolyn was going to pinch-hit as my plus one. Can you do the same?"

"I suppose."

His brow furrowed and he paused. "Will that be a problem?"

Dinner again with Ayden, except this time she would be his plus one? The evening prior she'd been able to justify it as two people sharing a meal after working late, but this felt different. Maya had to remind herself that this was business. Like Carolyn, she was attending to help him pitch Stewart Investments to his dream client. "No, it won't be a problem."

She hit the ground running the rest of day, working through all the emails, answering those that were urgent and forwarding those requiring Ayden's input. She set up a spreadsheet for his active deals that she'd studied up on yesterday. And thank God she had.

Later that day, Maya wanted to breathe a sigh of relief but fretted over what to wear. Having let her go an hour early to freshen up, Ayden planned on picking her up at 7:00 p.m. and she still hadn't selected a dress. Most of her clothing was still in storage, so her options were severely limited. Maya settled on a one-shoulder body-con dress. Callie had convinced Maya that with her slender figure she could pull it off. It wasn't like she had a lot of opportunities to dress up. Her life in San Antonio had been rather boring up to this point. At least the dress would hug the few curves she had. After adding some chandelier earrings, a spritz of perfume, and some mascara, blush and lipstick, she was ready.

Ayden was already in the lobby speaking with the security guard, which allowed Maya time to survey him. It was impossible to stop herself from staring at him like some love-struck teenager. He was powerfully built, and his suit fitted his broad frame like no other man she'd ever known. Maya felt breathless and her stomach was tied in knots. Ayden had the looks to go with his physique. Those stunning hazel-gray eyes, perpetual five-o'clock shadow and chiseled cheekbones caused her to suck in a deep calming breath.

The truth was, she could have kept looking at him forever, but as if sensing he was being watched, Ayden glanced up and his eyes fastened on hers. He shook the man's hand and walked toward her. Maya's heart rate began galloping at an alarming speed. Her mouth suddenly felt as dry as the Sahara Desert, but she managed, "I'm ready."

Ayden trapped her with his eyes. Helplessly she gazed up into those murky depths, which had suddenly darkened from hazel to something more mysterious. Maya's entire body burned from the look he was giving her. Then he blinked and it was gone, and Maya wondered if she'd imagined the lust she was almost certain was there.

Ayden offered Maya his arm and she took it. "Let's go."

They rode to the restaurant in companionable silence. Neither of them seemed too keen on talking until both their cell phones buzzed, indicating a text message. Maya pulled hers from her clutch. It was Carolyn. "She and the baby are okay," Maya said, turning to Ayden.

He glanced up from the road to reward her with a smile. "That's wonderful news. I'm glad to hear it."

The phone buzzed again and Maya quickly read the message. "But she's not returning to the office. The doctor has indicated her pregnancy is high risk and is putting her on bed rest."

"That's a shame because it leaves you in quite the lurch."

"Not really," Maya said. "I'm more than capable of stepping in, picking up the baton and running with it. I'm just glad I spent yesterday poring through those files."

"So am I, Maya. So am I."

When they made it to the restaurant, the hostess sat them at a table already occupied by Ayden's prospective client. "Mr. Kincaid. Ryan," Ayden said. He offered the elder Kincaid and his son handshakes. "Pleasure to see you both. And is this your lovely wife?"

"Yes, it is." The older man beamed with pride. "Sandy, I'd like you to meet Ayden Stewart..." The petite brunette rose from her seat and Ayden shook her hand.

"Nice to meet you."

"And of course, you know my son. Ryan, Ayden is the man who's going to make us millions."

"Mr. Stewart," Ryan replied, "my father thinks very highly of you. I'm curious to hear what ideas you have for us."

"Of course, but please let me introduce Maya Richardson." Ayden slid his hand to the small of her back and edged her over to the group.

"Ms. Richardson." Mr. Kincaid leaned over and clasped her hand. "You're looking quite lovely this evening. Isn't she, Ayden?"

Ayden's eyes glowed with fire when he looked at her, and Maya felt her belly clench in response. "She is."

"I agree with you, Father," Ryan commented, and Maya's heart started in her chest. There was naked interest in the younger Kincaid's eyes as he searched her face. She wasn't used to being the center of attention, especially from such a good-looking man with his tanned skin, shock of dark hair and stunning blue eyes.

Ayden reached for her then, tugging her forward. A sharp streak of sensation coursed through Maya at his touch. She nearly stumbled into the chair he'd pulled out for her.

Ryan reached for her to assist, but Ayden glanced up at him and said, "I've got her."

"Thank you." Maya hoped her blush wasn't showing at having both men so clearly interested in her well-being. Not that there was any competition. Her nerves had been shot the moment she'd seen Ayden in the lobby. She'd known it was going to be difficult working for Ayden again, but she hadn't realized that she would be thrown into a situation so quickly, especially when she still harbored residual feelings for him.

Before she could even gather herself, she felt the warm strength of Ayden's hand as he patted her thigh, probably in an effort to ease the tension that was no doubt radiating off her. His touch was oddly comforting, even though it made her tingle and brought her entire body to life. A tight coil formed in her tummy and was quickly racing upward toward her breasts, making them feel fuller, heavier. Maya willed her wayward body to relax. She grabbed her water glass and drank generously, hoping the chilled water would cool off her hot flesh.

"So how long have you two been seeing each other?" Mr. Kincaid inquired.

"It's not like that," Ayden quickly responded. "Maya is my assistant. She often entertains clients with me."

Mr. Kincaid wasn't fazed. "My wife was my secretary, too, and as you can see that didn't stop us."

"So you're single?" Ryan's question lingered in the air.

"Um, yes, I am." Maya offered Ryan a small smile.

"It's good to know there's hope for the rest of us mortals," Ryan said.

Was he trying to flirt with her? Because she'd never dated outside her race. She was woefully out of practice in the dating department. It was safer to change the topic. And she did. She discovered that the Kincaids had been married for thirty years and had a daughter, as well.

"Family is very important to me," Mr. Kincaid said. "Stewart Investments is one of the top investment firms in Texas, but it isn't all about money. I want to find someone who values family above the almighty dollar. I used to be all-business in the past and it nearly cost me my wife." He looked at Mrs. Kincaid. "That's why it's so important to work with people who are well-rounded and have work-life balance because, although I enjoy my money, I don't want to be consumed by it, or by the quest to make more. Tell me about your family, Ayden? Are you related to Henry Stewart of Stewart Technologies?"

Maya felt Ayden stiffen at her side, and everyone, including Ryan, seemed to be rapt waiting for his answer. She knew how much Ayden hated talking about his family, much less the father who'd never acknowledged him. It was a touchy subject and one she knew he didn't want to discuss with strangers. The only reason she happened to learn of the connection was because when his mother passed away, an arrangement had arrived from Stewart Technologies.

"He's my father, but we're estranged," Ayden said finally, after several long, tense moments. "I was very close with my mother, but she died about five years ago, so I'm in short supply on family."

"I'm sorry to hear that," Mr. Kincaid said.

Ayden nodded, but Maya couldn't let it go at that. "You won't find another investment firm that is more dedicated, honest and forthcoming than Stewart Investments. Clients are more than just numbers or facts and figures on a spreadsheet, Mr. Kincaid. Ayden cares about you and your family's future and wants what's best to grow your portfolio."

Mr. Kincaid turned to Ayden. "You've got quite the advocate sitting next to you."

Ayden turned to look at Maya. "Don't I know it."

Ayden was stunned by Maya's impassioned speech on his behalf. He'd never had someone have his back, except maybe Luke, and he was an ocean away. He'd always known that Maya was one in a million, but it was more than that. She was a truly exceptional person, and he doubted he'd truly realized just how exceptional up until this moment.

"You have quite the *assistant*," Mr. Kincaid added. Ayden caught his emphasis on the word *assistant*, because she certainly wasn't acting like one.

"Yes, I know." When he'd arrived in the lobby of her apartment, he'd been unable to mask the unadulterated lust that surged through him at seeing her in the slinky red dress. He'd never even seen Maya in color. She usually wore black, navy and beige, but then again, he hadn't seen her in five years. He was supposed to be keeping his distance and maintaining a professional decorum with Maya, but how was he supposed to when she looked sinfully sexy?

The dress showed off her long legs and incredibly fit physique. Running had done her body good. She was tall, graceful and perfectly proportioned. She had long legs, a waist that he could easily span with his hands and two round orbs for breasts. She had an understated beauty and Ayden was having a hard time ignoring her, as evidenced by the tightening of his body. He didn't need this now. Not when his energies had to be focused on securing Kincaid's business. And that wasn't the only problem: Ryan was making no attempt to hide his interest in Maya, and Ayden didn't like it one bit. He reached for his wineglass and drank liberally.

So he switched gears, charming the Kincaids well into the third course. Maya and Mrs. Kincaid were chatting quietly in the dining room about God knows what while he, Ryan and Mr. Kincaid had retired to the cigar room, so Kincaid could try one of the restaurant's Cubans they were known for. Ayden didn't care for cigars, so he opted for an aged cognac.

"There's nothing better than a fine cigar," Mr. Kincaid said, puffing on his cigar.

"I hear they are some of the best in town," Ayden said, and sipped on his drink.

"Speaking of the best…that assistant of yours," Mr. Kincaid responded. "She's a treasure, that girl."

"Yes, she is. And to be frank, I lost her some years back because I didn't appreciate what I had. I don't intend to make that mistake again."

"Is that right?" Ryan smirked. Ayden could see Ryan's mind working on whether that gave him an edge with Maya. It didn't. Maya was *his*. Well, not his, per se, but she was off-limits to the younger Kincaid.

Mr. Kincaid turned to him. "I appreciate a man who

can admit he made a mistake and not let pride come before a fall."

By the end of the evening, Ayden was shaking hands with the Kincaids and wishing them a good night as he sent them back in a limousine to their hotel. Meanwhile, out the corner of his eye, he could see Ryan speaking privately with Maya. He saw him hand her a business card and watched Maya give him a smile. Then Ryan touched her arm as he left. Ayden was not amused. He was thankful when Ryan got in the limo and they drove away. He handed the valet his ticket.

"That went rather well," Maya said. "Don't you think?"

Ayden gave a half smile. "Yes, it did. Thanks to you."

"Me?" Her voice rose an octave. "I didn't do anything."

"Of course you did. You had the Kincaids, each and every one of them, eating out the palm of your hand. I'm impressed and so glad I brought you along."

Maya shrugged and smiled smugly. "What can I say? We make a good team."

Ayden met her gaze. Their eyes locked, held. "Yes, we do."

Desire flared, hot and tangible, between them. Ayden didn't know what possessed him, but he stepped right into her personal space. He wished she hadn't looked at him like that. It heated his blood, and the cool air did little to settle the fever that was coursing through him. He caught her hand and pulled her toward him, compelled to do what he'd wanted to do all night, which was kiss her. He didn't know where this wildness was coming from because he was usually so composed, but Maya's proximity throughout the evening had gotten to him. Her eyes sparked and flared, radiating heat right through him. When she wet her lips with her tongue, Ayden found himself wondering what she would taste like again.

He was bending his head to brush his lips across hers when the valet pulled up in Ayden's Bentley, breaking the trance. He'd been just as enthralled by Maya as Ryan had been, perhaps more so because he knew her, had *been* with her. But he couldn't be again. He'd given her his word.

Slowly Ayden released her. He gave Maya a small smile because in her eyes he could see she'd been anticipating that kiss as much as he'd been. Would it have been light and sweet, or would it have been the frantic passion they'd shared so long ago?

They would never know because Ayden quickly moved to open the passenger door. Maya didn't say a word for several moments. She simply stared at him in confusion. He knew he'd given her mixed signals. One minute he was hot for her and the next he was pushing her away. But it was for the best. When he didn't say a word, Maya finally stepped toward the car and slid in. When she did, the skirt of her dress hiked up and Ayden couldn't resist feasting his eyes on her sumptuous thighs.

When he glanced up, Ayden found Maya watching him. Had she known where his thoughts had gone? If so, her eyes were shuttered and she didn't let on. He closed the door, came around to the driver's side and jumped in. After buckling up, he pulled away from the curb.

The drive to her apartment was fraught with pent-up tension. Awareness rippled through the air, but Ayden ignored it. He had to take Maya back home while he still could. He just couldn't walk her upstairs, because if he did, he'd be asking to come inside. In more ways than one.

They pulled up to the apartment's main entrance ten minutes later. He glanced at Maya. "Thanks for tonight. You did great. Sleep well."

She didn't even look at him as she said tersely, "Good night." Seconds later, she was out of the car without a backward glance. He stared at her retreating figure before pulling away to drive home.

Could he blame her for being angry at him?

He'd behaved horribly earlier, pulling her to him like he was going to start something he couldn't possibly finish. But Maya had been different tonight. He'd seen another side to her. A sexy siren. And it was contrary to what he'd always known about her. That mix had desire ripping through him, igniting a fierce desire to kiss her, claim what had once been his. Because there was no way Ryan Kincaid was going to have his woman. But did he really have a right to think this way? Wasn't this what had led him down the wrong path and caused Maya to leave in the first place? It had taken months to find the right person to replace her, and although Carolyn was awesome, she couldn't read his mind like Maya. He had to back off.

It was simply that talking and laughing with her tonight had caused memories to resurface. There were sparks of desire between them, of that there was no doubt. He would love nothing better than to kiss her, touch her and undress her. But there was no way he would or could allow them to burn as hot as they once had.

Maya had made it very clear that she wasn't interested in rekindling a personal relationship with him. And he had to respect her decision even if his libido didn't like it. And truth be told, she was too good for him anyway. She certainly wouldn't settle for a light and sexual affair, which was all Ayden was capable of. Maya was the kind of woman that you married and made the mother of your children. Ayden wanted no part of that life, and his penance was to go to bed longing for a woman he could never have.

Five

Maya was furious as she stormed through the apartment lobby toward the elevators. How dare he touch her like that? Look at her like that? Who the hell did Ayden think he was? Once again, he was showing that he could not be trusted. He'd told her that their relationship, going forward, would be strictly business, but tonight he'd changed the rules. Back at the restaurant, he'd pulled her to him, like... well, like he wanted her. Her stomach had lit up like a ball of fire, and she'd sparked at the desire that had lurked in those hazel-gray depths. Then, just as quickly, he'd cast her aside as if it hadn't happened.

Just as he had five years ago.

The elevator chimed and Maya entered. Leaning against the wall, she exhaled and closed her eyes. She was trying to force the kick of adrenaline she'd experienced to dissipate. Why had he done it? Stirred up a hornet's nest of emotions that she'd kept buried? For so long, she'd accepted that Ayden didn't want her. Never had. That he'd slept with her that night out of pity. And then tonight, he'd flipped the script, making her wonder if she'd gotten it wrong all those years ago. Had he wanted to make love to her? Had it been more to him? Is that what had scared him off?

No, no, no. She shook her head. She couldn't do this to herself. She'd dealt with this years ago. She couldn't resurrect those feelings of self-doubt. Not again. Maya had gone to therapy to deal with Raven and Thomas's betrayal and her night with Ayden. It had all done a number on her ego and self-confidence, but she'd picked up the pieces and finally felt as if she'd let go of the past. She'd faced those demons a few weeks ago when she'd gone to her niece's baptism.

Maya had hoped that taking this job again would not only help her mother financially, but exorcise those buried demons and remind her of her self-worth. She didn't need Ayden's mixed signals and she wouldn't abide it. Not anymore. She wouldn't just accept what Ayden or anyone else doled out to her. He would soon learn that she'd grown and was no longer a doormat.

The next morning, Maya arrived at the office ready to work and full of spice. She was prepared to give Ayden a piece of her mind, but he called to let her know that he had morning meetings and wouldn't be in until later. Maya was puzzled. There were no appointments on his calendar, so she could only assume he didn't want to face her. And perhaps it was for the best. Now she would have time to cool down and regain her composure.

By the time Ayden arrived midmorning, Maya had determined to put last night in the past, like an aberration, and move forward with the job. When he strolled into the office, walking with a lithe, purposeful gait, threading his way toward Maya, she was in control.

And so was Ayden.

"Maya—" he thrust a sheath of papers across her desk without looking in her direction "—I need copies of these immediately." He swept past her into his office and closed the door.

It didn't surprise her that he was ignoring what had transpired last night. He was good at that, acting as if nothing had happened. She would do the same. She did as instructed and made the copies. When she was done, she knocked on his office door. A terse "come in" was issued and she entered.

Ayden's office was as immaculate as the man himself. It held a dark walnut desk along with built-in bookshelves that spanned an entire wall. A sitting area with a leather sofa, low table and wet bar was in the opposite corner.

She headed to his desk. "Here you are." She leaned over to hand him the papers, but he seemed determined to act as if whatever he was reviewing on his laptop was more important than acknowledging her. So Maya dropped the copies with a flop on his laptop. That got his attention and he glanced up.

"Is there anything else, *boss*?" She said the last word with a measure of sarcasm, impossible to ignore.

His brow rose. "Actually, yes. Can you get Kincaid on the line?"

"I'll get right on that." Seconds later, she was slamming his door and returning to her desk. The jerk!

She was smarting over his casual disregard when a delivery man strolled toward her with one of the biggest bouquets of flowers Maya had ever seen. "Maya Richardson?" he inquired.

"Yes, that's me."

"These are for you. Sign here, please." He handed her a clipboard while he placed the fragrant bouquet on her desk. Maya signed for them even though she had no idea who they were from. She was still looking for a card when she heard Ayden's door open behind her, but she ignored him. She was curious who could have sent her flowers.

"Who are they from?" Ayden asked over her shoulder just as Maya found the card.

"Excuse me." She spun away from him, slid the small card from the envelope and read it. *Enjoyed your company last night. Have dinner with me, Ryan.*

A smile spread across Maya's lips.

"Well?" Ayden sounded annoyed when she still hadn't spoken. "Who are they from?"

"Ryan."

Ayden frowned. "Kincaid?"

Maya nodded and then swiveled around in her chair to face the computer. She'd suspected Ryan was interested in her personally, but she'd never thought he'd act on it.

"What did the card say?"

Inflamed, Maya spun back around. First, Ayden wanted to ignore what had happened last night, and now he wanted to play twenty questions with her personal life? "What business is it of yours?"

His face turned red and Maya could see she'd angered him, but she didn't care. "The Kincaids are a client, an important one, so it darn well is my business."

"It has nothing to do with work," Maya replied hotly.

Ayden leaned down. Both his large hands bracketed her desk and made Maya feel caged in. "Did he ask you out?"

Her brow furrowed. "How would you know that?"

Ayden rose to his full height and glared at her. "Because it's what I would do. I saw the way he was looking at you."

"And just how was he looking at me?" Maya folded her arms across her chest. She dared Ayden to say more.

Ayden turned away from her for several moments, and when he faced her again, his features were schooled. "It's unseemly for you to accept dinner with a client."

"That's not fair!" Maya rose to her feet to confront him. She didn't appreciate Ayden implying that she would do anything that would harm Stewart Investments. She'd been a valuable employee for five years. "You know I would never hurt you, I—I…" she stammered. "I mean hurt the company. And you *know* it."

Ayden colored. She'd hit her mark. "I apologize. I didn't mean to insinuate otherwise. So let me rephrase. It's not a good idea to mix business and pleasure."

"Is that a fact?" Her gaze met his and held. There was no mistaking she was referring to last night when he'd almost kissed her. Air bottled up in her lungs as she waited for a response.

Ayden had the grace to be embarrassed and looked away. "Do what you want!" He turned on his heel and slammed his door a moment later.

Maya told herself she didn't care how Ayden felt. She was being given an opportunity to go out with a good-looking, emotionally available man who was interested in her. Why not see where it led?

She glanced at Ayden's door. Because deep down, the man she wanted was closed off to her. Literally.

Ayden stared out his window for several moments before returning to his desk to concentrate on the figures and reports on his laptop, but it was useless. His brain was addled. Never before had he sat at his desk only to discover he'd wasted ten minutes thinking about a woman. And it wasn't just any woman. It was Maya. His Maya. He was imagining her going out with Ryan. Wondering if she'd kiss him. Let him touch her as he once had. He was jealous.

And he hated it.

He had no right to be.

He had no rights to Maya. But the thought of her with Kincaid stuck in his craw. He had seen the lust in the man's eyes when he'd looked at Maya. He had wanted to get to know her all right; he wanted to get to know her intimately! And worst of all, Maya didn't have a problem with it. He suspected she was doing it to give Ayden the finger for last night and today.

And she'd be within her rights.

He was falling back into old patterns. He'd acted as if he hadn't hauled her sensual, soft body against his hard one. Felt the pebbles of her nipples harden in response to their closeness. Heard her breath quicken as she anticipated a kiss between them. But he'd denied her. Denied them both. And now they were both miserable because they, or rather, *he* was trying to forget it happened.

It would have been easy if Maya was in her normal attire of navy skirt and button-down blouse. Except today, she'd chosen to wear a fuchsia-colored blouse that did wonders for her beautiful brown skin. He'd thought Maya returning to Stewart Investments was going to be easy. He had an active love life with plenty of women at his disposal. All he had to do was pick up the phone. There was no reason for him to feel like this; yet, he couldn't get his beautiful assistant out of his mind.

"Ayden?" Maya's voice rang through the intercom. "You have a call on line one."

He sighed. "I'm rather busy right now. Who is it?"

There was silence on the other end. "It's your sister, Fallon."

"I'll be with her in a moment." Ayden let go of the speaker button.

His *half sister*, Fallon. Four years younger than him, they shared the same DNA, but they had different mothers. He hated her witch of a mother, Nora Stewart, who was the cause of the downfall of his mother's marriage to Henry. The wily waitress had made sure she'd gotten pregnant and used it to lure his father away. Ayden had met Fallon a couple of times, but theirs certainly wasn't a normal brother-sister relationship. Why was she calling?

He had to know the answer. Ayden picked up the receiver. "Hello?"

"Ayden, it's so good to hear your voice. How are you?"

"I'm fine, Fallon. But I doubt this is a social call." The last time they'd seen each other had been six years ago when he'd expanded Stewart Investments and bought the building. Fallon had come to the grand opening. He'd been surprised by her appearance, as he was now by her call.

"Wow! I'd forgotten how you like to get to the point," Fallon said from the other end of the line.

"Yes, well, time is money."

"Of course. I was hoping if you had some free time, we might get together for lunch this week."

"I don't know." Ayden kept minimal contact with his half siblings. Although he couldn't blame them for their existence, Ayden still saw them as the chosen ones. The children that Henry deigned to acknowledge as his heirs while Ayden was left out in the cold to fend for himself.

"C'mon, Ayden. It's been several years. Aren't you the least bit curious about me? Dane?"

At times, he was. When he was lonely, Ayden wondered about his siblings and what they were doing with their lives. He knew Fallon ran Stewart Technologies, Henry's baby. Then there was his half brother.

Dane Stewart was an A-list actor in Hollywood. Ayden knew that Dane wanted no part of the Stewart family because he'd said so in several interviews. Ayden was certain there was a story behind Dane's estrangement and Fallon's absolute devotion. He'd even wondered what it would be like to have them as friends, but then he remembered that they'd had different lives. Ayden sighed heavily. "What is it that you want, Fallon?"

"Not over the phone," she whispered. "I need to speak with you privately. Can you meet me on Friday?"

Ayden was curious, so he agreed. "Yes, I'll have my assistant set it up."

"Thank you. I appreciate it. I'll see you then."

The line went dead, but Ayden was still holding the receiver. Exactly what did his sister want, and what did it have to do with him?

By Thursday, Maya was both giddy with excitement for her date with Ryan Kincaid this weekend and perturbed by Ayden's attitude the last couple of days. The only way she could describe his behavior toward her was *chilly*. Ayden was not happy about her spending time with Ryan. His interactions with her were strictly business. Email this. Call this person. There was none of the warm camaraderie they usually shared at the office.

He'd overheard Maya making plans with Ryan for Saturday night after she'd called to thank him for the beautiful arrangement. Since then, Ayden had been acting like a sullen child. He barely spoke to her. He'd been absent the last couple of days and was giving her a wide berth. Maya supposed it was a good thing. They'd gotten too close for comfort the other night. If dating Ryan kept her from obsessing about Ayden and wondering what might happen, it was for the best.

Callie agreed when she called Maya during lunch. Her best friend was happy she was getting back into the saddle and dating again. Maya knew Callie thought she was hopeless when it came to Ayden, but she was over him. Or that's the white lie she told Callie. If Ayden hadn't stopped that kiss, the heat between them would have consumed them. Maya refused to admit Ayden still held any power over her. She would sweep what happened under the rug just as he was doing.

After finishing lunch, she called her mother to check in. As usual, Sophia was saying everything was fine, but Maya knew better. True to her word, Raven had emailed her copies of her mother's outstanding medical bills, and since Raven had been authorized on the account, Maya had been able to pay the clinic directly without her mother being the wiser. She'd also set up a payment plan for future bills. In addition, Raven had sent her mother's schedule, so Maya knew her chemo treatments were every three weeks, but hadn't yet mustered the courage to make one.

When she finally came back from her lunch break, she found Ayden sequestered in his office with the door shut. Maya continued working and filtering calls like she always did. When he was ready, he would come out and talk to her.

Eventually, her intercom buzzed. "Maya, can you make reservations tomorrow for a late lunch with my sister, Fallon, at two p.m."

The line went dead.

Ayden was lunching with his estranged sister, Fallon? How could he just drop a bomb like that and not expect her to ask questions?

One day, years ago, when Ayden had just won a lucrative client that would put Stewart Investments on the map, he'd confided in her about his past and how it had shaped him into the man he was today. Everyone was lauding him as the man with the Midas touch. All except one—his father.

Ayden had shared that deep down, he'd thought he might hear from Henry to say how proud he was of his accomplishments even though he'd done nothing to help him achieve them. Ayden told her that he knew he'd never get his father's love, but he'd wanted his acknowledgment. Despite all his successes, that day never came. And year after year, as Stewart Investments had grown, Maya had watched Ayden's heart grow harder where the Stewarts were concerned, which was why it was surprising he would agree to lunch with Fallon.

Maya worried about him and his well-being. She wanted to know if he'd be okay, but Ayden was shutting her out. Would he ever let anyone in?

Six

The next afternoon, Ayden walked purposefully through the restaurant. He'd made sure to dress for the occasion of meeting his estranged sister, choosing a custom-made suit, red tie and Italian loafers. He'd even gone to the barber to ensure his scalp was smooth as a baby's bottom and his five-o'clock shadow was well-groomed. If the princess of the Stewart family was deigning to meet with him, he had to look his best.

Fallon rose from her chair as he approached, and Ayden was reminded of just how beautiful his sister truly was. With her dark brown hair with honey blond streaks and her smooth café au lait skin, his sister was a knockout. A designer dress revealed her slender but curvy figure.

"Ayden, I'm so happy you agreed to meet me." His sister stared at him through hazel-gray eyes, the same as his. It was a family trait.

"Did I have a choice?" he asked, coming toward her

and pushing her chair in as she sat down. If nothing else, his mother had raised a gentleman.

"I guess I didn't give you much of one," Fallon said after he sat across from her, "but given our relationship I wasn't sure you'd come."

"Curiosity brought me here," Ayden returned, placing his napkin in his lap. "I wondered why you would need anything from me, the black sheep of the family. The son our father can't be bothered to claim."

Sadness crossed her face and Fallon lowered her head. When she looked up again, tears were in the corners of her eyes. "I'm sorry Father has treated you this way, Ayden."

He shrugged. "What's it to you, anyway? You're his heir."

"And you're still my brother," she responded with a ferocity that shocked him.

"Now you want to claim me?" He smiled sardonically. "Why, Fallon? It's never been that important to you before."

"That's not fair, Ayden. I reached out to you when I went off to college, and you shot me down. You weren't interested in a little sister then."

"And I'm not interested in one now."

"Ouch." Fallon took that one on the chin, but bounced back, her eyes narrowing as she looked in his direction. "Despite having grown up away from Father, you're just like him. You know how to hit below the belt."

Ayden sucked in a deep breath. He deserved that. He hadn't meant to be unkind, but it was a little late to play brother and sister. That time had come and gone. But, at the very least, she deserved to be treated with respect like any human being. "I'm sorry."

She raised a brow.

"I am," he insisted. "This is all a bit disconcerting."

Fallon gave him a half smile, and Ayden felt a kick in the gut because it warmed his cold heart to see it. "It is for me, as well. It wasn't easy calling you for help, but I did."

"Help?"

"I'm in trouble, Ayden."

Ayden sat upright in his seat, training his gaze on her beautiful facial bones. "What kind of trouble? What can I do to help?"

"Careful, Ayden," Fallon said with humor to her tone. "You almost sounded like a big brother there."

His eyes narrowed. "What do you need, Fallon?"

"I don't know if you knew, but I'm CFO of Stewart Technologies. Have been a few years now."

"I'd heard."

"Have you also heard that the company isn't doing well? We've been in trouble for several quarters now. I've been doing my best to contain the damage, but bad investments and poor project planning have crippled the company. I've tried my best to turn it around, but there's little hope of saving it now."

Ayden frowned. He didn't like the direction this conversation was heading, but he was here now and he had no choice but to listen. It would be rude of him to get up and walk away, even though that's exactly what he wanted to do.

"For years, I tried to get Father to listen to me, but he's stubborn and pigheaded. Determined to do things his way, and now we're in a bind. We need a bailout."

And there it was, Ayden thought. The catch that had brought Fallon to contact him out of the blue. She needed money. "And what is it you expect me to do?"

"Ayden." Fallon reached across the table, which seemed as wide as an ocean, and took his hand. "I've heard great things about you. Everyone's calling you the miracle worker. If anyone can help turn this around it's you. And..." She paused as if searching for her words. "With some of your financial backing we could save the company."

Ayden stared at Fallon in disbelief. He glanced around the room to see if anyone had heard, because he wasn't sure he'd heard right. Fallon, Nora's daughter with Henry, was asking him, the son Henry had cast aside, to save *her* father's company. Surely, she had lost her mind. "And why would I want to do a thing like that?"

"Because it's our family business."

"No, Fallon. It's *your* family business. Stewart Investments is *my* business."

"But..."

"There's no buts. Henry chose to divorce my mother and walk away from us, and that's fine. That's his choice, but when he did, he washed his hands of me and subsequently any allegiance I had to this—" he made air quotes with his hands "—family."

"Ayden, I know you're upset with Father."

"Upset?" His voice rose and when it did, several patrons looked in his direction. "*Upset* is acting as if we had a minor disagreement, Fallon. I'm not upset. I *hate* him. I hate him for how he treated me, but most of all for how he treated my mother. He left her with nothing, even though she helped him start that damn company."

Tears sprang to her beautiful eyes—so like his own. "Wh-what? I thought—but my mother said..."

"Your mother lied, Fallon. Lillian Stewart was the woman behind the man, working two jobs to get Henry through college so he could work on his degree, helping build the capital necessary to open Stewart Technologies. And when he became successful, he kicked her to the curb for a younger model and cheated her out of her rightful share of the company. So Fallon, there's not a snowball's chance in hell I would ever help that man or his company and, unfortunately, that affects you." Ayden rose to his feet.

"Ayden," Fallon rushed out of her seat and placed a firm hand on his arm, stopping him before he'd taken two steps past her. "Please don't leave this way. I had no idea about what happened to you and your mother. I wasn't even born. Surely, you can't blame me?"

"I know that, Fallon, and I don't blame you. Henry's mistakes are his and his alone. I came here today out of respect for you even when I didn't have to. I heard you out, but there's nothing left to say." He glanced down at her hand on his sleeve, but she held on firmer.

Her eyes implored his and he saw the fear in them. "I need your help."

"I'm sorry, but the answer is no. Let the company crash and burn because, quite frankly, that's exactly what Henry so richly deserves." Ayden wrenched his arm away and spun on his heel. His heart was thudding loudly in his chest and his pulse was racing. He quickly threaded his way through the tables until he made it to the door. Once he was outside, he leaned against the building's facade and inhaled deeply.

Rage was coursing through his veins. Not at Fallon, but at Henry for ruining the company his mother helped build. Ayden wanted to punch something, *someone*, but instead he walked. And walked. He would walk back to the office so he could cool off and let calmer heads prevail.

Maya glanced down at her watch. It was well after five o'clock and the office was starting to clear out, but Maya couldn't leave. She hadn't heard from Ayden all afternoon and she was worried. He hadn't returned from his lunch with his half sister. Maya was dying to know how it went and if he was okay, but he hadn't so much as called to check in for messages.

It was nearly six when she finally gave up and began packing up her belongings. She was turning off the lights when she saw Ayden walking toward her from the reception area. Instead of his usual long and confident stride, his shoulders were hunched over. As he drew closer, Maya could see anguish etched across his face.

"Ayden?"

He glanced up, but looked straight through her and walked into his office. Maya was rooted to the spot as conflicting emotions tore through her. Should she go after him? He appeared so forlorn. Lost even, if she had to put a name on it. Or she should she go home and let him figure it out alone? They'd agreed to have a purely business relationship. Getting involved would complicate things.

But she couldn't leave him like that, could she?

Making a split decision, Maya threw down her things and headed for his door. She was surprised to find it ajar. He was sitting on the couch with his head hung low, a bottle of liquor on the table in front of him. A glass of dark liquid was in his hands. Maya suspected it was the aged cognac he kept on hand for celebrating a victory or sweet deal. But today was different. He was drowning his sorrows, whatever they may be.

She walked toward him quietly. He didn't say a word when she sat beside him. Instead, he continued drinking. When he'd finished the first glass, he poured himself another. They sat in silence for an eternity before Maya spoke. She was dying to know what happened. "Ayden?"

"Hmm…?"

"Are you okay?"

"No." He took another sip of his drink.

Ayden wasn't talkative by nature, but when he was in this mood, he would be even less forthcoming. "Did something happen at your lunch with Fallon?"

He turned to glare at her. The full force of his piercing hazel stare rested solely on her, and Maya squirmed in her seat at the intensity. "What do you think?"

Maya swallowed. She had to push and break through the barrier Ayden had erected to protect himself. She understood because she'd done the same thing herself. "What happened?"

"I don't want to talk about it."

"Perhaps if you didn't hold it inside, you might feel better," Maya offered.

"Feel?" Ayden huffed. "I don't want to feel anything."

Maya blinked several times, but tried again. "Ayden…" She touched his arm and he shrank away from her. Jumping to his feet, he made for the window on the far side of the room.

"Don't touch me, Maya. Not right now. You should go home." He turned away from her to face the window.

"I can't go home and leave you like this. You're hurting and I want to help."

He spun to face her. "You can't help me, Maya. No one can. Unless you can erase the last thirty years and make my father love me, want me—" he beat his chest with his fist "—acknowledge me as his son. His firstborn. The rightful heir to Stewart Technologies."

"Oh, Ayden."

"Don't!" He pointed his finger at her, tumbler still in hand. "Don't you dare feel sorry for me! I won't have it."

"Okay, okay." Maya held up her hands in surrender as she walked toward him. She took the glass out of his hand and placed it on a nearby table. He watched her with keen eyes, his chest rising and falling. "You don't have my pity. But I'm here for you, Ayden."

Heavy awareness surged through her as she locked gazes with him. Maya swallowed, but her mouth felt dry and parched. She inched forward until they were standing a breath away from each other. Something fundamental changed as they stared at each other, something that electrified the airspace. Maya was afraid to speak, afraid to break the interlude.

Maya touched his arm and when she glanced up, Ayden's gaze had turned from tortured to hot and burning. She should move away and get out of the office fast, but she couldn't seem to stop herself. There was so much tension inside him. Tension she wanted to help relieve. As if pulled by some imperceptible thread, her body moved closer to his. Maya felt the heat of him in her lower half as their bodies brushed once, twice. Then Ayden's hand flew to the small of her back and pressed her forward, clamping her tight against him.

Air whooshed out of Maya's lungs, but that didn't stop her from tipping her head upward and peeking up at him from beneath her lashes. She shouldn't have done that because with that movement, she swayed into his space. Ayden leaned forward until they were chest to chest, and then he kissed her. Their lips touched slowly, hesitantly at first, as if they were both unsure of whether they should continue, but then Ayden shifted, and Maya felt the strain of his erection against her middle and the kiss erupted.

Her mouth opened under his and he swept her into his embrace, kissing her deeply. Before she knew it, Maya's back was hitting the window, but she scarcely noticed because she was coming alive under Ayden's skillful mouth. His hands were threading through her hair and his mouth was devouring hers. Hunger coursed through her, and she thrust her hips involuntarily against his as an ache began to claim her lower region.

Ayden grasped her hips and tightened his arms around her, tipping her head to just the right angle so he could stroke his tongue with hers. Over and over again, he stroked her, deeper, harder and faster until he had Maya moaning in pleasure. She cupped the back of his neck and his hands roamed over her. When he found her breasts, he molded and kneaded them with his palm. He was luring her into a dark pit of need and Maya was drowning. She felt his hands snake under her dress, felt him touch her thigh.

Please, oh God, she wanted him to touch her there. She tilted her hips in silent invitation, begging him to do whatever he desired.

And just as his hands began inching to the damp place between her thighs, a knock sounded on the door. "House-keeping."

Maya jumped back as if a bucket of cold water had been thrown on them. She glanced at the door and then back at Ayden. His face was a storm of desire and Maya licked her lips.

"Do that again and I'll have you on the desk and to hell who sees us."

Maya blushed and, without saying a word, rushed for the door, swung it open and fled from the room. She ran past the stunned cleaner standing just outside the door, grabbed her purse and made for the elevator. She didn't dare look behind her because she couldn't look at Ayden. Not after what had just happened between them. If that cleaner hadn't knocked on the door when she had, who knew what would have happened.

Maya knew exactly what would have happened.

She would have allowed Ayden to make love to her again. And then where would she be? Back at square one.

* * *

Ayden slammed his fists down on his desk. He hadn't meant for that to happen, but Maya had gotten too close to the sun. And if she wasn't careful, she would get burned. That was exactly how he felt right now. Like scorched earth. Seeing Fallon had resurrected his demons. Ayden didn't talk about his family *ever* except the one time with Maya. She was the only person who knew he'd been abandoned by the great technical genius Henry Stewart.

But it wasn't exactly true. Ayden could remember a time when he was younger, before the divorce, when his father had been in his life. He'd been about five years old. He recalled his parents together, happy, but then Nora had come into the picture. Ayden had vague recollections of his mother and Henry arguing. His mother accusing Henry of being unfaithful. Ayden remembered finding Lillian crying in her bedroom because his father had asked her to leave.

Leave *her* house. And she had. She hadn't fought for what was hers—what was due her after she'd helped him build the company. Instead, she'd allowed that evil witch Nora to play lady of the manor in their home while he and his mother had been kicked out. Ayden blamed Henry for all the hardships they'd endured, the mental and physical abuse at Jack's hands. So there was no way in hell he would bail that man out of trouble. Let the company crumble. It was what Henry had coming. He was sorry Fallon was caught in the crossfire, but she was a grown woman and it was her decision to run the company. She would have to figure her own way out.

But Maya. Maya was another story. She'd only been trying to help, to lend a sympathetic ear, and he'd taken advantage of her. *You're weak.* The nasty voice of his conscience called him out. He'd let himself indulge in her when he'd given her his word that he would behave. If he couldn't keep the promises he'd made, he was no better than his louse of a father Henry, who hadn't kept his marital vows.

Ayden closed his eyes, but it did little to erase the imprint of Maya from his senses. He could still smell her sweet scent in the air. How in the world was he going to be able to forget how she tasted and go back to a professional relationship?

Seven

The next morning, Maya awoke feeling more exhausted than she'd been before going to bed. When she'd arrived home, she'd paced, unable to sleep because she couldn't get the kiss with Ayden off her mind. So she'd pretty much clock-watched the entire night, and time had seemed to stagnate.

Throwing back the covers, Maya showered and threw on her gear to go for a run. When she was in a mood like this, running was the best cure. She waved at her building's security guard and started for a nearby park about half a mile away. Maybe she could lose herself on the trail and feel invigorated afterward.

An hour later, Maya felt no better. In fact, she felt terribly silly for making a mountain out of a molehill. It was just a kiss. But was it?

Ayden wasn't just *any* man. He was the man of her dreams. The man whose face she had been unable to forget for five long years. And now, during her run, he was all

Maya could think of. The kiss had stirred up past feelings Maya thought she'd resolved. It had been earth-shatteringly passionate. It had rocked Maya to the core and made her wonder whether she could continue working for Ayden.

Maya realized that they'd never really resolved what happened five years ago. Instead, they'd acted like it was a one-time thing because she'd been upset over Thomas. She'd thought it had been pity, but now she realized that was a lie. If they'd both been bold enough, they'd admit there was something *there*. An attraction simmering just below the surface. Under the right circumstances and conditions, they combusted.

How else could she explain why Ayden had kissed her last night and she'd kissed him back? She'd been a willing and active participant in that kiss. Her heart thundered with excitement at how passionate Ayden had been. She'd felt the full force of that unleashed energy and doubted they would have stopped if not for the well-timed knock on the door.

Knowing that she felt this way, there was no way she could go out for dinner tonight with Ryan. Not when she had these swirling emotions surrounding Ayden on her mind. Once she made it to Starbucks for a coffee, Maya went to a quiet corner to make her call.

Ryan answered after several rings. "Maya, good morning."

"Good morning, Ryan. How are you?"

"I'm excited for our date this evening."

"Listen, about that—"

"Don't tell me you're canceling?" Ryan interrupted.

"I don't think it's a good idea that we go out," Maya said. "I really can't handle anything other than friendship right now. I have a lot going on in my life."

"Friendship sounds like a great start. Let's scratch dinner. How about attending a polo match?"

"Polo?" Maya had never been to a match and understood nothing of the game.

"Yes, polo. You can put on your Sunday best, well, in this case, your Saturday best, and meet me at the Austin Polo Club."

"I don't know...." Maya recalled that Ayden loved the sport. He used to talk about how he and Luke had played it during undergrad. Was he still playing for this club? But what if he were? Did it really matter? With all the people attending, it was highly doubtful he would even notice her.

"Do you have other plans?"

"No, but..."

"I'll see you at two then." Seconds later, the call ended and Maya was staring down at her phone. Ryan had hung up without giving her a chance to change her mind. Very sneaky of him. But she didn't have any plans, and if Ryan was okay that all she had to offer was friendship, then why not? She hadn't been out with anyone other than Ayden since she'd returned to Austin. It would be nice to have some male companionship, even if was a non-date. And who knows? Polo could be fun.

Ayden needed physical exertion to help clear his mind and give him some perspective on why he kept screwing up royally with Maya. He'd already gone to the gym this morning for two hours and was happy he had a polo match scheduled for even more punishment.

All morning as he'd hit the treadmill, weights, even the boxing ring, his mind kept wandering to Maya. And how he'd been greedy for her last night. He'd wanted to feel her skin against his. Had wanted to kiss her, touch her, and if that knock hadn't interrupted them, he would have taken her everywhere—up against the window, the desk, the floor, the couch in his office. He wouldn't have cared, because she'd spiked a need in him he couldn't recall feeling in…well….in five years. When that very same need had rocked him to his core and caused him to push her away.

Ayden hadn't understood it then and darn sure didn't understand it now. Maya was his assistant, his friend, yet she was the only woman who fired up a lust in him that was so profound he lost all thought or reason. She made him impulsive rather than cool and in control like he usually was in sexual encounters.

He had to get himself back on track, and today's match at the Austin Polo Club would help. After the gym, he'd gone home to shower and get ready for the game. He'd donned his usual ensemble of well-worn riding boots that fit just below the knees, white riding breeches and a black polo shirt with the number 3 for his position in the polo club. He liked being the attacker. And today, there was a tournament against a club out of San Antonio and he was ready for battle.

When he arrived at the club, he hopped out of his Bentley, gave his keys to one of the many valets and grabbed his gloves, kneepads and helmet with chin strap. He was looking forward to running his polo pony, a beautiful Thoroughbred he'd purchased some years back. He could thank Luke for introducing him to the sport in New England, because it had stuck. Ayden had found the polo club and been a member ever since. He typically tried to play twice a month to ensure he and his pony were one on the field, which in this case was the size of six soccer fields.

When he arrived at the stables, which housed two hundred Thoroughbreds, his team was already getting ready for the tournament. Ayden wasted no time saddling up his pony, and braiding and wrapping its tail. Once he was ready, he swung his leg around and into the stirrups. A club hand was on board to help, handing him his helmet and mallet.

"You ready to give those San Antonio boys a whooping and send them home?" Eddie, a venture capitalist and one of his team members, asked when he was mounted.

"Heck, yeah!" Ayden responded.

The first chukka went supremely well with Austin making the first goal. Ayden was really getting into the game. And when the umpire threw the ball between the two teams on the second chukka, Ayden took off after it with a fury, challenging the opposing San Antonio team member by riding him off. It worked. It moved his opponent away from the ball and out of the play so his teammate could score a goal.

"Good job!" Mateo, another of his team members, yelled as they began leading their ponies back to the equestrian facility for a break.

"Thanks, I was in the…" Ayden's sentence was cut short when he spied Maya and Ryan stepping out on the field to stomp the divots. What was she doing here? And with Ryan of all people?

Ayden was furious. Uncaring of who was watching, he began riding his pony across the field in Maya's direction.

"Having fun?" Ryan asked as he led Maya onto the green so they could stomp the grass.

"Oh, yes," Maya said, smiling from ear to ear. "Thanks for suggesting this." She hadn't the foggiest notion what to wear to a polo match. The only other time she'd seen one was when she'd watched Julia Roberts in *Pretty Woman*.

Did she need a big hat? She hadn't brought one with her. After rummaging through the closet, Maya had found a lace-embroidered off-shoulder white jumpsuit with wide leg pants. She'd matched it with some chunky wedges and large hoop earrings. She thought she looked pretty good. And when she'd met Ryan he'd agreed by giving her an appreciative whistle. He looked equally casual in a pair of Dockers, a polo shirt and a blazer.

"My pleasure." Ryan's mouth curved into a grin. "To be honest," he said, stomping the green with his foot, "I'd be happy with any time I got to spend with you."

Maya glanced up at him and there was no mistaking the interest in his gaze. Ryan wanted more than friendship, but that's all she had to give him. Her relationship with Ayden was too complicated for her to bring someone else into the picture, no matter how great he might be.

She wanted to say more, but then she heard hooves, and when she glanced up, she saw Ayden barreling down on them. Ryan grasped her by the waist and pushed her behind him as Ayden barely stopped his horse in enough time in front of them. Maya sucked in a deep breath at the near miss and noticed the lethal glint in Ayden's hazel eyes.

"Ayden, in God's name, man, you could have killed us," Ryan lashed out.

"Hardly," Ayden said, hurtling himself over the pony and pulling the animal forward by the reins. "I take care of what's mine."

The possessive look he gave Maya caused her stomach to knot up and her throat to suddenly become very dry. Was he talking about her? Because she wasn't his. She never had been and doubted she ever would be. He didn't do commitments. She'd always known that.

"What are you doing here?" Ayden inquired. There was an edge to his voice that Maya didn't understand.

"You invited me, remember?" Ryan replied. "At the restaurant."

"Ah yes." Ayden nodded and his voice became mellower. "I forgot. Though I had no idea you were bringing Maya." He glanced in her direction again, his gaze traveling from the wedges on her feet to the one-piece jumpsuit showing off her bare shoulders.

Maya finally found her voice even though her throat felt parched. "It was a last-minute thing, but I'm glad I came."

"Is that so?" Ayden's brow furrowed.

The level of tension between them ratcheted up and Maya's nerves were stretched tight. "Yes, that's right." She didn't appreciate his tone. He was acting as if she'd done something untoward when she'd only accepted a simple invitation to a polo match. *During the day.* It wasn't as if they were on a date. But weren't they? Even though Ryan had suggested it under the guise of "just friends," she knew he wanted more. But he also hadn't given her the chance to say no, having hung up before she could respond.

"Glad you're enjoying your date," Ayden said. "Be sure to watch me on the field." He jumped onto the back of the horse with ease and, after a swift kick, they were gone.

Ryan turned and eyed her. "What the hell was that about?"

Maya shrugged as if she didn't have a clue, but she knew. Ayden was jealous. Jealous over the fact that she was here with Ryan on what he thought was a romantic date when they were just friends. But why not let Ayden stew on it? He had no claims on her, and it would be good for Ayden Stewart to eat a little humble pie.

Ayden was angry. He didn't like how cozy Maya and Ryan were. Didn't like the level of intimacy he'd witnessed between them. Not one bit. He'd arrived back at the equestrian facility to cool the pony down and have a refreshment.

Although he didn't want a relationship with Maya, he

didn't want Ryan to have her, either. Which was totally unfair. Maya deserved someone better, who would treat her well, marry her and father a gaggle of babies. It's what she'd always wanted and thought she might have with the knucklehead who'd married her sister. Instead, she was in limbo with Ayden because he kept giving her mixed messages. They had a professional relationship one day. And the next, he was kissing her senseless and muddying the waters. Ayden couldn't make sense of it. He knew his jealousy was irrational, but he seemed powerless to control it.

"Are you going to keep daydreaming, Stewart, or are you ready to win this thing?" Eddie said from above him.

Ayden glanced up and found his team was already back in the saddle. "Yeah, I'm ready. I'm ready to pummel them." He hopped back onto his pony and they headed onto the field. He was going to win this thing. He had an audience and wanted to show Maya how skilled he was at polo. Of course, there were other skills he'd rather show her, which included the two of them on a bed or whatever surface was available.

He blinked. *Get your head out of the clouds, Stewart*, he reminded himself as the umpire threw the ball. Ayden took off down the field.

Unfortunately, the San Antonio team must have regrouped during halftime because they came back stronger than ever and won the third and fourth chukka, forcing a draw. Now they had to play another chukka, and the first team to score would win. Ayden wasn't playing his best and he knew it. Every time he got a chance, he was looking across the field, trying to find Maya, wondering what she was doing with Ryan. It was driving him crazy.

All four team members had gathered for a pep talk. "Come on, guys," Mateo commanded. "We've got to win this, otherwise we don't get to the Centennial Cup. So let's do this."

"Let's do it!" they all yelled.

Fired up, Ayden went all in. As soon as the ball was in the air, he rode toward his man. Ayden bumped the other player with his shoulder while simultaneously attempting another maneuver to hook his mallet when his opponent hit the ball. But their mallets got tangled together and both ponies began to get agitated. Before he knew it, Ayden was hurtling through the air and hit the ground with a loud thump.

Ayden had a splitting headache. Furtively he glanced around the room and that's when he realized he was at the hospital. The last thing he remembered was getting tangled up with the opposing player at the polo match and flying through the air. How long had he been out? He couldn't remember, he just knew he hated hospitals. That was where his mom had died. He tried to move, but felt immobile. Glancing down, Ayden saw a compression wrap around his ankle.

He couldn't afford any broken limbs. He led an active life and had a full workload. He wiggled his ankle. Thankfully, he could move it, but it was definitely swollen. He pressed the buzzer for a nurse. Several minutes later, one walked in. Dressed in blue scrubs and a white jacket, the young brunette came toward him to take his vitals.

"Ah, you've awoken from your slumber," she said.

"How long was I out?"

"For a while. You have a mild concussion, a contusion on your left eye and a sprained ankle, but otherwise, you'll be fine."

"Is that all?" he asked snarkily. "When can I get out of

here?" He used the remote to lift the bed upward into a sitting position. He hated feeling helpless.

"Not tonight," the nurse replied. "We're keeping you overnight for observation, but I'm sure the doctor will release you tomorrow into the care of a loved one."

The care of a loved one. He didn't have anyone here because Luke was across the ocean. His mother had been the only family he'd ever had. And as far as Fallon or Dane, he doubted either of them would come to his aid. The only person he could think of, the only person he would want taking care of him, was Maya. Maya cared for him and would be willing to help. And what better way to ensure she stayed away from Ryan than keeping her close by his side.

Oh, yes, Maya was the right person for the job.

Eight

Maya anxiously paced the hospital waiting room. How long was it going to take for them to tell her something? She'd been waiting for hours to hear about Ayden's condition and no one would tell her anything because she wasn't family. Ryan had stayed with her, but eventually she'd told him to go home. There was nothing he could do and she wasn't leaving until she could see for herself that Ayden was okay. Ryan had understood and advised her to sort through her feelings for Ayden.

When she thought about the accident, her heart turned over in her chest. She'd gasped in horror when Ayden had fallen from the horse. Immediately, she'd run to him, uncaring of how it might look to Ryan or anyone else. She'd just known she had to get to Ayden. He'd been lying motionless on the green and was unresponsive until the ambulance had arrived. He'd opened his eyes briefly on the ride to the hospital, and she hadn't seen those beautiful hazel-gray eyes since.

Once they'd arrived, she'd been treated like a second-class citizen and sent to the waiting room because she wasn't family. No one would talk to her until finally she'd pleaded for any word. They'd told her he was stable, but nothing more.

"Ms. Richardson?" a female voice called out from behind her.

Maya spun around and rushed toward the nurse. "Is there any news on Mr. Stewart?"

"Yes, ma'am. He's awake and asking for you."

Thank God! Maya closed her eyes and said a silent prayer. "Take me to him."

"Follow me."

The nurse led her into a private room. Ayden was sitting on the bed, fully awake with his ankle wrapped. He had one black eye, and a bandage was wrapped over the other side of his head, covering his left eye. Maya rushed toward him and, without thinking, flung herself into his arms. He clutched her to his hard chest.

"It's okay." Ayden patted her back as if he were comforting a small child. "I'm all right, Maya. I have a concussion and a sprained ankle, but other than that, I'm fine."

Inhaling, Maya counted to three and slowly rose to her feet. She'd overreacted and shown her true feelings. "I'm so relieved." Then she reached across the distance and swatted his arm. "Don't ever scare me like that again."

Ayden gave her a sideways grin. "Hey, I'm sorry. Didn't mean to give you a scare. Or sprain any ligaments." He nodded downward toward his ankle.

"Serves you right for those moves you pulled," Maya replied. "Ryan told me not many people try both those moves together."

"I had to do something. We were going to lose."

"And now look at you. You're going to have to take it easy. Maybe use the time for a much-needed vacation."

"I don't vacation," Ayden responded. "I have a business to run. I just need someone to help me while I'm..." He searched for the right word. "Incapacitated."

"Good luck. You're not an easy man to deal with."

"I don't need luck. I just need you."

"Me?" She hadn't been prepared for such a blunt, matter-of-fact statement.

"I need a nursemaid who can take care of me and help me navigate the next week, and I can't think of anyone more qualified than you."

"A-Ayden, that's crazy. I'm no nursemaid. I'm just your assistant."

"True, but you know me. You know what I like and dislike better than any other person," he replied. "You can do this, Maya. Unless there's a reason you can't?"

"What are you talking about?"

"I'm talking about Ryan Kincaid. You were with him at the polo match. In that outfit." He motioned toward her jumpsuit, which showed off her figure and a small swell of cleavage. "I know he's interested in you. Is the feeling mutual? Is that why you can't do me this favor?"

So he was jealous of Ryan. She knew it! But what would make Ayden think she could possibly get involved with another man after the kiss they'd shared last night? Ryan was just a friend, but Ayden didn't know that. It served him right that he was jealous. Over the years, she'd listened to him expound on plenty of other women.

Ayden's behavior didn't make any sense. He'd had a chance with her five years ago. But Ayden hadn't wanted her then. So what had changed?

Why now?

"Well?" Ayden was looking at Maya and waiting for an answer.

"I don't have to justify my actions to you or anyone, Ayden."

He glared at her and she could see he wanted to say more. She'd read between the lines with him long enough to know he was biting his tongue. He contemplated her for several long moments, his gaze scraping her from head to toe. It was a standoff that Maya intended to win.

"You're correct," he said, his voice softening. "I have no right to interfere in your personal life. I was out of line. But I am asking you for your help. You know me—and my needs and wants—better than anyone else. I want you."

Those words sank her. Her belly somersaulted in the air and did a triple axel like an ice skater, but she mustn't let it. She couldn't do this. There was no way that in spending time with Ayden, day in and day out, her true feelings for him wouldn't be exposed. "I'm sorry. I can't." Maya turned away. She couldn't look at him because doing so was playing tricks with her emotions.

"Maya, please," Ayden implored from the bed. "I'll double your salary. Whatever it takes. I *need* you."

Maya reminded herself to stay strong, but when she swirled around to face him, the pleading look in his eyes stopped her cold. There was no way she could deny this man anything even though it wasn't in her best interests. "Okay. Okay, I'll do it."

A large grin spread over his gorgeous face despite the bandage across his eye. "I knew you wouldn't let me down," he said smugly. "You should probably get back to the rental and pack up your things. I'll have a driver bring your belongings to my mansion."

"Your house?" she squeaked.

"Of course. You can't possibly take care of me from

your apartment. You'll need to move in, temporarily that is, until I get on my feet."

"I can't move in with you, Ayden."

"Why not?"

Because I'm in love with you. Because we kissed last night and almost had sex in your office the night before. Maya's face grew hot with a blush and she responded, "It's just not a good idea."

"Rubbish. It makes the most sense for you to be close by. So run along and collect your things and I'll have my driver meet you in a couple of hours."

"You can't just run roughshod over me, Ayden."

"I'm not trying to, but you must see how ridiculous it sounds for you to be my nursemaid from your apartment."

When he put it like that, it made Maya appear silly for suggesting such a thing. "Fine. Fine," she agreed begrudgingly.

"Good. I'm glad that's settled. Make yourself comfortable at my place. Feel free to choose any room you like. And then be back here tomorrow morning because that's when they're releasing me."

"Is there anything else, boss?" Because that was exactly the tone he'd used with her. Not the sexy way he said her name last night in the heat of passion.

"I'm sorry. I didn't mean to sound so formal, Maya. I really appreciate you doing this for me."

She nodded and before she could put a foot in her mouth again, Maya left the room. She needed some air anyway. Ayden had used her affection for him to lure her into his home. Now they would be sharing close quarters. How on earth was she supposed to keep her cool?

It didn't take long for Maya to pack up her meager belongings. And as promised, the driver called her when he arrived at the apartment building. He and the bellhop helped put all her suitcases into the limousine. Maya got in and leaned back against the buttery soft leather interior. It wasn't her first trip in a limousine. She'd accompanied Ayden on many occasions when they'd worked together. But it was quite different to be treated to this kind of luxury on her own.

Leaning back, she closed her eyes. Maya couldn't believe she was doing this. Not only had she accepted her old executive assistant position, but somehow she'd allowed Ayden to convince her to serve as his nursemaid *and* move into his home? It was insanity. But it had been impossible to deny him, especially after he'd said he needed her. *Wanted* her.

Of course, she knew he hadn't meant it like he had last night. That had been a moment in time, when he'd been in pain and reached for the nearest person to comfort him. She'd been convenient. She was a woman and he was a man. A man used to getting sex. Ayden had wanted to escape his past and she'd been willing. Like any red-blooded man, he'd accepted what she was offering.

She searched her purse for her phone. She'd called Callie after Ayden's accident and been beside herself. Callie had calmed her down, but would still be worried.

"Maya." Callie picked up on the first ring. "How is Ayden?"

"He's okay. He has a concussion and a sprained ankle, but he's okay."

"Thank God! I had no idea polo matches could be so dangerous."

"From what Ryan told me, they usually aren't, but Ayden was playing aggressively and making bold moves."

"Sounds like Ayden was jealous seeing you with another man. Do you think he was showboating to garner your attention?"

Maya was silent for a moment as she drank more of her champagne. "It's doubtful. He just wasn't exactly happy that I was with a client."

"A client? You mean another man?"

"I dunno," she fibbed. Because she'd thought the same thing. And she just had to spit out why she'd called. "Anyway, you should know I've agreed to move in and help Ayden around the house and at work until he's back on his feet."

"Sweet baby Jesus!" Callie retorted. "Out of the frying pan and into the fire. Don't you ever learn, girlfriend? What on earth possessed you to agree to such a thing?"

"He needs me. Please, be supportive, Callie. I need you to understand."

"Oh, Lord, Maya. I'm just scared that you're going to get hurt."

"I'll be okay. I can handle this." Or at least she hoped so, because if not, Callie was right. Ayden had the power to truly devastate her, so much so that she might never recover.

Nine

"Comfortable?" Maya asked once she'd settled Ayden in his master bedroom, fluffing his pillows and tucking the covers around him. She'd arrived late that morning to pick him up from the hospital. She'd come prepared with a change of clothes for him consisting of a tracksuit.

He smiled. He was more than comfortable. He was on cloud nine because Maya was here with him. Truth be told, when he'd made the outrageous suggestion, he'd expected her to turn him down flat. She'd put up some resistance, but in the end, he'd persevered and convinced her to move in with him. And with her tending to his needs day and night, there was no way she would have time to see Ryan Kincaid.

Was he really that jealous of his client?

Yes.

He hadn't liked seeing Maya spending time or having fun with another man. Her smile was reserved for only him.

"Yes, I'm comfortable, Maya. Thank you," he finally answered.

She'd been busy since last night. She'd placed crutches nearby to help him get around on his own. He could see her touches in the room, too. There were freshly cut flowers on the nightstand. His favorite spy books had been neatly stacked beside them along with a bottle of water and some pain pills. She'd filled his prescription. She'd literally thought of everything.

It was why he'd wanted her here with him.

Or at least it was one of the reasons. If he was honest with himself, it went deeper, beyond a friend caring for another friend, but he couldn't think like that. She was just doing him a favor.

"Is there anything you'd like?" Maya inquired.

You, Ayden thought as he peered at her through thick lashes. Today, she was dressed in slim-fitting jeans that showed off her sweet behind along with a long-sleeved sweater that had cutout shoulders. She was hardly wearing any makeup other than some mascara and some type of gloss that made her lips shine. He wanted to lean over, grab her by the waist and kiss it off. Although she might appear plain to some, Ayden thought she'd never looked lovelier. Lord, he was in a world of trouble.

"I'd like to go through any outstanding proposals including the Kincaids' to make sure they don't need tweaking before you send them out."

"You want to work?" Maya inquired with a frown. "For Christ's sake, you just got out of the hospital and are recovering from a concussion. Not to mention it's a Sunday, Ayden. I don't work on the weekends. So if you want this arrangement—" she pointed between the two of them "—to work, then you're going to have to remember those parameters."

"All right, what would you suggest we do? I can think of a few." Even with a bum leg, he had a few ideas, but they were certainly not PG-13.

"How about a movie? Or we could marathon a television show on Netflix."

"I don't watch TV."

Maya rose from her seat. "That's too bad because I'm going to find an activity for us that doesn't require the use of a bed."

He bowled over with laughter as he watched her scoot out of the room.

Maya was happy for some breathing room. She knew what other ideas he had because her mind immediately went to imagining the two of them naked, sprawled out over his sumptuous covers, kissing and making wild, passionate love. She'd felt her cheeks grow warm. Had Ayden sensed where her mind had wandered?

Probably not.

She was just a means to end, taking care of his immediate needs while making sure the office ran smoothly in his absence. Would he ever see her as more? Did she want him to?

Her mind was swirling as she set about locating the butler. She had to find some activity to keep the two of them busy on her day off. Because she was sure, come tomorrow, Ayden would be ready to get back to work, sprained ankle or not.

She found the butler downstairs in the kitchen talking to the chef about dinner. "Good afternoon, Ms. Richardson. Is there anything I can help you with?" he asked.

"First, you can call me, Maya." When he began to interrupt her, she held up her hand. "I'm going to be staying here while your boss recovers, so please call me by my first name."

"Very well, Maya. And second?"

"Do you have cable, internet, Netflix, anything to amuse us?"

A half hour later, Maya was armed and ready to entertain. The butler had secured a television and DVR on wheels and brought it into Ayden's master suite. Ayden had always told her he much preferred reading a good book or engaging in extracurricular activities with the opposite sex to watching mindless television. The butler had also found several board games like chess and dominoes and Taboo to keep their minds occupied until dinner. Meanwhile, she'd thrown some popcorn she'd found in the pantry into the microwave.

"What's all this?" Ayden asked when they brought in all the goodies.

"Your education on being an everyday joe," Maya said with a smile. "We're going to watch movies, eat popcorn and veg out all day."

"Really?"

"That's right, and you're going to love it."

And they did. While munching on popcorn, Maya joined Ayden on his bed—*above the covers*—and made him watch *Pretty Woman*. And instead of going downstairs to a formal dinner in his dining salon, dinner was served to them on television trays. Afterward, they ended up playing a game of chess. Ayden absolutely killed her.

"No fair," Maya said when the game was over. "You're a master at this. When did you learn how to play?"

Ayden shrugged. "I learned chess at boarding school. We didn't have much else to do. Thanks to my stepfather, I knew how to hustle those rich kids out of their money.

For them, it wasn't a hardship, but for me it ensured I had spending money because my stepfather didn't allow Mom to send me any money at school. He was just glad to be rid of me."

"What happened during school breaks?"

"I usually begged to go to friends' houses. Sometimes it worked. Sometimes Jack tolerated me coming home, but he made sure I knew that I was only there on his sufferance."

"That's terrible, Ayden. I'm sorry you had to endure that."

"I survived. And I don't want to end our fun evening on a sour note," Ayden said. "Plus, it's late and I'd like to get some rest so I'm ready for work tomorrow."

"You don't intend on going to the office, do you?"

Ayden shook his head. "No, not just yet. I'll work from home. At least until I get the hang of those." He nodded toward the crutches lying against a nearby chair.

"Those are easy. I taught Raven how to use them when she broke her leg in middle school."

"Have you spoken to your sister since the baptism?" Ayden inquired.

Maya greeted him with an icy stare. "I thought we were forgoing heavy talk?"

"I was just curious. I know how much she meant to you."

"My sister used to mean everything to me, but as you know, times have changed. We've spoken about my mom's care, but that's about it. You mind if we change the subject?"

"Okay," Ayden said. "I was just trying to be there for you like you've been there for me."

She offered him a smile. "Thank you, and I'm sorry if I bit your head off. I appreciate you caring. It's been a long night, and I'm going so you can get some sleep," Maya said. "I think you've done enough for today."

"I had fun. I can't remember the last time I honestly said that, so thank you." He leaned over and wrapped his arms around her in a hug. It should have been quick, but it lasted a little longer than was necessary. Maya felt her nipples instantly harden into bullets. Had he noticed she was turned on by a simple embrace? When he released her and she glanced up at him, Maya's heart stopped.

He'd noticed. His eyes were liquid, bottomless and filled with desire. She heard his breathing change ever so slightly and a throb of awareness coiled through her. He smiled and ran the back of his fingers down her cheek, and she shuddered. How had they gone from the friend zone to a heat flare in a matter of seconds?

"Ayden…" She didn't get the chance to utter another word because he closed the gap between them and sealed his mouth hungrily over hers. Maya responded to his kiss as every ounce of pent-up frustration from spending the day with him surged through her. She moaned and opened her mouth up to the onslaught of his kiss. She was just as eager as he was to taste, to lick and to twine her tongue with his. She drew him closer and he pushed her backward. Maya felt the pillows at her head as his torso pressed against hers, crushing her breasts against his magnificent bare chest.

Their mouths and bodies aligned perfectly and Maya parted her lips, inviting him in. Ayden took the cue and delved deeper. He took his time exploring, stroking his tongue back and forth against hers.

"This needs to come off," he said, and began tugging at the hem of her sweater. She obliged and tossed the offending garment over her head, revealing her breasts. Moaning, she captured his lips in a savage kiss, clattering her teeth against his as she sought more. Understanding her need, Ayden drew her closer against his body, settling her against his impressive erection. Maya tilted her hips back and forth and began rubbing shamelessly against his rigid length.

"Ayden…" she moaned.

His sizzling eyes sought hers and held. Then he began thrusting upward to meet her hip rolls. A fierce longing gripped Maya's insides. She knew she should slow things down, think about her actions, but she was powerless to fight the carnal desire he incited in her. She wanted to remove every stitch of her clothing and let Ayden make love to her, but she knew it would mean more to her than him. For him, it would just be a release and he'd treat her the same as before.

He sought her face with his hands and brought her closer, diving in to kissing her more thoroughly. Maya could feel herself losing control especially when he pushed his hips forward and ground his erection against her. And when she felt his hands at the zipper of her slim jeans, she didn't stop him. One of his hands snaked lower inside and she laced her fingers with his to guide him to her nub. When he dipped inside her and began stroking her inner walls, Maya was lost as pure pleasure raced through her.

Soon she was gasping and trembling and her muscles clutched his fingers as her climax rolled over her in waves.

"Did that feel good?" Ayden whispered as his lips left her mouth to nuzzle at her neck.

His words woke her up from the haze of desire she'd been under. Embarrassment flushed over her at how wantonly she'd behaved with him. She sat upright, pulling on her sweater as she went.

"Maya?"

"Please don't!" she exclaimed, scooting off the bed. "This…this should never have gotten this far. I told you it was a mistake for me to come here." She ran for the safety and cover of her bedroom. With a sprained ankle, Ayden wouldn't be chasing after her. She had to get some distance and figure out how she'd let the situation get so out of control.

Ten

Frustrated, Ayden sat upright, staring at the door Maya had just run through. Jesus! He rubbed his head. He'd really done it this time. The kiss in his office had been one thing, but tonight they'd had such a wonderful evening together talking, watching television and playing board games that it made Ayden realize just how much he wanted Maya. The heat between them was off the charts, so much so neither of them could deny the sparks when they were in such close quarters.

So he'd kissed her, not thinking about the complications of his actions. The sight of her half-naked body had jolted him. She was so beautiful, from her soft brown skin to her small breasts. She was exquisite and all he wanted to do was slake his thirst for her. Taste her very essence. He wanted to take those dark nipples into his mouth, to sink into her slick heat and let the passion between them explode. But he hadn't gotten the chance because Maya had run away from him *again*.

He wanted to go after her and bring her back to his bed, but he couldn't. Maya was skittish and he didn't blame her. He'd messed up last time when he'd appeared unaffected by their night together even though he'd been far from it. In fact, the desire he'd felt had scared him and he'd tried to marginalize it, brushing it off as good sex and nothing more.

It was certainly the best he'd ever had. And he wanted more. More of Maya. But how did he convince her to explore this side of their relationship when he'd hurt her before? Add the fact that he wasn't keeping the promise he'd made to her to keep their relationship professional and no wonder she was upset. Usually Ayden was a man of his word. He prided himself on it. But when it came to Maya, he didn't think with a level head. He'd been so convinced that night five years ago had been a fluke that he'd simply imagined how intense the attraction between them had been, but he was wrong. Years ago, he'd deceived himself, refusing to admit how much she meant to him, and now look at where they were.

Ayden glanced at the clock. It was after midnight and he was in no mood to sleep. His mind was racing, as he kept reliving the moment she'd come and the sounds she'd made when his fingers had been buried inside her. Jesus! Didn't she understand that she couldn't fight this attraction any more than he could? Because as sure as the sun rose in the morning, it was inevitable that they would fall into bed again. The chemistry between them would no longer be denied. It had probably always been there. Five years ago, they'd opened that door and there was no going back. Ayden had found the one and only woman who made him want to go back on his word.

Maya awoke the next morning knowing what she had to do. She had to leave Ayden, the job, Austin, all of it. Money be damned. She'd figure out a way to help pay her mother's cancer treatment bills. She was bright, and qualified assistants were always in high demand. She would find a job.

Throwing the covers off, Maya went to the bathroom. After brushing her teeth, showering and dressing, she packed up her minimal toiletries. Heading back to the bedroom, she pulled the suitcase out of the closet. She hadn't had time to unpack because she'd been so focused on caring for Ayden yesterday. Maya placed the luggage by the door and paused because she wanted to smell the flowers outside her balcony one last time before she left. When Ayden had said she could make herself comfortable, she'd chosen the room above the gardens. Opening the door, she walked to the railing and looked out over the colorful plants in full bloom, taking in the fragrance wafting in the air around her.

Her arrangement with Ayden was untenable. She couldn't continue doing the same thing and expecting a different result. Ayden was her Achilles' heel and she had to face it that being his nursemaid would undoubtedly have her winding up in his bed. Maya accepted that she had no willpower when it came to resisting him. Callie was right. She was in over her head.

She heard a creak behind her and turned to find Ayden on crutches behind her. Maya didn't speak and turned back around to stare at the garden.

"Maya, I recognize that last night the situation got out of control."

"You mean that boundary we crossed, that *you* said wouldn't happen again?"

She heard his sharp intake of breath. It wasn't fair to blame him entirely for what had happened. She'd played an active role. She whirled around. "I'm sorry. That was unfair."

He shook his head. "No, you're right. I promised to keep my hands to myself, but failed miserably. And if we're being honest, I can't promise that I'm not going to touch you, not kiss you, and not make love to you."

All of Maya's tingly parts came alive at his bold declaration. "So then you're in agreement that we can't work together and it's best we terminate this agreement."

"Far from it."

"Pardon?" She didn't understand. He'd just said that he wasn't going to keep his promise for their relationship to remain professional.

"I think we need to acknowledge there is something between us and *act* on it. Stop denying it exists and just see where it goes."

"Straight to your bed," she countered. "Because we both know where it will lead."

"And is it so wrong that we enjoy each other?" Ayden asked, hopping toward her until they were a few feet apart. "Don't you think it's high time we started acting like adults and admit we're attracted to each other?"

"Ayden…"

"You want me. Don't you?"

Maya lowered her gaze. She couldn't believe they were having this conversation. Right now. He was putting everything out in the open and pulling no punches. When she didn't answer, she felt him throw the crutches to the ground and move over to the railing until he was inches from her face.

"I dare you to say you don't."

Maya rolled her eyes upward. "Yes, I want you. There. Are you happy? I admit it."

"No, not really because you're too far away from me to kiss you properly."

Maya leaned over and Ayden rewarded her with a hot,

deep kiss. She moaned softly, opened her mouth, allowed his tongue to dip inside and mate with hers. *What was she doing?* Maya wrenched herself away and when he leaned in again, she put her hand against his hard chest. "Are you sure about this?"

"Yes. Don't deny us this pleasure when we both want this."

She did want him more than she had any other man, and he was offering her the opportunity to have unfettered access to him. But what did it all mean? What happened once he tired of her?

"Stop thinking, Maya. For once, just feel, allow yourself to let go and be *mine*."

His words startled her. Be his. They'd only been together once and it had been the most amazing sexual experience of her life. If she allowed herself to go there again, Maya was afraid she'd never be the same again. The first time she'd been completely devastated and had had to move away because she couldn't stand to be near him. What would happen this time?

"Come away with me."

She frowned in consternation. "Where?"

"To Jamaica. You were right. I never take a vacation and now, with this bum ankle, it's a prime opportunity to take some time off and explore us." He wound his hands around her neck and pulled her closer, bringing her into his air space. He leaned his forehead against hers. "Come away with me."

"I don't know, Ayden." She pulled away. "You're moving too fast. You want me to fly to Jamaica at a moment's notice? I have responsibilities now. You know I want to be here for my mother's next treatment."

"Of course, I understand that. It would be a short getaway. Plenty of time for you to get back, but enough time for us to discover our feelings in paradise without any outside influences."

Maya was torn. She did want to go with Ayden, but she was also afraid to jump into the deep end of the ocean without a life vest. Even though he'd admitted his desire for her, Ayden had the power to hurt her because she still had unresolved feelings for him. Feelings that went deeper than lust. Yet, if she didn't take this opportunity she would always wonder what could have been.

"All right, I'll go with you."

Maya couldn't believe she was on a recliner in a living room–style cabin of a private plane on her way to Montego Bay with Ayden. Once she'd agreed, Ayden had contacted his pilot to file a flight plan. In her wildest dreams, she would never have imagined that he would want to spend time alone with her or that she'd readily agree. But one devilish yet sinfully sexy look from him had her abandoning her principles and packing a suitcase for Jamaica. And she knew full well what was in store during their stay—mind-blowing, toe-curling sex the likes of which she'd never experienced except with him.

Maya was both excited and terrified. She was by no means a virgin, but she'd only been with a handful of men. And none of them had ever made her feel the way Ayden did. One look, one touch from him set her on fire. She didn't want to disappoint him.

A lump formed in her throat. She regarded him from across the aisle where he lay sprawled out on the couch with his ankle up, playing with his tablet. He seemed perfectly content, as if he didn't have a care in the world. Was he used to whisking women away on getaways to paradise so he could wine and dine them and take them to bed? Or maybe there would be no wining and dining, just sex. Full stop.

She hazarded a glance at him and found his eyes on her. "What are you worrying about, Maya? I hope you're not regretting your decision to come with me."

She shook her head. "I'm just wondering what you have in store for me."

He chuckled, showing off his winsome smile and perfect white teeth. "If you're asking if I intend to let you come up for air after I've had my wicked way with you, the answer is yes. We're going to Jamaica on vacation. I may not be able to do everything like climbing Dunn's River Falls, but we can certainly take in the sights and enjoy the culture."

Maya smiled brightly. "All right, that sounds good."

"You're too far away over there. Why don't you come over here." He gave her a wink and patted the empty seat beside him.

"Ayden Stewart, I have no intention of becoming a member of the mile-high club. Plus, the crew is just in the other room." She inclined her head toward the front of the cabin where the pilots and flight attendant were assembled.

"I promise to be good."

"I highly doubt that."

"Come here," he commanded. The tone of his voice had Maya rising from her seat and moving to him, but she stopped a few inches away from him. It forced Ayden to sit upright, grasp her arm and haul her forward. "This is much better," he said when she was in his lap. "And this will be even better." He lowered his head and brushed his lips across hers. She was fast becoming addicted to his kisses. He used everything in his arsenal to make her his willing captive.

When he finally lifted his head, he smiled as he looked

at her. "You look thoroughly kissed. Every man will know that you're with me."

He sat her upright and for the rest of the flight wouldn't let her leave his side. Maya supposed she should be flattered by all this attention, but what happened at the end of their vacation? Where did they go from there? She shook her head. She wouldn't think of the future, only the here and now with Ayden for the scant time she had with him.

They arrived in Jamaica later that afternoon and were met on the tarmac by a limousine. A driver took care of their luggage and his crutches while Ayden leaned on Maya for support to help him to the limo. Soon they were leaving Montego Bay and heading through the countryside. Maya peered out the window taking in the sights of the island country.

"You look like a kid in a candy store," Ayden said.

Maya turned away from the window. "I'm sorry, am I being too gauche? I've only been out of the country once during spring break when I let Callie talk me into going to Cancun."

"And how did that go?"

"Terrible. Callie was wasted half the time and when she wasn't, she was curled up next to several guys. I spent much of the time reading on the beach. The best part of that vacation was the fact that I was of legal drinking age and could partake in the cocktails."

Ayden stared at her for several long moments. "Have you ever done anything out of your comfort zone?"

"This," she responded. "I'm running off to an island to have an affair with my boss."

"Is that all I am to you—your boss?" Ayden asked.

His question startled her. She hadn't meant to offend him. If she had, it was a bad start to their journey. "No, of course not." She moved away from the window. "I'm sorry, you're more than just my boss." She took a deep breath and said what she truly felt. "You're about to become my lover."

He grinned and the light returned to his eyes. "That's right. And I intend to ensure I satisfy your every need."

"I can't wait."

They arrived at a beautiful villa built on the side of the mountain. It was the epitome of romance. The home was surrounded by long clinging vines, bougainvillea, fragrant flowers and dense green trees. There wasn't another house for miles. They would be secluded in this love nest. Tucked away from the world. Just the two of them.

Once their bags were taken inside, Ayden grabbed the crutches and showed Maya the grounds. "You've stayed here before?" she asked.

He nodded. "I come here sometimes when I need to be alone."

Maya wondered if he'd ever made peace with what happened, but chose not to ask. She just followed behind him. The inside of the home was white and clean with modern furnishings. The large kitchen and living area were open to the great outdoors which overlooked a terrace that had a luxurious infinity pool for their use. "I can't wait to slip into my bathing suit and get in."

"Who says you need a bikini?" Ayden replied, "We're the only ones here, Maya. You can feel comfortable in your birthday suit."

She turned away and began walking down the corridor to see the rest of the home. He wanted her to walk out in the open completely nude? She could never do that. She'd feel too self-conscious. Raven had always had the rocking body with curves for days that men liked, while Maya had always had a slightly boyish figure. Thank God, she'd finally gotten boobs.

Ayden caught up with her at the master suite, which housed a raised platform bed with a silky duvet in deep red and loads of cream pillows strewn over it. Swaths of fabric hung from the ceiling, draping the bed. They were gauzy and sexy. It clearly wasn't a bed made for sleeping.

"Maya!"

"Hmm?"

"Sit." He motioned to the bed and Maya took a seat so they could be eye to eye. "You have nothing to be ashamed or embarrassed about. You have a beautiful body."

"You don't have to say that, Ayden. I know that I'm not like the curvaceous women you usually date."

He cupped her chin, tilting her head so he could peer into her eyes. "Maya, I love your body."

"You do?"

"Yes, and I can't wait to show you just how much."

"When?" she asked expectantly, eagerly.

He gave her a wolfish grin. "Later, after dinner."

"Promise?"

"Oh, it's a promise I intend to keep all night long."

Eleven

Ayden ignored the jolt of arousal that had been surging through him from the moment they'd arrived. He wanted to give Maya the romantic evening she deserved rather than immediately throwing her down on the bed and thrusting inside her wet heat until she called out his name. It was crazy to think that for years he'd been blind to her beauty until that night five years ago opened his eyes. Ayden always had boundaries and each person had their proper place, but he'd been unable to put Maya back into the box he'd had her in. Instead, all their time together was marked by sexual tension and awareness.

Tonight was no different. After arriving, they'd both showered—*separately*—and were now in the living room having a drink before dinner. Ayden had arranged for a local catering company to drop off meals for them during their stay. A candlelight dinner was set up on the patio along with a bucket of champagne so he and Maya could eat underneath the stars. When they were ready, all they had to do was pull the food out from the warmer on the counter. Soup was in a heated container nearby and salad plates were already in place.

But he wasn't sure he wanted dinner. He wanted to devour Maya. Her beautiful dark brown hair was stylish, sleek and straight. She'd changed into a print sundress with spaghetti straps that stopped at the knee, giving him an unfettered view of her long legs.

It wasn't easy navigating, but he managed to pull out her chair. "Thank you," Maya said once she was seated.

Ayden shuffled to the other side, tossing down his crutches. "You're looking exceptionally lovely this evening, Maya."

She blushed. "Thank you."

"Would you like some champagne?"

"Love some."

He took care of pouring the bubbly into their glasses and, once filled, leaned both elbows over and held up his flute. "A toast."

"To us."

"And unexplored territories," Ayden finished, sipping his champagne.

Maya drank her champagne, regarding him from under mascara-coated lashes. He noticed she wasn't wearing much makeup and he liked that about her; she was comfortable being herself. He wanted her to feel that way, but he sensed her tension from across the table.

So he began talking about the fun things they were going to see and do in Jamaica while he ladled soup into the bowls on the table. "I've hired a tour guide for the day after tomorrow. Thought he could show us around the island. You can take some photos."

She smiled as she accepted her soup bowl. "I'm looking

forward to it. Hopefully, we'll get to eat some authentic jerk chicken. I hear Jamaica has some of the best."

"I didn't realize you liked spicy food."

"Then you need to catch up on all things Maya. Starting with how I like my pizza."

Ayden appreciated this feisty side of Maya, and over the next hour as they tucked into their dinner of Caribbean-style fish with grilled pineapple, shrimp and vanilla-rum butter sauce, he learned even more about her. He knew she loved running but didn't know she listened to Audible during her runs. Or that she had a fear of heights due to falling off the monkey bars when she was six years old. In his prior relationships, if he could call them that, he'd never taken the time to get to know their likes and dislikes, but Maya made him want to go deeper, know more.

By the end of the evening, they'd adjourned to a large chaise and removed their shoes to stargaze. They'd imbibed the entire bottle of champagne, along with a fair share of wine with their meal. They were both feeling relaxed, so it was only natural when Ayden leaned over and brushed his lips across Maya's. Hers were soft and sweet like the creamy custard of the crème brûlée they'd had earlier for dessert.

She tasted so good he dipped his head for another taste. Maya wound her arms around his neck and he pressed his body against hers. Feeling her against him was electrifying and he slid his hands down her bare arms to her breasts. He caressed the small mounds and felt her nipples pebble to his touch. And when she shuddered, he knew Maya was ready to take their relationship to the next level.

He rose up on one arm and looked down at her. "Why did you stop?" she asked, looking up at him in bewilderment.

"I just want you to be sure, Maya."

"I'm sure, Ayden. I want you. So stop talking and make love to me." She clasped his head and brought his mouth down on hers. He tried to keep it gentle, but the kiss deepened and desire bloomed. He wanted to explore her, taste every inch of her. His mouth left hers and found a path to her shoulders. He kissed the soft blades, sliding the straps of her sundress down as he went until her dress was lowered to her waist and he could feast his eyes on her breasts.

He bent down and closed his mouth over one round globe. Maya nearly jackknifed off the chaise as he sucked it deep into his mouth, swirling the rock-hard tip with his tongue. He alternated between sucking and licking and tugging the sensitive nipple with his teeth, causing Maya to squirm underneath him. The fact that she was so turned-on pleased him tremendously and he intended on giving her a lot more pleasure. He splayed his hand across her stomach to keep her down, so he could lean over and palm the other breast and give it the same ministration.

While his mouth played havoc with her upper body, his hands roamed lower, aiming for the place between her legs. His fingers slid underneath her dress, which had shifted up to her waist with all her squirming. He snatched the tiny scrap of fabric from her hips and tossed it aside, then plunged deep inside. Ayden found her deliciously hot and wet. He was thrilled with the knowledge that she was ready for him. His groin tightened in anticipation of what was to come.

"Ayden," Maya cried out when his fingers teased her, stroking in and out of her core.

"I want to taste you," he said gruffly. He moved lower to kiss her abdomen and stomach until he came to her hips and thighs. He splayed them open with his arms, pushing them wider to make room for what he wanted to do. He teased her first not giving her what she wanted. He licked the inside of both of her thighs, the back of her knees, even kissed her feet before he came back to her core. He licked the seam and Maya let out a sob of pleasure that only made Ayden want more. His tongue slid in farther, teasing the sensitive nub with soft flicks and licks. Her legs began to shake and she began to shiver uncontrollably.

She was close.

"Please," she begged him. Her moans and mews were driving Ayden crazy. He knew what she wanted, but he wasn't about to give it to her. Not yet. If he did, he wouldn't be able to hold himself together and would climax almost immediately because that's how hard his erection was. He needed to sate her first. Otherwise, if he took her now, it would be over too quick.

"Easy, love," he whispered, and returned to feverishly stroking her with his tongue until her entire body spasmed and she clutched around him. Her honeyed taste filled his senses and he lapped her until she eventually subsided.

Maya couldn't believe she'd just let Ayden make love to her out in the open. She'd always been somewhat of a prude. It was like she was outside her body, but couldn't stop herself. The man made her wanton and greedy for whatever he had in store. And if she allowed herself to think about it, she'd stop, and she didn't want to. She was enjoying being with Ayden and exploring this side of herself.

"Are you all right?" he asked, glancing up at her as he eased upward to kiss her.

She could taste herself on his lips. It was heady stuff. She ached to touch him, but she wanted to do so when they were skin to skin. She rose onto her knees and quickly threw off her sundress, tossing it to the floor.

Ayden grinned as she sat before him, completely and

unabashedly naked while he was still fully clothed. "So beautiful." His eyes darkened and Maya felt the words through every part of her.

She leaned forward and began unbuttoning his shirt. He shrugged it off his broad shoulders, bringing into view his beautiful torso along with his muscular biceps and trim waist. Her fingers tingled to touch more. She moved to his belt, loosening each loop, until finally she could unzip him. He stood and dropped his pants and they fell to the floor by her dress. Then he worked off his boxers to reveal the most spectacular erection she'd ever seen.

He was beautiful and *large*.

She would gladly take all of him inside her because she'd wanted this for so long. She hadn't thought it would ever be possible to be with Ayden again, yet here she was. He crawled onto the chaise beside her, covering her body with his, and Maya lost all coherent thought except that she was exactly where she wanted to be. In the moonlit darkness, Maya felt it was safe to say exactly what she wanted. "Please, Ayden."

"Please what?"

"Make love to me."

He gathered her in his arms and claimed her mouth. His fingertips caressed her all over with feather-soft strokes, up and down her side and then lower until his fingers slid along her crease. He teased her core, testing her yet again, making sure she was wet. And when he locked gazes with her, she knew he was seeing if she had any last-minute regrets. But she didn't have any. Then she watched as he retrieved a condom from his pants pocket and sheathed himself.

Soon she felt the ridge of his shaft, notching at her entrance. He eased forward inch by delicious inch and she gasped. But she wanted him even deeper and lifted her knees to help guide him in farther. He braced himself on his elbows and in one fell swoop surged inside her.

"Oh, yes," Maya moaned. It felt right to be joined with Ayden this way.

"You feel so good, Maya. And so tight," he panted as he began moving inside her. "Why did I ever think I could resist you?"

Maya didn't have an answer because she too had been denying the pull between them. But he'd been right. It was inevitable that they would end up like this. And so she gave into the moment, wrapping her ankles around his back and lifting her hips to move to the rhythm he set. Ayden flexed his powerful body and she sensed he was struggling for control because he began thrusting frantically. She parted her thighs wider, wanting him to fill her as completely as only he could.

"Maya…" He rasped out her name and his hold tightened around her as he pumped faster and faster.

"Yes," she cried as tension began building inside her. She could feel her body begin to tremble and she grabbed his buttocks and clutched him closer to her. And when he pulled back, only to thrust in again, she greedily met him as he pushed their pace. When her climax hit, she became undone and screamed his name.

He continued pounding into her until, moments later, she heard a loud groan rip from deep inside him and he fell on top of her. Maya tried to suck in air, but it was impossible. She gasped for breath as he rolled to her side.

Maya lay still, afraid to look at him, staring at the stars overhead. Had he felt the intensity of their coupling as she had? They'd been frenetic, more intense than five years ago. Yet it had been a totally sublime experience that she couldn't wait to relive over and over throughout their days in Jamaica.

"That was over much too quick," Ayden said softly from beside her.

With a small grin, she turned to him. "It was sensational."

"I'm sorry. I'm usually more in control, but with you…" His voice trailed off.

"With me what?"

"I can't seem to find it anymore."

She was happy that he felt he could be honest with her. "I've felt the same way for a long time."

"How long?"

"C'mon, Ayden, are you saying you didn't notice that I pined for you for years before I met Thomas? Maybe even after…"

He rose up on an elbow to look at her. "No, no, I didn't. I've always been aware of you, Maya—" he stroked her cheek "—but you were always so composed and buttoned up. And then when you came to me upset and broken-hearted, I don't know, something snapped and all I wanted to do was make you feel good. Special. Adored."

"You did that then. And now," she whispered as the warmth of his words enveloped her. She was eager for him to tell her more. Instead, he reached for her, closing the gap and sealing her mouth hungrily with his. She reciprocated, responding to him with abandoned enthusiasm. His arms wrapped tightly around her and Maya felt the hard ridge of his shaft against her middle. She couldn't believe he'd recovered that quickly. Or that she was just as desperate to feel him inside her again.

A maelstrom of unbridled lust and passion that only Ayden could quench took over. She crawled up the length of his body and straddled him, settling against his bulge. Ayden's gaze was dark and intense and filled with desire. He reached for yet another condom and rolled it on. She watched him, spellbound. And when he grasped her hips firmly, she sank down on him, drawing him in. He filled her in the best possible way. "Yes," she purred.

She enthusiastically began grinding hard against him, eager to feel his powerful body pressing against hers. Her hair fell into her face, but she didn't care. She put her hands on his chest for leverage and adjusted the angle, taking him even deeper inside her. And when she found the right rhythm, she rode him.

"Damn it, Maya." Ayden stared up at her, his skin glistening with sweat. She could feel him trying to slow down the pace, but she kept undulating against him. That's when he began to devour her, holding her more tightly as he nudged his hips higher, thrusting harder and faster into her. When her orgasm struck, her back arched like a bow, and only seconds later, a loud guttural groan burst from his beautiful lips. He thrust one final time and her entire chest constricted as yet another tidal wave of pleasure surged through her. All Maya could see was a flash of lightning as she closed her eyes and fell forward, drifting into another dimension.

Twelve

Maya stirred awake the next morning on the platform bed in the master suite as light streamed through the windows. How had she gotten here? Then she recalled that sometime during the night, Ayden had scooped her into his arms and carried her to the bedroom where he'd proceeded to make her come again and again. But where was he now? When she glanced over at his side of the bed, he was gone and the sheets were cool to the touch.

Last night had been an incredible night of lovemaking and snuggling next to Ayden. He'd been voracious in his appetite for her. Her underutilized muscles were slammed while several intimate areas felt sore, but she welcomed that if it meant Ayden wanted her as much as she wanted him.

Determined to go find him, she sat up, threw off the covers and went in search of something to wear. She was rummaging through her suitcase when Ayden returned carrying a tray laden with food and coffee mugs.

"Where do you think you're going?" he asked.

"To find you." Maya grabbed her silk robe and slung her arms through it, knotting it at the waist.

"Did I say you were allowed to get dressed?" Ayden asked as he laid the tray on the bed and took a seat.

She grinned. "I can't very well walk around naked."

"Why not?"

Maya flushed. She didn't answer him; instead, she walked toward the bed and sat beside him. "What do you have here?"

"Some omelets, toast, fresh squeezed orange juice and coffee."

"You made all this?"

"Oh, heck no, the catering company stopped by this morning."

"Did they? I didn't hear them."

He grinned. "That's because you were exhausted."

"I wonder why."

He rolled to his side and leaned over to kiss her. "I can think of a number of reasons, but you need to eat. And I'll draw you a bath. I suspect you're a bit sore this morning." He searched her eyes for confirmation. "We, were, um, very vigorous last night."

Maya flushed. He was right. He hadn't been gentle, but she hadn't wanted him to be. Nevertheless, she'd never spoken so openly about intimacy with another man. "Thank you. That would be lovely."

He hopped off the bed and headed for the en suite while Maya continued nibbling on toast and the delicious Denver omelet. She heard the tap running and smiled at his thoughtfulness. When she was done eating and Ayden hadn't returned she went to the bathroom. He had not only drawn a bath, but he was in it.

"Are you coming in or do I have to come and get you?"

"That won't be necessary," Maya said, relieving herself of her robe and sinking into the steaming water. She leaned back against Ayden, pressing her backside against his shaft. He was semi-erect, but that was quickly changing. She opened for him, letting him take any liberties he chose, but he didn't. Instead, he washed her thoroughly and then eventually swaddled her in a towel and carried her back to the bed.

Maya was a bit disappointed. She'd thought he would gather her against his chest so she could straddle him and go for another round, but instead, he laid her down on the bed. Desperate not to lose the connection, she circled her arms around his neck. He kissed her then, openmouthed, with such raw passion that her brain short-circuited. Heat pooled at her core, making her want him all over again. "Ayden…"

"Hmm…" He'd moved from her mouth and was nibbling at the sensitive spots on her nape and neck. When he dipped his tongue inside her ear, Maya moaned.

"Feel good?"

"Yes…"

"I'd like you to feel even better." He shifted down her body and Maya parted her legs, letting him in.

He glanced up, his eyes locking with hers momentarily before he began to pleasure her. He teased her with his tongue and fingers, arousing her so much so that she thrashed and begged him to take her, but he didn't. Instead, he licked her until her orgasm struck hot and fierce and she came apart. Her entire body trembled and he kissed through the aftershocks until lethargy took over and she closed her eyes.

But as she drifted off, the truth hit her hard in the chest. Maya had allowed herself these moments to enjoy Ayden and all he could offer because deep down she knew it wouldn't last.

Ayden hadn't made any promises. He'd only offered her this week, this moment in time when it was just the two of them away from the world. She'd taken it and she wouldn't surrender to regret now.

She was here in Jamaica with Ayden, the man she loved. Oh yes, that was the truth. There was no denying it.

She loved him.

Ayden stared down at Maya's sleeping figure. Her mass of hair was spread across the pillows like a fan. He gently lifted a strand and breathed in the fresh citrus scent. It smelled like Maya, and his chest felt tight and his breathing became harder. He rubbed his forehead.

He'd thought coming to Jamaica would help clear up this insatiable need he felt for Maya, but it appeared he'd only stoked the flames. Waking up with Maya by his side should have been alarming because he typically never stayed the night with other lovers. Once his lust was sated, he left and returned to his own home to sleep. But, with Maya, he felt like he was home. And when he'd turned to her during the night, she'd welcomed him with open arms, all too eager to please.

And she had pleased him immensely.

With each orgasm, her tight, slender body had blown his mind into a million pieces. He'd watched her responses, heard her cries and moans as he'd extracted every ounce of pleasure he could from her pert breasts to the thatch of hair between her thighs. She was his fantasy come to life and he'd made sure to taste every inch of her.

Just now, he'd wanted to take her again and she'd been willing, but he'd needed to regain some composure. He felt off his game. Felt as if he was diving into the deep end of the ocean without knowing how to swim. They would have to get out of this house tonight. If they didn't, Ayden feared he'd keep her naked and writhing on the bed for the entire length of their stay.

Eventually, Maya did awake and he arranged for them to go to Rick's Café, one of the famous bars in Jamaica. They arrived before sunset so they could see the brave souls willing to jump off the highest cliff into the Caribbean. They'd dressed casually for the night out; he was wearing linen trousers and a matching button-down shirt while Maya had opted for a filmy dress that left her shoulders bare.

"We're here," the driver announced when the limo stopped.

"Ready for a fun night?" Ayden asked, squeezing Maya's hand, which had been resting in his for the entire drive from the villa.

"Absolutely."

The well-known bar was alive with activity, full of bikini-clad and bare-chested patrons. After a well-slipped tip, the host was able to find them a table overlooking the West Cliffs. The view was spectacular, and Ayden was looking forward to the sunset as well as time spent with the woman across from him.

"This is great, Ayden. I'd heard about this place and always wanted to come."

"Are you feeling adventurous?" He inclined his head toward the top of the cliff divers were jumping from.

Maya shook her head. "No, thank you. I'll leave it to the daredevils. But I'll cheer them on from here."

"My kind of gal."

He appreciated Maya even more when instead of ordering a cocktail, she got a Red Stripe like a local and indulged in jerk chicken and Jamaican beef patties. The woman was full of surprises. He doubted any of the well-coiffed women he usually dated would be caught dead in an establishment like this. For them, it had to be five-star all the way, but Maya was content with just being normal. Ayden didn't realize just how much he'd been missing out on until now.

They didn't stay and close down Rick's Café. After watching the colorful and vibrant sunset and dancing hip to hip to reggae music from the live band, Ayden was horny as hell. When Maya had put her rear to his groin and begun grinding her hips to the rhythmical music, he'd been in both heaven and hell. Hell because he was getting turned on by a dance in front of too many people and heaven because it would take hours to get back to the villa so they would have plenty of time to enjoy each other in the limo.

After finding the condom in his wallet, he knew he wasn't even going to try. Once they were seated in the limo, he hauled Maya into his lap and crushed her mouth to his. He indulged himself in her with long sweeps of his tongue, thrusting and stroking until eventually he had to come up for air. All he could think about was touching her, kissing her. He leaned his forehead against hers.

"I want you," he murmured.

"We're in a limo." The blacked-out divider had been lifted as soon as they'd entered.

"I don't care." He lifted her so she was straddling him. Then he ran his hands through her hair and brought her mouth forward to his. And when he'd tasted his fill, he bent his head to suck her through the fabric of her dress. He reveled when she arched to meet him, pressing her nipple into his mouth so he could take a nip. Ayden reached underneath the dress to find the thong, the only piece of underwear he knew she was wearing. He was delighted to find it damp with desire and, with a tug, ripped it from her body. Then he plunged a finger inside her.

"Ayden…"

He stopped her cries by closing his mouth over hers and let his hands do all the talking. He began feverishly stroking her and she bucked against him, her breathing coming in short gasps, but he had no intention of letting her climax without him. He reached between them and tugged at the zipper on his trousers until he got himself free, then lifting his hips, he shoved them down with one hand while holding Maya in the other.

"Maya," he groaned, and handed her the condom. "Put it on."

She looked at him, her eyes glazed with desire, and complied. Once he was sheathed, he kissed her again and thrust inside her.

"Oh, baby, you feel so good," he said, before withdrawing slightly and slamming back in again. He repeated the process over and over and Maya lifted her hips to meet him as he went as deep as he could. But this couldn't be just about him and his release. Slipping his hand between their bodies, he found her sweet spot and pressed his thumb there. Maya's entire body began to shake, her muscles contracting around him.

Ayden was lost and all he could do was continue pumping inside her until he felt the familiar tension build in his body. He stiffened and then exploded inside of her, triggering yet another orgasm for Maya. She collapsed against him, clutching his shoulders and circling her arms around his neck.

Neither of them spoke for the remainder of the drive. They just tidied themselves up as best they could until the driver eventually pulled up in front of the villa. Ayden glanced over at Maya. Her hair was unkempt and her dress was wrinkled with damp spots at her nipples. There was no denying she looked as if she'd been made love to. And even though he'd just had her, Ayden wanted her again.

He was in big trouble. If this was how he felt after a few days with Maya, how was he going to feel when their short time in Jamaica was over? He was quickly losing his head to this beautiful, amazing woman, and it scared the living daylights out of him.

Maya sat across from Ayden as they played a game of dominos on the deck outside the villa. She'd enjoyed these lazy days in Jamaica with Ayden. Waking up and going to sleep, making love or just lounging by the pool.

When she had time, she'd called her sister to check in on their mother. They didn't talk long, only enough for Raven to inform her that Sophia was lethargic and nauseous, but otherwise hanging in there. Maya wished there was more she could do, but they had to allow the chemo to do what it was designed for. After the call, she was down in the dumps, so she was especially excited when Ayden had told her they would tour the island and visit Dunn's River Falls.

Ayden hadn't been able to climb the falls with a bum ankle, but he'd waited for her at the bottom while she'd soldiered up the cliff. Afterward, however, he'd been sore and achy from the hiking and she'd had to give him a foot rub and put him to sleep. That hadn't lasted long and he'd woken up in the middle of the night as hungry for her as he'd been that night in the back seat of the limo. She blushed thinking of the encounter.

She lifted her fingers to her lips, recalling the feel of his mouth and how magical his kisses were.

"And what are you thinking about?" Ayden asked as he moved another domino.

"Oh, nothing. What are we going to do on our last night here?"

"Anything you want."

"How about we find the nearest hot spot and hang out with the locals?"

"You sure?"

"Why not? Could be fun."

"I'm game if you are."

Just then Ayden's cell phone buzzed beside him. He glanced down at it but didn't answer, as he'd done for several days now. Although she wanted to ask him who was trying so urgently to reach him, she was afraid to delve too deep.

"Important call?"

He shook his head. "Yes…no…maybe so."

"Which is it?"

Ayden shrugged again and she could see his shoulders stiffen as if he didn't want to answer, but he did. "It's my sister, Fallon. She's been trying to reach me to convince me to help her."

"But you can't."

"*Won't* would be a more accurate word." Ayden made another move. "I won."

Maya glanced down and, indeed, he had, but her mind hadn't been on the game. It had been on him. "Maybe you should talk to her."

"It won't change my mind, Maya. I'll give the Stewart family exactly what they gave me. Nothing. I owe them no allegiance."

"True, but she is your sister."

"In blood only. And why are you pushing this anyway?" He glared at her. "You more than anyone know how my mother and I were treated by Henry Stewart."

Maya was surprised by the icy glare Ayden was giving her. She knew it was a touchy subject, but she was trying to help. She cared deeply for this man and his well-being. "Yes, of course I do."

"Then why?" he pressed.

"Because…" Her voice trailed off.

"Speak your mind, Maya. You obviously have something to say."

"I just want you to be happy, and settling things with your family might bring you the peace you crave."

"I *am* happy," he replied. He reached across the distance between them, grabbed her arm and pulled her into his lap. "Here with you." He grasped both sides of her face and kissed her hard on the mouth.

Maya could see what he was doing. He was effectively ending the conversation and shutting her out like he always did. And she let him because it was what he needed. But some day—some day soon—there would be a reckoning that he wouldn't be able to turn away from.

Thirteen

About an hour before arriving home in Austin, Ayden looked out the window of his private jet and reflected. He had enjoyed Jamaica and spending time alone with Maya, but it was time for him to get back to work. He'd never been gone this long from Stewart Investments. It was his baby. A dream he'd accomplished on his own with no help from Henry Stewart.

Which was why Fallon's request was so misguided. She had to have known he would turn her down. Ayden had been estranged from the Stewart family for decades. Had it really come as a surprise to her? It must have, because she'd been trying to reach him on and off for the last three days.

He glanced across the cabin at Maya, who was lying on a reclining chair sleeping soundly with her Kindle in her lap. He'd been banking on having a little fun while airborne and seeing if he could convince her to become a member of the mile-high club. Over this week, she'd not only been an extremely passionate lover, she'd been open to trying new things, like when he'd pulled some silk sashes from his luggage and tied her hands... Christ! He needed to get a grip. They were going back to Austin to work. Now that his ankle was starting to feel better, he wouldn't need any help at home. Maya could go back to her apartment if she wanted. The problem was, he didn't want her to. His emotions had become entangled and he wanted her with him. But for how long? He didn't know, but surely they could figure out something. He sat up straight, frustrated by the circumstances.

She stirred in the recliner and glanced over at him. "How long was I out?"

"Not long." He closed the report he'd been reading on his tablet. "We'll be landing in another hour."

She rubbed the sleep from her eyes. "Great. That will give me time to freshen up."

"You look beautiful, as always."

"If you say so."

"Maya, I would think after a week in Jamaica with me that you know I find you utterly ravishing."

A grin spread across her face. "Yes, I suppose."

"Suppose? Why don't you come over here and I'll convince you."

She shook her head. "Oh, no, you don't. The limo was bad enough, but not the airplane."

He laughed. "All right. You can't blame a man for trying. So listen. I think we should discuss what happens when we get back."

Maya's eyes grew large and he saw genuine fear in their depths. He would have to tread carefully because he didn't want to hurt her. Not now. Not ever.

"Yes?"

"You're moving in with me."

Her mouth turned down in a frown. "Is that a question or a statement?"

"The latter."

"I don't recall being asked."

"You agreed to take care of me," Ayden replied, annoyed by her response.

"And now you're healed."

"Are you saying you don't want to come back home with me?" Ayden wasn't ready to let her go, not by a long shot. She'd come to mean more to him than just a lover. She was his friend.

"Of course not, but we hadn't really discussed it."

"We're discussing it now." Why was she being so noncommittal? This wasn't like her. Now that the shoe was on the other foot, was she done with him? He couldn't believe that. He'd been with her, he knew Maya cared a great deal about him. Surely this wasn't the end of the road?

She sighed. "Yes, we are. I just wasn't sure of what you wanted. I just assumed that Jamaica was Jamaica, and I would move back to my place."

Ayden couldn't believe he'd misjudged the situation so entirely. Unbuckling his seat belt, he walked over and sat beside Maya. He grasped her delicate hand in his. "I'm sorry if I wasn't clear about what I wanted and how absolutely hot I am for you. I want you to come back with me to my home. Please say that you will."

Maya stared into his hazel eyes. Any girl would jump at the chance to have what he was offering, but she was hesitant. She knew Ayden didn't share her feelings. He hadn't said he was in love with or even that he was falling for her. He'd said he was *hot* for her. Meaning that as long as she was willing to be his bedmate, he'd happily have her. But again her mind went back to that age-old question: *how long?*

"Maya?" He sounded unsure. It saddened her that she was making him feel this way, but she also had to protect her heart.

"Maybe it's best if I go back to the apartment. I mean, you're better now and you don't really need a nursemaid."

"Or a lover?" he asked coldly, pulling his hand away from her and rising to his feet. "Are you saying you've tired of me after one week?"

"No, that's not what I'm saying at all," Maya responded hotly, jumping to her feet. "Don't put words in my mouth, Ayden Stewart."

"Then what? Why are you turning me down? I know it's not because you didn't like the sex. I lost count of your orgasms."

Tears sprang, stinging her eyes. How could he speak to her this way after the week they'd shared? She spun away from him and began walking to the lavatory, but he called after her. She couldn't face him because she feared he would see the tears fall.

"Maya, wait! I'm sorry. I shouldn't have said that." He reached her with two long strides and caught her at the door. "I'm truly sorry. You didn't deserve that. I guess I don't know how to do this." He rubbed his head in frustration.

"Do what?"

"Be casual with you about sex. You're not like the other women I've been with. You're Maya."

"And that's a bad thing?" Her voice cracked when she looked at him.

"Yes. No. God! I don't know, you're making me crazy." He began pacing the cabin.

"See." She pointed to him. "You don't know how to do this any better than me."

"I know I want you with me."

"So Ayden gets to have everything he wants. Me at the office. Me in your bed. What about what I want?"

"C'mon, Maya. That's not fair. I rewarded you handsomely to get you back at Stewart Investments, and as for being in my bed, you wanted me as much as I wanted you."

Maya turned away from him. He was right. It was unfair of her to put her expectations on him. "You're right. There. Are you happy?"

He stared at her intently. "Not in the slightest. Not unless you're agreeing to come back with me."

"For tonight, yes," she countered. "All my stuff is there."

"And after?" he pressed.

"We'll just have to see."

Have to see? Ayden was still reeling from Maya's words earlier on the plane as he got ready for bed. She'd refused to give an outright yes or no to his request for her to stay with him. Or had he meant *live* with him? He hadn't really defined what he meant. Was that why she was unsure?

Since they'd returned from the airport, he'd been busy catching up on phone calls and emails in his study. There were several from Fallon, as expected. Maybe Maya was right. He should call her, if for no other reason than to make sure she was okay, because despite what he'd said, he did care.

As for Maya, when they arrived, she'd immediately gone upstairs to unpack. Or pack? Ayden didn't have a clue. Just like he didn't know where to go from here. It was all so confusing. Maya was confusing. Bringing her back to Stewart Investments was supposed to be straightforward. He needed an assistant and with a little coaxing she had become available. He'd never anticipated that the attraction he'd felt for her so long ago would rear its ugly head. He'd thought he'd worked through those feelings. It had been a one-time thing because she'd been hurt and he'd wanted to console her. He'd moved on with his life, dated other women and relegated that night to an indiscretion not to be repeated.

He'd never anticipated becoming so taken with her that he'd whisk her off to paradise and make love to her day and night. Or that he would feel a deep yearning to commit to her in some form or fashion.

No one could have foreseen it.

Or could he have? If he'd just dealt with the insatiable lust he'd had for her back then, maybe it would have fizzled out and they'd have gone their separate ways. Now it was complicated because he knew what it was he'd been missing out on all these years. Now Stewart Investments needed her—or rather, *he* needed her—and he'd do anything to keep her.

With renewed purpose, he strode to his library door and took the stairs two at a time until he reached the second floor, where Maya's room was located. The door was ajar and he watched from the doorway as she *unpacked* her suitcase. Surely, this must mean she'd decided to stay? His heart began thundering in his chest, but Ayden refused to analyze what it might mean. "Knock. Knock."

Maya whirled around on her heel to face him. She was holding a sexy little teddy that she'd worn for him in Jamaica, though it hadn't stayed on her long. "Come in."

Ayden smiled as he came toward her, only stopping when he was in her personal space. Maya stepped backward, dropping the teddy, and he advanced. He loved this dance between them. It was a sort of foreplay he would never get tired of. "You're unpacking."

"No, I was just getting out something to wear for tonight..."

He grinned. "Oh really? Well, what do you say you leave that teddy here and come to my room? Because you won't really need it for what I have planned." He circled his arm around her waist and led her out of the room.

"What about dinner?"

"I'll have dinner sent up."

Maya felt oddly out of sorts Monday morning as she went through her usual routine of getting Ayden's calendar settled for the week. Could it be because her sinfully sexy boss and the best lover she'd ever had in her life had kept her up half the night doing wicked things to her? Although she hadn't agreed to move in with him, she had enjoyed the last few nights at Ayden's with unadulterated relish. She even had the whisker burns on her thighs to prove it. Maya blushed. She knew she was expected to jump back into work even after a week and multiple nights spent in Ayden's arms.

He didn't seem to have any problem getting back into the swing of things. She glanced at his door, which had been closed for most of the morning. Ayden had one meeting after another with department heads after their vacation. Eventually the door opened and he emerged. He was wearing a charcoal suit that made him look every bit as powerful as he was. Several other men departed after him.

"Maya, can you come into my office?" He went back inside.

She picked up her tablet and followed him. Ayden was standing by the floor-to-ceiling windows staring out over Austin.

"Close the door."

She did as instructed and when he spun around to face her there was only one thing she saw in his stare. Red-hot desire. She swallowed.

"Come here." He breathed his command.

Maya battled with herself—her pride demanding that she deny him. He'd already gotten his way by having her stay at his house. She couldn't give him everything. But her own lust for him won out.

She stepped toward him until she was close enough for him to grasp her waist and pull her against him. She arched her neck and glanced up into those eyes she always got lost in. He lifted his hand and curved it around her neck, bringing her face closer to his. Then he bent his head to kiss her until she softened against him. She felt powerless and gave in to the passion he aroused. His lips were firm and sure and took everything. When they broke the kiss, their breathing was shallow and unsteady.

"I've been dying to do that all morning," Ayden said. "I've been in those damn meetings thinking of nothing but kissing you." He stroked her already swollen lips with his thumb.

"We can't do this here." Maya tried pulling away, but Ayden wouldn't let her go.

"You're right. I'm sorry. I should have been more discreet."

She let out a sigh of relief. "Thank you. I don't want everyone to know we're an item." She glanced behind her at the door. "They'll think I got this job back because we're sleeping together."

"But you and I know that not's true. You're back as my EA because you're the best."

"Even better than Caroline?" she asked with a smirk.

His dark eyes stared back at her. "You know the answer to that."

"Good, because this assistant needs to leave early today. My mother is trying a new treatment and I'd like to be there." When they'd been in Jamaica, she'd shared her mother's condition with Ayden.

"Of course. You didn't even need to ask. I wish I had been there when my mom was ill. Take whatever time you need. I'll see you back at the house later?"

She nodded. "Thank you."

He kissed her on the forehead and released her.

After finishing up some last-minute items for Ayden, Maya drove to the cancer center where her mother would be getting her treatments. When she arrived, she found Sophia, Raven and Thomas sitting in the waiting room. They all rose when she approached.

"Maya, I'm so glad you could come," Raven said. "Mama, aren't you happy Maya's here?" Her sister looked up at her and smiled for the first time in a long time.

"You told her about my condition?" Her mother turned to Raven. "I thought you had it covered?"

"Of course, I told her. She had a right to know," Raven responded. "It can't all be me mom, you have another daughter."

"I didn't want Maya burdened especially starting her new job. Or should I say her *old* job." Her mother attempted a laugh, which turned into a coughing fit that required Thomas to help her into a nearby chair.

Maya immediately rushed to her side, kneeling in front of her. "Are you okay?"

"Why are you all hovering over me?" Sophia huffed, coughing again into a handkerchief she pulled out of her purse.

"Because we care," Raven said from beside her. "We all do." She glanced in Maya's direction. "And it's about time you know how much."

Her mother frowned. "What do you mean?"

"It means Maya has been helping pay for your treatments since she returned to Austin. They were too expensive for us to manage with a new baby, and we needed her assistance."

Tears sprang to Maya's eyes. She couldn't believe Raven was taking up for her when she never had in the past.

"So *you're* paying for my continued therapy?" her mother asked, staring at Maya.

"Yes, Mom. I am." Maya wiped away a tear with the back of her hand. "Is that a problem? Or would you rather your favorite daughter and son-in-law continue to struggle?"

"Of course not," Sophia stammered, with tears in her eyes. "I just never thought you cared."

Maya rolled her eyes upward and prayed for strength. She couldn't stand on the sidelines while cancer ravaged her mother. And the monetary assistance wouldn't help only her mother—it was about healing herself. She truly needed to let go of the past. "You're my mother. And although we don't see eye to eye and never have, I do care. I love you."

Tears filled her mother's eyes. "Thank you. I know I may not deserve it, but I'm glad you're here." She squeezed Maya's hand back.

"Good, because you have both your daughters here to support you." Maya glanced over at Raven, who gave her a reassuring smile. They were a long way from reconciliation, but they'd get there. And for the first time in years, Maya was open to it.

A nurse appeared several moments later to take her mother away for the treatment. When they advised that one person could come with her, Maya fully expected Sophia to ask for Raven, but she looked at Maya.

"Would you come with me?"

Maya rose to her feet. "Yes, Mama. I will."

Fourteen

Ayden prowled around his enormous house, glancing at his Rolex every few minutes. It was after eight o'clock and he hadn't heard from Maya. He knew she'd gone to be by her mother's side, but that had been hours ago. She hadn't called or texted and it was driving him crazy. She didn't answer to him after hours, but the least she could have done was let him know everything was all right.

Eventually, after working through the evening, he flopped on the couch and made himself comfortable by turning on the television and flipping through the channels. He never watched TV; it was just noise. Even though he knew his staff was down the hall, he felt lonely without Maya. His voracious hunger for her was not subsiding; he wanted her more than ever. He loved the way she stood her ground, telling him off when she didn't agree with him. Or the way she found joy in the simple things in life like playing dominos or drinking a Red Stripe.

He'd tried to ignore his feelings for Maya, but they kept resurfacing. She was smart and funny and beautiful, with her sexy, tight body. He recalled how she'd looked in a bikini with her skin sun-kissed from the Jamaica sun. He was craving her something fierce and he knew she felt the same, but she was erecting barriers between them. She hadn't agreed to permanently move in with him and had kept her short-term rental. Why was she holding on to it? Was her coming to San Antonio only temporary? It brought a pang to his chest to think of her leaving him. It reminded him of the loss he'd felt when his mother had moved him away from his father, from the only place Ayden had known as home, into a sad one-bedroom apartment. He didn't want to lose Maya. She made him feel alive. Ayden felt like he could do anything when he was with her, like he was worthy. But, more importantly, he'd never been this content or this relaxed with another woman.

He drew a deep, ragged breath. Ayden couldn't remember the last time he'd been truly happy like he'd been these last couple of weeks with Maya. Before her, he'd worked around the clock, stopping only to eat, work out or have the occasional dinner with any number of nameless, faceless women, then leave their beds in the middle of the night. None of them had held a candle to Maya. He stayed with Maya *every night*. He looked forward to drawing her close and spooning with her. And when he did, it was the best sleep of his life.

Eventually, he retired to the master bedroom to shower and get ready for bed. He'd changed into black silk pajama bottoms when he heard Maya's car pull into the driveway. He waited for the click of her heels on the marble floor as she climbed the stairs. Her steps were silent on the plush carpet in the hallway, but he finally sensed her outside his room. Was she trying to decide if she should come in? He hopped off the bed and padded barefoot to her room. "Maya?"

She jumped. "You—you startled me."

"I'm sorry." His gaze swept over her face as he looked for signs of distress. Her eyes were glassy. "Is everything okay? "

She looked downward and when she lifted her head back up, he could see tears staining her cheeks. It made him feel as useless as a rag doll to see her so upset. "Maya, Maya." He pulled her to him, grasping the sides of her face to make her look at him. "Did something happen today?"

She shook her head. "No, it's just…" Hiccupping, she tried to speak through her crying. "I can't…" Her voice trailed off, and she leaned into him and began softly sobbing.

"It's okay." He held her firmly, desperate to give some of his strength to her. "I'm here for you."

When she finally quieted, she spoke softly. "The treatment they're giving Mom is aggressive. Very aggressive. But it's the only way they can try to rid her of the cancer. It didn't seem real when I found out, but today… There was no denying that my mother could die."

"But she's not going to," Ayden murmured in her ear. "Because of you, she's getting the best treatment available."

"I know that, but it's still so scary. I—I could lose her. And even though we haven't been close, I've always known she was there. And if something happens to her, I'll be all alone because I don't think Raven and I can ever go back to being sisters again, not after her betrayal."

Without hesitation, Ayden said, "You won't be alone, Maya. You'll always have me."

As soon as he said the words, he wished he could take them back.

He wanted them to be true because he cared deeply for Maya, but he couldn't guarantee her that their relationship would always be like this.

He didn't do commitments because there was too great a risk of getting hurt.

Had he just doomed their relationship by telling his first white lie?

You'll always have me.

Ayden's words kept replaying in Maya's head the next day even though she tried to keep her mind on work. Ayden had left hours ago, leaving her to her own devices and thus giving her plenty of time to recount last night. After making love, she'd slept in his embrace as he held her, unable to sleep because his words were in her head like a nursery rhyme she could never forget. She knew he didn't mean them. Couldn't possibly. She didn't have a future with Ayden. She'd been living in an alternate yet blissful universe while ignoring the obvious.

Ayden was an attractive, wealthy man whose interests lay in making money. But it was inevitable that Ayden would return to his former ways. She had to look on their time as the precious gift that it was. He'd made her feel beautiful, sensual and desirable, and she would always be grateful. She would remember their time in Jamaica fondly. The time they'd shared, however, had an expiration date.

Maya was steeling herself for that moment when Ayden would want her to go back to being only his trusted assistant instead of his lover. When he looked to her to make appointments and spreadsheets rather than being desperate for their next kiss or lovemaking session. When she'd have to go back to her boring life in which no other man would ever measure up to Ayden. She knew that when that time came, she'd leave again. There was no way she could see him day in and day out after the time they'd shared. Except this time, she wouldn't go far. Her mother needed her.

She'd started over once. She could do it again. She just didn't want to. She'd set aside most of her sign-on bonus to help with her mother's treatments. There was some left over in her savings, and with her new salary and generous stock options, she could make it until she found a new position.

"I'm back." Ayden startled her as he strode toward her desk.

"How was your meeting?"

"Successful. I convinced Kincaid to bring his portfolio over to Stewart Investments." He grinned from ear to ear. "It was a big day for me."

"That's wonderful, Ayden." She was happy he'd finally landed the elusive client.

"I want to celebrate. What do you say we take off early for a night out on the town?"

Her eyes fixed on his beautiful face and her heart began galloping in her chest. "Why, Ayden, are you asking me out on a date?"

He smiled wolfishly. "Well, ma'am, it appears I am." He rubbed the perpetual five-o'clock shadow on his chin. "Would you like to accompany me to dinner?"

Ayden's infectious mood was catching and Maya felt herself getting excited. "I would love to."

An hour later, Maya was staring back at her reflection in a dressing-room mirror. Rather than navigate the Austin traffic during the middle of rush hour, Ayden had driven her to a stylish boutique where he'd given her her own *Pretty Woman* experience complete with a designer dress purchased right off the rack. Maya had balked at such an outrageous gesture. She had plenty of dresses back at the house, but Ayden wasn't taking her back home. The saleswoman had been happy to assist when he'd pulled out his platinum credit card and told her price was no object.

Now Maya was in a teal halter dress that clung to her slender curves and did wonders for her complexion. She'd touched up her makeup with subtle eye shadow, mascara and lipstick she carried with her. The clerk had insisted she add shoes and a bag, so Maya was ready for the night with a clutch and beaded sandals with straps that wrapped her delicate ankles.

Ayden was waiting for her at the curb, having stepped out to take a phone call earlier while she got dressed. "You look stunning." He whistled as she approached the Bentley.

"You should know. You paid an outrageous sum for this dress."

"I wanted you to not only look good, but feel good."

His words put a smile on her face. "I feel like a million bucks."

"Good." He opened the passenger door and pulled her inside. "Get in."

Ayden took Maya to a popular restaurant known for its wealthy clientele. It was the first time they were going out in public as a couple. Since they'd become lovers, they hadn't been seen by anyone other than the housekeeping staff at the villa in Jamaica and his estate.

Did this mean Ayden might want more from her than a short-lived affair?

Maya didn't want to be hopeful, but it was hard not to read between the lines when he was going out of his way to impress her. First with the couture dress and designer shoes, and now with a fine dining experience. Upon arrival, he showered her with the most expensive bottle of champagne and treated her to the finest meal she'd had in a long time. Each plate was a tiny work of art created by a master chef. Maya felt like she was floating, weightless, carried away on a tidal wave. She knew what was happening. She was falling deeper and deeper in love with Ayden.

Her mind warned her to be cautious, prudent even, to not outwardly portray her true feelings, so she focused on the easy, undemanding conversation they had a tendency to share. She loved the melodic sound and timbre of his deliciously masculine voice. Every now and then she would glance up, only to find his eyes fixed on her, and she was helpless to tear away her gaze.

When the exquisite meal was finally over and they were drinking cappuccino with their intricately conceived desserts, someone called his name. "Ayden!"

Ayden turned and smiled, then rose to his feet to greet half a dozen suited gentlemen coming toward them. It was late, but clearly they'd just had a business meeting. He shook the men's hands. "Good to see you. You enjoyed your dinners?"

"Of course. This place has the best duck in Austin," one of the men answered.

Several of them glanced in Maya's direction and Ayden motioned her over. "Gentlemen, I'd like you to meet Maya Richardson, the best executive assistant in all of Austin."

"Is that why you're taking her out to a meal here?" There were snickers.

Ayden cleared his throat. Maya could see he was uneasy with the conversation, yet he was allowing it, feeding into it. "You misunderstand. We're colleagues."

Maya was stunned and stared at Ayden in anger and bewilderment. Tears pricked the back of her eyes, but she refused to let these Neanderthals see it. He hadn't even defended her when they had snickered. And she couldn't believe Ayden had just told these men that she meant nothing to him. He might as well as have put a neon sign on her that read Booty Call. Maya had to get away before she said something that embarrassed them both. "Excuse me. I need to visit the ladies' room."

She heard several of the men laugh behind her. "Does she know, Ayden, that you're not the settling-down kind?"

Laughter followed her as she left the dining room, Ayden's included.

Maya nearly slammed the door against the wall as she pushed the door to the restroom open. Not only had Ayden not introduced her as his girlfriend, but he'd laughed about it. Hell, she would have even accepted his describing her as his date, but his *assistant*? Clearly he valued these men's opinions so much that he wasn't even willing to acknowledge she meant more to him than someone who just worked for him. She was furious!

She clasped both her hands to her face and inhaled, trying not to cry. She couldn't make a scene or fall apart. Not here. Not now. Damn! Why did she still care about his reputation after he'd just treated her so shabbily? Because she loved him, and despite everything, she wouldn't embarrass him like he'd just done her. She glanced at herself in the mirror. Her makeup was still intact; she'd held it together. *Just barely.* Now all she had to do was get out there. She just hoped the other men were gone.

As she entered the dining room, she saw Ayden sitting alone. Thank God.

He stood when she approached. "Maya..."

"I'm ready to go." She didn't bother sitting down. "I'd like to go now."

Ayden nodded. "I figured as much and have already taken care of the bill."

Maya didn't wait for him to continue and strode toward the door. She wanted to get away from him as soon as possible. Go back home and lick her wounds. But she wasn't truly going back home. She was going to Ayden's, where she wouldn't have a moment alone to process what had happened.

He must have followed her because he slid beside her at the valet counter, handing the attendant his ticket. Maya folded her arms across her chest and waited for them to fetch Ayden's car. Surprisingly, he was silent beside her. Maybe he knew she was peeved and was in no mood to talk. She did have one question for him.

Why?

Why bring her to a fancy restaurant?

Why romance her at all if all she was to him was a damn good assistant that he just happened to sleep with?

The Bentley arrived at the curb and she didn't wait for Ayden's assistance. She opened her door herself and slammed it shut. He took the hint and walked around to the driver's side. Once it was just the two of them, he turned to her. "Maya. About earlier... I'm sorry."

"I don't want to talk about it."

"Please don't let what happened ruin a great night."

"You did a fine job of that all by yourself."

She heard him suck in his breath. Score one for her. But she really wasn't interested in winning a battle of wills with Ayden. The real reason she was upset was because he didn't love her. Never would. And she was fooling herself to think otherwise. It was the same as she'd done with Thomas all those years ago. She'd foolishly thought he loved her. When, actually, he'd been sleeping with her sister behind her back. It was humiliating and she'd felt those exact same feelings tonight standing by Ayden's side when he relegated her to nothing more than the help. She couldn't look at him, much less talk to him.

The ride back to his mansion was fraught with tension. As soon as the car stopped, Maya hopped out, but

Ayden was hot on her heels. He caught her in the foyer and snagged her hips to him, but she refused to be *handled*. She knew exactly what Ayden would do: he would try to brush aside what had occurred at the restaurant. Make it appear as if she was blowing it out of proportion. And because she was so weak, when it came to him, she'd succumb and he would carry her off to bed where they'd have sex all night long. But then where would they be? Exactly where they'd started.

She continued twisting and turning in his arms in an attempt to get away, but all she did was spin herself around until her backside was against his swelling erection.

"Stop fighting me," he whispered, clasping his arms around her.

"Let me go." Her steely tone must have soaked through his brain, because he released her and they faced off. His hazel eyes were searching her face. For what? She wasn't sure. She just wanted to go to bed. *Alone*.

"I'm going to bed." She grasped the railing of the staircase and started to ascend.

"Maya, I don't want to end the night like this. Can't we talk? Please?" he implored.

She stopped on the staircase. "Talk? About what? That after nearly two weeks spent in bed together that there's nothing between us? Is that what we're going to talk about?"

He frowned. "That's not fair, Maya. Some of them are my colleagues as well as clients. Did you honestly expect me to tell those men that we're an item? To spill my guts to them and tell them how I truly feel?"

She descended the stairs until she was back facing him. "Actually, I did, Ayden. I expected you to acknowledge that I *meant* something to you."

"You do. You know that. I wouldn't have been with

you this entire time, giving up work and obligations, if you didn't."

She felt confused. "But yet you couldn't bring yourself to tell those men that you were *with* me, *dating* me. But I get it, okay? What we do in the dark is supposed to be for our eyes only and no one else. What I don't understand is why take me out for dinner? Why not just keep me in the house to service you at your beck and call?"

His eyes blazed fury and she could feel the anger emanating from his every pore. "That was a cheap shot, Maya."

"But well deserved." She spun on her heel and ran up the stairs, but Ayden refused to let sleeping dogs lie and she heard his footsteps behind her. When she made it to her room, she slammed the door, shutting him out. She heard the latch give way on the door and sensed Ayden's presence behind her as much as she heard the door click closed behind him. She didn't want to look at him. He'd hurt her. She just wanted to go to bed and forget. To block out the pain until morning, when she would be forced to face reality, which was that Ayden was never going to love her.

When Maya began unzipping her dress and it stuck, she let him come behind her and help. He stilled her by placing his hands on her shoulders. Then he easily slid the zip down until he reached her bikini panties. Despite the tension between them, she stepped out of the dress, removed her undies and turned around to face him, naked.

Desire and hunger shot through her as it always did when she looked at him.

Maya didn't speak and neither did he. Instead, she allowed him to tug her toward him until she was lost once again in the bliss she always found in his arms.

Fifteen

The next morning Ayden was gone from her bed before Maya woke up. She was thankful because last night shouldn't have happened. She'd been so upset with him for how he'd treated her in front of his colleagues. How could she have allowed him to make love to her afterward? He must think her a fool, ruled by her libido rather than her head. She'd allowed the physical pull Ayden had on her to make her go completely left when she meant to go right.

After showering and dressing for the day, Maya packed her things. It was time for her not only to get out of Ayden's house, but out of his orbit. She should never have allowed him to convince her to come back to work for him, not with the feelings she'd had. Knowing that he'd desired her, too, did little to soften the blow that Ayden wasn't the type of man she was looking for. And there was no way she could lie or pretend otherwise. If she did, she wouldn't be true to herself and it would suck away her soul.

Maya felt like a raw and open wound. The time they'd shared in Jamaica had been real, so real that it had changed *everything*. Ayden had made her want more than he was capable of giving to her, plain and simple.

Her task was complete in under a half hour because she hadn't brought that many belongings to Ayden's. She called downstairs and the butler ensured her luggage was taken to her car. When she inquired where Ayden was, he informed her he was in the morning room having breakfast. Maya saw no better time than the present to let him know her plans.

She had to do this for her own self-respect and self-worth. Somehow, she'd survive this, just as she had when he'd crushed her spirit five years ago.

She found Ayden reading the newspaper, a cup of coffee along with a half-eaten plate of food on the table in front of him.

He glanced up when she walked into the room. "Good morning." He put down the paper. "I didn't want to wake you, so I came downstairs. I hope you don't mind." He eyed her warily as she sat down next to him.

She shook her head.

"Would you like some breakfast? I can have Cook whip you up something, an omelet perhaps or some crepes. He makes the best crepes you've ever had in your life."

Again, she declined with a headshake. Was Ayden Stewart nervous? Because he was babbling about breakfast when he had to know there was more to be said between them.

"We need to talk."

He chuckled quietly. "Whenever a woman says those words, it can't be good."

She stared at him incredulously.

He held up his hands in defense. "Don't bite my head

off. It was just a joke to lighten the mood because I suspect I'm not going to like this conversation very much, am I?"

He fixed his gaze on hers and Maya reminded herself that she'd made up her mind and there was nothing he could do to change it. "I'm leaving and moving back into my apartment."

He nodded. "I suspected as much when I saw your bags were brought down."

"You know why?"

"You're upset about last night. You feel like I disrespected you and this is your way of punishing me."

Maya rolled her eyes in frustration. She wanted to strangle him because he wasn't getting the point. "I'm not trying to punish you, Ayden."

"Then why?" He pounded the table with his fist, startling her. "Why isn't what we have good enough? Why are you leaving me? I know you like it here. *With me.* I know you want to be here and I don't want you to go. So why leave, if not to punish me?"

"Because I want *more*, Ayden. And I'm not willing to take whatever scraps of yourself you're willing to give me."

"I don't understand. What is it that you want? Whatever it is, I'll give it to you."

"Don't you see? You can't. You and I are on different pages. Yes, I've been happy here with you. Cut off from the world in our idyllic little slice of heaven. But it was never real. It was never going to last. I know that and so do you. I want marriage, babies and a white picket fence. I want a family."

"A family?"

"Yes, I've always wanted one. When I was with Thomas, I thought we were headed in that direction. But he went and married my sister and gave her all the things I've always craved. Especially someone to love me." There, she'd said the word aloud. The *L* word that she hadn't dared to speak or make mention of, but she had to now. She couldn't go on making the same bad decisions. Something had to give.

"I wish I could give you all those things, but I can't."

"You mean you *won't*. Because you're not capable of anything more than immediate gratification. And like an idiot, I went along with it, accepting less than what I wanted because I wanted to be with you. Because I never truly got over you the first time." She shook her head. "Why did I do this to myself? Maybe it's because I've never felt like anything special. I never have been for any other man, so why should now be any different? My own mother said as much for most of my life. And as for you, I'm a convenience who just happens to be compatible with you sexually."

"Don't say that!" Ayden shot to his feet. "I don't ever want to hear you say that you're nothing special, Maya. Because you are. You are to me."

Then why won't you love me? She wanted to scream at him, but instead she stared back at him and felt the tears of unrequited love trickle down her face.

"Maya, please don't cry…"

He reached out to touch her, but she bunched her shoulders and moved away. She couldn't let him touch her. Not now. Not when she was weak and vulnerable. He would use it to his advantage to pull her back into his web. She barely had enough strength to have this conversation and demand the things she wanted, whether he was able to give them to her or not.

"It's okay. I walked into this affair with my eyes wide open. I knew who I was dealing with."

He frowned in consternation. "What the hell is that supposed to mean?"

"Nothing." She rose to her feet and began to walk toward the doorway. "I've said what I have to say and it's best I left."

"Oh, no, you don't. You're not getting the last word. At least not until you tell me what you meant."

"You want to go there, Ayden?"

"Yes," he stated unequivocally. His eyes blazed a fire through her.

"All right then. How about we start with the fact that you've never had a serious relationship a day in your life. You flit around from one affair to the next."

"That's because I haven't had the time. I've been building Stewart Investments."

"Rubbish. It's because you're scared. Scared of getting close to anyone or anything because you're afraid of getting hurt. But guess what, Ayden? I'm equally scared, but I'm willing to put myself out there on the off chance that one day—one day—I might find someone who loves me just as much as I love them. And I know that's not you."

"Maya…" His tone softened, "I—I'm just not capable of anything more. I wish to God I were because you're an incredible woman, deserving of happiness. But I just don't believe in happily ever after."

"That's because you're still holding on to the past and the anger you have toward your father. Until you make peace with your family, you'll never be able to move forward."

"You know nothing of my family, not really, other than the few tidbits I told you."

"You're right. I only know the scraps you've chosen to share with me or that I've garnered from working with you all these years, because you've closed yourself off, Ayden. To the world. To your sister, Fallon. And most of all to me. I can't just be the woman you sleep with anymore, no matter how pleasurable that might be. I want more. And I *deserve* it."

"Yes, you do," Ayden said finally in a quiet, defeated tone. "You deserve more than I could ever give you and that, my precious Maya, will be my greatest regret."

Maya nodded and then quietly left the room.

Ayden stared at the doorway Maya had departed through. He'd been sitting there for the last hour in utter shock. She'd walked out on him. He'd woken up this morning with a deep sense of foreboding of her departure, but he'd told himself it couldn't possibly be true. Maya, *his Maya*, would never leave him. During breakfast, he'd told himself that Maya was upset. Understandably so. He could have handled last night better, but at the time, he just hadn't known what to say.

Were they on a date?

Was she his girlfriend?

They certainly hadn't discussed the ramifications of becoming intimate. Seeing his colleagues had caught him off guard. He'd been that way from the moment she'd walked out of the boutique. She'd looked sensational. Beautiful. Stunning. But mere words did little to describe her. Unfortunately, he'd behaved like an utter jerk. He'd hoped making love would be a salve to her tender spirit, but it hadn't been, even though for him it had been magical. He couldn't recall another time in which he'd felt so connected to another human being.

This morning he'd planned on asking her to make their living arrangement permanent. It was the best he could offer when he didn't do commitments, but for Maya he'd been willing to make an effort. But he hadn't gotten the chance to even ask, because she wanted marriage and babies. And a darn white picket fence! Why did women always want the moon and the stars? Why couldn't she let him have his say and just move in? It might not be exactly what she was looking for, but at least it would have given her some kind of commitment.

But marriage?

Babies?

Oh, hell, no!

Ayden didn't ever plan on getting hitched. He'd seen how married people, supposedly in love, treated each other. When the dust settled, the only ones hurt were the babies, the innocents that had been pulled into their parents' unholy matrimony.

No, thank you. He was content with the single life.

Or at least he had been until Maya had come roaring back into his world with a vengeance.

Now what was he supposed to do? Was she cutting him off entirely? Although, it would be devastating not to make love to her again, he supposed he could get through it if he buried himself in work. But what of Stewart Investments? The last time she'd left him, it hadn't been just him, but her position. It had taken him nearly half a year to find someone. He couldn't go through that again. He *wouldn't* go through that again.

He'd lived with his father's betrayal all these years, accepted he would never be acknowledged as his son. But he couldn't bear it if Maya turned her back on him, too. Because this time, it would destroy him, and Ayden wasn't sure he'd ever recover.

Ayden didn't know what to do. They couldn't go back to their working relationship. They couldn't be lovers anymore. And he doubted she wanted his friendship. There was nothing he could offer her that would entice her to stay and that was the greatest travesty of all.

Maya hated the letter she'd just penned to Ayden and sent by courier. Once again, she'd resigned her position as his executive assistant. The only difference was that this time she was offering her services via virtual assistant until he could find someone permanent. She was prepared to draft his presentations, handle his schedule, make appointments and take his calls *remotely*. She'd thought it through and, logically speaking, they didn't need to see each other. She could do her job without ever laying eyes on him.

It was the best she could come up with on short notice. She knew he was working with several important clients, especially Kincaid, and she was invested in his success. So she was willing to listen to his voice over the phone giving her instructions or read an email with his name on it so long as they had no interaction face-to-face.

She was weak when it came to Ayden. If she were in the office, he'd use every weapon in his arsenal to break down her defenses, and Maya knew herself. Knew she would crumble. So she was offering this olive branch. Either way, the signing bonus was hers free and clear according to the offer letter she'd signed.

She wondered how he would react when he received her resignation. Would he blow his top? Or would he be thankful because she was out of his hair and he wouldn't have to worry about dealing with her demanding any more of him?

Maya found out when her cell phone rang nearly an hour later.

"What the hell is this?"

Maya knew exactly who was on the other end of the line and what he was referring to. "Ayden, you must have received my letter."

"Yes, I did. And I don't accept it."

"C'mon, Ayden. You know it's best if we keep our distance. As a virtual assistant, I can still assist you with the important deals on the table, giving you plenty of time to interview and find my replacement."

"I don't want to replace you, Maya."

She sucked in a breath. "Well, those are your options. You can take them or leave them." She held her breath as she waited for his response.

"I will leave them. Thank you very much. If you want away from me so bad, go ahead, but I warn you, you signed a contract."

"An offer letter," she corrected. "Besides, when I signed, you stated our relationship would be professional only. We crossed that line, Ayden, and no court in the land would uphold that document if they heard what went on between us in Jamaica."

"Damn it, Maya. Don't do this."

"I'm truly sorry, but it's the only way. We both want different things out of life. You're content with the status quo. Me in your bed. While I, on the other hand, lose out on finding my happily-ever-after. Well, no more, Ayden. I'm going to chase after what I want until I find it. Don't stand in my way."

He sighed heavily. There was silence for several long moments in which she heard his slow and controlled breathing before he said, "I will miss you."

"I—I'll miss you, too." Then Maya ended the call. She had to. It was torture to both of them if she let it continue. She would forgive Ayden the same way she had Raven and Thomas, because he was her past and she had to look toward the future. A future that included a husband and children someday. The problem was, her heart was breaking in two and only Ayden could put it back together again. But he wasn't willing or able.

Sixteen

Ayden sat at his desk befuddled. He'd lost ten minutes because he'd been daydreaming about Maya. He told himself it would get better.

But it didn't. The ghost of Maya was everywhere. In his bed. At the office.

He still wanted her, in his life, in his bed, but she wanted marriage and babies. Ayden couldn't give her that. Yet he didn't want to live his life without her. So he'd let her walk away when he didn't want her to go. Did it mean he was in love with her? He wasn't sure. He'd never been in love before. But if there was anyone he wanted to love, it was Maya. He thought about her day and night. And with each passing day, he missed her more and more. Nothing eased the ache in his heart. Not even work, which had been his cure-all for loneliness. The sense of loss was so acute it physically hurt to breathe.

It had been nearly two weeks since Maya had left the mansion, calling him out on his failure to commit. They had been the worst weeks of his life since his mother passed away. Back then, he'd felt alone in the world and emotionally battered. He felt the same way now.

And work was going horribly.

He wished he'd taken Maya up on her virtual assistant offer, but he hadn't. The recruiter had sent a candidate who had emailed the wrong proposals to two different clients earlier in the week. And when he'd yelled at her for the mistake, she'd left the office crying, vowing never to return. The second temp hadn't been much better, but at least she'd lasted a few days. Could no one handle the simple requests he made of them? It was late Friday evening and he would have to muddle through on his own.

Ayden reached for the phone on his desk and called Luke. He didn't care what time it was in London. He needed a sounding board.

"Do you know what time it is?" Luke said.

"No, I didn't look," Ayden responded.

"Well, it's past midnight here," Luke said groggily.

"Sorry."

"No, you're not. So what's going on? I haven't heard from you in over a month so I assumed everything was going swimmingly."

"It was."

"And now it's not?"

Ayden sighed heavily. "Far from it."

"What's happened?"

"Maya left me."

"I could have told you that was going to happen," Luke replied. "It's barely been a month and I bet you ran the poor girl ragged. I warned you about easing up."

"That's not the reason she left."

Silence ensued on the other end of the line before Luke said, "Don't tell me you shagged her again?"

Ayden snorted. "We had a consensual and mutually gratifying relationship. But she still left me. Can you believe it?"

"Are you daft or what, mate? The woman came back because she's had the hots for you, probably did from the get-go, and the first thing you lead with is sex? You don't offer her any kind of commitment other than a good shag—even though you know she's the settling-down kind? Instead, you choose the easy way out? And for the life of me, I don't understand why she went along with it. But go figure. Love is blind."

"Love? No one said anything about love."

"Oh, bloody hell, Ayden! The woman is in love with you. She wouldn't have agreed to come back otherwise. Not after the way you treated her after that one-off five years ago."

"I offered her a lot of money, which she needed to take care of her ailing mother."

"And that might have played a role in her accepting the job, but you and I both know that she came back for *you* and only you. Because deep down she wanted to see if there was a chance for a future with you, and you blew it!"

"Luke, you know I don't believe in love and marriage and all that crap."

"That's a real shame, Ayden, because you're going to miss out on the best thing that ever happened to you, mate."

"Luke..."

"The next time you call me in the middle of night, at least be ready to take my advice. 'Cause right now I'm telling you to sod off," Luke growled.

"Thanks a lot."

"You know I love you like an adopted brother, but I'm going back to bed. Call me tomorrow when you gain some common sense."

Ayden hung up the phone and leaned back in his chair. He felt like all the energy had been zapped out of him. If anyone could give it to him straight and he would listen, it was Luke. With the exception of Maya, Luke was the only person Ayden implicitly trusted.

Was he right?

He'd spent the last fifteen years of life not only surviving, but trying to meet some expectation in his mind that if he was smart enough and rich enough, Henry Stewart would give him the time of day. He had to face facts: Henry was never going to love him. He had to stop looking back on what could have been, *should* have been. It was time to look at what was right in front of him.

Maya.

He'd kept up a shield with every other woman he'd ever been with, keeping them at arm's length, never allowing them the chance to get close—but not with Maya. He couldn't pretend with this woman. She saw straight through him, not just to his triumphs and successes, but to his failures. She knew he liked his coffee black with two sugars, but she also knew his deep, dark secrets, which made it impossible for him to deny that there was something between them. Something strong and powerful had been forming, but because of Ayden's hang-ups, they were dead in the water. Like Luke, Maya had told him that he needed to resolve his past. Make peace before they could have a future.

Maybe they both had a point.

Ayden knew exactly what he had to do to get started.

Ayden arrived unannounced at Stewart Technologies. He wasn't interested in seeing Henry Stewart, but he was determined to see his sister. After her repeated phone calls, texts and emails had gone unanswered she'd stopped contacting him. And he couldn't blame her; he'd acted like a complete ass toward her. He couldn't give her the financial bailout she needed, but at the very least, he owed her an apology for ignoring her.

When he told her assistant that he was her brother, however, the woman politely said, "Nice try." Fallon had one brother and that was international superstar Dane Stewart. But Ayden hadn't budged from the spot until she'd finally agreed to tell his sister he was standing outside her door.

In time, Fallon emerged from her office in an elegant red pantsuit. Her blond-streaked brown hair was flat ironed and her makeup was flawless. She was the epitome of class and sophistication. She stood in the doorway and regarded him. "I'm shocked you've deigned to darken my doorstep, Ayden Stewart."

"I deserve that," Ayden said, walking toward her, "but I'd like to talk if you have a moment."

Fallon glanced at her assistant. "No interruptions, please. My brother and I have some unfinished business."

Ayden couldn't resist a smirk as he passed the woman, whose mouth hung open in shock. He strode into the room, and Fallon closed the door behind him. Then she folded her arms across her chest and stood rooted to the spot.

"I have to admit, big brother, I'm surprised you've come into enemy territory. Because that's what I am to you, right? Your enemy. So what gives? Why are you here? And what's happened to you? You look god-awful!"

Ayden knew he looked tired and there were lines under his eyes. He hadn't slept in the weeks since Maya left him. He answered her first question. "You're not my enemy, Fallon."

She rolled her eyes upward. "You could have fooled me, Ayden. Your actions speak louder than any words. And, trust me, those were enough. I know my mother did yours wrong and you blame my family for every bad thing that happened in your life. But guess what, Ayden? I didn't harm you. I wasn't even born when all that went down. Yet you blame me as if I had some control over the past."

"You're right."

"Excuse me?"

"I said you're right," Ayden replied, raising his voice. "I was wrong to blame you, Fallon. You and Dane are innocent in this." She nodded but didn't speak, so he continued. "Our parents are to blame for what went down back then, and I'm sorry that I put you in the middle of that. You've tried to extend an olive branch to me and I've never wanted to take it."

"Because you're angry that I got the life denied you?"

"Yes." Ayden was man enough to admit that. "You and Dane not only got my father—" Ayden beat his chest with his fist "—but you got the good life. The houses, the cars, the travel, the fancy clothes and schools. While I had to work my butt off for everything I've ever achieved."

"But I bet it's all the more sweet," Fallon replied.

"What do you mean?"

"I know you had a hard life," she responded. "But my life hasn't been a picnic, either. I admit I've had every material possession, but you want to know something? I've also had a disinterested, self-absorbed mother who couldn't be bothered to raise the two children she had in order to keep our demanding father. And Henry Stewart? He hasn't been an easy man to love, constantly pushing me to excel. I've had to bust my tail for years to prove I'm the best person to run this company. I've always been in Dad's shadow, unable to run Stewart Technologies how I see fit without constant input and criticism. And right when I make it to the top, I see my whole life's work on a weak foundation and the sand is crumbling underneath my feet."

Fallon walked over to the couch and sank down onto it.

Ayden rushed over. "I had no idea how hard it's been on you."

"Father wanted Dane to take over the company, but my baby brother is only interested in making movies. He's never wanted to be a businessman, much to father's chagrin."

"So he pushed you."

"Yes. And don't get me wrong, I love what I do. And I love this company. It's why I came to you for help."

"And I turned my back on you," Ayden replied. "I'm sorry for that, Fallon. It's just that…"

She reached for his hands and grasped them. "It's okay. I had no right coming to you. Not after what father did to you. But I felt I had no choice and was out of options. The reason I called was to let you know I'd had it out with my mother and she admitted to ensnaring father. I only wanted to say that I was sorry."

"Thank you for that," Ayden said. Hearing that Nora had admitted to part of the blame was something, but what about Fallon? "What are you going to do about the company? If you really need the money, I could loan it to you. Not to the company directly, but as a personal loan with a good interest rate."

"Ayden, that's very generous of you considering the circumstances, but I could never accept, not knowing how Daddy treated you and your mother. This isn't your cross to bear. It's mine."

"But you're my sister."

"And I will find a way and might already have. Anyway, the fact that you've come here today—" her voice caught in her throat "—you have no idea how much this means to me."

"It means a lot to me, too, Fallon. I've been alone for a long time. Hell, since before my mother even passed.

And, well, I've felt adrift without a family, but if you and Dane are willing… I'd like to try to have a relationship with you both." He was never going to forgive Henry for abandoning him or his mother, but he could try to forge a bond with his siblings.

A warm smile spread across her lips. "Ya know, I wouldn't mind having a big brother. Someone I could look up to. Maybe even call for advice?"

Ayden returned her grin. "I'd like that. I'd like that very much."

Fallon glanced down at her watch. "Now I have to get to a meeting, so let's plan on having dinner sometime soon, okay? I won't push. We can do this in baby steps."

"Baby steps." Ayden laughed. He opened his arms and, after several seconds, Fallon came into his embrace, returning his hug. It was a small gesture, but meant everything to Ayden.

After leaving Stewart Technologies, Ayden felt a heavy burden had been lifted off his shoulders. Clearing the air with Fallon and agreeing to start anew as a family was one the best decisions he'd made in a long time. He hadn't realized just how much the hatred and anger was eating him up inside and taking up room in his heart. To acknowledge that he needed Fallon and Dane was a big step for him. He was used to being on his own, staying in control, feeling nothing, but being with Maya had changed him.

He'd been pretending for years that Maya was just an assistant, a friend, even a lover, but she was more than that. She was everything to him. He had to talk to her. Tell her that he was a fool. Tell her that he loved her. Tell her she was his other half, his soul mate, and pray that she would take him back. He was prepared to lay down every vestige of his pride, *do anything*, if she'd just give him another chance.

* * *

It was essential that Maya keep her mind occupied. It was time she got settled and moved on with her life. It had taken a couple of weeks, but she'd found a permanent apartment in an area of Austin she liked and given up her short-term rental. Callie had driven from San Antonio to help her unpack her belongings from storage over the weekend so it would feel like home.

Maya had to admit the added benefit of being in Austin was that she was closer to Sophia. She'd already been able to make it to her mother's last couple of treatments.

This time she wasn't running from her problems. She was sticking around to spend time with her mother and develop some semblance of a relationship with Raven. Just that weekend, she'd met up with her sister at a baby store to shop for baby clothes and they'd gone for coffee afterward, which allowed Maya to coo over her niece. It was a small step toward mending their relationship, but one she never would have taken if she hadn't come back home.

She wasn't desperate for money, and was keeping herself busy until she could find a new job. Busy cleaning and decorating her new home. Grocery shopping to fill her refrigerator. Running in the early-morning hours. Focused on the books she read. Any activity she could think of that would take up room in her mind. Because if she didn't, the memories would arrive. And what purpose was there in reliving the nights she'd spent making love with Ayden. Because that's exactly what it had been. It hadn't been sex.

She was in love with Ayden and had given him a part of herself, but he didn't love her back. What was wrong with her? Why couldn't she find a man who would love her? She'd thought Thomas had, but he'd chosen Raven over her. And now Ayden. He was everything she wanted and could ever need. She wanted to be his wife, the mother of his babies, but he didn't want her forever. Just right now. It made Maya realize that she'd never really loved Thomas because he paled in comparison to Ayden, the man she'd secretly loved for the last decade. And she had to face the facts: she couldn't force him to love her back. She had to accept that he was never going to love her like she loved him. Heck, he didn't want to even try. She understood he'd been hurt, but would he ever allow love in?

Thoughts of Ayden were still invading her subconscious on Monday morning when she started a temp job a head-hunter found for her. Maya tried to block Ayden from her mind and concentrate on typing. Tap, tap, tap on the keyboard. She could and would do what was necessary to move forward by keeping focused on the spreadsheets and reports she was assigned.

The elevator door chimed and Maya didn't know what made her look up. Maybe it was the powerful force field surrounding Ayden that required her absolute attention. Because there he was, striding toward her desk. Maya's stomach hollowed at the sight of him. She tried to quell the feeling, but there was no point. The effect of seeing him after weeks of going without was too much.

Ayden was standing in front of her in the flesh!

The man she'd loved, who'd once held her in his arms, kissed her passionately, made love to her tenderly, cuddled with her quietly was here. He'd been her entire universe that week in Jamaica. She would have probably continued to carry on their affair, grateful for whatever piece of himself he was willing to give her. Who knew how long she would have gone? "How did you find me?"

"An investigator."

"Why? We're over, Ayden. There's nothing left to be said."

"I disagree. I need to talk to you," he whispered.

She chuckled to herself at his arrogance, but why should she be surprised? "It's always about you, isn't it? Well, no more, Ayden. I choose me and my happiness. You should go."

"That's fair, but I'm not leaving. If I have to, I'll camp out until we have an opportunity to talk. I miss you, Maya."

A tear slipped down her cheek at his honest admission. "All right, we can talk."

She moved from behind the desk and walked toward the elevator. Ayden's hand closed around her elbow.

"I miss you, too, by the way," Maya commented, giving him a sideways glance, "but that changes nothing."

Ayden snorted. "It changes everything, Maya. It means there's still a chance."

"A chance for what?" She sniffed.

"For us."

They were silent as they waited for the car. Maya didn't know what to say. She had no idea why Ayden had come. She still wanted love and commitment, marriage and children. The whole enchilada. And she wasn't willing to settle for less.

The elevator arrived and Maya stepped in. She stole a glance at Ayden and found his eyes fixed on her. Watching her. She didn't want to look too closely at him. She would hear what he had to say and then leave. The car dinged again and several more people entered, forcing Ayden to move closer. Far too close for her liking. Her breath tightened in her lungs at his nearness.

The ride ended several moments later. Maya walked quickly through the lobby toward the revolving doors and across the cascade of steps that led to a large courtyard housing a green space where workers came to eat their lunch. Since it was still late morning, it was deserted.

Maya broke away and sat on a nearby stone bench. She needed to put distance between them. It hadn't been long enough for her to become immune to being near him. As it was, she'd had a hard time in the elevator because she'd felt his hard chest pressed against her back as it became overcrowded.

"What do you want, Ayden? I thought our conversation at your mansion and then again over the phone was pretty clear."

"Not quite," he responded, taking a seat beside her. "There's a lot I need to say to you and you need to hear."

She shrugged. "All right, I'm all ears."

He turned to face her. "For years, I was used to not having any emotions because feelings equaled weakness. If my stepfather saw me have any kind of emotion whatsoever when he was verbally abusing my mother or smacking us around, he'd hit us harder. Yell louder. So I learned to control my emotions to show none. Become impenetrable so I wouldn't get hurt."

"I'm sorry, Ayden. I can't even imagine how horrible it was. But I still don't understand what this has to do with us."

"A lot, if you'll give me a chance to explain. When you walked into my office ten years ago, I sensed you were something special, someone different from the other women I'd met. You weren't looking for anything from me, so you fit perfectly as my assistant. But as the years went on, you became less of an assistant. You became my friend." When she began to speak, he held up his hand. "I know I made your life hell back then. Having you send flowers and gifts to my dates. I think in my own way I was trying to test you to see if you would crack and throw yourself at me, but you never did. You just quietly let me be myself. Soon, I was opening up to you about the childhood I'd endured. I know it wasn't everything, but it was more than I'd told anyone."

"I remember I was surprised when you shared your story with me."

"You listened. You didn't judge or offer platitudes. It meant the world to me. And I think part of me knew that I had to keep you at arm's length. Otherwise, I would fall head over heels for you."

"But you didn't, Ayden."

"Five years ago, you cracked my armor when you came to me distraught over Thomas. I honestly never meant for anything to happen between us. I wanted to comfort you. Make you see how beautiful you were inside and out. And then you kissed me. Leading to the most spectacular night of my life up to that point."

"Yet you still showed me the door," Maya pressed. She hadn't forgotten the hurt she'd felt.

"Because I was scared. Scared of the feelings you'd evoked in me. Feelings I'd never felt before with another woman. So, of course, I did what I knew best. I pushed them down. Acted as if they didn't exist. I hurt you immeasurably and you left, with good reason. But then you came back, and all those old feelings resurfaced, Maya." He leaned in to cup her face with his large hands. "Don't you see they'd never really left? They'd been buried this entire time. But that week in Jamaica brought them to the forefront. It changed everything. I could no longer hide how much I wanted to be near you, mouth to mouth, skin to skin. I finally had you in my life and didn't want to let you go."

"Neither did I. You made me ridiculously happy in Jamaica and afterward. I thought surely you must feel something. Maybe even love me, just a little. But then you were willing to let me walk out the door, out of your life."

"I'm sorry, Maya. I was afraid I wouldn't be able to give you everything you might need. Marriage? Children? It terrifies me because I never wanted to do what my father did to me, Maya. He ripped me apart. Destroyed our family. Took away my home. Abandoned me. Gave away *my* inheritance to his new family. Never acknowledged me."

She touched his cheek with her hand. "Then don't be that man, Ayden. Be better than him."

He nodded and she saw tears glistening in his eyes. "It's why I'm here. I took your advice. I met with Fallon and we talked. We're going to try to make a go of this brother-sister thing. Hopefully, Dane will be on board, too."

"And your father?"

He shook his head. "That ship sailed a long time ago, Maya. And I can live with that. What I can't live without is you. I love you, Maya. And if you'll have me, I want to be your friend, your lover, your partner, your *husband*."

A sob worked its way upward and she let it out. *Had she really heard him correctly?* "Husband?"

"Yes, I want to spend the rest of my life with you, Maya. I don't want my life to be consumed with work. I want it to be full and rich. I want someone to share it with. I want you. Please tell me it's not too late. Though even if it is, I'm going to try my best to win you over."

She placed her palm flat on his chest. "You don't have to try to win me over, Ayden. You've had me from the moment I stepped foot in your office ten years ago and every moment thereafter. I love you. I always have and I always will."

Her entire body swayed toward his and Ayden swept her into his arms, kissing her fiercely, passionately. His faint stubble teased her skin and she moaned at the realization of a dream come true. When they finally parted, he reached into his suit pocket, and before she knew it he was down on one knee, pulling out a ring box. "Will you marry me, Maya? Will you make me the happiest man on earth by agreeing to grow old with me and have lots of babies that look just like you?"

With the back of her hand, Maya wiped the tears that were sliding uncontrollably down her face. "Yes, yes, yes, I'll marry you, Ayden."

His mouth moved over hers, slow and warm. "I promise I will treasure you for the rest of our lives."

"As will I. You won't be alone anymore, Ayden, because we're family."

"And you, my dear Maya, are my home. I love you."

Epilogue

"I can't believe I'm going to meet *the* Dane Stewart," Maya said when she and Ayden sat down to dinner at an exclusive restaurant in Austin known to cater to the wealthy. "And that we'll be related!"

"That's right." Ayden smiled. He couldn't wait to make Maya his wife. She would be his and vice versa. Since they'd gotten engaged several weeks ago, he'd been eager to get started planning their wedding. He was just sorry he'd wasted so much time, taking five long years before he'd finally admitted that she was the best thing to ever happen to him. But they were together now and that's all that mattered.

"Are you nervous?" Maya asked, peering up at him from under thick lashes.

Maya was intuitive. She must have noticed him tapping his foot underneath the table. "I would say I'm anxious," Ayden responded evenly. "Fallon has always been open to accepting me as her brother while Dane, up to this point, has steered clear of the family, same as me. So I don't know what to expect."

"You can expect that I won't judge you for our parents' shortcomings," a deep male voice said from behind him, "like you did Fallon."

"Dane!" Fallon muttered from behind him, swatting him on the arm. "You promised to behave." She wore a scowl that didn't match the vibrancy of her orange midi-dress, which was tailored to perfection on her slender figure.

"I was just joking," Dane said, laughing as he turned to face her.

Ayden rose to his feet and faced his baby brother. Dane Stewart was as tall as Ayden, well over six feet, with an athletic physique hidden in all-black attire: jeans, T-shirt and leather jacket. He had the same caramel complexion as Fallon, but didn't share Ayden and Fallon's eye color. His were dark brown and mischievous. Ayden could see why he was America's favorite actor.

"Dane." Ayden offered his hand and Dane snorted.

"We're brothers, Ayden. I think a hug is in order."

Ayden was stunned when Dane walked toward him and wrapped his arms around him in a bear hug. He'd never had a family before. Never thought he'd ever have one. Or even needed one. But now that they were here, Ayden wondered how he'd ever survived like that. He patted Dane's back. "Yes, we are. Yes, we are."

They parted, and a surge of emotion welled in Ayden. He could feel tears at the back of his eyes. Sensing he was overcome, Maya came and stood beside him, sliding her hand into his. It was a simple act, but meant the world to him. He smiled down at her and she rewarded him with a beaming grin.

"Where's the champagne?" Dane glanced around for the waiter. "I believe there's an engagement to celebrate."

"Bring it on," Fallon concurred with a grin. "It's time we welcome Maya into the family."

As champagne soon followed, Ayden sat back in his chair and thought about how thankful he was to finally get to know the brother and sister he'd once refused to claim, with the woman he loved by his side. Life couldn't get any better.

* * * * *

SECRETS, LIES & LULLABIES

HEIDI BETTS

To Rob and Michelle (Timko) Massung, for all of their amazing computer help recently. You saved my butt more than you will ever know, and I just can't thank you enough.

One

Alexander Bajoran swiped his key card and pushed open the heavy oak door to his suite. He'd been halfway down the winding mile-long drive leading away from the luxurious yet rustic resort—aptly named Mountain View Lodge—when he realized he'd forgotten a stack of much-needed paperwork. Now he was late for his meeting, and it was going to be nearly impossible to make it into downtown Portland on time.

He let the door swing closed behind him as he marched toward the large cherrywood desk on the far side of the sitting area. Six steps in, he stopped short at the sound of someone else moving around in the suite. Turning toward the bedroom, he paused in the doorway, taking note of the woman stripping his bed and shaking her rear end to a song only she could hear.

She was wearing a maid's uniform, but sadly not one of the sexy French variety. Just a simple gray dress that did nothing to compliment her figure or coloring.

Her blond hair was pulled up and twisted at the back of her head, held in place by a large plastic clip, but he could still see bits of color peeking out here or there. A thin streak of black, then auburn, then blue running down one side and blending into the rest.

Yes, blue. The woman had blue hair. At least a few bits of it.

She was humming beneath her breath, the occasional odd lyric tripping off her tongue as she whipped back the top sheet, then a corner of the fitted one. The quilted coverlet was already in a heap on the floor.

As she danced around, oblivious to his presence, he noticed the glitter of earrings lining the entire length of one ear. Studs, hoops, dangles; there must have been seven or eight in her right ear alone. The left had only four that he could see—three near the lobe and one higher up near her temple.

Despite all the silver and gold and jeweled settings, he knew they had to be fake. No way could a chambermaid afford the real thing. Which was a shame, because she'd look good in diamonds. And he should know—diamonds were his business.

Soiled sheets balled up in her arms, she turned suddenly, jumping back and giving a high-pitched shriek when she saw him standing there.

He held his hands up in the universal I-mean-you-no-harm gesture. "I didn't mean to startle you," he offered by way of apology.

Reaching up, she yanked the buds from her ears and tucked them into the pocket of the white apron that must have held her MP3 player. He could hear the heavy beat of her music as she fumbled to turn down the volume.

Now that he could look at her straight on, he noticed she wasn't wearing makeup...or not much, at any rate. Strange, considering her hair and jewelry choices. She even had a small gold hoop with a tiny fleck of cubic zirconia hanging from the outer edge of her right eyebrow.

Eyes still wide from the scare he'd given her, she licked her lips. "I'm sorry, I didn't know anybody would be here. I didn't see the sign on the knob."

He shook his head. "There wasn't one. I expected to be gone for the day, but forgot something I need for a meeting."

He didn't know why he was telling her this. He didn't normally spend a lot of time explaining himself to anyone. But the longer he stood here talking, the longer he got to look at her. And he did enjoy looking at her.

That, too, was unusual for him. The women he dated tended to be socialites from wealthy families. Polished and sophisticated, the type who spent their days at the garden club doing nothing more strenuous than planning their next thousand-dollar-a-plate fundraiser for the charity du jour.

Never before had he found himself even remotely attracted to someone with multicolored hair and excessive piercings. But the young woman standing in front of him was fascinating in an exotic-animal, priceless-piece-of-artwork way.

She seemed to be slightly disconcerted by his presence, as well, staring at him as if she expected him to bite.

"Is there anything you need, as long as I'm here?" she asked, nervously licking her lips over and over again. "Extra towels or glasses, that sort of thing?"

He shook his head. "I'm fine, thank you."

Then, because he couldn't think of anything else to say or any other reason to stand there, staring at the help as though she was on display, he moved away, heading back across the sitting room and grabbing up the file he'd forgotten. It was her turn to stand in the bedroom doorway while he slapped the manila folder against his free hand a couple of times.

"Well," he murmured, for no particular reason, "I'll leave you to it, then."

She inclined her head in acknowledgment, still watching him warily.

Walking to the suite's main door, he pulled it open and set one foot across the threshold into the hall. But before walking off, he couldn't resist turning back and taking one last glance at the intriguing young woman who had already returned to her job of changing his sheets.

"It was Alexander Bajoran," Jessica said in a harsh whisper, leaning so far across the small round deli table that her nose very nearly touched her cousin's.

"You're kidding," Erin returned in an equally hushed voice, her eyes going wide in amazement.

Jessica shook her head, crossed her arms over her chest and flopped back in her chair, causing her cousin to move forward in hers. Their sandwiches sat untouched in front of them, their ice-filled fountain drinks slowly producing rivulets of condensation down the sides of the paper cups.

"Did he recognize you?" Erin asked.

"I don't know. He didn't say anything, but he *was* looking at me a little funny."

"Funny, how?"

Jessica flashed her a tiny grin. "The usual."

"Well, you do tend to stand out."

Jessica stuck her tongue out at her cousin's teasing. "We can't all be prim and proper Jackie O wannabes."

"Nobody's asking you to be Jackie O. The family just wishes you weren't quite so intent on being the next Courtney Love."

Following through on the natural instincts that had probably earned her that reputation in the first place, Jessica flipped her cousin a good-natured hand gesture. Not the least offended by the response, Erin merely rolled her eyes.

"Actually, your unique personal style may work in our

favor. You don't look at all the way you did five years ago. Chances are, Bajoran won't have a clue who you are."

"I hope not. I'll try to switch floors with Hilda, though. That should keep me from accidentally bumping into him again."

"No, don't do that!" Erin said quickly. "The fact that he doesn't recognize you is a good thing. You can move around his suite freely without arousing suspicion."

"Arousing suspicion?" Jessica repeated. "Who am I— James Bond?"

"If I could do it, I would, believe me," Erin told her with no small amount of bitterness leeching into her voice. "But you're the one he already thinks is a chambermaid."

Jessica narrowed her eyes. "Why does that matter?"

"Because it means you can move around the lodge without being noticed. You know what men like Bajoran are like. Rich and self-absorbed…to him, you'll be all but invisible."

Jessica understood her cousin's anger, really she did. Fifty years ago, Alexander Bajoran's grandfather and great-uncle had launched Bajoran Designs. Soon after, they'd begun a partnership with Jessica's and Erin's grandfathers, who owned Taylor Fine Jewels. Both companies had been based in Seattle, Washington, and together they'd been responsible for creating some of the most beautiful and valuable jewelry in the world. Million-dollar necklaces, bracelets and earrings worn by celebrities and royalty across the globe.

The Taylor-Bajoran partnership had lasted for decades, making both families extremely wealthy. And then one day about five years ago, Alexander had taken over Bajoran Designs from his father, and his first order of business had been to steal *her* family's company right out from under them.

Without warning he'd bought up a majority of shares of Taylor Fine Jewels and forced Jessica's and Erin's fathers off the Board of Directors so he could absorb the company into his own and essentially corner the market on priceless jewels and their settings.

Thanks to Alexander's treacherous move, the Taylor family had gone bankrupt and been driven out of Seattle almost overnight. They were far from destitute, but all the same, the Taylors were *not* used to living frugally. Jessica didn't think her mother was used to her new, more middle-class lifestyle even now, and Erin's mother had taken the reversal of fortune hardest of all.

Jessica was doing okay, though. Did she *enjoy* being a maid at a resort where she used to be a guest? Where she used to stay in a three-thousand-dollar-a-night suite and that her family could easily have purchased with a flick of the wrist?

Not always. But being a maid, working at a normal job like a normal person, gave her a freedom she'd never felt as a rich, well-known socialite. No way could she have gotten away with streaks in her hair and pierced everything when she'd been one of *those* Taylors. When she'd been attending luncheons at the country club with her mother and been the subject of regular snapshots by local and national paparazzi.

Money was good, but she thought anonymity might be a little bit better. For her, at least. For Erin, she knew the opposite was true.

"Why do I need to be invisible?" she asked finally. "It's lucky enough he didn't recognize me the first time. I should switch floors and maybe even shifts with one of the other girls before he does."

"No!" Erin exploded again. "Don't you see? This is our chance! Our chance to get back at that bastard for what he did to us."

"What are you talking about?" Thoroughly confused, Jessica shook her head. "How could we possibly get back at him for that? He's a millionaire. Billionaire. The CEO of a zillion-dollar company. We're nobodies. No money, no power, no leverage."

"That's right, we're nobodies. And he's the CEO of a zillion-dollar company that *used* to be ours. Maybe it could be again."

Before Jessica had the chance to respond, Erin rushed on. "He's here on business, right? That means he has to have business information with him. Paperwork, contracts, documents we could use to possibly get Taylor Fine Jewels back."

"Taylor Fine Jewels doesn't exist anymore. It's been absorbed into Bajoran Designs."

"So?" Erin replied with a shrug of one delicate shoulder. "It can always be un-absorbed."

Jessica didn't know how that would work. She wasn't sure it was even possible. But whether it was or it wasn't, what Erin was suggesting was insanity.

"I can't go poking around in his things. It's wrong. And dangerous. And corporate espionage. And *definitely* against Mountain View policy. I could lose my job!"

Her cousin made a sound low in her throat. "It's only corporate espionage if you're employed by a rival company. Which you're not, because Alexander Bajoran *stole* our company and put us all out on the street. And who cares if you lose that stupid job? Surely you can scrub toilets for the wealthy elite at some other high-priced hotel."

Jessica leaned back, stunned by the venom in her cousin's voice, as well as her obvious disdain for Jessica's occupation. Yes, she scrubbed toilets and stripped beds and vacuumed carpets instead of folding scarves and dressing mannequins at an upscale boutique like Erin, but she kind of liked it. She got to spend most of her time alone, got along well with the rest of the housekeeping staff and didn't have to claim her sometimes quite generous tips on her taxes.

And it kept her busy enough that she didn't have time to

dwell on the past or nurse a redwood-size grudge against an old enemy the way her cousin obviously did.

"Come on, Jess. Please," Erin begged. "You have to do this. For the family. We may never get another opportunity to find out what Bajoran is up to, or if there's some way—*any way*—to rebuild the business and our lives."

She wanted to refuse. *Should* refuse. But the pain in Erin's voice and in her eyes gave Jessica pause.

She could maybe poke around a little.

"What would I have to do?" she asked carefully. "What would I be looking for?"

"Just...see if you can find some paperwork. On the desk, in his briefcase if he leaves it. Interoffice memos, maybe, or documents outlining his next top secret, underhanded takeover."

Against her better judgment, Jessica gave a reluctant nod. "All right, I'll do it. But I'm not going to get caught. I'll *glance around.* Keep my eyes open. But I'm not going to rummage through his belongings like a common thief."

Erin's nod was much more exuberant. "Fine, I understand. Just look around. Maybe linger over fluffing the pillows if he's on the phone...listen in on his conversation."

She wasn't certain she could do that, either, but simply acting like she would seemed to make her cousin happy enough.

"Don't get your hopes up, Erin. This has 'Lucy and Ethel' written all over it, and you know how their crazy schemes always turned out. I'm not going to jail for you, either. A Taylor with a criminal record would get even more press than one having to work a menial, nine-to-five job cleaning other people's bathrooms."

Two

This was insane.

She was a former socialite turned chambermaid, not some stealthy spy trained to ferret out classified information. She didn't even know what she was looking for, let alone how to find it.

Her cart was in the hall, but she'd dragged nearly everything she needed to clean and restock the room in with her. Sheets, towels, toilet paper, the vacuum cleaner… If there were enough supplies spread out, she figured she would look busier and have more of an excuse for moving all over the suite in case anyone—specifically Alexander Bajoran—came in and caught her poking around.

The problem was, his suite was pretty much immaculate. She'd been cleaning it herself on a daily basis, even before he'd checked in, and the Mountain View's housekeeping standards were quite high. Add to that the fact that Alexander

Bajoran was apparently quite tidy himself, and there was almost *nothing* personal left out for her to snoop through.

Regardless of what she'd let her cousin believe, she was not going to ransack this room. She would glance through the desk, under the bed, in the nightstands, maybe inside the closet, but she was not going to root through his underwear drawer. Not when she didn't even know what she was supposed to be looking for.

Business-related what? Compromising...what?

Jessica couldn't blame her cousin for wanting to find *something* incriminating. Anything that might turn the tables on the man who had destroyed the Taylors' livelihood and a few members of the family personally.

But how realistic was that, really? It had been five years since Bajoran's hostile takeover. He had moved on and was certainly juggling a dozen other deals and business ventures by now. And even if *those* weren't entirely on the level, she doubted he was walking around with a paper trail detailing his treachery.

The sheets were already pulled off the bed and in a heap on the floor, so it looked as though she was busy working. And since she was close, she quickly, quietly slid open one of the nightstand drawers.

Her hands were shaking, her fingertips ice-cold with nerves, and she was shivering in her plain white tennis shoes. Sure, she was alone, but the hallway door was propped open—as was lodge policy—and at any moment someone could walk in to catch her snooping.

She didn't know which would be worse—being caught by Alexander Bajoran or by her supervisor. One could kick up enough of a stink to get her fired...the other could fire her on the spot.

But she didn't need to worry too much right that second, because the drawer was empty. It didn't hold so much as a

Bible or telephone directory. Mountain View wasn't *that* kind
of resort. If you needed a Bible or phone book or anything
else—even items of a personal nature—you simply called
the front desk and they delivered it immediately and with
the utmost discretion.

Closing the drawer on a whisper, she kicked the soiled
sheets out of her way and shook out the clean fitted sheet
over the bare mattress as she rounded the foot of the bed.
She covered one corner and then another before releasing the
sheet to open the drawer of the opposite nightstand.

This one wasn't empty, and her heart stuttered in her chest
at the knowledge that she was actually going to have to follow through on this. She was going to have to search through
her family's archenemy's belongings.

The bottom drawer of the bedside bureau held a decanter
of amber liquid—scotch, she presumed, though she'd never
really been in charge of restocking the rooms' bars—and a
set of highball glasses. The top drawer held a thick, leather-
bound folder and dark blue Montblanc pen.

She swallowed hard. Once she moved that pen and opened
the folder, that was it…she was invading Alexander's privacy
and violating the employee agreement she'd signed when
she'd first started working at the lodge.

Taking a deep breath, she closed her eyes for just a split
second, then reached for the pen. As quickly as she could
she flipped open the folder and tried to get her racing mind
to make sense of the papers inside.

Her eyes skimmed the print of the first two pages, but
nothing jumped out at her as being important or damaging.
And the rest was just pictures of jewelry. Snapshots of finished pieces and sketches of what she assumed were proposed designs.

Beautiful, beautiful jewelry. The kind her family used to
create. The kind she used to dream of being responsible for.

She'd grown up pampered and protected, and was pretty sure her parents had never expected her to do anything more than marry well and become the perfect trophy wife. But what she'd truly aspired to all those years she'd spent primping and attending finishing school was to actually work for Taylor Fine Jewels. Or possibly more specifically their partner company, Bajoran Designs.

Like any young woman, she loved jewelry. But where most of her peers had only wanted to wear the sparkly stuff, she'd wanted to *make* it. She loved sifting through cut and uncut gems to find the perfect stone for a setting she'd drawn herself.

All through high school her notebooks and the margins of her papers had been filled with intricate doodles that were in reality her ideas for jewelry designs. Her father had even used a few for pieces that had gone on to sell for six and seven figures. And for her sixteenth birthday, he'd surprised her with a pearl-and-diamond ring in a setting that had always been one of her very favorites.

It was still one of her favorites, though she didn't get many opportunities to wear it these days. Instead, it was tucked safely at the bottom of her jewelry box, hidden amongst the much less valuable baubles that suited her current level of income.

But, heavens above, these designs were beautiful. Not perfect. She could see where the size of one outshone the sapphire at its center. Or how the filigree of another was too dainty for the diamonds it surrounded.

She could fix the sketches with a sharp pencil and a few flicks of her wrist, and her palms itched to do just that.

When she caught herself running her fingers longingly across the glossy surface of one of the photographs, she sucked in a startled breath. How long had she been standing there with a target on her back? All she needed was for Alexander or another maid to walk in and catch her staring at his portfolio as if she was planning a heist.

Slamming the folder shut, she returned it to the bedside drawer and placed the pen back on top in exactly the same position it had been to begin with. She hoped.

With the nightstand put to rights, she finished stretching the fitted sheet over the other two corners of the mattress, then added the top sheet. She needed to get the room cleaned, and the best way to snoop was to search the areas nearest where she was working, anyway.

So she got the bedroom fixed up and cleaned but didn't resupply the bathroom before moving back into the main sitting room. She ran the vacuum over every inch of the rug, just like she was supposed to, but took her time and even poked the nose of the sweeper into the closet near the hallway door. The only thing she found there, however, was the hotel safe, which she knew she didn't stand a chance of getting into.

The only place left that might hold something of interest to her cousin was the large desk along the far wall. She'd avoided it until now because she suspected she didn't really want to find anything. She didn't want to be put in that spot between a rock and a hard place; didn't want to hand something over to Erin that might put her cousin in an even more precarious situation; didn't want to stir up trouble and poke at a sore spot within her family that *she'd* thought was beginning to heal over. She'd thought they were all moving on.

Apparently, she'd been wrong.

Leaving the vacuum nearby, she did a quick sweep of the top of the desk. There were a few sheets of hotel stationery with random notes written on them, but the rest seemed to be the typical items supplied by the lodge. Hotel directory, room-service menu, et cetera.

Inside the desk, though, she found a heck of a lot more.

Namely a small stack of manila folders and a laptop computer.

Jessica licked her lips, breathing in shallow bursts that matched the too-fast beat of her heart against her rib cage.

She was not opening that laptop, she just wasn't. For one thing, that would be *too much* breaking and entering, and sticking her nose where it didn't belong, for her peace of mind. For another, it would take too long. By the time it booted up and she figured out how to explore the different files and documents, her supervisor would surely be kicking in the door demanding to know why she was still in this suite when she should have been done with the entire floor.

She was sticking to her guns on this one. Erin might not like that decision, but she would just have to deal with it.

So she stuck with the folders lying beside the laptop, opening them one at a time and scanning them as quickly as possible.

Nothing jumped out at her as being out of the ordinary— not that she really had a clue what she was looking at or for. It was all just business jargon, and she certainly hadn't gone to business school.

But there was no mention of Taylor Fine Jewels in any of the papers…not that she'd expected there to be. And there was no indication of anything else that put her instincts on red alert.

She was just letting out a huff of air that was part frustration, part relief when she heard a creak and knew someone was entering the suite behind her. Her eyes flashed wide and she all but slammed the desk drawer shut—but slowly and quietly to keep from looking as guilty as she felt.

Putting her hand on the rag that she'd left on top of the desk, she started to wipe it down, just as she was supposed to. *Act natural. Act natural. Try not to hyperventilate. Act natural.*

Even though she knew darn well someone was behind her…likely standing there staring at her butt in the unappealing, lifeless gray smock that was her work uniform…she didn't react. She was alone, simply doing her job, as usual. The trick would be to feign surprise when she turned around and "discovered" that she *wasn't* alone.

Schooling her breathing…*act natural, act natural*…she hoped her cheeks weren't pink with the guilt of a kid caught with her hand in the cookie jar. Luck was on her side, though, because as she finished wiping down the desktop and twisted toward where she'd left the upright vacuum cleaner, whoever was standing behind her, silently monitoring her every move, cleared his throat.

And it was a he. She could tell by the timbre of that low rumble as it reached her ears and skated straight down her spine.

The air caught in her lungs for a moment, and she chastised herself for having such a gut-level, feminine response to something so simple. This man was a complete stranger. Her family's sworn enemy. And since he was a guest of Mountain View, and she worked for the lodge, he might as well be her employer.

Those were only the first of many reasons why her breathing should not be shallow, her blood should not be heating, and the clearing of his throat should not cause her to shiver inside her skin.

Doing her best to snap herself out of it, she straightened and twisted around, her hand still on the handle of the vacuum cleaner.

"Oh!" she exclaimed, letting her eyes go wide in mock startlement, praying the man standing in front of her wouldn't see right through it. "Hello again."

"Hello there," Alexander Bajoran returned, his mouth curving up in a small smile.

Jessica's pulse kicked up a notch.

It was nerves, she told herself. Just nerves.

But the truth was, the man was devilishly handsome. Enemy or no enemy, a blind woman would be able to see that.

His ink-black hair was perfectly styled, yet long enough in places to look relaxed and carefree. Eyes the color of blue ice glittered against skin that was surprisingly tan for a resident of the Pacific Northwest. But she knew for a fact it wasn't the result of time spent in tanning beds or spray-on booths; the entire Bajoran family leaned toward dark skin, dark hair... and ruthless personalities.

She had to remember that. The ruthless part, anyway.

Never mind how amazing he looked in his black dress slacks and dark blue blazer. Like he belonged on the cover of *GQ*. Or *Forbes,* thanks to his ill-gotten millions.

Never mind that if she saw him on the street, she would probably give herself whiplash spinning around to get a second look.

"We seem to have conflicting schedules this week," he said in a light, amused tone. His voice immediately touched deep, dark places inside of her that she *really* didn't want to think about.

He gave her a look, one she'd seen thousands of times in her adult life and had no trouble recognizing. Then his voice dropped a fraction, becoming sensual and suggestive.

"Or maybe they're matching up just right."

The heat of his voice was like sunshine on budding little seedlings, making *something* low in her belly shiver, quiver and begin to unfurl.

Oh, no. No, no, no. No more charming-but-dangerous men for her—and Alexander Bajoran was the most dangerous of all.

She'd been hit on and leered at by any number of male guests in her time at Mountain View. Traveling businessmen, vacationing husbands with a wandering eye, rich but useless playboys with a sense of entitlement.... But whether they'd pinched her on the rear, slipped her hundred-dollar tips or attempted simple flattery, she had never once been attracted to a single one of them.

Yet here she was, face-to-face with the man who had stolen her family's company and whom she was supposed to be spying on, and caterpillars were crawling around under every inch of her skin.

He took a step toward her, and her hands fisted, one around the handle of the vacuum, the other near her right hip. But all he did was set his briefcase—which was really more of a soft leather messenger bag—on the nearby coffee table before sinking into the overstuffed cushions of the sofa behind it.

Releasing a pent-up breath and sending some of those annoying creepy-crawlies away with it, Jessica reached down to unplug the sweeper and started to coil up the cord. The sooner she got out of there now that he was back, the better.

"I can leave you alone, if you need to work," she said, because the growing silence in the room was killing her.

But even though he had the brown leather satchel open on the glass-topped table and had pulled out several stacks of paperwork, he shook his head.

"Go ahead and finish what you were doing," he told her. "I've just got a couple of things to look over, but you won't distract me. In fact, the background noise might do me some good."

Well, shoot. How was she supposed to make a smooth but timely exit now?

She guessed she wasn't.

Dragging the vacuum across the sitting room, she set it in the hallway just outside the door of the suite. Then she gathered up an armful of fresh towels and washcloths for the bathroom.

It wasn't hard to go about her business this far away from Alexander. It was almost as though the air was normal in this tiled, insulated room instead of thick with nerves and guilt and unspoken sexual awareness. From her standpoint, at any rate. From his the air probably seemed absolutely normal. After all, he wasn't the one snooping, breaking the law, fighting a completely unwanted sexual attraction to someone he was supposed to hate.

She spent an inordinate amount of time making sure the towels hung just right on the towel rods and were perfectly even in their little cubbies under the vanity. Even longer putting out new bottles of shampoo, conditioner, mouthwash and shaving cream.

There were decorative mints and chocolates to go on the pillows in the bedroom, but she didn't want to go back in there. From the bathroom she could wave a hasty goodbye and get the heck out of Dodge. But if she returned to the bedroom, she would have to pass by Alexander. See him, smile at him, risk having him speak to her again.

That was one corner she was willing to cut today. Even if he complained to her superiors and she got in trouble later, missing mints were easier to apologize for than snooping or blushing herself into heat stroke in front of a valued guest.

Stepping out of the marble-and-gilt bathroom, she rounded the corner and was just congratulating herself on a narrow escape when she lifted her head and almost ran smack into Alexander, who was leaning against the outside wall waiting for her.

She made a tiny *eep* sound, slapping a hand over her heart as she bounced back on her heels.

"Sorry," he apologized, reaching out to steady her. "Didn't

mean to scare you, I just wanted to catch you before you took off."

If ever there was a word she didn't want to hear pass this man's lips, it was *catch*. Was she caught? Had he noticed something out of place? Figured out that she'd rifled through his things?

She held her breath, waiting for the accusations he had every right to fling at her.

Instead, as soon as he was sure she wasn't going to topple over, he let go of her elbow and went back to leaning negligently against the wall. It was a casual pose, but all Jessica could think was that he was standing between her and the door, blocking her only exit from the suite.

"I know this is probably out of line," he murmured, "but I was hoping you'd have dinner with me tonight."

His words caused her heart to stutter and then stall out completely for several long seconds.

"I'm here on business, so after I finish with meetings and such during the day, my evening hours are a bit…empty."

He shrugged a shoulder, and because he'd taken off the blazer, she could see the play of muscle caused by the movement beneath his crisp white dress shirt. Something so minor shouldn't make her hormones sit up and take notice, but they did. Boy, howdy, did they ever.

Licking her lips, she cleared her throat and hoped her voice didn't squeak when she tried to speak. It was bad enough that her face was aflame with nerves; she could feel the heat all but setting her eyelashes on fire. She already looked like a clown, in many people's estimation—she didn't need to open her mouth and sound like one, too.

"Thank you, but fraternizing with guests is against resort policy."

Ooh, that sounded good. Very confident and professional—and squeak-free.

Alexander lifted a brow. "Somehow I find it hard to believe a woman with blue hair is afraid of breaking a few rules."

She reached up to toy with the strip of chemically altered hair he was referring to. "It's not *all* blue," she muttered.

That bought her a too-handsome grin and flash of very white, perfectly straight teeth. "Just enough to let the world know you're a rebel, right?"

Wow, he had her pegged, didn't he? And he wasn't taking no, thank you, for an answer.

Dropping the hank of hair, Jessica pushed her shoulders back. She was a rebel, as well as a confident, self-reliant woman. But she wasn't stupid.

"I could lose my job," she said simply.

He cocked his head. She wasn't the only self-assured person in the room.

"But you won't," he told her matter-of-factly. Then, after a brief pause, he added, "Would it make you feel better if I said I won't let that happen?"

With anybody else she would have scoffed. But knowing who Alexander Bajoran was and the power he held—even here in Portland—she had no doubt he meant what he said and had enough influence to make it stick.

"You'll be on your own time, not the resort's," he pointed out. "And I'll let you decide whether we order from room service or go out somewhere else."

She should say no. Any sensible person would. The entire situation screamed danger with a capital *D*.

But she had to admit, she was curious. She'd had male guests proposition her before, give her that salacious, skin-crawling look reserved for when they were on out-of-town business trips without their wives and thought they could get away with something.

Alexander was the first, though, to ask her to dinner without the creepy looks or attempts at groping. Which made her wonder why he was interested.

Did he suspect her of snooping around where she didn't belong, or was he just hitting on a pretty, no-strings-attached maid? Did he recognize her as a Taylor and think she was up to something, or just hope to get lucky?

Of course she *was* up to something, but now she wanted to know if *he* was up to something, too.

So even though she knew she should be running a hundred miles an hour in the opposite direction, she opened her mouth and made the biggest mistake of her life.

"All right."

Three

Jessica didn't get many opportunities to dress up these days. But she was having dinner this evening with a very wealthy, very handsome man, and even though she knew it was a terrible idea, she wanted to make the most of it. Not so much the man and the dinner but simply the act of going out and feeling special for a little while. Putting on something pretty rather than functional. Taking extra time with her makeup and hair. Wearing heels instead of ratty old tennies.

She even went so far as to dab on a couple drops of what was left of her favorite three-hundred-dollar-an-ounce designer perfume, Fanta C. Alexander Bajoran might not be worth a spritz or two, but she certainly was.

She was wearing a plain black skirt and flowy white blouse with a long, multi-strand necklace and large gold hoop earrings in her primary holes. The others held her usual array of studs and smaller hoops.

As she strode down the carpeted hallway, she fiddled with

every part of her outfit. Was her skirt too short? Did her blouse show too much cleavage? Would the necklace draw Alexander's eye to her breasts? Or worse yet, would the earrings pull too much of his attention to her face?

Flirting—even flirting with danger this way—was one thing. Truly risking being recognized by her family's greatest enemy, though... No, she didn't want that.

Which was why she'd chosen to meet him here, in his room at the resort, rather than going out to a public restaurant where they might be seen by someone they—especially she—knew.

Getting caught in a guest's room after work hours would be bad, but being spotted out on a date with Alexander by one of her relatives or somebody who might tell one of her relatives would be exponentially worse. She would rather be fired than deal with the familial fallout.

Reaching the door of his suite, Jessica stopped and took a deep breath. She straightened her clothes and jewelry for the thousandth time and checked her small clutch purse to be sure she had her cell phone, a lipstick, a few bucks just in case. She didn't know if she would end up needing any of those things, but wanted to have them, all the same.

When there was nothing left to double-check, no other reason to put off the inevitable, she took another deep, stabilizing breath, held it and let it out slowly as she tapped on the door.

The nerves she'd tamped down started to wiggle back toward the surface as she waited for him to answer. Then suddenly the door swung open, and there he was.

Six foot something of dark, imposing good-looks. Slacks still smooth and pressed, despite being worn all day. Pale, pale lavender dress shirt unbuttoned at his throat and sleeves rolled up to his elbows, but no less distinguished than when he'd been wearing a tie and suit jacket.

He smiled in welcome and a lump formed in her throat, making it hard to swallow. Suddenly she was almost pathologically afraid to be alone with him. It was two mature adults sharing a simple meal, but almost as though she was watching a horror movie, she could see around all the corners to where scary things and maniacal killers waited.

A thousand frightening scenarios and terrible outcomes flitted through her brain in the nanosecond it took him to say hello—or rather, a deep, masculine, "Hi, there"—and step back to let her into the suite.

She could have run. She could have begged off, hurriedly telling him she'd changed her mind, or that something important had come up and she couldn't stay.

She probably should have.

Instead, a tiny voice in her head whispered, *What's the worst that can happen?* and showed her images of a lovely, delicious meal at an establishment where she worked but never got the chance to indulge, with an attractive man the likes of which she probably wouldn't meet again for a very long time. Not given her current circumstances.

So she didn't run. She told herself she was here, he was a gentleman, and everything would be fine.

"Thank you," she murmured, surprised when her voice not only didn't crack, but came out in a low, almost smoky tone that sounded a lot sexier than she'd intended.

She stepped into the suite, and he closed the door behind her with a soft click. More familiar with these rooms than she cared to admit, she moved down the short hallway and into the sitting room where there was already a table set up with white linens and covered silver serving trays.

"I hope you don't mind, but I took the liberty of ordering," Alexander said, coming up behind her. "I thought it would save some time."

True enough. Mountain View employed one of the best

chefs in the country and served some of the best food on the West Coast, but room service was room service. It sometimes took longer than guests might have liked for their meals to arrive, especially if the kitchen was busy trying to get food out to the dining room.

Cupping her elbow, he steered her around the table and pulled out her chair. She tried not to let the heat of his hand do funny things to her pulse. Of course, her pulse had a mind of its own.

He helped her get seated, then began uncovering plates of food. The smells hit her first, and they were divine. Even before she could identify them all, she saw that he'd ordered a sampling of some of the very best culinary creations the resort had to offer.

From the appetizer section of the menu he'd asked for watermelon gazpacho with tomato; cucumber and borage; seafood tomato bisque; eggplant ravioli; and oysters in red wine mignonette.

As entrées, he'd gone with pheasant with green cabbage, port wine-infused pear and black truffle shavings, and something she could rarely resist—crab cakes. Mountain View's particular recipe consisted of large chunks of Dungeness crab, tiny bits of lobster, corn and faro lightly seared to a golden brown.

He had no way of knowing they were one of her all-time favorites, though. Most likely he'd ordered them because they were nearly world renowned and one of the most popular items on the resort's menu.

But her stomach rumbled and her mouth began to water at the very sight. She might work here, might have skated past the kitchen or dining room a time or two, but since she couldn't exactly afford fifty-dollar-a-plate dinners any longer, she'd never been lucky enough to actually taste them.

"I hope there's something here you'll like."

Like? She wanted to take her clothes off and roll around on the table of food, then lick her body clean.

Because she wasn't certain she could speak past the drool pooling on her tongue, she merely nodded and made an approving *mmm-hmm* sound.

"I ordered dessert, as well, but let's wait until we finish this before we dig into that."

Oh. She'd heard wonderful things about Mountain View's desserts, too.

"So..." he murmured, "where would you like to start? Or should I just hand over the crab cakes before someone gets hurt?"

The mention of crab cakes and the slight amusement in his tone brought her head up, and she realized she'd been concentrating rather intensely on that particular platter.

"Sorry, they just...smell really good."

He grinned at her candid response. Reaching to the side and lifting the plate, he set it back down directly in front of her.

"They're all yours," he told her. "As long as you don't mind if I keep the pheasant to myself."

Well, she would have liked at least a *tiny* bite—she'd never had the pleasure of trying that particular dish, either—but if the crab cakes were as delicious as they looked, smelled and she'd heard they were, she supposed it was a sacrifice worth making.

Her silence seemed to be answer enough. He moved the pheasant to his place setting, then reached for the bottle of wine in the center of the table and pulled the cork. While she shook out her napkin and laid it across her lap, he poured two glasses of the rich, dark liquid and handed one to her.

She took it with a murmured thank-you and brought it to her nose for a sniff. Mmm. It had been a while since she'd enjoyed a glass of really good, expensive wine. This one was full-bodied, with the scents of fruit, spice and just a hint of chocolate.

She was tempted to take a sip right away, but didn't want to ruin her first taste of the crab cakes and had also promised herself she would be careful tonight. A little bit of wine with dinner wouldn't hurt, but she didn't want to risk drinking too much and forgetting who she was...who he was... and exactly how much was on the line if she accidentally let any part of the truth slip past her lips.

So she set the glass aside and picked up her fork instead.

"At the risk of scaring you off now that you're already here," Alexander said, shaking out his own napkin and placing it across his lap, "it occurred to me that I invited you to dinner tonight without even knowing your name. Or introducing myself, for that matter."

Jessica paused with her first bite of crab cake halfway to her mouth. Uh-oh. She hadn't been concerned with introducing herself to Alexander because she already knew who he was. And keeping her own identity under wraps was critical, so she hadn't exactly been eager to share that information, either.

Now, however, she was cornered, and she'd better come up with a response soon or he would start to get suspicious.

To buy herself a little bit of time, she continued the trajectory of her fork and went ahead with that first bite of food she'd so been looking forward to. Her anticipation was dampened slightly by the tension thrumming through her body and causing her mind to race, but that didn't keep her taste buds from leaping with joy at the exquisite spices and textures filling her mouth.

Oh, this was so worth the stress and subterfuge of pretending to be someone she wasn't. With luck she would only have to lie to him for one night, and not only would he be none the wiser, but she'd have the experience of a lovely meal with a handsome, wealthy playboy-type tucked away in her memory banks.

The part about deceiving him and searching his suite like a wannabe spy would maybe have to be deleted, if she hoped to live with herself for the next fifty years, though.

Making a satisfied sound deep in her throat, she swallowed and finally turned her attention to Alexander—since she couldn't justify ignoring him any longer.

"My name is Jessica. Madison," she told him, using her middle name instead of her last. If he questioned anyone at the resort, they would either deny knowing her or correct her little fib without realizing they were revealing anything significant. He obviously hadn't asked around about her or he would already know her name, and she doubted he would bother after this, as long as she didn't give him cause to become curious.

He offered her a small grin and held his hand out across the table. She had to put her fork down to take it.

"Hello, Jessica. I'm Alexander Bajoran. You can call me Alex."

A shiver of heat went through her at both the familiarity of his invitation and the touch of his smooth, warm hand.

Darn it! Why did she have to like him so much? And she really did. He was charming and good-looking and self-assured. Knowing he had a nice, hefty bank account certainly didn't hurt, but it was his easy friendliness that made her regret her bargain with Erin and the fact that she was a Taylor.

If she didn't have that baggage, she suspected she would be extremely flattered by his apparent interest in her and excited about tonight's "date." But she would be self-conscious about the fact that she was a lowly chambermaid, while he was clearly blessed financially, even though there was a time when her fiscal worth possibly rivaled his own.

She would have been fidgeting in her seat, careful to say

and do all the right things in hopes of having him ask her out again.

And she probably also would have been imagining going to bed with him. Maybe not tonight, on their first date, or even on their second or third. But eventually—and sooner rather than later considering her deep and sudden hormonal reaction to him.

Shifting in her chair, she returned her attention to her plate, playing with her food in an attempt to get her rioting emotions under control. Not for the first time, she realized how truly foolish it was for her to have agreed to spend any more time alone with him than absolutely necessary.

Alexander—Alex—didn't seem to be suffering from any such second guesses, however.

"So…" he muttered casually, digging into his own perfectly roasted pheasant. "Tell me something about yourself. Were you born here in Portland? Did you grow up here? What about your family?"

All loaded questions, littered with pitfalls that could land her in very hot water. Without getting too detailed or giving away anything personal, she told him what she could, stretching the truth in some places and avoiding it altogether in others.

Before long, their plates were clean, their glasses of wine had been emptied and refilled at least once and they were chatting comfortably. More comfortably than Jessica ever would have expected. Almost like new friends. Or new ones, hoping to become even more….

Four

Reaching across the table, Alex topped off Jessica's glass before emptying the rest of the bottle into his own. He leaned back in his chair, watching her, letting the bouquet of the expensive wine fill his nostrils while his eyes took in every detail of the woman sitting before him.

He couldn't remember a time when he'd enjoyed a dinner more. So many of his meals were spent with business acquaintances, hammering out a new deal, discussing the aspects of a new publicity campaign or simply blowing smoke up someone's proverbial skirt in an effort to preserve continued goodwill. Even dinner with his family tended toward business talk over anything personal.

Jessica, however, was a breath of much-needed fresh air. Without a doubt she was a beautiful woman. It was hard to miss her streak of blue hair or the multiple piercings running along her ear lobes and right eyebrow, but rather than detracting from her attractiveness, they added a unique flare to her classic good looks.

She was also much smarter and more well-spoken than he would have expected from a hotel maid. Truth be told, he hadn't known what to expect from the evening after his completely impromptu invitation. But Jessica was turning out to be quite entertaining. Not only were her anecdotes amusing, but her warm, whiskey-soft voice was one he wouldn't mind hearing more of. For how long, he wasn't sure. The rest of the night might be nice. Possibly even in the morning over breakfast.

Jessica chuckled at whatever she'd just said—something he'd missed because he was preoccupied by the glossy pink of her bow-shaped mouth, the smooth half-moons of her neat but unmanicured nails and the soft bounce of her honey-blond curls. She tucked one of the shoulder-length strands behind her ear and licked those delectable lips, and Alex nearly shot straight up out of his chair. And while he managed—barely—to remain seated, other portions of his anatomy were beginning to inch their way north.

Knowing his behavior probably came across as bordering on strange, he shot to his feet, nearly tipping the heavy armchair over in the process. In the next instant he'd grabbed her hand and yanked her up, as well.

She made a small sound of surprised protest, but didn't resist. She did, however, dig in her heels and catch herself on the edge of the table just before she would have smacked straight into his chest.

Too bad; he would have liked to feel her pressed against him for a moment or two. Her warmth, her curves, the swell of her breasts.

When he'd walked into his suite to find her making his bed that first time, he'd caught a whiff of lemon and thought it came from whatever cleaning solutions she'd been using.

Now he realized the tangy scent had nothing to do with dusting or scrubbing. Instead, it came directly from her. From her shampoo or perfume, or maybe both. It was a peculiar blend of citrus and flowers that he'd never smelled before, but that seemed to suit her perfectly.

He took a deep breath to bring even more of the intoxicating fragrance into his lungs, then reached around her to pick up both glasses of wine.

"Come on," he invited, tipping his head toward the French doors and the balcony beyond.

He left her to follow—or not—but was pleased when she did. Even more pleased that it seemed to take her no time at all to decide. No sooner had he turned and started walking than she was on his heels.

Though Jessica had arrived while it was still light out, the sun had long ago slipped beyond the horizon, leaving the sky dark and star dappled. A slight breeze chilled the evening air, but nothing that required jackets or would hinder them from enjoying being outside for a while.

Moving to the stone balustrade, he set down the two glasses, then turned, leaning back on his rear and crossing his arms over his chest. As large as the Mountain View resort was, and as many guests as he was sure were in residence, the wide balcony that ran the entire length of his suite was completely private.

Tall, waffle-patterned trellises protected either side from the balconies beyond. He didn't know what the lodge did about them in the dead of winter, but at this time of year, they were covered with climbing flowering vines, creating a natural barrier to sound and sight.

When Jessica came close enough that he could have reached out and touched her, he uncrossed his arms and reached behind him instead. "Your wine," he offered in a low voice.

She took it, raising it to her mouth to sip. For long minutes neither of them said anything. Then she moved to the low chaise longue a few feet away and carefully lowered herself to its cushioned seat.

Her skirt rode up, flashing an extra couple of inches of smooth thigh. More than he'd been able to see while she'd cleaned his rooms in that frumpy gray uniform. A shame, too, since she had *amazing* legs. Long and sleek and deliciously toned.

He had the sudden urge to sit down next to her and run his hand along that silken length. Even through her stockings he wanted to feel the curve of her knee, the sensitive dip beneath, the line of her outer thigh and the perilous trail inside.

Alex sucked in a breath, his mouth gone suddenly dry.

When was the last time he'd been this attracted to a woman? Any woman?

He'd had affairs, certainly. A few relationships, even. At one time, he'd dated a woman long enough to consider marrying her. He hadn't loved her, not really, but it had seemed as if it might be the right thing to do. The most sensible next step, at any rate.

He was no stranger to lust, either. He'd been with women who'd caused it to flare hot and fast. But to the best of his recollection, he'd never been with a woman who stimulated his libido *and* his brain both at the same time.

Oh, it wasn't as though he and Jessica were waxing poetic about astrophysics or the effect of global warming on penguins in Antarctica. But that was just the point: he'd *had* those discussions—or similar ones, at least—with certain women without a single erotic nerve ending tingling to life. Just as he'd found himself burning with passion and rolling around on the sheets with others without a single intelligent thought passing between them.

And then there was Jessica Madison. Nearly anonymous

housekeeper at a resort he'd only decided to patronize a week and a half ago. If he'd booked a suite at the downtown Hilton instead, as had been his first inclination, he never would have bumped into her.

Damned if he wasn't glad they'd been booked up and someone had recommended Mountain View as a second choice. This dinner alone was worth every penny of the added expense and every extra mile it took to get into downtown Portland for his scheduled meetings.

Jessica wasn't just lovely to look at, but entertaining, too. Not only conversationally but in her silent self-assurance.

The hair and jewelry choices were the physical aspects of that, he supposed; a way to tell the world without words that she knew who she was and didn't care what anyone thought of her or how she lived her life. But whether she realized it or not, her body language conveyed the same message.

Once she'd spotted those crab cakes and decided she wanted them, it had been difficult to draw her attention away from the plate. And when he'd told her she could have them all to herself, she'd set about eating them as passionately as an artist struck by sudden creative inspiration.

No worries about how she'd looked or what he might think. Which wasn't to say she'd been a ravenous wolf about it. Her table manners had been flawless. But she'd enjoyed her meal the way he enjoyed a quick bout of neat, no-strings lovemaking.

And there it was. Sex. No matter where his mind started to wander when he got to thinking about this woman, it always seemed to circle right back around to *S-E-X*.

It didn't help that she was stretching now, lifting her legs onto the long seat of the chaise and leaning back until she was nearly sprawled out like a virgin sacrifice.

Blood pooled in his groin, heating, thrumming, creating a beat in his veins that matched the one in his brain. *Pa-dump.*

Pa-dump. Pa-dump. His heart, his pulse and his head kept the same rhythm, one that he could have sworn was saying, *Do it, do it, do it.*

He was very afraid "it" could be defined as something ill-advised. Like kissing her. Touching her. Taking her to bed.

Indulging in another sip of wine, Jessica let out a breathy sigh and crossed her legs—those damn tempting legs—at the ankle. She rested her arms on the armrests and her head back against the chaise.

"I'm sorry," she said. "I've been doing all the talking and not letting you get a word in edgewise."

Something he'd noticed, but certainly hadn't minded. He'd much rather listen to her speak than himself. On his best day he was a man of few words, and his only response now was to arch his brow and lift his own wine to his mouth for a drink.

"So..." she prompted. "Tell me about yourself. What do you do? Why are you in town? How long will you be staying at our fine establishment?"

"How long will you be making my bed and restocking my wet bar, you mean?" he retorted with a grin.

She chuckled, the sound filling the night air and doing nothing to quiet the pounding in his blood, his head, his gut.

"I don't stock the bars," she told him, returning his grin. "They don't trust us near the pricey liquor—because they're afraid we'll either steal it...or drink on the job."

He laughed at that. "I might be tempted to drink, too, if I had to clean up after strangers all day. Especially the kind who stay here. I imagine a lot of us come across as quite demanding and entitled."

She shrugged a shoulder. "It's not so bad. For one thing, I don't usually have to interact with you demanding, entitled types. Most of the time the rooms are empty when I clean, and I get to work alone. The pay could be better—and for rich people, you guys sure can cheap out when it comes to tipping—but I like my coworkers, and the view is stunning when I get the chance to stop and actually enjoy it."

He inclined his head. "Duly noted. In the future, I'll be sure to leave a generous tip anytime I stay out of town."

"Every morning before you leave your room," she clarified, "not just the day you check out. Shifts change, and the same maids don't always clean the same rooms every day."

As hard as he tried, he couldn't completely hold back the hint of a smile. She was a pretty good advocate for her fellow service workers.

"I'll remember that. Have my tips so far been acceptable?" he asked, half teasing, half genuinely curious of her opinion.

She slanted her head, thinking about it for a minute. Then she shrugged a shoulder. "You've been doing well enough. And tonight's dinner definitely makes up for any corners you may have cut."

"Glad to hear it," he drawled.

"You never answered my question," she said after a moment of silence passed. The only sounds in the growing darkness were the muted voices of guests far off in the distance, perhaps strolling along one of the lodge's moonlit paths, and the occasional chirp of crickets.

"Which one?"

"Any of them. All of them." She uncrossed her ankles only to cross them again the other way. "Just tell me something interesting so I won't feel like I monopolized the conversation tonight."

"All right," he replied. Pushing away from the stone barrier, he strode toward her, dragging the second chaise closer to hers one-handed and sitting down on the very end to face her.

"My family is in jewelry. Gems and design. Maybe you've heard of us—Bajoran Designs?"

Her eyes widened. "*You're* Bajoran Designs?"

"I'm one of the Bajorans of Bajoran Designs," he clarified. "As much as I might feel or wish otherwise at times, it isn't a one-man operation."

"Wow. Your jewelry is amazing."

"You're familiar with it?"

"Isn't everybody?" she retorted. "Your ads are in all the magazines, and on TV and billboards everywhere. Didn't you design a bracelet for the Queen of England or something?"

"Again, *I* didn't, but our company did."

"Wow," she repeated. And then her head tilted to one side and she raised a brow. Her lips curved. "I don't suppose you have any free samples you'd like to share."

The sparkle in her eyes told him she was teasing, but he wished suddenly that he had more than just a few proposed design sketches with him. He wished he had a briefcase full of priceless jewels surrounded by exquisite settings to regale her with.

He would love to see her draped in emeralds and platinum or diamonds and gold. Earrings, necklace, bracelet, perhaps even a small tiara to tuck into those mostly blond curls.

He could think of any number of his companies' designs that would look stunning with what she was wearing. But he imagined that they'd look even better on her while she was utterly naked.

Naked in his bed, her skin alabaster against dark sheets, her hair falling loosely about her shoulders. And at her lobes, her throat, her waist...maybe her ankle, too...*his* jewels, *his* designs, in essence his *marks* lying cool on her warm, flushed flesh.

The picture that filled his head was vibrant and erotic and so real, he nearly reached out to touch her, fully expecting to encounter nothing but the blessed nudity of a gorgeous and waiting female.

Arousal smacked into him with the force of a freight train

late to its final destination. His fist closed on the wine in his hand, so tight he was surprised the glass didn't shatter. Every muscle in his body turned to iron, and that most important one—the one that desired her most of all—came to attention in a way that made its wishes clearly known.

Sweat broke out across Alex's brow and his lungs hitched with the effort to breathe. Jessica was still staring at him, the amusement at her teasing about the jewelry slowly seeping from her eyes as she realized he wasn't laughing.

She probably thought she'd insulted him. Or come across as a gold digger. The difference in their stations—her minimum wage chambermaid to his multimillionaire business tycoon—was patently obvious, and something he supposed she hadn't forgotten for a minute. Add to that the fact that he felt ready to explode, and he probably looked like Dr. Jekyll well on his way to becoming Mr. Hyde.

Forcing himself to loosen his grip on the wineglass, he concentrated on his breathing. *Relax,* he told himself. *Breathe in, breathe out. Don't scare her off before you have a chance to seduce her.*

And he was going to seduce her. He'd been attracted to her from the moment they'd first met, which, of course, meant he'd thought about sleeping with her about a thousand times since. But thinking about it and making a conscious decision to go through with it were two different things.

He hadn't realized until just this minute that he *was* going to make a move on her. He *was* going to kiss her and do his best to convince her to go to bed with him.

Pushing to his feet, he leaned across to set his wine on the wrought-iron table that had been between the two chaises. He locked his jaw and cursed himself when she jerked at his sudden movements. His only hope was that he hadn't frightened her so much that he couldn't smooth things over. Seducing a woman on the first date could be hard enough without adding "acted like a jackass" to the mix.

"Sorry," he said in a low voice, hoping the single word would be suitable as a blanket apology. And then in answer to her earlier question, "I don't have any samples. I'd need a 24/7 armed guard to carry that kind of merchandise around with me."

At his friendly tone, she seemed to relax. And when she did, he did.

"If you like, though, I can arrange a tour of our company. You can see how the pieces are put together, watch some gems being cut, maybe even catch a peek at a few designs that haven't been released yet. You'd have to come to Seattle, though. Think you can get the time off?"

If he'd expected her to be impressed, he was sorely disappointed. Her expression barely changed as her tongue darted out to lick her lips.

"That's all right," she said, instead of "Oh, wow, that would be awesome!" "I was just joking. I could never afford anything of yours, anyway. Better not to tempt myself."

It was on the tip of his tongue to tell her he'd gift her with a piece while she was there. He'd never done anything of the sort before, never even been tempted. Yet suddenly he didn't want to just imagine her covered in his family's fine jewelry, he wanted to literally cover her with it. Throw it at her feet like a humble servant making an offering to the gods. Diamonds, emeralds, opals, sapphires... Whatever she wanted. As much as she wanted.

He wasn't sure exactly when he'd become such a weak-kneed sycophant. He'd certainly never given women jewelry before; at least not easily or as willy-nilly as he was envisioning doing with Jessica.

To be honest, he wasn't sure he liked these feelings and the lack of control she seemed to evoke. It was the number one reason he thought he should probably call it a night and get as far away as possible from this woman.

That would be the smart thing to do, for certain.

So why didn't he?

Desire? Lust? Sheer stupidity?

But rather than thank her for coming and seeing her to the door, he held out his hand, indicating that she should give him her wineglass. When she did, he set it aside, then held out his hand again, this time inviting her to take it. He was equal parts surprised and relieved when she did so without a hint of reservation that he could detect.

Her fingers were cool and delicate. For a moment he savored the simple touch, not letting himself ruin it by imagining more just yet.

Then he gave her a tug, urging her to the edge of the chaise. A second tug pulled her to her feet.

She came into his arms as though she was tied to him and he was drawing on the string that bound them. Another step and she was pressed to his chest the way he'd wished she could be earlier.

Her blouse was silky against his palms and the front of his own dress shirt, her breasts rubbing just enough to give him ideas and get the blood pumping hot and thick to his groin once again. He held her there, enjoying the feel of her, stroking his hands up and down the line of her spine.

To his great delight she didn't pull away, but sank into him even more, her breath blowing out on a soft sigh.

With one hand at the small of her back, he brought the other up the length of her arm and the side of her throat until he cupped her jaw, his thumb brushing along the baby-soft curve of her cheek.

"I want to kiss you," he told her in a low, graveled voice, "but I'm afraid you'll think I'm moving too fast."

Afraid he was moving too fast and that he would scare her

off. Afraid that this overwhelming need he felt for her wasn't normal, wasn't the typical interest he felt when he was in the mood for a one-night stand.

"Did you notice my hair?" Jessica asked in little more than a murmur, reaching up to finger a few strands of blue.

His brows knit. What did her hair have to do with anything?

Still, he answered, "Yes."

"And my ears? My brow?" She flicked her wrist at both.

"Yes," he said again, more confused than ever.

"These are not the piercings and hairstyle choices of a girl who scares easily."

For a second, he didn't move, didn't dare breathe while her words sank in. Then a slow smile spread across his face.

"No," he murmured, even as his head lowered toward hers. "I guess they aren't."

Five

The minute Alex's lips touched hers, she was lost.

She knew this was a mistake. Everything was, from the moment she'd stepped into his suite tonight, to letting her guard down over wine and a moonlit stroll onto the secluded balcony. Maybe even before that, when she'd recognized him and not gone running, or when she'd agreed to her cousin's ridiculous scheme.

It hadn't been easy to sit still and pretend she didn't know who he was, but it *had* been somewhat enlightening to listen to him talk about himself and his business. Knowing what she did about him—namely that he'd stolen a portion of the company out from under her family—she would have expected him to be proud, arrogant, boastful.

Instead, he'd been humble, speaking highly of Bajoran Designs, but not taking any of the credit for the company's success for himself.

She thought that might have been when her head had

started to go fuzzy and stars had formed in her eyes. Her skin had been flushed with heat, too, but that was nothing new; that was just part of the attraction that had flared to life as soon as she'd walked into his arms.

She shouldn't be kissing him...or rather, allowing him to kiss her. It was a worse idea than agreeing to dinner with him, but she just couldn't seem to help herself.

The entire time they'd been talking, all she'd wanted was to cross the balcony and lay a hand on his chest. To see if it felt as hot and hard as it looked. And then to touch his mouth with her own to see if he tasted as delectable as she imagined.

The good news was, his chest *did* feel as hot and hard as she'd thought it would. Better, even, pressed up against her breasts and her belly.

And his lips were as delicious as she'd expected. Warm and soft but with a firmness that spoke of power and total self-confidence. He also tasted of the lush wine and food they'd shared earlier.

The *bad* news was that his chest felt exactly as she'd imagined, his mouth tasted even better, and instead of allaying her curiosity, it only made her want more.

With a groan she leaned farther into him, letting his heat and strong arms surround her, letting the passion sweep her away.

It was just a kiss, just one night, and he had no idea who she really was. What could it hurt to surrender to whatever this was igniting between them and just let go?

She didn't let her mind wander past that, didn't let her brain actually consider all the things that really could go wrong. She didn't want to think about it, didn't want to slow down—or worse, stop. For once she wanted to let go, be wild, be free and not worry about the consequences.

Besides, it wasn't as though anyone would ever find out. Erin would think she'd searched Alex's suite and come up with nothing, and Alex would think he'd gotten lucky with a near-anonymous hotel maid. No strings, no ties, no awkward morning after.

His mouth possessed her, but she certainly didn't mind. If anything, her moan, the melt of her body, her meeting his tongue swipe for swipe and thrust for thrust told him exactly how much she liked it.

Liked it? Loved it and was eager for more.

Not bothering to breathe—who needed oxygen?—Jessica wrapped her arms around Alex's neck, running her fingers through the hair at his nape and hanging on for dear life.

It was Alex's turn to groan. He hugged her tight and she felt his arousal standing proud, leaving no doubt that he was just as turned on as she was, just as carried away on this wave of uncontrollable lust.

Thank goodness. She would hate to be coiled in a haze of desire, only to discover he'd been after nothing more than a quick kiss.

But she needn't have worried. He was all but sucking her tonsils down his throat. And then his hands went to her waist, her hips, her thighs a second before he scooped her into his arms.

They broke apart, only because the change of position forced it, and it turned out people really did need oxygen eventually. They both gasped for breath as he carried her across the balcony and through the French doors, his long strides eating up the thickly carpeted floor all the way to the bedroom.

Once there, he set her on the end of the wide, king-size bed with more gentleness than she would have managed if their roles had been reversed. Standing over her, he stared into her eyes, his own crystal-blue ones blazing like hot ice.

With both hands, he cupped her face, tipping her head

back a fraction of an inch. Then he leaned in and kissed her softly, almost reverently.

Jessica's eyes slid closed, letting the sensation of his lips on hers wash over her, carrying her away.

A moment later, his mouth left her, but she felt his hands at her throat, his fingers trailing down the sides, over her collarbones and the slope of her chest. Goose bumps broke out on her skin as he grazed the insides of her breasts and started to unbutton her blouse.

She held her breath while he worked. This wasn't the first time a man had undressed her, but it was certainly the first time one had done it so slowly and had seemed to take such pleasure in the act. Either that or he was torturing her, but even the torture brought exquisite pleasure.

When he reached the last of the buttons, she straightened enough for him to tug the blouse from the waistband of her skirt. He flicked it over her shoulders and arms, then tossed it away completely.

Sitting there in her skirt and bra, Jessica suddenly realized she didn't have to be so passive. As much as she was enjoying his seductive treatment, she wanted to be in on the action. And, yes—if she was soon going to be naked in front of him, then she wanted to see him out of his clothes, too.

While he went for the zipper at the back of her skirt, she went for his belt buckle. He sucked air through his teeth, and she was delighted to see his nostrils flare, his jaw tic.

After undoing his belt, she got to work on his fly. She slid the tab down so slowly, each individual snick of the zipper's teeth echoed through the room. He was just as deliberate unzipping her skirt.

He pulled her to her feet by the elbows, tugging her against his chest again while he slipped the skirt past her hips. At the same time, he kicked off his shoes, letting her push his pants down so that both items of clothing fell to the floor together.

He set her back on the bed, then stepped out of the pants and kicked their clothes out of the way, unbuttoning his shirt and shrugging out of it all with urgent efficiency. Standing before her totally naked, Alex stared down at her with fire in his eyes and a set to his tall frame that told her without words that there was no turning back now. No escape.

As though she'd even want to. If she hadn't been sitting already, Jessica was pretty sure she would have melted into a steaming puddle on the floor. Her knees were jelly, her stomach doing somersaults worthy of an Olympic gold medal.

Her mouth felt as if it was filled with sand, and she licked her lips, swallowing in an attempt to bring some moisture back before the dehydration went to her head and sent her into a dead faint.

His gaze zeroed in on that tiny gesture, and she could have sworn she saw smoke spiraling out of his ears. He took a single, purposeful step toward her, bringing himself flush with the foot of the bed. Leaning in, he towered over her, fists flat on the mattress on either side of her hips.

"Scoot up," he told her in a low voice.

Even though her bones felt like rubber, she put her hands under her and did as he'd ordered, slowing moving back across the mattress toward the head of the bed. He followed her every inch of the way. Hovering over her, crawling with her, plucking the heels off her feet and pitching them over his shoulder as they went. She stopped when she reached the pillows, letting her head sink into one of the feather-stuffed cushions, still covered by the spread she'd tucked around them that morning.

"You're overdressed," Alex murmured a moment before he tucked his thumbs into the waistband of her barely there satin-and-lace panties and drew them down her legs. She helped him by kicking them off, then lifted up so he could unclasp and remove her bra.

For several long seconds he drank her in, his gaze so intense, she could hardly breathe. Just when she was about to hide her breasts self-consciously with her arms, Alex reached around her, loosening the bed's comforter and dragging it down, uncovering the pillows and sliding the slick fabric under her body until they were resting only on cool, freshly laundered sheets.

Once he was happy with the state of the bed, he lowered himself down on top of her. From chest to ankle he covered her like a blanket, the heat of his skin warming her and the hairs on his legs and chest tickling in all the right places.

He offered her a small, confident smile, and she couldn't resist rubbing against him, loving every single seductive sensation. Then she looped her arms around his shoulders and met him for a long, deep, soul-rattling kiss.

Alex ate at her mouth like he was enjoying their succulent dinner all over again. And she licked back as though she had moved on to the most decadent of desserts.

Alex's hands skimmed her body, up and down, all around, learning her shape and form and sweet spots. Her breasts swelled at his touch, and he rewarded them with added attention, squeezing, caressing, teasing until her nipples tightened into pebble-hard buds.

Tracing his mouth over her brows, her closed eyelids, the line of her jaw, he made his way down to suckle those pert tips, making her moan and wriggle beneath him.

She let her knees fall open, pulling him farther into the cradle of her thighs. He came more than willingly, settling against her, rubbing in all the right places.

Soon they were panting, writhing, clawing each other like wild animals. With a strangled groan, Alex grasped her waist, sitting back as he tugged her up to straddle his hips. Her arms tightened around him, her nails raking his skin.

The flats of his hands swept up either side of her spine,

sliding under her hair to cup the back of her skull. His fingers massaged, then dug in as he captured her mouth.

Long minutes ticked by while the only sounds in the room were their mingled breaths, their bodies moving together and the staccato interruption of deep growls and desperate moans.

Even though she was perched inches higher than Alex, he was definitely driving their passion. Which was fine, since he was really, *really* good at it. But she didn't want to be just a passenger on this bus, passively riding along wherever he decided to take them.

She wanted to *drive,* baby, and show him that a resort cleaning lady could blow his socks off just as easily as some silver-spoon socialite strumpet. Better, even, since she didn't give a flip about messing up her hair.

Bracing her legs on either side of him, she gripped his shoulders and pushed, toppling him backward and coming to rest over him with a satisfied smirk on her face. He returned her smile with a grin of his own, letting her know he was just as game for this position as any other.

"A take charge kind of woman," he said, running his hands along her torso until they cupped her breasts. His thumbs teased the undersides, coming just close enough to her nipples to make her bite her bottom lip in longing. "I like it."

Well, then, he should *love* her. She'd been taking charge of her life for as long as she could remember—to her parents' continued consternation. Even before it had become a necessity, Jessica had been more headstrong than was probably wise. Lord knew, it had gotten her into trouble on more than one occasion. She only hoped tonight wouldn't prove to be the biggest mistake of them all.

"So you're in charge," Alex told her, breaking into her fractured thoughts. His thumbs were growing bolder, finally brushing the very tips of her oversensitized breasts, causing them to grow almost painfully tight. "What's next?"

That pesky act-before-you-think gene had backfired on her again. Because her liberal, uninhibited streak seemed to have abandoned her, along with all the strength in her limbs. She no longer wanted to tower over him, but thought she would be better off sinking into the bedclothes in a pile of boneless flesh and nerve endings. That's what Alex's touch did to her—turned her to mindless, quivering mush.

But she needn't have worried. Alex might *say* he liked a strong-willed, take-charge woman—at least in bed—but he had no problem taking the reins when necessary. Abandoning her breasts, he splayed his palms at her waist and down her hips. Raising her slightly, he centered her over his burgeoning erection, brushing lightly between her folds with just the tip.

Jessica sucked in a breath, and Alex bared his teeth, nostrils flaring. Taking her hands, he wrapped them firmly around his hardened length. He was hot to the touch, soft velvet over tempered steel and throbbing beneath her fingers.

"Take me," he told her through gritted teeth. "Show me what you want, how you want it."

How could she resist? He was like a holiday buffet and she was a very hungry reveler.

Angling her hips just so, she brought him flush with her center. Then slowly…slowly, slowly, slowly…she sank down. Inch by inch he filled her, and the feeling was exquisite. To him, too, she guessed, judging by his long, low moan of satisfaction. His eyes fluttered closed, his hands clutched at her hips and beneath her rear, his thighs were as tense as iron beams.

She, however, was loose, almost liquid. Warmth spread through her veins, filled her belly, and surrounded him with moisture where they were connected. His body jerked, driving him higher inside of her, causing her internal muscles to spasm in response.

Though he was still breathing heavily, still holding himself gallantly in check, he smiled up at her, blue eyes flashing with devilish intent.

Oh, my. How had she resisted him for so long? Granted, their "relationship" had pretty much moved at the speed of light as it was. But gazing down at him now, knowing that he was not only movie-star handsome, but oozed sophistication and charm from every pore, she wondered how she hadn't fallen at his feet the very first day—first moment— they'd met. How every woman he came in contact with didn't simply drop to the nearest surface flat on her back like an upturned beetle.

That was the power he possessed—at least over her. He had the power not only to seduce her with barely a whisper, but wipe every ounce of sense straight out of her head.

What they were doing here tonight, in this room, in this bed, had nothing to do with good judgment and everything to do with pure, raw, primal instinct and desire.

Tossing her head from side to side, she shook her hair back over her shoulders and wriggled atop him to find just the right position. Alex growled, fingers digging into her flesh, and tensed even more between her thighs.

"Don't do that unless you're ready to relinquish control," he warned in something akin to a hiss, "because I'm about two seconds from rolling you over and finishing this, whether you like it or not."

A shiver rolled down her spine at his deep-throated threat. Oh, she suspected she would like that very much, indeed. She was tempted to say *yes, please* and let him do just that.

But staying in charge—at least for a while longer—was the only way she knew she'd be able to look herself in the mirror tomorrow. She wanted no doubts, no cracks in the story she might tell herself that would allow her to alter facts. She didn't want to wake up with enough doubts to convince herself that he'd taken advantage of her.

No, she wanted to be sure that if guilt was going to set in, it would rest squarely on her own shoulders. And that if anyone—especially anyone in her family, such as Erin—ever found out, she wouldn't give them further reason to paint Alexander Bajoran as a bad guy.

Running her tongue across her lip—slowly...from one side to the other...first the top...then the bottom—she watched his pupils dilate and his chest hitch with his ragged breathing.

"Poor baby," she murmured in her best sex kitten voice. "Am I being too rough on you?"

On the word *rough,* she flexed the inner walls of her feminine channel, squeezing him like a vise.

He moaned.

"Making this too...*hard?*"

She flexed again, this time coming up on her knees so that the friction, the rasping of their flesh drew sparks, sending currents of electricity outward to shock them both.

He groaned, snarled, muttered a colorful oath. And Jessica grinned at the knowledge that if their social circumstances were reversed—if they'd been doing this five years ago while her family still had control of their company—she could probably have gotten *him* to sign his company over to *her.*

That feeling of superiority, though, was short-lived. While he lifted off the bed and she continued to cant her hips back and forth in a slow, methodical motion, Alex reached for her breast again with one hand. To rub and squeeze and caress. He tweaked her nipples, making her shudder. Then, when it was her turn to let her eyes slide closed, he dropped his other hand between her legs and found the secret, swollen bud sure to send her spiraling out of control.

She moaned, biting her tongue until she thought she might draw blood, as ecstasy built to an almost unbearable pressure inside of her.

Alex stared at Jessica, fighting his own need to moan, pos-

sibly even whimper. Had he ever seen a woman so beautiful? Ever met anyone quite like Jessica Madison? He'd never
gone to bed with one, of that he was certain.

He couldn't explain his overwhelming attraction to her,
but he was sure as hell grateful for it—as well as her mutual enthusiasm. If she'd turned him down out there on the
balcony, walked away after only a single too-brief kiss, he
suspected he'd have spent the rest of the night taking out his
frustrations by trying to punch a hole in one of the suite's
walls with his forehead.

But she hadn't turned him down. She'd turned him *on,*
then stuck around to do something about it.

Her skin was alabaster silk, running like water under his
fingertips. Her mouth was equally soft: warm and inviting
and sweeter than anything he'd ever tasted.

And the rest of her... He didn't think words had yet been
invented to describe the rest of her. How she moved with him
and around him. How she welcomed him and made him want
to cherish her and ravish her both at the same time. How her
hazel eyes turned dark and liquid when she looked at him.
They were so wide and inviting, he thought he could drown
in them without a single regret.

Those weren't exactly the thoughts he wanted to be thinking about a one-night stand, but they were there all the same.

And then he couldn't think at all because she was moving on him like sin itself. Long, sure strokes that drove him
deeper. Made his jaw lock and his eyes roll back in his head.

He clutched her hips tight enough to leave bruises and had
to make a concerted effort to loosen his hold before he did.
Not that Jessica seemed to notice. Her straight white teeth
were locked on her lower lip...her lashes trembled like butterfly wings as she struggled to keep her eyes open while
passion coaxed them closed...and her pace never faltered as
she undulated above him.

His own hips rose and fell with her movements, meeting her stroke for stroke, thrusting as deeply as possible and trying for more. Her hands flexed and curled on his chest until her nails dug into the muscles like claws and then released as she reached up to cup her breasts.

The sight of those slender fingers with their neatly trimmed but unmanicured nails curving over her soft, cushiony flesh, touching herself, bringing herself added pleasure, nearly sent him over the edge. Then she tweaked her nipples, arched her spine, and threw her head back on a rich-as-hundred-year-old-scotch moan, and he knew he was a goner.

In one sharp, fast motion, he flipped her to her back, drawing a yelp of surprise from those pink, swollen, delectable lips. Rising over her, he shifted her legs to his waist, encouraged when she linked them together at the base of his spine, heels digging in.

"Hold on, sweetheart." The endearment slipped past his lips before he could stop it, but he couldn't say he regretted it, not when her grip tightened around him, both inside and out.

"Yes," she gasped when he began to pound into her. Long, sure strokes, as deep as he could go to bring them both to the keenest, highest peak of satisfaction.

He moved faster, thrusting in time with her rapid-fire murmurs of *yesyesyesyesyes* until the world tilted, an invisible surf crashed in his ears and everything washed away to nothing except the woman beneath him and the startling, intense, overwhelming pleasure rocketing through him like a meteor crashing to earth.

When he came down, Jessica was breathing rapidly against him, her body splayed on the mattress in proverbial rag-doll fashion.

Well, wasn't he a heel. He'd enjoyed himself to the nth degree, but hadn't bothered to make sure she'd reached her completion first. So much for being a gentleman.

Then she lifted her gaze to his, arms going around his neck while her fingers combed through his hair near the nape. And she smiled.

"Better than dessert," she said just above a whisper.

Blowing out a relieved breath, he returned her grin before leaning in for a soft, lingering kiss. "Who says we can't have both?"

Six

Jessica had been right about the resort's desserts—they were delicious.

So how scary was it that she hadn't enjoyed that indulgence nearly as much as getting naked and rolling around with Alex?

Three times.

After that first amazing encounter, they'd only made it to the bathroom for a quick potty break before somehow ending up back in bed, getting sweaty all over again.

An hour after that, Alex had regained enough strength to reach for the phone and call for room service. She'd told him it wasn't necessary, that she wasn't even particularly hungry anymore. At least not for food.

But he'd insisted. The dishes had been preordered, so the kitchen was simply waiting for his call to send them up. Besides, he'd said, no dinner date was complete without dessert.

She thought heart-stopping, pulse-pounding, coma-inducing sex probably qualified as a decent substitute.

The fruits and pastries, crèmes and sauces that he'd spooned and then hand-fed her had been pretty yummy, too, though. She'd especially enjoyed the bits he'd eaten off her bare skin, and then let her lick off his.

Which had led to that third and final incredible experience that had started on the sitting room sofa...and somehow ended on the very desk she'd snooped through earlier.

Afterward he'd picked her up and carried her back to bed. Good thing, since she'd been doing her best impression of a jellyfish by that point.

She'd drifted off, tucked snuggly against Alex's solid warmth, his strong arm holding her close. And for a while she'd let herself pretend.

That it meant something.

That what they'd shared had a longer shelf life than expired milk.

That she wasn't deceiving him and he hadn't ruined her family.

But all too soon she came awake, reality slapping her hard across the face. Careful not to disturb him, she'd slipped from the bed, from his arms, and gathered her clothes, dressing as quickly and quietly as possible.

Tiptoeing from the bedroom, she moved through the sitting room, praying she could find her purse and get out before Alex noticed she was missing. Then she saw his briefcase, lying open on the coffee table. Frozen midstride, she stood staring at it, battling with herself over what to do next.

Should she turn around and leave, as she'd planned, ignoring the blatant invitation to snoop just a little more? Or should she peek, check to see if there was anything even remotely incriminating inside?

She felt like a dieter standing over a plate of fresh-baked chocolate chip cookies. Tempted. So very tempted.

With a quick glance toward the open bedroom door, she decided to risk it. Rushing forward, she put her clutch down beside the case and started riffling through the papers and manila folders.

It was too dark to see much, her eyes adjusting as best they could to the bit of moonlight shining through the French doors leading to the balcony.

As far as she could tell, it was more of what she'd found in the nightstand. Interoffice memos, contract notations, design sketches. Nothing worthy of fueling Erin's proposed plan of corporate espionage.

Then, at the very bottom of the case, she spotted one final packet. Not a plain manila folder, but a darker manila envelope stamped with giant red block letters she couldn't have missed, even if the room had been pitch-black: CONFIDENTIAL

Jessica's heart stopped. It was sealed. Well, tied closed with a thin red string, at least. But it was obviously private, not meant to be viewed by anyone but Alex and other authorized Bajoran Designs personnel.

Sparing another glimpse toward the bedroom, she took a deep breath and hurried to untie the stringed closure.

She didn't know what she'd been expecting...a treasure map or stack of secret security codes, maybe. Or maybe that was just her vivid imagination, replaying various scenes from her favorite action-adventure movies in her head while she pretended to be a poor man's Indiana Jones.

But what she found was no more surprising than anything else she'd stumbled upon so far. A stack of papers labeled Proposed Princess Line, with sketches of a dozen or so fresh designs included. They were for earrings, necklaces and rings, all in matching sets with similar design elements.

Obviously these were suggested pieces for a new line Bajoran Designs intended to launch in the near future. Likely a multimillion-dollar business venture.

Jessica couldn't have said what possessed her, but before she even realized what she was doing, she set the envelope under her clutch and replaced the other papers and folders inside the briefcase, making sure to leave it open exactly as she'd found it.

She was tired and maybe not thinking straight. But she would take the proposed designs with her to study more carefully in the safety of her apartment, and decide then whether or not to show them to her cousin.

With luck she could sneak them back into Alex's briefcase in the morning when she cleaned his room, long before he even noticed they were gone.

Pushing to her feet, she grabbed her purse and the envelope and rushed to the door, careful not to make a sound as she slipped out of Alex's suite, leaving him sleeping peacefully and hopefully none the wiser.

Seven

One Year Later

Alexander made his way down the hall toward his office with his nose buried in the company's latest financials. Not bad for a year when the country's economy was pretty much in the toilet, but he suspected they would have done better if someone else hadn't gotten the scoop on their Princess Line.

A deep scowl marred his brow. It had taken him a while to figure out, but now he knew exactly who was responsible for that little betrayal, too.

He was digging into his anger, mentally working up a good head of steam, when a peculiar sound caught his attention. Pausing midstride, he tilted his head to listen. Heard it again.

The unfamiliar noise seemed to be coming from the conference room he'd just passed. Backing up a few steps, he glanced through the open doorway.

His arms, along with the papers he was holding, fell to his sides. He blinked. Shook his head and blinked again.

He knew what he was seeing, and yet there was a part of his brain that refused to function, that told him it couldn't be what he thought it was. Obviously he was imagining things... but did illusions usually come with full surround sound?

The noise he'd heard earlier came again. This time he identified it easily, mainly because the source of that sound was sitting right in front of him.

In the center of the long conference table that was normally filled with high-ranking Bajoran Designs' employees sat a white plastic crescent-shaped carrier. And in the carrier, lined with bright material covered in Noah's ark cartoon animals, sat a baby.

A baby.

In his boardroom.

While the child continued to kick his legs and coo, Alex double-checked to be sure the room was empty. It was. No mother or father or grandparent or nanny in sight.

Stepping out of the room, he looked in both directions up and down the hall. It was completely deserted.

Since this was the floor where his office was located, it tended to be quiet and not heavily trafficked. Just the way he liked it. The majority of Bajoran Designs' employees were stationed on other floors of the building.

But that didn't mean someone wasn't visiting, child in tow. He couldn't say he thought much of their parenting skills, considering they'd left what looked to be their months-old infant completely unattended on a tabletop.

"Rose!" he shouted down the hall toward his personal assistant's workstation. He couldn't see her from where he was standing, but knew she would be there. She always was. "Rose!"

"Where's the fire?" she asked in an exasperated voice, coming into sight as she headed his way.

He ignored her tone. Having worked together for years, they knew each other better than some husbands and wives. He might be demanding and short-tempered at times, but Rose was twenty years his senior and only let him get away with so much before putting her foot down.

Rather than responding to her question, he pointed a finger and asked one of his own. "What is *that?*"

Rose paused beside him in the doorway, blinked once and said, "It's a baby."

"I *know* it's a baby," he snapped. "What is it *doing* here?"

"Well, how should I know?" Rose replied, equally short. "*I* didn't put it there."

A beat passed while Alex ground his teeth and struggled to get his growing outrage under control.

This was getting him nowhere. His secretary might be a woman, but she apparently wasn't teeming with maternal instincts.

Fine. He would handle the situation himself.

Stalking forward, he turned the baby carrier slightly to face the child head-on. Cute kid. Alex couldn't say he—or she—was any more or less cute than any other baby he'd ever seen, but then, he didn't pay much attention to children one way or another. They were—in his opinion—smelly, drippy, noisy things, and he didn't know why anybody would want or purposely set out to have one of their own.

Which still didn't explain why somebody had left *this one* in his conference room.

The baby smiled and blew a tiny spit bubble as it kicked its feet, sending the carrier rocking slightly. That's when Alex noticed the piece of paper tucked beneath the safety strap holding the infant in place.

Careful not to touch the baby any more than necessary, he removed the paper, unfolded it and read.

Alex—
I know this will come as a shock, but Henry is your son. I'm sorry I didn't tell you about him before now, but please don't hold that against him.

As much as I love him, I can't keep him with me any longer. He deserves so much more than I can offer right now.

Please take care of him. And no matter how you feel about me, please tell him that I love him very much and never would have left him if I'd had a choice.

It was signed simply "Jessica."

Jessica. Madison? Mountain View Jessica Madison?

The timing was right, he would admit that much. And he hadn't forgotten a single thing about their encounter, despite the year that had passed since she'd sneaked out of his hotel room—his bed—in the middle of the night.

A muscle ticked in his jaw as he clamped his teeth together more tightly than nine out of ten dentists would probably recommend.

She'd left without a word, which was bad enough. But it wasn't until later, much later, that he'd discovered the proposed designs for his company's Princess Line were also missing.

It hadn't taken more than three seconds for him to realize she'd taken them. That she'd apparently been some kind of spy, either sent by a competing corporation or come on her own to ferret out Bajoran Designs secrets.

And she'd found herself a doozy, hadn't she? He might be CEO of the family business, but it had been none too comfortable standing in front of the Board of Directors and explaining that he'd lost the Princess Line prospectus. Not just lost them, but had them stolen out from under him by what he could only assume was the competition.

Not that he'd told them the whole truth. He hadn't wanted to admit that he'd let himself be seduced and then robbed. He'd also hoped to get to the bottom of the theft on his own before coming totally clean. Which is why he'd talked them out of taking legal action or filing an insurance claim.

But he'd seethed for months. And though no one had said anything to his face—no one would dare, unless they had a death wish as well as a desire to be on the unemployment line—he knew he'd lost a certain amount of respect from his colleagues.

He wasn't sure which bothered him more—that, the loss of revenue for the company or his apparent gullibility at the hands of a beautiful woman.

Now, just when he'd finally begun to get his impromptu affair with Jessica the Chambermaid-slash-Evil Seductress out of his system and memory banks enough to focus more fully on the theft itself, here she was again. Popping into his life and claiming he'd fathered her child.

Not a single fiber of his being told him he could believe the note in his hand. If it was even from Jessica...or the woman he'd known as Jessica. After all, he had no proof that was her real name. Or that she'd actually written this letter...or that this was really her child...or that this was really *his* child.

Even so, he found himself studying the infant's features. Was there any hint of himself there? Any hint of Jessica?

"Call security," he told Rose without bothering to look in her direction. "Tell them to search the building for anyone who doesn't belong—especially a lone woman."

A lone woman with a streak of wild blue in her blond hair and eyes the color of smoky quartz. He thought the words, but didn't speak them.

"I also want to see the video footage from this floor."

Wrapping his fingers firmly around the handle of the carrier, he lifted the child off the table and marched away, certain his orders would be followed to the letter.

"I'll be in my office."

What the *hell* was he supposed to do with a baby?

At the moment, he was pacing a hole in the carpet of his home office, bouncing the squealing, squalling infant against his chest and shoulder. He still wasn't convinced this was his son, but the evidence certainly did point in that direction.

Security had searched Bajoran Designs' entire building—including the floors and offices that had no affiliation with the company. Nothing.

Then they'd reviewed the security tapes from Alex's floor, as well as the building's main entrance. Sure enough, there had been a woman who rang all kinds of bells and whistles for him.

She'd been wearing sunglasses and a knit cap pulled down over her ears, the collar of her denim jacket flipped up to cover as much of her features as possible. But her attempts at anonymity couldn't conceal the blond curls peeking out from beneath the cap, the high cheekbones holding up the shades or those lips that reminded him of sinful, delightful things better shared in the dark of night.

So while he couldn't say with one hundred percent certainty that the woman on the security tapes—toting a baby carrier on the way in but not on the way out—was the Jessica he knew from Mountain View Lodge, it was sure as hell looking that way. Which meant this *could* be his child.

According to Rose's best nonmaternal guess, she pegged the infant to be three or four months old. And given that he'd spent the night with the child's alleged mother a year ago... Yeah, the timing was more right than he cared to contemplate.

The question was: What did he do now?

Rose had been no help whatsoever. She'd told him to get himself some diapers and formula, and then take the baby out of the office because his coos—which were headed much more toward fussing by that point—were getting on her nerves.

Not having a better game plan, he'd done just that. Called his driver and ordered him to stop at the nearest grocery store on the way home.

Normally, he'd have sent his housekeeper out for baby supplies—and he probably still would. But at that very moment, he'd somehow known that he shouldn't wait much longer to have food for this kid's belly and clean Pampers on his bottom. Babies, he was quickly learning, were both demanding and smelled none too fresh after a while.

Thank God a clerk had come to his aid and pointed out a dozen items she insisted he couldn't do without. He'd been in no position to argue, so he'd bought them all.

No matter how rich he was, however, he learned the hard way that he couldn't snap his fingers and get a nanny to appear on his doorstep within the hour. He'd tried—asked Mrs. Sheppard to call every nanny placement agency in the city and offer whatever it took to have someone at his estate that night. She'd run into nothing but one stone wall after another.

No one was available on such short notice, and even if they had been, the agencies insisted he had to go through the official hiring process, which included filling out applications and running credit and background checks. He'd gotten on the phone himself and tried to throw his weight around in a way he rarely did, but suspected that had simply bumped him to the bottom of their waiting lists.

In a growing series of things that were just not going in

his favor today, it turned out Mrs. Sheppard was no more maternal than Rose. The minute she'd spotted him walking through the door carrying a whimpering child, she'd scowled like a storm cloud and firmly informed him with more than a hint of her usual Irish lilt that she "didna do babies," hadn't signed on to care for children and wasn't paid well enough to start now.

He *paid* her well enough to care for every child who passed through the gates of Disneyland on a daily basis, but understood her point. Until today he "didn't do babies," either.

Maybe that's why all of the people in his employ were less willing to volunteer for child-care duty than he was. Having an aversion to infants himself, he'd apparently hired staff who felt the same.

Which had worked perfectly well up to now. Suddenly, though, he wished he'd surrounded himself with more of the ticking-biological-clock types. A few women who couldn't wait to take a crying baby off his hands and work whatever natural magic they possessed to restore peace and quiet to his universe.

Before running out for a few more things he thought he might need before morning, Mrs. Sheppard had at least helped him stumble his way through his first diaper change and bottle preparation. He'd gotten the baby—Henry...the child's name was Henry, so he'd better start remembering it—fed and thought he was in the clear.

Still in the little rocking seat with the handle that made for easier toting around, the baby had started to drift off, eyes growing heavy as his tiny mouth tugged at the bottle's nipple like...well, like something he had no business thinking in the presence of an infant. Especially if that infant turned out to be his son and the image in his head was of the child's mother.

And then, just a few minutes after he'd emptied the bottle of formula, Baby Henry had jerked awake and started screaming at the top of his lungs. Alex had rocked the baby seat…shushed him in a voice he'd never used before in his life…and tried every trick he could think of—which weren't many, he was frustrated to realize.

Finally, having run out of options, he'd lifted the child from the padded seat and tucked him against his chest.

Surprised by his own actions, he'd begun patting the baby's back and bouncing slightly as he crossed the room. Back and forth, back and forth, back and forth in an effort to soothe the bawling child.

He didn't know where any of this came from, but it seemed the natural thing to do. Not that it was working. The baby was sobbing so hard, his little chest was heaving and his breaths were coming in hiccuping gasps.

If this lasted much longer, Alex was going to dial 9-1-1. It was the only option he could think of, given that he had no nanny and no personal knowledge of child rearing. Especially if it meant the difference between being thought a fool for overreacting or letting the poor kid suffocate on his own tears.

He was headed for the phone, intent on doing just that, when the doorbell rang. Halting in his tracks, he took a second to wonder who it could be at this hour—he wasn't expecting anyone except Mrs. Sheppard, and she had her own key—before Henry gave another hitching sob, driving him to action. Whoever it was, he hoped to hell they knew something, *anything* about babies.

Please, God, let this be Mary Poppins, he thought as he stalked out of his office and across the gleaming parquet foyer.

Yanking the door open, he jerked to a stop, shock reverberating through his system.

The person standing on the other side of the threshold was better than Mary Poppins…it was the baby's mother.

Jessica.

Eight

Jessica's heart was pounding like the bass of a hard rock ballad in her chest, tears pouring down her face. Coming here hadn't been part of the plan. And the last thing she'd intended was to knock on the front door.

But she couldn't stand it anymore. Henry's sobs were tearing her apart, causing a deep, throbbing physical pain that couldn't be ignored one second longer.

She'd been crying since she'd sneaked into Alex's office and left her sweet little baby on his boardroom table. No choice, nowhere else to turn.

She'd done everything she could on her own, and finally realized that turning Henry over to his father was the only option left unless she wanted to raise her child in a homeless shelter.

But doing the right thing, the *only* thing, didn't mean she could just walk away. She'd left Henry with a note for Alex to discover, praying he would believe her words and accept the baby as his son. That he would love and care for him the way their son deserved.

Then she'd sneaked back out of the building, but had stood across the street, waiting and watching. And crying. Crying so hard, she'd been afraid of attracting unwanted attention.

When she'd spotted Alex coming out of the building to meet his car at the curb, baby carrier balanced at his hip, her pulse had spiked. She'd taken it as a good sign, though, that he'd had the baby with him. And that he hadn't called the police to turn her in as an unfit mother, as well as for child abandonment.

She hadn't known where he was going, though, and suddenly she'd *needed* to know. Not that she could afford to hail a cab, and she'd sold her own car months ago.

With no other options, she'd taken a chance, using public transportation, then walking the rest of the way to Alex's estate. A gorgeous, sprawling sandstone mansion on fifteen private, perfectly landscaped acres in an area she was well familiar with from her own time living in Seattle.

It was also gated, but she'd lucked out—huffing and puffing from the uphill climb, she'd reached the entrance to Alex's property just as someone else had been leaving. The car had pulled out, turning onto the main road, and Jessica had slipped through the iron gate as it was slowly swinging closed.

Then she'd rounded the house, looking in every window she could reach until she'd spotted Alex and Henry. Heart in her throat, she'd used a less-than-sturdy hedge as a stepping stool, standing on tiptoe to watch. Just…watch.

She'd wanted so badly to go inside and hold her baby. To take him back and tell Alex it had all been a horrible mistake. But even if she had…even if it *was*…her circumstances would be exactly the same.

No choice. She had no choice.

It was when Henry had started crying—sobbing, really—and had refused to be calmed, that she couldn't stand it any longer. She wanted her baby, and he obviously needed her.

So here she stood, face-to-face with the one man she'd had no intention of ever being face-to-face with again.

She didn't know what to say to him, so she didn't mince words. "Give him to me," she said, plucking the baby out of his grasp.

She wasn't the least bit familiar with the layout of the house, but she didn't particularly care. Moving across the foyer, she headed in the direction she thought would take her to Alex's spacious office den. The one she'd been hiding outside of for the past half hour, spying on her child and ex-lover.

Pulling off her knit cap and shrugging out of her jacket—one arm at a time while balancing Henry in the other—she tossed them aside, bringing the baby even closer to her chest, tucking him in and crooning. From the moment he heard her voice, he began to relax.

It took what seemed like forever for his cries to die down, but she continued to sway, hum, pat him on the back. She whispered in his ear, telling him in a low, singsong voice how much she loved him, how sorry she was for leaving, and that everything would be okay. She wasn't sure she believed it, but she promised all the same.

A long time later, his tiny body stopped shuddering and she knew he was sleeping, his face turned in to her neck, his warm breath fanning her skin.

It was the most amazing sensation, one she hadn't thought she'd get to experience again anytime soon…if ever. Her own chest grew tight, moisture gathering behind her closed eyelids.

As much as she was trying to absorb every precious moment, she knew she was also stalling. Because Alex was standing behind her. Watching and waiting and likely fuming with fury.

She couldn't hide behind the baby forever, though. Time to pay the piper.

On a sigh, followed by a deep, fortifying breath, Jessica turned.

She'd been right. Alex was standing only a few feet away, arms crossed, blue eyes as cold as a glacier glaring at her. That look cut through her, chilling her to the bone.

Swallowing hard, she kept her voice low to avoid waking the baby, hoping Alex would take the hint and do the same.

"I'm sorry," she told him. "I shouldn't have abandoned him like that."

Abandoned. God, that made her sound like such a bad mother. But it was the truth, wasn't it?

She expected him to jump on that, throw all kinds of nasty accusations at her—though in a subdued tone, she hoped.

Instead, he pinned her in place with a sharp, angry stare. "Is he mine?"

"Yes," she answered simply. Honestly. "His middle name is Alexander, for you. Henry was my grandfather's name."

Without responding to that bit of information, he asked, "Are you willing to take a blood test to prove it?"

It hurt to have him ask, but she wasn't surprised. She'd lied to him—so many times, about so much…things he didn't even know about yet, let alone the things he did.

"Yes," she murmured again.

That seemed to give him pause. Had he expected her to refuse?

She wasn't exactly perched soundly on the higher ground, here. She had no room to complain and no right to be offended. If there were hoops he wanted her to jump through, and punishments he wanted to dole out, she had no choice but to acquiesce.

"I'll make an appointment first thing in the morning."

She nodded, though she knew he neither needed nor was waiting for her to agree.

"You'll stay here tonight," he continued, his tone brooking no argument. "In fact, you'll stay here until I know what's going on and have decided what to do about it."

As uncomfortable a prospect as that was, she was oddly okay with it. It wasn't as if she had anywhere else to go. Even after leaving Henry at Alex's office, her only plan had been to look for work here in Seattle or catch a bus back to Portland and try to find something there, but she suspected she probably would have ended up sleeping in the bus terminal instead. Provided Alex didn't intend to lock her in a dungeon somewhere in this giant house of his, it might be nice to sleep in a real bed for a change.

When she offered no resistance to his demands, he tipped his head and moved toward the door. "Follow me." He didn't look back, assuming—or rather, *knowing*—she would do exactly as he said.

Still holding a sleeping Henry, she trailed him out of the office, across the cavernous foyer and up a wide, carpeted stairwell to the second floor. He led her down a long hallway lined with what she could only assume was priceless artwork and credenzas topped with fresh-cut flowers in crystal and Ming-style vases.

Stopping suddenly, he pushed open one of the doors and stood aside for her to pass. It was a beautiful, professionally decorated guest room, complete with queen-size four-poster canopy bed and private bath. Done in varying shades of sage-green, it was unisex; not too masculine or too feminine.

"If you try to leave," Alex said from behind her, "I'll stop you. If you try to take my child from me—if he really is my child—I'll have both the police and my attorneys on you faster than you can blink."

She had no doubt he was rich enough, powerful enough and bitter enough to carry through with the threat. While she was broke, powerless and too exhausted to walk much farther, let alone attempt to run away.

Turning to face him, she continued to rub the baby's back. "I'm not going anywhere, Alex. I handled this badly, and for that, I apologize. This isn't how you should have found out you're a father. So whatever you need me to do…within reason," she added with a raised brow, "well, I figure I owe you one."

His raised brow told her he thought she owed him more than just one. And maybe he was right. But her response seemed to reassure him. Some of the tension went out of his shoulders and the lines bracketing his mouth lessened a fraction.

"Tell me what you need for him."

His eyes darted to Henry and she *thought* she saw a hint of softness there. Although she might have imagined it.

She had next to nothing. By the time she'd decided leaving Henry with Alex was her last resort, she'd been out of formula and down to her last diaper. If she hadn't, she probably wouldn't have been able to go through with it.

She could have gone to her parents, but that was still a can of worms she was trying to avoid opening. And the guilt of not alerting Alex to the fact that he was a father had started to eat at her, so she'd decided that he was a better "last resort."

"Everything," she said dejectedly.

"Make a list," he told her. "My housekeeper is picking up a few things right now. I'll try to catch her and have her get whatever else you need while she's out."

Jessica nodded, expecting him to go…unless he intended to pull up a chair and stand guard at the door all night. Instead, he remained rooted to the spot, his features drawn in contemplation.

"Will this be all right for him?" he finally asked. His arms swept out to encompass the room. "I don't have a crib or anything else...nursery-ish."

She offered a small smile. As angry as he was, he was still concerned about his son's safety and comfort. She found that endearing. And it gave her hope that his resentment would one day give way to understanding.

"We'll be fine," she assured him. "Henry can sleep in the bed with me, and I'll use pillows around the edges to keep him from rolling off."

He considered that for a moment, then said, "I'll make arrangements for someone to come by tomorrow and baby proof the place. Make a list for that, too—whatever you and Henry will need for an extended stay, and whatever needs to be done to keep him safe."

She wasn't sure what he meant by that. How *extended* a stay did he have in mind?

But now wasn't the time to question him. She was on thin enough ice as it was.

"We still have to talk," he informed her. "But you look tired, and I know he is. It can wait until tomorrow."

With that, he turned on his heel and walked out, closing the door behind him.

Jessica let out a breath, wishing it was one of relief. Instead, it was only...a short reprieve. As she set about readying the room, herself and the baby for bed, she felt as though a noose was hanging over her head.

Because as bad as today had been...tomorrow promised to be even worse.

Jessica didn't know what time it was when she finally came awake the next morning. Henry had had her up a few times during the night, needing to be changed or fed or simply lulled back to sleep. But she suspected yesterday's stress level had impacted him, as well, because he'd slept like a stone the rest of the time.

Stretching, she glanced beside her to find him awake and smiling around the pacifier in his mouth. His legs were kicking, and when he saw her looking down at him, he waved his arms, too.

"Good morning, sweetheart," she greeted him, unable to resist leaning over and kissing his soft cheek. He made a happy sound from deep in his belly, and she took a minute to blow raspberries on his tummy through his thin cotton T-shirt until he giggled.

Laughing in return, she scooped him up and finally looked at the clock. Ten-thirty. Later than she normally woke, but not quite as late as she'd expected, given the bright sunlight peeking through the drawn floor-to-ceiling curtains. As she started moving around, using the restroom and changing the baby, she heard noises from outside the bedroom door.

Last night, before she'd gone to bed, Alex's housekeeper had arrived with several large fabric totes bulging with baby items. Formula, bottles, pacifiers, toys, onesies, baby lotion, baby shampoo, baby powder...everything. More than Jessica would need to get through just the next few days. And now it sounded as though Alex had a construction crew in the house, building a nursery—or possibly an entire day care center—to his exact specifications.

With Henry at her hip, she opened the door only to find the hallway filled with oversize boxes and shopping bags. She stood rooted to the spot for a minute, stunned and confused.

Noises were coming from next door, and before she could decide which direction to turn—left toward the sounds of the pounding or right toward the stairs—Alex appeared. He strolled down the hall with two men on his heels who were carrying a large, flat cardboard box between them.

"In there," Alex instructed, pointing to the room where all

the building noises were coming from. He waited for them to pass, then waved her ahead of him.

They paused in the doorway of the room beside hers, where several men were busy putting furniture together and attaching shelving to the walls.

"What's all this?" she asked, though she could certainly guess. The half-assembled crib and changing table in the corner were dead giveaways.

"I'm putting a nursery in between our two rooms. That way we'll both be close to the baby in case he needs us during the night."

Jessica swallowed, not quite sure how to respond. Should she be more concerned that Alex's room was apparently only two doors down from where she'd spent last night...or that he seemed to believe she and Henry would be here long enough for a separate nursery to be necessary?

She owed him answers, and, of course, knew that he would want to spend time with his son now that he was aware of Henry's existence, but that didn't mean she—or the baby—were going to stick around forever.

Before she could decide how to respond, he continued.

"I've called Practically Perfect Au Pairs, the premiere nanny agency in the city. They'll be sending potential nannies out over the next few days to be interviewed. You can be there, if you like."

This time she wasn't at a loss for words. Her spine went straight and tight as outrage coursed through her system.

"Henry doesn't *need* a nanny. I'm his mother. I can care for him just fine by myself."

"As evidenced by the fact that you left him in the boardroom of my office building, with a note begging me to take him in," he replied, deadpan.

Jessica's chest squeezed. He was right, and they both knew it. But she'd changed her mind. She was here now, and damned if she'd let him foist her child off on some complete stranger.

"That was yesterday," she told him. "Today, I'm perfectly capable of watching out for my own child. I don't *need* a nanny," she stressed again.

She expected an argument. Worse, she expected him to toss more "unfit mother" accusations at her. Instead, he shrugged one shoulder encased in the fine silk-wool blend of a tailored dark blue suit.

"Humor me," he said in a tone that could only be described as wholly polite. "This is all rather new to me, and I'd feel better having a trained professional on hand for those times when you or I can't be with Henry."

Again the thought crossed her mind that she probably wouldn't be staying with him for long. Certainly not long enough to hire extra staff.

But what she asked him was, "Why wouldn't I be with him?" Her back was still stiff as a rod, her voice carrying more than a hint of wariness.

"We have a lot of ground to cover. You may need a nap after the grilling I plan to give you."

Her eyes widened at that, and suspicion gave way to fear.

"You missed breakfast," he added, jumping so easily from one topic to another that her head started to spin. "But I'm sure Mrs. Sheppard can see that you're fed."

"Oh, that's all right. I don't want to be a both—"

Alex took her elbow, forcibly turning her toward the other end of the house and leading her in that direction.

"Feed the baby," he told her. "Then get yourself something to eat. After that, we'll talk."

He said "we'll talk," but what Jessica heard was, "Let the inquisition begin."

Nine

Alex thought he deserved a damn Academy Award for his performance so far. Every second that he'd been with Jessica, he'd wanted to shake her. Every word that he'd spoken in calm, even tones, he'd wanted to shout at the top of his lungs. It had taken every ounce of control he possessed to hold a normal, mundane conversation with her rather than demand answers. Right there, right now, regardless of how many witnesses might hear.

But he'd bitten his tongue, fisted his hands so tightly he'd nearly drawn blood. Reminded himself that in most situations, one got further by keeping a cool, level head than losing one's temper and raging like a maniac.

As hard as it was to resist turning the full force of his fury on her, he told himself that would only frighten her and possibly cause her to run off again. This time taking *his son* with her.

Oh, there were going to be DNA tests to prove—or disprove—that claim. In addition to the nannies who would be dropping by on and off over the next several days, he had a doctor scheduled to stop in and conduct a paternity test as quickly as possible.

But until he knew for sure, he was going on the assumption that he *was* the child's father. Better safe than sorry, and if he was, he wanted to get a jump on being a dad.

He'd already missed… He didn't know how long. He did know, though, that he'd missed the entire pregnancy, the birth and any number of firsts. First feeding, first diaper change, first time being awakened in the middle of the night and rocking Henry back to sleep.

Alex clenched his teeth until they ached. One more thing to hold against Jessica. The list was getting pretty long.

Biding his time, he led her downstairs to the kitchen and asked Mrs. Sheppard to see to it that Jessica and the baby were both taken care of. Then he'd returned to the foyer to oversee the rest of the baby preparations.

He'd waited thirty minutes. Thirty-two to be exact, before returning to the kitchen, ready to get some answers to the questions burning a hole in his gut.

Walking into the room, he stopped short, taken aback by the sight before him.

Jessica sat at the table of the eat-in nook near the windows, a half-eaten plate of scrambled eggs and toast in front of her. She alternated between taking a bite of her own meal and slipping a spoonful of goopy gray cereal into the baby's mouth. He was perched on her thigh, nestled and in the crook of her arm.

"Why isn't he in the high chair?" Alex asked, his voice reverberating through the room more loudly than he'd intended, startling both Jessica and Henry. He'd ordered the expensive piece of infant furniture, though, so his son should darn well be using it.

Dipping the tiny spoon back into the baby goop, she said, "He's only three months old. He's not quite ready to sit up on his own yet."

Well, there was one question answered. Henry was three months old. The math worked.

He also made a mental note to buy some baby books. He didn't want to learn from Jessica or anyone else what his child could or couldn't do, or what he needed.

Feeling suddenly uncomfortable and slightly self-conscious, he cleared his throat. "When you're finished, come to my office. It's time to get down to business."

As she crossed the front of the house toward Alex's den, Jessica felt for all the world as if she'd been called to the principal's office. Her feet were lead weights and her heart was even heavier. Henry at her hip, in comparison, was light as a feather.

He was also happy today. She shouldn't have been quite so delighted about it, but from the moment she'd arrived last night and plucked him from Alex's arms, Henry had been relaxed and content. Something to be said for her mothering skills, she hoped, as well as their strong mommy/baby bond.

On the heels of that thought, though, came a wave of guilt. She'd had nine months of pregnancy and the three months since Henry was born to bond with him, while Alex had had only yesterday. And that hardly counted, since she'd sprung the baby on him with no warning and hadn't even stuck around to explain.

Which was why she was letting him get away with the strong-arm tactics. He was angry—with good reason. And she was guilty—for bad reasons.

The door was open when she arrived. Alex was seated behind his desk, another man—older and balding—sat in one of the guest armchairs with his back to her.

Alex spotted her almost the moment she stepped inside and stood to greet her.

"Come in," he said, rounding the desk as the other man also got to his feet.

"This is Dr. Crandall," he introduced them, closing the door behind her with a soft click. "Dr. Crandall, this is the young woman I was telling you about."

To Jessica, he added, "Dr. Crandall is here for the paternity test."

Having her integrity called into question stung, but in Alex's shoes she would have insisted on the very same thing. So she extended her arm and shook the doctor's hand.

"Nice to meet you, Doctor."

"You, too, my dear," he said, smiling gently. "And I don't want you to worry about a thing. This is a relatively painless procedure. Just a quick cheek swab, and I should have the results back from the lab by the middle of next week."

"I appreciate that, thank you."

The idea of having Henry's blood drawn hadn't appealed. He'd survived worse, of course, but that still didn't make it a fun prospect.

"Dr. Crandall assures me that the cheek swab tests are just as accurate as blood tests," Alex put in. "The only reason we'd have to have blood drawn later is if the initial tests come back as inconclusive or problematic."

Jessica nodded. "Whatever you need."

Ten minutes later, Alex was walking the doctor to the door, DNA samples labeled and tucked safely into his medical bag. She stood in the doorway of Alex's office, watching as he shook the physician's hand, then ducking back inside before Alex returned.

When he arrived, she was sitting in one of the leather guest chairs, bouncing a giggling Henry on one knee.

Alex stood for a moment, simply watching them. The

woman who'd seared some of the most passionate memories of his life into his brain, and the child they'd most likely made together.

His chest contracted. Without a doubt, he was furious. She'd used him, stolen from him, betrayed him and lied to him. Yet part of him wanted to cross the room, drop to one knee and wrap his arms around them, holding them close and cherishing them the way a family should be cherished.

He wondered what would have happened if his relationship with Jessica had played out differently. If she hadn't spent the night with him simply to steal company secrets. If she'd stuck around instead of running off before the sun rose the next morning so they could share breakfast, get to know each other better, perhaps agree to keep seeing one another.

Alex wasn't a man of fickle emotions, so when he'd awakened that morning after making love with her, looking forward to making love to her again…and possibly again…he'd known he'd found something special. Or thought so, at least. Reality had proven to be quite different.

But deep down, he knew the possibility of a good, old-fashioned romance had existed. They might have dated, shared a short engagement and walked down the aisle before deciding to start a family. Baby Henry would still have been part of the big picture, just a little further down the road.

Fate had a way of turning things upside down, though, then sitting back for a good chuckle at the expense of the humans who had been played with like marionettes.

Which meant he was now faced with fatherhood first and…he didn't know what else second.

Clearing his throat, he strode across the room, returning to his seat behind the desk. It was awkward to put such cold, professional distance between himself and the mother of his child, but he felt comfortable there, and if it intimidated Jes-

sica at all, kept her on the level, then it was the right position to take.

"I think I'm going to need a quick rundown of events,"
he told her, careful to keep his tone level and unaccusatory.
"Why did you take off in the middle of the night? And if
Henry is my son, why didn't you contact me when you found
out you were pregnant?"

He watched her eyes, saw the pulse in her throat jump as
she swallowed.

"It was a one-night stand. I didn't think you'd want me to
still be there in the morning," she murmured. "And then when
I went back the next day to clean your room, you were gone."

"My business in Portland wrapped up a few days early,
and I was needed back here in Seattle. I wanted to ask about
you," he admitted—albeit against his better judgment, "or at
least leave a note, but was afraid it might get you in trouble."

He very intentionally didn't mention the missing Princess Line prospectus. It was a subject that definitely needed
to be discussed, but not now. Not until he knew for certain
whether or not Henry was his son.

For the time being, the child and his possible unexpected
fatherhood trumped everything else.

She nodded somewhat ruefully. "It probably would have
gotten me fired."

Just as he'd suspected. "I called a while later, but whoever
I talked to claimed there was no one by the name of Jessica
Madison working at Mountain View. And that the only Jes-
sica they'd had on staff had quit the week before."

He'd considered digging deeper, perhaps hiring a private
investigator to track her down. But then he'd realized how
that would look: desperate. Especially since he hadn't yet
hired a P.I. to look into the theft. If their one night together
hadn't meant enough to her to make her stick around, then
he'd look pretty pathetic chasing after her like a lovelorn pup.

So he'd put her and what he still considered a spectacular intimate experience behind him. Or tried, at any rate. And he'd succeeded at putting her out of his everyday thoughts, if not his late-night, private ones.

"You must have called soon after I discovered I was pregnant," she said.

His mouth turned down in a frown. "You quit because of that?"

A strange look passed over her features, and it took a second for her to reply.

"I had to. It wouldn't have been long until I was unable to keep up with the workload, and the chemicals we used to clean wouldn't have been good for the baby. Besides, the owners of the resort weren't too fond of unwed mothers being on the payroll. They thought it tarnished the resort's pristine reputation and would have come up with a reason to let me go before long."

Alex made a mental note never to stay at Mountain View Lodge again. If anything, single and expectant mothers needed their jobs more than other employees. And considering some of the behavior that often took place at those types of high-scale resorts—adultery topping the list—he didn't think the owners had a lot of room to point fingers.

Getting back to the subject at hand, he said, "Why didn't you tell me when you found out? You knew who I was and where to find me."

It wasn't always easy to get in touch with him—Rose was an excellent guard dog—but if Jessica had left her name and at least a hint of what she needed to talk to him about, he would have returned her call. Hell, he would have relished the chance to see her again—for more reasons than one.

He didn't know how he would have handled the news of her unexpected pregnancy. Probably much the same as he was handling the news of Henry's existence now—with a fair dose of skepticism and trepidation. He liked to think he would have done the right thing, though, once he'd established the veracity of her claim. Much as he was trying to do now.

He was playing it smart, getting medical proof before accepting parental responsibility, but if Henry turned out to be his, he would do more than put a crib in one of the extra guest rooms and make sure his name was on the child's birth certificate. He would be laying full claim, taking whatever steps were necessary to be sure his son stayed with him. Whether Jessica liked it or not.

Why didn't you tell me when you found out you were pregnant?

It was the question Jessica had been dreading ever since she'd made the decision *not* to tell him.

It had been the wrong decision. Or at the very least, the wrong thing to do. There had been so many factors to consider, though, and she'd been so very frightened and alone.

To Alex, however, she said simply, "I didn't think you'd want to know. Most men wouldn't."

A muscle ticked in his jaw, and she got the distinct impression he was grinding his molars together to keep from doing—or saying—something violent.

"I'm not most men," he said slowly and very deliberately, almost as though each word was a statement unto itself. "I would have stepped up to the plate. And I most certainly would have wanted to know I'd fathered a child."

"I'm sorry."

Jessica didn't know what else to say, not without saying far too much. He was angry enough with her already; she didn't think telling him she was a Taylor and that she'd been poking around his hotel room looking for company secrets would do much to improve his mood.

So she kept her mouth shut, knowing he would find out eventually but hoping he would hate her a little less by then.

Ignoring her apology, both physically and verbally, he went on. "If you didn't want me to know about Henry, why did you dump him at my office yesterday?"

She flinched at his less-than-flattering description of her actions, even though that's exactly what she'd done—in his eyes and in her own.

"I didn't feel I had a choice," she told him quietly. "It's been rough being out of work and trying to care for a baby all by myself. I can't find a job until I put Henry in day care, and I can't afford day care until I get a job."

"Don't you have family to turn to? Parents? Relatives who could help you out?"

The short answer was no. The long answer would mean admitting she was a Taylor, and that rather than telling her family she was pregnant by Alexander Bajoran, she'd chosen to run away. Disappear and live one step up from on the streets.

She'd thought so many times about going home and telling her parents everything. But she hadn't wanted to see the disappointment on their faces when they found out who the father of her baby was. Even if she refused to tell them, she was afraid her mother would eventually wear her down and drag the truth out of her.

And if she'd managed to hold out against her mother's badgering, she'd been very much afraid her cousin would come along later and figure it out.

Because Erin knew what she'd been up to in Alex's room at the resort. And she knew that Jessica hadn't been dating anyone around that time. She'd have done the math in her head, become suspicious and started badgering Jessica until she confessed everything. Then Erin would tell Jessica's folks for sure, damn her meddling hide. Her cousin was the impetus behind all of this, yet Jessica was the one to suffer the consequences.

To Alex she said carefully, "No one who could help me out, no."

He considered that for a moment, the tension in his jaw easing slightly. "You should have come to me sooner. *Come* to me," he emphasized. "In person rather than sneaking around like a cat burglar."

"At least I left something instead of stealing something," she quipped in an attempt at levity.

"I'm not sure the authorities would see it that way," he replied with a withering glance that immediately wiped the lopsided smile from her face.

Before the adrenaline from his veiled threat made it into her bloodstream, however, he added, "You were actually pretty good at getting in and out of the building without being seen. How did you manage that?"

"Just lucky, I guess."

If *luck* included practically growing up there while her family was still part of the business, and knowing not only where all the security cameras and blind spots were, but also how the building's security functioned. Or how it *had* functioned, anyway. She'd taken a chance and hoped not much had changed in the past few years.

Alex's eyes narrowed, and she could see the questions swirling there, knew the interrogation wasn't even close to being over. And while he'd certainly earned the right to some answers, she didn't know how much longer she would be able to get away with partial ones and half-truths.

Then as though heaven actually heard her silent pleas, she was saved by the bell. Literally.

From the front of the house the doorbell rang. They heard footsteps, followed by muted voices, and then more footsteps. A minute later there was a soft knock at the office door.

"Come in," Alex called.

Mrs. Sheppard poked her head in. "One of the applicants from Practically Perfect Au Pairs is here," she said.

"Give us two minutes, then show her in," Alex instructed. "Bring us a tray of coffee and hot tea, as well. Thank you."

The housekeeper nodded, pulling the door closed behind her.

"This is only the first interview of many," Alex told Jessica. "Would you like to take Henry off to do something else, or would you like to stay?"

Another woman interviewing for the privilege of taking care of her son when she wasn't readily available? Oh, there was no way she'd leave that decision to anyone else. Not even her baby's father.

Ten

By the end of the day, they'd interviewed half a dozen nannies. They ranged in age from eighteen to probably forty-five or so; college-age girls needing a job and a place to stay while they attended school, to lifelong caregivers. Each of them came with a resumé and the stamp of approval from either Practically Perfect Au Pairs or one of the other professional nanny placement services Alex had contacted.

As nice as most of the people were, though, Jessica found herself balking at the idea of Alex hiring any of them. Credentials, references and background checks aside, none of them seemed quite good enough to be left alone with her child.

She stood in the foyer, waiting while Alex saw the last of the potential nannies out. Shutting the door behind him, he turned to face her.

"So...any possibilities?" he asked, his footfalls echoing on the parquet floor as he crossed to her.

She shrugged a shoulder, not saying anything.

One corner of his mouth quirked up in a half grin. A sexy half grin, she was troubled to note.

Damn him for being so attractive, even when he hated her. And damn herself for still *finding* him attractive when she had so very much to lose at his hands.

"Come on," he cajoled, raising a hand to rub one of Henry's cheeks with the side of his thumb before letting it drop... and stroking her arm with his cupped palm all the way down. The touch made her shiver as goose bumps broke out along her flesh.

"There has to be someone you liked at least a little. You can't be with Henry 24/7, and every child needs a babysitter at some point. So if you had to pick, who would it be?"

Taking a deep breath, she thought back to each of the interviews, the details playing through her memory. One jumped out over all the others.

"Wendy."

His gaze narrowed. "Why?"

"She was friendly and smart," Jessica told him. "And she engaged Henry almost as soon as she walked in. Spoke to him, smiled at him, played with him, split her attention evenly between the three of us. The others seemed more concerned with remaining professional and impressing you."

A beat passed while he digested that. Then he offered a curt nod. "I thought exactly the same thing."

"Really?" Jessica asked, more than a little surprised.

Taking her elbow, he turned her toward the stairs, leading her to the second floor.

"Absolutely. I may not know much about babies, but I do know that a nanny will be spending ninety percent of her time with Henry. Which means that whoever we hire should be more concerned with impressing him, not me."

He smiled at Henry while he spoke, earning himself a giggle and kick, which only made Alex smile wider.

Tweaking the baby's bare toes as they strolled down the hall, he said, "Besides, I noticed the same things you did. She was really quite good with him. I especially liked that she cleaned his toy giraffe with an antibacterial wipe from her purse before handing it back to him after it fell on the floor. All without a hitch in her conversation with us."

"Me, too," Jessica admitted. Actually, she'd loved that part of the interview. Even Jessica's first instinct would have been to simply take her chances that the floor wasn't that dirty, or maybe run the toy under some water if she was near a faucet. The fact that Wendy had come so well prepared before she'd even been hired definitely earned her bonus points.

"So we'll put her at the top of the list," Alex said. "There are still a few more potentials to meet with tomorrow, and then we can decide. But I think we should strike that Donna woman from the pool entirely. She was downright frightening."

Jessica chuckled, even as a shudder stole down her spine. "Definitely. She should be running a Russian prison, not caring for small children and infants."

Alex gave a short bark of laughter. "Maybe I'll mention that to the agency when they ask how the interviews went."

Jessica's eyes widened. "Don't you dare!" she exclaimed, slapping him playfully on the chest with the back of her hand.

She stopped in her tracks, both shocked and horrified at what she'd done. Dear God, what was she thinking? She was joking with him as if they were old friends. Never mind that he held her future in his hands and could decide to punish her in a million alarming ways at the drop of a hat.

She swallowed past the lump in her throat and forced her gaze up to his, an apology on the tip of her tongue. But his expression kept it from going any further.

Rather than looking annoyed or upset, his features were taut, his eyes blazing with something she hadn't seen since their time at the resort. It made her heart skip a beat and sent heat rushing through her system.

Or maybe she was imagining things. Maybe that blaze in his eyes really was annoyance, and she'd amused herself right into a boatload of trouble.

Chest tight, she licked her dry lips and wondered if she could distract him with a change of subject.

"What are we doing up here, by the way?"

For a moment, he continued to stare with that same barely controlled intensity. Then he pulled back just a fraction and gestured behind her.

"The nursery is ready," he said, leading her in that direction. "I thought you might like to see it."

The general decor of the room was the same as it had been before. Pale yellow walls, lacy white curtains at the windows and gleaming hardwood floors. But any original pieces of furniture had been replaced with top-of-the-line baby items.

A spacious oak half-circle crib rested against one wall, a large changing table and storage unit along another, and in the corner sat a beautiful rocking chair she'd be willing to bet was hand carved.

"What do you think?" Alex asked from just over her shoulder.

"It's lovely," she told him. Like something out of *House Beautiful* or *Babies Born with Silver Spoons in Their Mouths*. She was almost afraid to touch anything for fear she'd leave a smudge on the pristine interior. "I can't believe you had all of this done in only one day."

"Getting things done is easy when you have money and know the right people."

A fact she knew quite well from the good old days before Alex had destroyed her family.

"If there's anything else you or the baby need, anything you'd like to change, just say so," he continued. "I want everything to be perfect, and I'm afraid you're my only source of information at the moment where Henry is concerned."

He said it without a hint of censure. At least none that she could detect. But the guilt and underlying threat were there all the same.

"Why are you doing this?" she asked softly. Shifting Henry from one arm to the other, she turned to face Alex more fully. "You don't even know for sure that Henry is yours."

She did, of course, but she'd assumed that was the point of the paternity test they'd taken that afternoon.

Alex shrugged. "Better safe than sorry."

A very simple, off-the-cuff answer, but she suspected there was more to it than that.

"You're going to make us stay, aren't you?" she asked barely above a whisper.

"For the time being," he said without hesitation.

Then, surprising her yet again, he reached out and slid his hands beneath Henry's arms, lifting him out of her grasp and into his own.

For a split second, Jessica held her breath and nearly tried to tug the baby back. She had to remind herself that Alex *was* Henry's father. He *did* have a right to hold him, if he wanted to.

As distant as he'd been up to now, he didn't seem the least bit nervous about it. There was no hesitation, no pause while he considered the best way to position Henry against his thousand-dollar suit.

He was a natural. Either that, or he'd learned on the job during last night's screaming fit. Still, she couldn't resist stretching out a hand to smooth the baby's shirt down his back, making certain everything was just right and he was okay.

It was odd not holding her own baby, not having him almost surgically attached to her side when she was the only person who'd held him for any length of time since he was born. She didn't know what to do with her arms.

Letting them drop to her sides, she dug her hands into the front pockets of her jeans and told herself to leave them there, even though the urge was to fidget like crazy.

As hard as it was to admit, she made herself mumble, "You're really good at that."

"I've been watching you," he said, his gaze meeting and locking with hers. "I figured I should probably get the hang of it if I'm going to be responsible for this little guy from now on."

There it was again, the hint of a threat—or maybe just a reminder—that if Henry was his, Alex intended to exercise his full parental rights.

On the one hand, Jessica was impressed and sort of proud of him for that. A lot of men wouldn't have been the least bit pleased to discover they might have a child they hadn't known anything about.

On the other, she was scared almost spitless at what it might mean for her and Henry. What if Alex tried to take her son away from her? What if he wanted to keep Henry here with him, under his roof, but informed Jessica she was no longer welcome?

Jessica would fight—of course she would. But she already knew her chances were slim to none of winning any kind of battle against a man like Alex, let alone a custody one. Not given his money and influence and her total lack of either, not to mention her past actions and behavior where he was concerned.

Not for the first time she wanted to kick herself for bringing Alex into their lives. She hadn't had a choice; rationally, she knew that. And even more rationally, she knew he had the right to know about and *know* his own child.

But being here, disclosing Henry's existence to Alex, changed everything. It turned their world upside down and shook it like a snow globe.

To make matters worse, Jessica was afraid Henry was already showing signs of being a Daddy's Boy. He was leaning into Alex, completely trusting, completely content. One of his tiny hands was wrapped around Alex's silk tie, likely wrinkling it beyond repair, while his cheek rested on Alex's shoulder, his bow of a mouth working around his pacifier, his fine, light brown lashes fluttering toward sleep.

"He's getting tired," she told Alex, even as her heart cramped slightly at the sight. Until now she'd been the only one to see him get sleepy and doze off. She'd been the only one those miniature fingers had clung to.

"He missed his afternoon nap because of the interviews. We should probably give him a bottle and put him down for a while. If we don't, he's likely to get extremely cranky and keep us both up half the night."

"Only half?"

There was a twinkle of amusement in Alex's blue eyes. One Jessica couldn't help but respond to with a small smile of her own.

"If we're lucky."

Alex nodded. "Why don't you go downstairs for a bottle. I'll stay here with him. While you're down there, tell Mrs. Sheppard we'll be ready for dinner in thirty minutes. You'll join me, I hope."

That caught her off guard. "You're giving me a choice?"

"Of course."

"Would that choice happen to be eat a four-course meal

downstairs with you or enjoy a lovely serving of bread and water alone in my room?"

He chuckled. "My home isn't a prison, and you're not a prisoner."

"Are you sure?" It was a pointed question, one that had her holding her breath while she waited for the answer.

"After the way you've been living, I'd think staying here would almost be a vacation. Why don't you just enjoy it."

As responses went, it wasn't exactly a *You're free to leave anytime you like.* Although he did have a point; staying in this beautiful mansion was a far cry from worrying about where she was going to sleep that night or where her next meal might come from.

And yet she felt just as trapped as she would if he put her in her room and turned the key in the lock on the way out.

"You can't honestly refuse me this," he said when the silence between them had stretched on for several long seconds. "If Henry is my son, as you claim, I've missed the past three months of his life. The *only* three months of his life. I just want to spend some time with him, make up for a bit of that."

When all else fails, throw out a guilt bomb, she thought. And it hit its mark dead center. How could she possibly deny him time with his newly discovered son? Besides, it wasn't as though staying in a million-dollar house on a multimillion-dollar estate was going to be a hardship. Not physically, anyway.

Mentally, there was no telling yet what the toll would be. But she owed him at least this much.

Tipping her head, she kept her thoughts to herself, but let him know he'd won her over by saying, "I guess I'll go down for his bottle, then, and tell Mrs. Sheppard we're almost ready for dinner."

She patted Henry's tiny back, then stepped around them

and headed for the door. Just as she reached it, his voice stopped her.

"You can request bread and water, if your heart is set on it."

Her lips pursed as she fought a grin, but *his* chuckle of amusement followed her halfway down the hall.

Despite the beautiful new nursery just next door, Jessica couldn't bring herself to put Henry down in there for the entire night. He napped in the expensive new crib after his bottle and while Jessica and Alex ate dinner. But even though she left him there as she showered, changed into pajamas and got ready for bed, she hadn't been under the covers for ten whole minutes before leaping back up and marching next door to get him.

She hoped Alex hadn't gone into the nursery during the night to discover what she'd done. Or if he had, that he wouldn't say anything. She didn't feel like explaining her mild case of separation anxiety or the nagging worry that if she didn't have the baby in her sights at all times, Alex might take Henry away from her, hide him from her and never give him back.

Despite those very real concerns, however, Jessica had to admit that Alex had been perfectly pleasant at dinner. She'd been afraid to go down to the dining room with him, afraid to sit across the table from him—just the two of them alone in an almost cavernous room.

She'd expected more of the third degree. Inquisition, Part Two—only this time without the interruption of nanny interviews.

To her surprise and immense relief, he hadn't brought up even one uncomfortable topic of conversation. He'd asked about the baby. A few not-too-personal questions about her pregnancy. Even about where she'd been and what she'd done to support herself before Henry was born. And he'd spoken a bit about how he'd spent that time himself—mostly changes or new developments at Bajoran Designs.

It had actually been almost enjoyable, and she'd flashed back more than once to the only other meal they'd ever shared—that night at the resort. The night she'd let herself be led by her heart and her raging hormones instead of her head. The night Henry was conceived, though neither of them had had a clue about that at the time.

By the time dessert had been served—a simple but delicious fruit tart—he could have asked for her social security number and internet passwords...well, when she'd had use for internet passwords...and she probably would have turned them over as easily as she'd give someone the time of day. She was that comfortable, that lulled into a false sense of security.

But he hadn't. He'd remained a perfect gentleman, seeing her out of the dining room, then asking if she would be all right going back to the nursery and her room on her own while he went to his office to catch up on a bit of work.

It was the ideal opportunity to escape and put some distance between them. That should have made her happy, right? Just being this close to him, under the same roof, was dangerous with a capital *D*.

But she couldn't help feeling just a little disappointed. That what had turned out to be a lovely dinner had come to an end... That her memories of the last time they'd eaten together had been stirred up, warming her, yet leaving her somewhat frustrated by the fact that *this* meal wouldn't be ending the same way.... And possibly even that he wouldn't be accompanying her upstairs to check on Henry and say good-night.

Why she would want Alexander Bajoran to wish her a good-night, she had no idea. It was craziness to even imagine it. If anything she needed him to spend *less* time with her, watch her *less* closely.

In that, her prayers were answered, because he hadn't knocked on her door in the middle of the night to demand she return Henry to the nursery. He wasn't even waiting outside in the hall when she awoke the next morning and stepped out to begin the day.

Jessica did go to the nursery then, changing Henry's diaper and putting him into one of the matching baby-boy outfits Alex had had delivered the day before. He hadn't only ordered items for the baby, either, but had bought a good deal of stuff for her, as well. New clothes and toiletries; even a stack of puzzle books for her bedside table. Ostensibly in case she grew bored—something that rarely happened while caring for a three-month-old infant. Most nights she was asleep before her head hit the pillow.

But Alex's kindness hadn't gone unnoticed.

Henry was his son, a son he had every intention of laying claim to if those paternity tests came back with his name on them. So purchasing things for the boy was to be expected. Maybe not to the extent Alex had gone—"starting small" obviously wasn't a term that existed in his vocabulary—but buying diapers and formula and a few new pieces of clothing was completely within the realm of understanding.

He had absolutely *no* reason to feel the least bit generous toward her, however. He could have stripped the guest room of every creature comfort and left her to wear the same clothes she'd arrived in for the entire stay, and she would have considered it fair punishment for her deceptions.

But he was a bigger man—a kinder, more considerate man—than she could have anticipated. She only wondered how long it would last once he had the confirmation that Henry really was his son. Would he shower her with roses or take back everything and send her packing?

Hitching Henry higher in her arms, she strolled down the carpeted hallway and wide set of stairs, taking a right on her way to the kitchen. It was early yet, with the sun just beginning to cast purplish light through the windows as she passed.

But Henry was an early riser, especially when he was hungry. So she'd get him some cereal and juice, and make sure he was happy before looking for Alex and finding out what was on the agenda for the day. Likely more nanny interviews and questions from his long list of continued demands.

Half an hour later, she was sitting in the breakfast nook with Henry in his baby seat, his face and bib covered in splots of sticky and drying cereal. Mrs. Sheppard bustled around the center island, readying items for the meal she was about to prepare while Henry kicked his feet and sent the plastic seat rocking on the tabletop with every bite.

Jessica couldn't help grinning at her child's antics. He was so darn cute when he was happy and his belly was full. He was also extra adorable in the little choo-choo train overalls Alex had provided. He probably hadn't picked them out specifically, but whoever he'd put in charge of buying baby clothes had done an excellent job.

Raising a tightly closed fist into the air, Henry suddenly let out a squeal and jerked so hard, his seat scooted a good inch across the table. Jessica jumped, dropping the tiny Elmo spoon full of cereal and grabbing the seat before it could move any closer to the edge. Then she turned her head slightly to see what had gotten Henry so excited.

Alex stood only inches away, dressed in a charcoal suit and electric-blue tie that made his eyes pop like sapphires. He looked as though he'd just stepped off the pages of a men's fashion magazine. Or was maybe on the way to a photo shoot for one.

"Jeez, you scared me," she told him. Then she turned

back to Henry, picking up the fallen spoon and wiping up the spilled cereal with a damp cloth she had nearby.

When he didn't respond, and the awkward silence stretched from seconds into minutes, she craned her neck in his direction again. That's when she noticed the hard glint in his narrowed eyes and the still line of his mouth.

She swallowed and took a breath. "What's wrong?"

She'd never seen an expression like that on the face of anyone who wasn't there either to chew her out or tell her somebody had died. And with Alex she was betting on getting chewed out. What was it this time? she wondered.

"We need to talk," he told her simply, his voice sharp as a razor blade.

Uh-oh.

She looked back at Henry, her hand still on his carrier. His food-smeared smile was wide, his feet continuing to dance.

"Mrs. Sheppard," Alex intoned. "Can you please watch the baby while I have a word with Jessica?"

The housekeeper didn't seem thrilled with the prospect of babysitting duty, but dried her hands on a dish towel and crossed to the table, plucking the small plastic spoon from Jessica's fingers. Taking that as a sign that she didn't have much choice in the matter, Jessica relinquished the spoon and her seat, reluctantly following Alex from the kitchen.

Wordlessly, they walked to his office, where he waited for her to enter ahead of him, then shut the door behind them with a solid click of finality.

Much like the day before, she expected him to move behind his desk, and for both of them to sit down before he said whatever it was he had to say. Instead, he remained near the closed door, legs apart and arms crossing his chest in what could only be described as an aggressive stance.

"You're a Taylor," he blurted without preamble.

Her heart stuttered in her chest. "Excuse me?"

His eyes went to slits, a muscle ticking on one side of his jaw.

"Don't play dumb with me," he bit out. "Your name isn't Jessica Madison. It's Jessica Madison *Taylor*."

Eleven

The blood drained from Jessica's face. She felt it flush down her neck and through her body all the way to her toes, leaving her dizzy and light-headed.

Afraid she might actually faint, she took a step back, relieved when she bumped into one of the armchairs standing in front of his wide desk. She leaned her weight against it, reaching behind to dig her nails into the supple leather to help hold her upright and in place.

Licking her lips, she swallowed past the overwhelming drumbeat of her heart. Barely above a whisper, her voice grated out the only thought spiraling through her mind. "How did you find out?"

A flash of anger filled his expression. "DNA isn't the only thing I had tested. A friend on the police force ran your fingerprints for me, and they came back as Jessica Madison Taylor. No criminal record, I'm pleased to say, but it turns out you aren't at all who you claim to be. Your prints showed up as a former employee of both Mountain View and Bajoran Designs."

Well, not Bajoran Designs so much as Taylor Fine Jewels, when it existed. Still, she didn't know what to say. Shock that he'd found her out reverberated through every bone and nerve ending.

She certainly hadn't expected to be called out quite so soon. She'd actually been hoping she could find a time and place and way to tell him on her own. Eventually, when she couldn't keep it under wraps any longer.

"So what was your plan, exactly?" Alex asked, bitterness seeping into every syllable. "Seduce me for company secrets so you could sell them to the highest bidder? Or was the goal all along to get pregnant so you could blackmail me later with an heir?"

What little blood had worked its way back to her brain seeped out just as quickly. Her breath came in tiny, shallow gasps as her chest tightened and she swayed on her feet.

"What are you talking about?" she said, her jaw clenched. Partly because she was angry and partly because she was literally shaking. Her arms, her legs, her teeth. Every inch of her was quaking with the effort to hold back the maelstrom of emotions raging through her like a tidal wave. "I didn't get pregnant *on purpose*. And I didn't sell anything to anyone."

Alex didn't look as though he believed her.

"But I didn't get lucky with just a single, uninhibited chambermaid, did I? You're the daughter of Donald Taylor, granddaughter of *Henry* Taylor, both of whom used to be in partnership with Bajoran Designs. Aren't you?"

A beat passed before she answered. "Yes."

"And you just happened to be at the resort, cleaning *my* room."

She raised a brow, her grip on the chair at her back loosening as she began to regain some of her equilibrium.

"Actually, yes."

Doubt filled his stony features and was evident in his snort of derision.

"Call Mountain View. Give them my real name, and they'll tell you I was employed there long before you checked in. And the suite where you stayed was part of my regular rounds."

"Lucky for you that I landed there, then, wasn't it?"

"I wouldn't use the word *lucky,* no."

The day Alex had checked in to the resort was the beginning of her life's downward spiral. Except for Henry. He may have been unexpected, tossing her headfirst in a direction she wasn't ready to travel, but he was also the single greatest gift she'd ever been given.

"It was the perfect opportunity for you to take part in a bit of corporate espionage, though, hmm?"

Her pulse skipped in her veins. Wasn't that the exact term she'd used when Erin had first concocted her appalling plan? Of that, at least, she *was* guilty.

"I suppose you could say that, yes," she admitted. She wasn't proud of it, but the jig was obviously up, and she didn't intend to lie or deny any of it any longer.

"I recognized you the minute I saw you," she told him. "My family was devastated when you cut them off from Bajoran Designs and drove them out of business. I was okay with it, believe it or not. I might have ended up as merely a hotel maid, but I was happy and making enough of an income to live on. Unfortunately, the rest of my family didn't handle things quite as well."

Taking a deep breath, she released the rest of her hold on the armchair and moved on stiff legs to perch at the very edge of its overstuffed cushion. She was no longer facing Alex, cowering beneath his withering glare, but she didn't need to. His angry judgment filled the room like poison gas.

"When I mentioned to my cousin that you were staying at the resort, she convinced me to poke around your room. No excuses," she put in quickly, putting up a hand to hold off whatever his next verbal assault might be. "It was a stupid idea and I was wrong to ever agree to it, but I did. She wanted me to look for something that would hurt you—or rather, hurt Bajoran Designs. Something that could be used against you or put Taylor Fine Jewels back in operation."

"The design specs for the Princess Line," he said, his voice sharp as tacks.

Her head snapped up. So he knew she'd taken them. She'd kind of hoped she wouldn't have to confess that. But...

"Yes. I'm sorry about that."

"You seduced me to get them, and then sold the proposed designs to our competition."

The accusation struck her like a two-by-four. Her brows knit and she shook her head.

"No. No," she insisted. "I took them, but I didn't sell them. I never did anything with them."

"But you don't deny seducing me to get your hands on them," he tossed back with heavy sarcasm.

Spine straight, she lifted her chin and held his icy gaze. "Of course I do. I'm not a prostitute. I don't use my body to obtain information or anything else."

In for a penny, in for a pound, she thought before forging ahead. "I slept with you because I wanted to, and for no other reason. I'm also pretty sure *you* seduced me, not the other way around."

"I wouldn't be so certain of that," he muttered.

Stalking across the room, he rounded his desk and took a seat in front of the laptop set up there for his regular use. He tapped a few keys, waited a moment then turned the computer a hundred and eighty degrees so she could see the screen.

"Seduction aside, how do you explain this?" he asked.

She studied the images in front of her, growing colder by the second.

"I don't understand," she murmured.

Sliding forward, she looked even closer, narrowing her eyes, trying to figure out what was going on, how this had happened.

It had been months since she'd seen the original designs for the Princess Line, but she remembered them in acute detail. She'd even redesigned portions of them mentally and sketched changes in the margins of numerous pieces of paper that had passed through her hands since she'd taken them from his briefcase.

Nearly the *exact* designs from that folder were on the screen in front of her now, though, in rich, eye-popping color.

"What is this?" Swinging her gaze to Alex, she frowned. "Did Ignacio Jewelers buy the line concept from you? They needed work, but you shouldn't have given them up. They were perfect for Bajoran Designs."

His eyes turned to chips of blue glass, his fingers curling until the knuckles went white. "What kind of game are you playing, Jessica? I already know who you really are. I know what you were doing in my suite that night. You can stop with the lies."

"I'm not lying about anything," she said, growing more confused by the moment. "What are you talking about?"

"What are *you* talking about?" he demanded. "You know damn well you stole those designs from my briefcase that night after we slept together and sold them to Ignacio. I assume as part of your plot for revenge. Though why the hell you would have it in for me or my family's company, I'll never know."

Closing her eyes, Jessica shook her head and rubbed a spot near her temple where a headache was forming at record speed.

"No. This is…this is insane."

Opening her eyes again, she met his gaze head-on. "I told you I made a mistake in taking those designs. But I never did anything with them. I tried to return them the very next day, but you were already gone. Do you really think that if I'd sold them, I would be here now? That line of jewelry was worth millions. Even with a baby to care for, I couldn't have gone through that kind of money in under a year."

"I don't think you did," Alex told her. "I think you decided that showing up with a baby and telling me he's mine is all part of your plan to get even more money out of the Bajorans."

Tears prickled behind Jessica's lashes. "I'm sorry that I lied to you and betrayed your trust by taking those sketches," she said, struggling to keep her voice even and unwavering. "But no matter what you think of me, Henry *is* your son. I'm here because of him, *not* because I want anything from you. And I don't know what happened with that line," she rushed to add. "I don't know how Ignacio Jewelers got hold of it, but…I'll find out. Or at least I'll try."

Alex watched the myriad emotions playing over Jessica's delicate features. She looked truly distraught. Guilty and confused and hurt by his rapid-fire accusations.

It was no less than she deserved, of course, he thought to himself, clenching his jaw and refusing to be swayed by the moisture gathering in her eyes.

He wasn't sure what angered him most—the fact that she'd stolen the plans for one of his company's million-dollar ventures, or that she'd slept with him to get them.

That night might have been a one-night stand, but it sure as hell hadn't been meaningless. Not to him. Now he felt like a first class fool for ever thinking there was more between them than simply sex.

Crossing his arms in an attempt to rein in his temper, he arched a brow. "How, exactly, do you intend to do that?"

He could see the wheels in her head turning, desperately searching for a solution, a way out of the fix she was in.

Finally, she took a deep breath, her expression filling with resolve. "I left the proposal with the rest of my things when I stored them at my parents' house before leaving town. It should still be there."

"And who's to say you didn't simply make a copy before selling it out from under me?"

"I—" She screeched to a halt, blinking in confusion. "Why would I do that? I'd have no reason to keep a copy once I sold it for millions and millions of dollars to keep me in the wonderful lifestyle to which I've become so accustomed."

For having started out on a stammer, she ended with more than a fair note of snark. He had to bite the inside of his lip to keep from laughing aloud at her spunk.

Not for the first time, he was impressed by her resilience. She was in trouble, here. With his power and money, he could squash her like a bug if he so desired. Yet she was standing in front of him with her chin out and her "dare me" attitude wrapped around her like a shawl.

It also got him thinking. She was challenging him, and no one in their right mind would do that—not in this manner, about something so vital—unless they could back it up. Would they?

"So your assertion is that if the file is still there, hidden amongst your other belongings, then you couldn't have betrayed me and my family's company by selling it, is that it?"

"Yes."

"How do you intend to prove that?"

She took a deep breath, causing her breasts to rise beneath the lightweight material of her daffodil-yellow top. He wondered if it was one he'd had delivered for her, or if she'd brought it stuffed in that ridiculously small knapsack she'd been carrying when she'd arrived.

"I guess I'll have to go home and dig it out." A beat passed as she narrowed her gaze on him and pursed her lips. "Would you believe me if I did?"

Another challenge. Damned if he didn't like that about her. Not enough to give her a free pass, but the benefit of a doubt was a possibility.

"I'd consider it," he said carefully, not ready to promise anything he wouldn't later be willing to deliver.

"Well, that's encouraging," she mumbled half under her breath. Shaking her head, she straightened and looked him in the eye. "Tell me what you want me to do. Should I go to Portland and look for the file, or would you prefer to continue hating me for wrongs you *think* I committed?"

"Oh, you've committed plenty of wrongs, with or without the sale of that design line to our competitors," he reminded her even as he battled a grin.

She was guilty of so much, but she didn't let that hold her back one bit when it came to sticking up for herself. Arguing business with his contemporaries was definitely never this exhilarating.

Then again, no one at Bajoran Designs was as attractive or compelling as Jessica, and he'd never had quite as much to lose —or gain—if he suffered a defeat at their hands.

"We'll go together," he told her. "We can take the corporate jet. Be down there and back in a matter of hours."

Sucking her bottom lip between her teeth, she worried it for a moment, her face reflecting sudden alarm.

"What?" he asked. "Change your mind already? Decide to confess and put an end to the charade before we waste any more time or a load of jet fuel on a wild-goose chase?"

"You're an arrogant ass, do you know that?"

His brows rose. So much for the effectiveness of his harsh features and intimidating demeanor.

"If you must know," she continued sharply, "my parents don't know about Henry."

The shock must have shown in his expression because she flushed crimson and shifted guiltily in her chair.

"I know. I know how terrible that sounds," she admitted, tucking her hair behind one ear and running her fingertips through to the ends. "I'm a horrible daughter. It will crush them when they find out I've been lying and keeping a grandchild from them all this time."

"Then why did you?"

She cast him a glance meant to singe him on the spot. "Can you just hear that conversation? 'Hey, Mom and Dad, I know this will disappoint you, but I'm pregnant from a one-night stand. Oh, but that's not the best part. The *best* part is that the baby's father is our family's arch nemesis, Alexander Bajoran, the man who single-handedly ruined Taylor Fine Jewels and destroyed our lives. Surprise!'"

"Archenemy is a bit strong, don't you think?" he asked with an arched brow.

She gave a snort of derision. "Not amongst the Taylor clan. Your name might as well be Lucifer Bajoran, as far as they're concerned."

Which seemed to be an awfully harsh sentiment to have for a former business associate who hadn't had much at all to do with the split between their families. All of that had taken place quite literally before his time. Alex had been working at Bajoran Designs, of course, but hadn't taken over as CEO until well after the Taylors' departure.

He frowned to himself. Perhaps there was more to the story than he knew, more that he *should* know. He made a mental note to look into it when he got back to the Bajoran Designs offices. Out of curiosity, if nothing else.

"Then what do you propose?" he asked, focusing instead on the matter of visiting Portland so they could retrieve the Princess Line proposal. If it was even still where she claimed it was.

"If we go on Sunday, my parents will be at my aunt's house for brunch. They're usually gone three or four hours, so we should be able to get in and out before they get home."

He thought about that for a minute. "You're really going to sneak into town without letting your parents know you were there? After not seeing them in almost a year?"

Her chest shuddered as she took in a deep, unsteady breath. "If I have to, yes. I told you I was a terrible daughter," she added when he tipped his head quizzically. "I need to tell them, I know that. And I will. Soon. I just...I need time to work up to it, and frankly, I can only deal with one major crisis at a time. At the moment, *you* are the main crisis I'm dealing with."

"Then the sooner we get to the bottom of some very important facts, the better."

"Agreed."

"In that case, let me know exactly what time we need to be at your parents' house, and I'll make all of the arrangements for the trip, including someone to stay here with Henry."

He expected an argument over that, but all she did was nod. Apparently she, too, saw the wisdom in not dragging an infant along on a mission one step up from breaking and entering.

Twelve

"I don't understand. They were right here."

Jessica hoped her voice didn't reflect the panic beating in her chest and at her pulse points.

They were at her parents' home in Portland. A lovely two-story brick house at the end of cul-de-sac in a modest development.

The flight down had been uneventful, and only uncomfortable because Jessica didn't like being alone in such close quarters with Alex. If "alone" included a pilot in the cockpit and one very discreet flight attendant who made herself scarce between serving drinks and asking Mr. Bajoran if there was anything else he required. And if the private plane could be described as "close quarters." It wasn't as large as his mansion, but it wasn't exactly a broom closet, either.

She'd blamed her antsiness on a mild fear of flying and being away from Henry. Only one of those factors actually bothered her, but Alex didn't need to know that. And the sooner they found the folder and got back to Seattle, the better.

Back to her baby, who was probably even now being rocked to sleep by Wendy the nanny. She liked Wendy well enough; she was actually the nanny Jessica would have hired if it had been her choice alone. But that didn't mean she was keen on another woman caring for her child when she should be there with him instead.

The garage attached to her parents' home was large enough for two midsize cars—one of which was currently absent—and all of her belongings from when she'd had to clear out her apartment. Thankfully she didn't own much by way of material possessions.

Even so, she'd gone through everything. *Everything* because the folder with the Princess Line designs inside wasn't where she was almost positive she'd left it. She specifically remembered tucking it away with some of her other important papers and legal documents. Not only for safekeeping, but because she knew it would blend in and wasn't likely to be noticed if anyone snooped through her things.

She couldn't imagine her parents going through her stuff.

Her mother would be like a dog with a bone about the paternity of her first grandchild, but they weren't the nosy sort otherwise. For heaven's sake, she'd quit her job, given up her apartment and taken off for parts unknown, all on a whim, and they hadn't asked a single question. As far as they were concerned, she was traveling, sowing the female equivalent of wild oats and would call if she needed them. Otherwise they assumed no news was good news.

"Maybe they were never there to begin with, and this is just part of your elaborate ruse to convince me they were," Alex said from two or three feet behind her. He'd been standing there, hovering less than patiently while she searched.

"You'd like that, wouldn't you?" she retorted without turn-

ing around. She was still on her knees, digging through the
same banker's box for the third time in thirty minutes. "One
more nail to drive into my coffin. One more reason you'll
give the courts to convince them I'm an unfit mother—a
criminal, even—and that you deserve full custody of Henry."

Frustrated, angry and increasingly frightened he would
do just that, she climbed to her feet, brushing off the knees
of her jeans.

Facing him, she said, "Well, that isn't going to happen. I'm
not lying, and this isn't a ruse. They were *there,* dammit, and
I'm going to find out why they aren't anymore."

Big talk when she had no idea how to go about it. But she
couldn't let Alex see her uncertainty, not when there was so
much at stake.

Think. Think. Think.

Her erratic pulse suddenly slowed, and she realized she
wasn't the only person who had known about the Princess
Line proposal. She'd told her cousin. Shown her the designs,
even.

Not to use them against Alex, but to prove she *had* poked
around his room the way she'd promised, and also because
she'd simply loved the designs. The artist in her had been
impressed and unable to resist sharing them with someone
she'd thought would appreciate their beauty and intricacy
as much as she did. With a few notations on how she would
improve upon them, if she could.

That's what they had discussed the morning she'd shown
Erin the design sketches. *Not* how they could best go about
selling them out from under Bajoran Designs. She would
never have done that, regardless of what Alex might think.

As much as she wasn't looking forward to what she had
to do, it needed to be done. She owed it to Alex, and at this
point, to Henry and herself, too.

"Can I borrow your cell phone?" she asked.

Alex's eyes widened a fraction, the blue of the irises stormy and nearly gray. Whether due to mistrust or the dull light in the interior of the garage, she wasn't sure.

Without a word, he reached into the inside pocket of his suit jacket and removed his phone, handing it over.

Dialing by memory, she waited through three rings for her cousin to answer.

"Erin, it's Jessica." It was strange having this conversation in front of Alex, especially considering what she was about to say, but it wasn't as though she had much choice.

"Erin, this is important," she bit out, cutting into her cousin's fluffy, drawn-out greeting. Once Erin quieted, she said, "What did you do with the design folder I stole from Alexander Bajoran?"

Lord, it hurt to use that word—*stole*. But she'd taken it without permission, so she had to call it what it was.

"What do you mean?" her cousin asked. Too innocently. Even through the phone line, she could tell Erin was feigning naïveté.

"Don't play dumb with me, Erin. I mean it. This is important. I need you to tell me *right now* what you did with the Princess Line designs. I put them with my things in Mom and Dad's garage, but they're missing, and *you* are the only other person who even knew they existed."

Silence filled the space between them for several long seconds. Jessica didn't look at Alex. She couldn't. Instead, she pressed her fingers to the bridge of her nose and prayed she wouldn't break down in front of him, no matter how close to tears she felt.

Finally, in a tone of complete entitlement, her cousin said, "I sold them."

Jessica's heart sank. "Oh, Erin," she groaned, "tell me you didn't. *Please* tell me you didn't really do that."

"Of course I did," Erin replied without a hint of apology.

"That was the plan from the very beginning, after all. To stick it to those Bajoran bastards."

Despite her best efforts, tears leaked from Jessica's lashes. "No, it wasn't," she told her cousin, voice cracking. "That was never the plan. I *never* agreed to anything even close to that."

"Why else were you poking around the man's room, then?" Erin asked haughtily. As though she had any right to be offended.

"Because I was an idiot," Jessica snapped. "And because you convinced me I needed to do something to avenge the family against the evil Bajorans. Which is the most ridiculous idea in history and the stupidest thing I've ever done."

Taking a deep, shuddering breath, she dropped her hand from her face and turned away from Alex. She couldn't bear to look at him or have him look at her, at least directly, while she was making such a soul-shattering confession.

"You had no right to go through my things, Erin. No more right to take that proposal from me than I had to take it from Alex." Her voice was ragged, and she was skating close to the very edge of hysteria. "You have no idea what you've done, Erin."

"Oh, what did I do?" her cousin retorted, snottier than Jessica had ever heard her. "Get a little revenge against a corporate tycoon who used his money and influence to put our family out of business? Make some well-deserved money of my own while screwing the Bajorans out of another couple million they *didn't* deserve? So what."

"No," Jessica murmured, forcing herself to speak past the lump in her throat. "What you've done is betray my trust. Worse, you've done irreparable damage to my life. My reputation. My *son's* life. I can't forgive you for this, Erin. Not ever."

She clicked the button to end the call just as her voice

broke and her lungs started to fight against her efforts to draw in fresh oxygen.

How could Erin have done this to her? She'd convinced Jessica to do the wrong thing, true. And Jessica took full responsibility for having actually done the snooping and taking of the papers.

But she hadn't truly planned to do anything with them. Had fully intended to put them back, and suffered months of guilt when she hadn't been able to. She'd almost traveled all the way to Seattle to return them in person, but had been too afraid Alex would call the police and have her arrested.

That, in fact, had been one of her greatest fears about returning to Seattle with Henry. She'd been beyond lucky that he'd put their son first and not called the authorities on her the moment she stepped into his house.

"Are you all right?"

He spoke softly, his tone kinder than she would have expected given the circumstances. In fact, he hadn't sounded quite so nice since that night at the resort when he'd been intent on getting her into bed. Or according to him, open to allowing her to seduce him.

His hand touched her shoulder. Lightly, almost comfortingly.

Fresh moisture glazed her vision. How could he be so understanding *now* when the evidence was clearly stacked against her? He should be furious. Sharp and accusing, just like before.

"Jessica?" he prompted again.

She shook her head. "I am definitely not all right," she told him with a watery laugh.

Turning back to the stacks and boxes of her things, she started replacing lids and putting everything back in order. It was busywork, something to keep her hands occupied so she wouldn't sit down right in the middle of the hard con-crete garage floor and sob uncontrollably.

"I guess that's it," she threw over her shoulder in Alex's general direction. "You win. Erin took the proposal and sold the designs to Ignacio, just like you thought I had. So there's no way to prove my innocence. No way to convince you I'm not the lying, thieving bitch you accused me of being."

"I don't remember using the term *bitch*."

Sliding the last cardboard box onto a short pile of other boxes, she turned to face him. Calmer now, more composed. Resigned.

"I'm pretty sure it was implied," she said, emotionless now.

"No, but perhaps it was inferred," he replied.

Moving toward her, he stopped mere inches away. She still couldn't bring herself to meet his eyes, so she stared at a spot on his blue-and-black-striped tie instead.

"I should probably apologize for that," he continued, sur-prising her enough that she lifted her head. "I might have been a bit more critical of your actions than was warranted."

Jessica's mouth didn't actually fall open in a big wide O, but she was certainly shocked enough that it should have.

He was apologizing? To her? But she didn't deserve it. She may not have been guilty of *exactly* what he'd accused her of, but she'd undoubtedly put it all in motion.

She hadn't set out to seduce him or to get pregnant, but both had happened because she'd been poking her nose where it didn't belong.

And she hadn't sold the designs for the Princess Line to a competing company, but she had taken them and shown them to her cousin, who'd done just that.

Cocking her head, she studied him through narrowed eyes. "Did I accidentally drop one of those boxes on your head?"

she asked him. And then, "Who are you and what have you done with Alexander Bajoran?"

She was too upset and emotionally wrung dry to mean it as a joke, but one corner of his mouth lifted nonetheless.

"I heard both sides of the conversation. Enough to get the general idea, anyway, and to accept that it was, indeed, your cousin who sold the line proposal to Ignacio Jewelers. Which isn't to say you don't still carry some of the responsibility," he added with a note of severity he wasn't sure he felt.

"What are you saying?" Jessica asked, justifiably suspicious. "That you just...forgive me? Absolve me of guilt for everything I've done since we first met?"

"I wouldn't go quite that far," he replied dryly. "But I'd be a hypocrite—as well as a heel—if I held you responsible for something you didn't technically do. I'll talk to our attorneys, see if there's anything we can do about your cousin's spin at corporate espionage."

He paused to gauge her reaction to that, expecting anything from a heated defense of her family member to hysterical tears and begging for leniency. Instead, her full lips pulled into a taut line and her shoulders went back a fraction.

"I'm sorry," he said, "but we have to at least look into it. Losing those plans cost us millions of dollars."

"No, of course," she responded quickly. "What Erin did was wrong. What *I* did was wrong, but I never would have taken it as far as she did. She made her bed...I guess she'll have to lie in it."

"Strange as it might sound," Alex told her, "I actually believe you."

And he did. Not only because of what he'd heard with his own two ears, but because if she'd made a dime off the Princess Line prospectus, she would have shown at least a modicum of guilt. Or been dancing like a spider on a hot plate trying to wiggle her way out of trouble.

He even had to wonder about his assertion that she'd seduced him that night back at Mountain View to get her hands on company secrets. If that were true, she wouldn't have wasted a moment now trying to seduce him into letting her transgressions slide.

But she wasn't fast-talking, and she didn't have her hand down his pants. More's the pity on the latter. She'd simply admitted her part in the whole ordeal, all but assuming the position and waiting for the cops to slap on cuffs.

That was not the behavior of a liar, a cheat or—quite frankly—a gold digger. The verdict was still out on Henry and her purpose in leaving the baby in his boardroom. But since she'd been telling the truth about the majority of charges he'd leveled against her…well, there was a fair chance she was telling the truth about the rest.

Clearing his throat, he stuffed his hands in the front pockets of his slacks to keep from doing something stupid like reaching out to touch her. And not to console her.

He wanted to brush the lock of loose blond hair dusting her cheek back behind her ear. Maybe slide his hand the rest of the way to her nape, thread his fingers into the soft curls there, tug her an inch or two closer….

And from there his thoughts took a decidedly hazardous turn. Better to keep his hands to himself before he risked complicating matters even more than they were already.

"Just because I believe you about your cousin doesn't mean you're off the hook," he told her in a voice that came out rougher than he would have liked.

That roughness wasn't caused by anger but by the fact that he was suddenly noticing the bounce of her blond curls—sans the blue streak of a year ago. The alabaster smoothness of her pale skin. The rosy swell of her lush, feminine lips. And the slight dusting of gray beneath the hazel brown of her eyes, attesting to the stress she'd been under for...he suspected months now.

He hadn't exactly helped alleviate that stress, either, had he? No, he'd added to it in every possible way from the moment she'd walked into his home.

With good reason, he'd thought at the time. But not such good reason now that he knew she wasn't quite the conniving witch he'd made her out to be.

"At the very least," he intoned, "I'd say you owe me one."

She stared at him with eyes gone dull with wariness. "Owe you one...what?"

Rather than answer that question directly, he shrugged a shoulder and finally reached out to take her hand. "I've got something in mind. In the meantime I think we should get out of here. The jet is waiting, and your parents will probably be back soon."

With more familiarity than he thought she realized she was showing, she grabbed his wrist and turned it to glance at the face of his watch.

"You're right, we should go."

She didn't look any happier about leaving than she had when they'd arrived.

"I'm sorry we didn't find what we came here for," she muttered softly as they headed for the garage's service door.

"That's okay." He let her pass first, then followed, closing and locking the door behind them. "I know just how you'll make it up to me."

Thirteen

Though she asked a handful of times on the flight home exactly how Alex expected her to "make it up to him," he wouldn't give her so much as a hint of his plans. Rather than put her out of her misery, he merely smiled a cruel and wicked smile and let her squirm.

Hmph. He was probably enjoying her suffering. He probably didn't have a single clue yet what he was going to ask of her as so-called "repayment"—he just liked having her dangle like a little worm at the end of his hook.

And there was nothing she could do about it. She was at his mercy.

Hunched in the plush leather window seat, the sound of engines roaring in the background, she tried to hold on to her indignation and put on a full pout. The only problem was, she'd never been much of the pouting type. She also knew she deserved a bit of payback for what she'd done to Alex, both the intentional and the unintentional.

That didn't mean she was going to let him walk all over her. If he said he wanted her to assassinate the president or be his sex slave for a month, she'd know he was a crazy person and wasn't as interested in compensation as simply using and abusing her. But if he just wanted her to eat a little crow, she would do her best to sprinkle it with seasoning and choke it down.

Twenty minutes later the plane landed, and Alex accompanied her onto the tarmac and straight to the shiny black Lexus waiting for them. A private airstrip employee opened the passenger-side door, waiting for her to slide inside before rounding the hood and handing the keys to Alex.

They rode in silence until Jessica realized they weren't headed for Alex's estate. At first she thought she just wasn't familiar enough with the area. And then that he was taking a shortcut...except that it turned out to be a long cut. She remembered the route they'd taken from the house to the airport, and this wasn't the reverse of that.

"Where are we going?" she finally asked, finding her voice for the first time in more than an hour.

"You'll see," was all he said, strong fingers wrapped around the steering wheel.

She didn't sigh, at least not aloud. But she did sit up straighter, fiddling with the safety strap crossing her chest while she studied each of the street signs and storefronts as they passed.

Before long, he slowed, easing effortlessly into a parking space in front of a shop called Hot Couture. Sliding out of the car, he came around, opened her door and pulled her up by the hand.

She began to ask again where they were going, but bit down on her tongue before she started to sound like a broken record. He led her across the wide sidewalk and inside the upscale boutique.

Okay, she had to say something. "What are we doing here?"

Everywhere she looked, headless size-zero mannequins were draped in costly bolts of silk, satin, sequins and a dozen other expensive materials she couldn't begin to identify. She'd been away from this sort of extravagance for too long…and hadn't cared for it all that much when she'd been expected to wear gowns like these on a regular basis.

"This is Step One of your penance," he told her as they were approached by a saleswoman who looked as though she'd had her facial features lifted one too many times. Her eyes were a tad too wide, her brows a tad too high, her lips a tad too pursed.

"Good afternoon," she greeted them, focusing her attention much more firmly on Alex than on Jessica. With good reason—Alex looked like every one of the million-plus dollars he was worth, while Jessica was dressed in a pair of worn jeans and a stylish but nondesigner top. They were Daddy Warbucks and Little Orphan Annie…Richard Gere and Julia Roberts…the Prince and the Pauperette.

She rubbed her palms nervously on the legs of her jeans. "This isn't necessary, Alex," she murmured so that only he could hear.

At full volume, he replied, "Yes, it is." Then to the other woman, "We need a gown for a very important gala fundraiser. Shoes and handbag, as well."

The woman looked positively giddy at the prospect of a large commission.

"Alex…" Jessica began.

"I'll take care of the jewelry," he said over the beginning of her protests.

"What kind of fundraiser?" she asked, wanting to know at least that much before she began trying on a year's worth of dresses in the next couple of hours.

"Sparkling Diamonds," he said, naming the well-known charitable organization founded and run by Washington State's most notable jewelers. Since its inception only a few years ago, Sparkling Diamonds had raised hundreds of thousands of dollars to support a variety of worthwhile causes, from childhood cancer to local animal shelters.

"Tuesday night's benefit is being sponsored solely by Bajoran Designs. Some of Seattle's deepest pockets will be there, and we want to rake in as much as possible for this year's literacy campaign. I was planning to go stag, but now that you're here and—as we established—owe me one," he tacked on with an uncharacteristic wink, "you can be my plus-one."

Jessica wasn't entirely sure how she felt about that. Getting dressed up and going to a swanky party with Alex? Hanging on his arm all night with a smile on her face while they mingled with people who might recognize her as a Taylor Fine Jewels Taylor? Oh, the rumor mills would be rife with chatter after that. Word might even get back to her parents.

She thought she might prefer to undergo an extra hot bikini wax. But then, she didn't have much of a choice, did she? And after her conversation with Erin, the cat was pretty much out of the bag, anyway.

"Literacy is important," she said by way of answer.

"Yes," he agreed, rare amusement glittering in his too-blue eyes, "it is. The event is also a chance to show off a few of the company's latest designs. Ones we've been unveiling instead of the Princess Line."

There it was. Knife inserted and twisted forty degrees clockwise. It pinched, just as he'd known it would.

"You'll be wearing the most significant pieces. Yellow gold and diamonds, so they'll go with almost anything."

Turning his attention back to the saleslady, he said, "I want her to look absolutely stunning. Find a dress that showcases her natural beauty."

Inside her chest, Jessica's heart fluttered, heat unfurling just below the surface of her skin. If she weren't fully aware of the situation and where each of them stood, it would be all too easy to be flattered by that comment. After all, Alex was a very charming man. Isn't that how she'd ended up in bed with him in the first place?

But he wasn't trying to be charming. He wanted her dressed up and pretty to impress donors at his charity event. She was sorely out of practice, but that was something she could definitely do.

"Yes, sir," the woman replied, money signs glowing in her eyes along with her wide smile.

Jessica followed her silently to the rear of the store, listening with only half an ear to the older woman's cheerful chatter. Leaving Jessica in the changing room to strip, she went in search of gowns that would meet Alex's high standards.

An hour later, Jessica felt like a quick-change artist. She was tired and out of sorts, and just wanted to get home to see Henry.

She'd tried on so many dresses, she couldn't remember them all. After viewing the first few, even Alex had seemed to lose interest. He'd made low, noncommittal noises, then told her he trusted her to make a final decision before wandering off to talk on his cell phone.

Another six or eight gowns later, Jessica was pretty sure she'd found one that would pass muster. It was hard to be sure how anything would look with the jewelry he had in mind, since she hadn't actually seen the pieces for herself, but he'd described them briefly and she did her best to imagine them with each of the gowns she modeled.

She needed just the right color, just the right neckline. Just enough sparkle to shine, but not *out*shine the jewelry itself.

She'd forgotten how stressful the whole socialite thing could be. There was a reason she hadn't missed it. Much.

It didn't help, either, that her performance needed to be perfect this time. It wasn't just a public appearance or a high-priced fundraiser. It was one of her only options for redemption with Alex and getting into his good graces. There was still so much he could hold against her. So many ways he could punish her, if he so desired.

Licking her dry lips, she finished putting on her street clothes, then carried the gown she'd decided on—albeit uncertainly—out of the dressing room.

"We'll take this one," she told the sales lady.

"Excellent choice," the woman agreed, taking the gown and carrying it to the counter.

Jessica was pretty sure she'd have said the same thing about a gunny sack, as long as Alex was willing to pay a high four figures for it.

A few minutes, later she had shoes and a matching clutch, all of it wrapped up with tissue paper in pretty boutique boxes, ready to go. When the sales woman recited the total, Jessica's eyes just about bugged out of her head and her throat started to close.

It was almost as though she was having an allergic reaction to spending so much money for *one* night out on the town. She had half a notion to tell Alex that if everybody who planned to attend the fundraiser would simply donate the amount they would have spent on getting dressed up for the evening, they wouldn't need to hold the event at all.

It had been a long time since she'd poured money like that into anything that couldn't be eaten, driven or lived in, but the outrageous total wouldn't make a man like Alex so much as blink.

As though to prove her point, he seemed to appear out

of nowhere, passing his platinum card to the clerk over her shoulder.

The sales woman flashed a delighted grin. Thirty seconds later, Alex and Jessica were headed back to the car, expensive packages in tow.

"You found something you like, I take it?" he said once they were on the road again, finally on their way to his estate.

A knot of eager anticipation tightened in her stomach. She couldn't wait to get there and see her baby. They'd only been gone a day—not even a full day, really—but she wasn't used to being away from him. She'd missed him and wanted to see how he'd fared with the nanny Alex had hired—possibly on a permanent basis.

"Yes," she responded, trying to keep her mind focused on the conversation rather than the fact that Alex was driving the speed limit. He could have gone a *few* miles over without risking a ticket, for heaven's sake.

"I hope it's all right. It was hard to pick something to go with the jewelry you have in mind when I couldn't actually try them on together."

"I'm sure they'll be fine. The fundraiser starts at eight. Dinner will be served around nine-fifteen. Can you be ready to leave by seven?"

"Of course." It wasn't as though she had anything else to do or anywhere else to be aside from wandering around Alex's enormous house and spending time with Henry. She could be ready by seven o'clock *tonight,* if he needed her to be.

And in a way, she wished they were attending the charity function tonight. At least then it would be over and she wouldn't have to spend the next day and a half dreading the evening to come.

Alex stood in his den, one hand braced against the mantle of the carved marble fireplace, the other slowly swirling the ice cubes in his glass of scotch. He studied the empty hearth, lost in thought.

Jessica would be down soon to leave for the Sparkling Diamonds fundraiser. How the evening would proceed wasn't at the forefront of his mind, but Jessica certainly was.

After discovering that she wasn't the mastermind behind the theft of the Princess Line designs, he'd begun to wonder what else he might have been wrong about where she was concerned. Could she be telling the truth about everything?

She wasn't one hundred percent innocent, that was for sure. But for each wrongdoing he knew about or had accused her of, she'd come clean.

So what if she was also telling the truth about Henry being his son? He hoped she was, actually. It was a can of worms just waiting to be opened, but having Jessica and the baby under his roof had turned out to be a unique and surprisingly enjoyable experience.

He was just as attracted to Jessica now as he had been the first time he saw her. No matter what had happened in the year since, he still wanted her. His mouth still went dry the minute she walked into the room. His fingers still itched to stroke her skin and peel the clothes off her warm, pliant body.

And the baby...well, he'd been more than a little put off at first, but now he had to admit he was quite smitten. It was hard as hell to wear a mask of indifference, waiting to find out *for sure* whether or not Henry was his son. Not when he spent every day wanting to shed his suit and get down on the floor to tickle the baby's belly, dangle brightly colored plastic keys or play hide-and-seek behind his own hands just to hear the little boy giggle.

Then at night he lay in his big king-size bed imagining Jessica down the hall, sleeping alone. More than once he'd nearly tossed back the covers and marched over to join her...

or drag her back to sleep with him. Not that he had any intention of letting her fall asleep.

Pushing away from the fireplace, he crossed to his desk, setting aside his drink to flip open the file he'd read once before. He needed time to digest the information inside, figure out exactly what to do about it. But even as he rolled it over in his head, he looked the papers over again and was just as stunned and sickened as he'd been when he'd first seen them.

Jessica had mentioned that her cousin blamed him for the Taylors being driven out of business with Bajoran Designs. To his knowledge the decision had been mutually arrived at by the individual heads of each company. At the time that had been Jessica's father as CEO and her uncle—Erin's father, as it turned out—as CFO on the Taylor Fine Jewels side, and Alex's father as CEO and Alex's uncle as CFO on the Bajoran Designs side.

Both companies had been started separately by brothers— Alex's and Jessica's grandfathers and great-uncles. Then they'd joined together because all four brothers had met, formed a strong bond of friendship and thought Fate was trying to tell them something. And it had been a wonderful, very lucrative partnership for many years.

As far as Alex knew, the Taylors had simply decided to go back to being a separate business. His father had assured him the split was amicable and that everything had been taken care of before he'd retired and Alex had taken his place.

Of course what Alex and his family had learned only *after* his father had stepped down, and a few months before his death, was that the elder Bajoran's memory had started to slip. From the moment Alex had taken over the role of CEO, he'd been putting out small fires that his father had unintentionally set ablaze.

This, though...this wasn't a small fire, it was a damn inferno.

Oh, nothing that would harm Bajoran Designs. On the contrary, Bajoran Designs had come out miles upon miles above Taylor Fine Jewels.

But that made Alex far from happy. The bottom line was not more important to him than honor, integrity and proper business ethics. He didn't feel good about the fact that they'd apparently forced the Taylors out of the partnership and probably screwed them out of millions in profits.

The question now became *who* was responsible for that turn of events. It wasn't his father. The man might not be here to defend himself or even question, but Alex knew in his bones that his father would never have done something like that. Not to a business partner, and especially not to one he also considered a friend.

He highly doubted it had been his uncle, either. The two brothers were cut from the same cloth—honest and trustworthy to a fault.

The company investigators he'd put on the case had turned up these initial records fairly quickly, but they hadn't yet tracked down the name of the person who had put this ball in motion. He expected the information to come through any day now, and then he would have to deal with it.

But that was business. Jessica was personal, and he wasn't quite sure what to do about her or the way this information impacted her, as well as the rest of her family.

At the very least an apology was in order, even though he'd awakened that morning thinking she still owed him one.

A soft tap at his office door had him straightening up, closing the file and slipping it into one of the desk drawers for safekeeping. Then, clearing his throat, he called, "Come in."

Mrs. Sheppard poked her head in and said, "Miss Taylor asked me to tell you she's ready and waiting in the foyer."

"Thank you."

The nanny—who was turning out to be an excellent

choice, despite Jessica's original protests—was already upstairs with Henry, and his driver had been sitting outside in
the limo for the past half hour. Grabbing the jewelry box he'd
brought home with him that afternoon and the lightweight
camel hair coat he'd had special ordered for Jessica for this
evening, he headed toward the front of the house, his footsteps echoing in the cavernous emptiness.

He saw just the back of her head over one of the main
stairwell's newel posts as he rounded the corner. Then, as
he drew closer, she heard his approach, turned and took a
step in his direction.

His heart lurched, slamming against his rib cage hard
enough to bruise, and he faltered slightly, nearly tripping
over his own two feet.

This was why he'd had to walk away at the boutique on
Sunday. He'd waited while she'd changed into two different
gowns, then stepped out of the dressing room looking like a
supermodel hitting the end of a Paris runway...or an angel
dropped straight from Heaven.

His heart had thudded then, too, threatening to burst right
out of his chest, and other parts of his body had jumped to
attention. Whether it was a white spaghetti strap sheath or
long-sleeved red number, she'd made everything she put on
look like a million bucks.

He'd had to feign indifference and use phone calls as an
excuse to escape before he'd done something phenomenally
stupid, like giving the saleslady a hundred dollars to take off
and lock the door behind her so he could push Jessica into
the changing room and make love to her right up against the
wall. He'd broken into a cold sweat just thinking about it.

And that was before she'd landed on *the* dress, added ac-
cessories and done her hair and makeup to match. She was
so beautiful, she literally took his breath away. His lungs
burned from a lack of oxygen, but he couldn't have cared less.

The dress she'd chosen was a sapphire-blue that leaned toward turquoise and made the hazel of her eyes positively pop. It would have clashed horribly with the rebellious near-navy blue stripe that used to be in her hair. Her now all-blond tresses were swept up from her nape, held in place by invisible pins to leave her shoulders and the column of her long neck bare.

The gown was classically understated. A strapless, slightly curved bodice hugging the swell of her breasts...a wide swath of sparkling rhinestones circling the high waist...and yards of flowing blue fabric falling to the floor, with a sexy slit running all the way up to reveal a mouthwatering expanse of long, sleek leg when she moved.

Though she'd balked, Alex had finally convinced her to go into town for a quick mani-pedi. The pampering had done her good, and he'd been sure to spin the suggestion as part of the payback for her lies and thievery. And now her freshly painted toes peeked out of the strappy, diamond-studded heels that poked out from beneath the hem of the gown.

Alex didn't know how long he'd been standing there, drooling like a dog over a particularly juicy steak, but it must have been a while because Jessica's eyes narrowed in concern and she glanced down the line of her own body, checking for flaws. Of which there were absolutely none.

"What's wrong?" she asked, returning her gaze to his. "Don't you like the dress? I told you I shouldn't be the one to choose. It's *your* fundraiser, you should have—"

He cut her off midrant. "The dress is fine. More than fine," he said, grateful his voice came out only a shade rusty and choked.

Her chest rose as she inhaled a relieved breath, drawing his attention to all that lovely pale skin and the shadow of her cleavage. He couldn't decide if he was delighted or annoyed that he now got to decorate it with some of the shining jewels from Bajoran Designs' most recent unveiling.

He knew they would look amazing on her, even if she outshone them just a bit. But on the downside, draping her neck with shimmering diamonds would drag everyone else's eye to something he preferred to keep to himself.

"Do you have the jewelry you want me to wear?" she asked, seeming to read his mind.

He held out the large leather case, embossed in gold with the Bajoran Designs logo. Flipping open the lid, he let her see what lay on the blanket of black velvet inside.

"Oh," she breathed, reaching out red-tipped fingers to touch the necklace's center gem. "They're beautiful."

And yet they paled in comparison to the woman standing in front of him.

Tossing the coat he'd gotten for her over the banister, he set the jewelry box on the flat top of the newel. "Here, let me put them on you."

He started with the bracelet, slipping it on her wrist, and then the oversize dinner ring on the middle finger of her opposite hand. Her ears, normally glittering with multiple studs and tiny hoops, were completely bare, leaving room for his earrings and his earrings alone. Since he didn't want to hurt her, poking around trying to get the fish hooks into the proper holes, he handed the three-inch dangle earrings to her and let her insert them on her own.

"Spin around," he told her, reaching for the pièce de résistance.

Lifting the necklace up and over her head, he waited for her to arrange it in just the right spot before fastening the latch at the back of her neck. He let his fingers linger on her smooth skin, lightly stroking the tendons that ran from nape to shoulders, down to the delicate jut of her collarbones and then back up to cup her shoulders, stroking all the way down the length of her arms.

Circling one wrist, he lightly tugged her around to face him once again. The diamonds at her throat and ears twinkled in the light of the giant chandelier far overhead. But his gaze wasn't locked on the priceless set of jewels that were supposed to be the focal point of tonight's event. Instead, he was struck mute by the brilliant facets of Jessica herself.

Her fingers fluttered up to touch the netted V-shape of the necklace crossing her chest. Even without seeing them ahead of time, she'd chosen the most ideal gown possible to display the jewelry he'd intended to have her wear.

"Would you be offended if I said this set is much prettier than most of the pieces in the Princess Line?" she asked.

He gave a low chuckle. Leave it to Jessica to speak her mind, even when she thought she was in the doghouse.

"It better be. We really had to scramble to make up for that loss. We needed something to release in its place that would make just as much of a splash. Or so we hoped."

She tugged one corner of her lower lip, glossy with red lipstick, between her teeth. "Are you trying to make me feel worse about that than I already do?"

"Actually, no. I wouldn't give up this moment, seeing you in this dress wearing these particular pieces, for anything in the world."

She blinked at him, eyes round with disbelief. He was a little surprised that the words had come from his own mouth, but he wasn't sorry. After all, it was the absolute truth.

Another absolute truth was that if he'd had a choice in the matter, he'd say to hell with the Sparkling Diamonds fundraiser, scoop Jessica into his arms and carry her upstairs to his bed where she belonged. Or where he wanted her, at any rate. Almost more than his next breath.

His hand tightened on her wrist and he had to make a concerted effort to lighten his grip before he hurt her. Or followed through on his baser instincts.

"We should go," he murmured reluctantly. Lifting his free hand, he brushed the back of his knuckles along her cheek to her ear, pretending to straighten an earring.

She gave a small nod, but didn't look any more eager to move than he was.

"Here," he said, reaching for the ladies' camel hair coat. He was glad now that he'd chosen to order one in black. It went beautifully with her gown, but would have gone with a dress of any other color, as well.

He held it for her and she turned to slip her arms into the sleeves. Pulling the front closed, she lightly knotted the belt at her waist then took his elbow when he offered.

Crossing the polished parquet floor and stepping outside to climb into the waiting limousine, Alex let himself imagine, just for a moment, that this was real. That Jessica was his and that going out with her for a night on the town was the most normal thing in the world.

As would be coming home late, crawling into the same bed together and making love until dawn.

Fourteen

Two hours into the fundraiser, Jessica was ready to go home. Not because it wasn't enjoyable, but simply because she'd forgotten how exhausting events like this could be.

Once the thousand-dollar-a-plate dinner had been served and consumed, it was all about mingling. Rubbing elbows, making polite conversation, promoting your company and raising money for the cause du jour.

To his credit, Alex was a pro at it. There must have been close to two hundred people in attendance, but he acted as though each person he talked to was the *only* person in the room. He was charming and handsome, and positively oozed self-confidence.

Everyone they met was treated to the same suave greeting, which included introductions, questions about the other person's family and/or business, and then idle chitchat until Alex found an opening to bring up both a reference to Bajoran Designs and a request for a healthy donation. Jessica didn't know who was in charge of collecting checks, but she would be willing to bet his or her head was spinning in delight by now.

She was also relieved that even though Alex was introducing her by her real name, and she was sure most of the guests recognized her for exactly who she was, nobody seemed to be giving her curious looks or talking behind their hands about a Taylor returning to the fold on the arm of a Bajoran.

That wasn't to say the grapevine wouldn't be ripe with fresh rumors by morning, but at least no one was making an issue of it this evening.

Breaking away from the latest group of smiling faces, Alex put a hand at the small of her back and led her on their continued circuit of the room.

In addition to key Bajoran Designs executives and board members wearing the latest pieces of jewelry to show off, there were blown-up full-color signboards on easels arranged throughout the large ballroom featuring other Bajoran designs. It was an enticing display. Jessica had noticed more than one woman already decked out in her weight's worth of gold and jewels admiring what Jessica suspected would be her—or more likely, her husband's—next acquisition.

And for some reason she was inordinately pleased. She loved the jewelry business, loved the sparkle of priceless gems and the intricacies of the designs themselves. Hadn't realized just how much she'd missed it, actually. And even though she and her family were no longer involved in it the way they'd once been, she still wanted Alex's company to be successful.

Alex slowed his step when he noticed her studying one of the extraneous designs more closely than the others photographed on a background of bright pink satin.

"Do you like it?" he asked softly.

"Of course. Your company does very nice work."

"Very nice?" he replied.

When she tipped her head in his direction, she saw that one dark brow was notched higher than the other.

"Shouldn't you be swooning and dreaming of the day you can wear that necklace around your own neck?"

She gave a low chuckle. She was already wearing a lovely necklace from Bajoran Designs worth probably twice as much as the one in the oversize photo. Not that either of them would be very practical in her day-to-day life unless she sold them for things like food and diapers.

To Alex she said, "You forget that I used to be around jewelry like this all the time. After a while it loses a bit of its allure."

He leaned down to whisper in her ear. "Shh. Don't let anyone hear you say that or we'll lose customers."

She laughed again. "Sorry," she returned in an equally low, equally conspiratorial voice.

"So why were you studying this one so intently?"

Shrugging a bare shoulder, she turned back to it. "There are just a few things I would have done differently, that's all."

It took a second for Alex to reply. Then he asked, "Like what?"

She worried her bottom lip for a moment, not sure she should say anything. Then with a sigh, she decided she probably couldn't get into any more trouble with him than she already was.

"The metalwork is a bit heavy-handed," she said, pointing to the spots she was talking about. "These stones don't need that thick a setting. If the gold were a bit thinner, more of the emeralds would show and the whole thing would have more sparkle to it."

One beat passed, then two.

"What else?" he asked.

"I might have gone with more slope to the design." She ran

her finger over the outline of the piece to illustrate her point. "This is very boxy, whereas more curvature would lay better against a woman's chest and be more appealing to the eye."

This time, more than a couple of beats passed in silence. She'd counted well past ten and begun to sweat before she twisted slightly to face him.

His expression was inscrutable. The only thing she could tell was that his eyes had gone dark and he was studying her as though he expected her to burst into flames at any moment. And she just might, if her embarrassment grew much hotter.

She opened her mouth to apologize, backpedal as much as possible, but he cut her off.

"How do you know so much about this stuff?"

Caught off guard, she rolled her eyes and said the first thing that popped into her head. "Hello? Jessica Taylor, Taylor Fine Jewels. I told you, I grew up around all of this. Before my family and your family went their separate ways, I was in line to start designing for the company on an official basis. But even before then, my father let me offer suggestions on existing design specs."

She turned toward the crowd, watching until she spotted just the right example. "See that woman standing over there in the too-short red dress?"

Alex followed her line of sight. "I don't think it's too short."

With a snort, Jessica murmured to herself, "Of course you don't." He probably didn't think the dress was too tight for the woman's build, either, considering how much of her breasts were popping out.

Then to him she said, "The earrings and necklace she's wearing are mine. Marquise-cut diamonds in a white gold setting, with a lone ruby as the main focal point. My father made me work with one of the company's design teams, but only to be sure everything was done correctly. Otherwise, he told them to give me free reign."

Jessica could feel that she was smiling from ear to ear, but she couldn't help it. Perfecting and designing those pieces, working at her family's company and having her father show so much faith in her had been one of the happiest times of her life. She'd so been looking forward to doing that every day. Not just on a whim or trial basis, but as a career.

For the first time, she realized she shouldn't have given up on that dream so easily. She'd been so busy starting a new life that she'd lost sight of those goals. Even if it had been in another city, for another company, she should have found a way to continue designing.

Once again the stretch of silence from Alex brought her head around. His sharp blue gaze made her pulse skitter and sent a shiver rippling under her skin.

"The only other time I've ever seen you smile like that is when you're playing with Henry," he told her, his tone so low and intense, her chest grew too tight for her lungs to draw in a breath. "Why didn't I know about any of this before?"

Jessica blinked, her fingers curling into the palm of one hand and around the rhinestone-studded satin clutch in the other. He was moving too fast for her, jumping from business to personal, personal to business, too quickly for her to keep up. Not with the conversation, but with the feelings he was stirring inside of her and with what she *thought* he might be conveying with his suddenly severe expression.

Was the heat of his gaze banked passion or tightly controlled anger? She couldn't tell for sure, but from the arousal coiling low in her belly, she found herself hoping it was the former. As dangerous as that thought was.

Licking her dry lips and swallowing until she thought she could manage clear and normal speech, she said, "I guess my father never told anyone. Maybe he was waiting to see how I performed and whether my pieces actually sold before taking steps to hire me into the company officially."

Reaching out, he brushed a tendril of hair away from her face, letting the backs of his fingers skim her cheek. Sparks of electricity went off in her bloodstream at the contact, raising goose bumps over every inch of her flesh.

"We didn't manufacture very many of that design," he said softly, the words barely penetrating her hormone-addled brain. "But they sold very, very well."

She blinked, pleasure flooding her at his admission.

"I even remember commenting that we needed to put out more pieces like that on a larger scale, but I never thought to ask for more from the actual designer. I simply assumed they were the result of a design team's efforts."

"If you're saying all of this just to be nice or to butter me up for something, please don't tell me the truth yet," she murmured, letting her eyes slide closed on the riot of sensations washing through her. "Let me savor this feeling just a while longer."

Eyes still closed, she smelled Alex moving closer a second before she felt his warm breath fan her face. His aftershave was an intoxicating mix of spicy citrus and sandalwood that she remembered intimately from their single night together. Now, as she had then, she inhaled deeply, wanting to absorb his scent and carry it with her from that moment on.

His mouth pressed against hers. Soft, but firm. Passionate, but not at all inappropriate given their current location and how large an audience they might be attracting.

He pulled away long before she was ready, leaving her cold and lonely. Her eyes fluttered open and she almost moaned with disappointment.

Still standing close enough to draw undue attention, he whispered quietly, "I meant every word. Although I do have a question for you that you might think I *was* buttering you up for."

His thumbs stroked the pulse points at her wrists, which she was sure were pounding harder than a jackhammer.

"For the record, I wasn't. You can say no, even though I sincerely hope you'll say yes."

Yes. Yes, yes, yes! She didn't even know what the question was yet, but the word raced through her mind, anyway, rapidly multiplying like furry little bunnies. She almost didn't care what he asked— Will you marry me? Will you sneak into the ladies' room and let me take you against the vanity? Would you like brown sugar on your oatmeal?—she wanted to say yes.

Her voice cracked as she made herself say, "All right. What is it?"

So many words. And she sounded so reasonable, when inside she was flailing around like a passenger on a tilt-a-whirl.

"Will you come home with me?"

Some fragment of her brain thought that was a silly question.

"I have to," she told him. "You're making me stay with you until the paternity results come back."

His lips curved in a patient smile. "No," he said softly. "You know what I mean. Let me take you home, to my bed. Spend the night with me the way I've been wanting you to since you came."

She nearly wept. Inside she actually whimpered. If he only knew how hard it had been to lie in bed all those nights, alone, knowing he was only two doors away. She'd thought about him, fantasized about him, even cursed him. And then, once she'd fallen asleep, she'd dreamed about him.

"What about your fundraiser?" she asked, needing to buy a little time for her heart to slow its frantic gallop and her mind to be sure—really, really sure—she could deal with the consequences of her answer.

"There are others here who can see it through to the end. And if we don't get out of here soon, it's possible they'll be in for more of an evening than they bargained for. We're talking full-out, triple-X public displays of affection right here in the middle of the ballroom."

He emphasized his point by pressing against her, letting her feel the full state of his arousal through his tuxedo slacks and the fall of her gown. She leaned into him, reveling in his palpable desire for her. Though her response wasn't nearly as noticeable, it was just as intense, just as overwhelming.

She also wasn't sure she'd mind if he threw her down on the nearest banquet table and had his wicked way with her, but it might turn into a public relations nightmare for his people.

"Then maybe it would be best if we left," she murmured.

She felt his chest hitch as he sucked in a breath.

"Is that a yes?" he asked, his voice sounding like sandpaper on stone.

"Yes," she answered easily. "It's definitely a yes."

She wanted to laugh at the endearing, lopsided grin he beamed at her. And then they were moving. He spun her around, keeping her in front of him as he steered her across the room, making excuses and lining up others to oversee the rest of the fundraiser in his place. Depending on who he spoke to, he blamed their premature exit either on *his* early meeting schedule the next morning or *her* phantom headache.

Finally they were in his limo, pulling away from the hotel portico and racing toward his estate.

As soon as the chauffeur had closed the door behind them, Alex was on her, devouring her mouth, running his hand up and down her leg through the slit in her gown, anchoring her to him with an arm around her back.

Her fingers were in his hair, loving the silky texture and holding him in place while her tongue tangled with his. The plush leather of the wide seat cushioned them and brushed against the bare skin of her shoulders and back, making her realize they'd left the benefit without a thought for the coats they'd checked at the beginning of the evening or the chill in the late-night air.

Breaking the kiss, Alex panted for breath, his hands never pausing in their rabid exploration of her body through the sleek material of her gown.

"I want to take you right here," he grated, "so I'll never again be able to ride in this car without thinking of you."

Her heart did a little flip. "Then what are you waiting for?" she asked in a soft voice. Thankfully the privacy window was up—and she hoped soundproof.

His teeth clicked together, a muscle throbbing in his jaw. "Not enough time," he bit out. "But soon. Believe me—very soon."

With that, he pulled away, tugging her down to lie almost flat along the wide seat.

"What are you—?" she started to ask, but his hands were beneath her skirt, finding the elastic waistband of her panties.

In one swift, flawless motion, he had them down her legs and off. Then he was pushing aside the folds of the dress, leaving her naked from the belly button down except for the diamond-studded heels strapped to her feet.

Sliding to the limousine floor, he knelt there, a wolfish grin slashing his face and flashing straight white teeth. His hands at her hips tugged her forward, then gently parted her knees.

A quiver of anticipation rushed over her, pooling low in her belly. "Alex—" she whispered in a halfhearted protest, but it was already too late.

Lowering his head, he brushed kisses along the insides of

both thighs, leading upward until he reached her mound and pressed one there, as well. His lips moved over her, nuzzling the sensitive flesh and burrowing between her damp folds swollen with arousal.

He tortured her with long, slow strokes of his tongue that made her back arch and her nails dig into the leather seat cushions. She whimpered, writhed, panted for breath. Alex merely hummed his approval and redoubled his efforts to drive her out of her mind.

He licked and nibbled, flicked and suckled until Jessica wanted to scream. She was pretty sure *that* sound wouldn't remain on this side of the privacy window, however, so she squeezed her eyes shut and bit her lips until she tasted blood.

A second later, the limousine started uphill, rolling them together even tighter and pressing Alex more fully between her legs. His lips and tongue and fingers hit just the right spot with just the right amount of pressure to make her shatter, her insides coming apart in sharp, mind-blowing spasms of pleasure.

When she regained consciousness—because she truly believed she might have fainted from pure physical delight—Alex was hovering over her, smiling like a cat who'd just figured out how to unlock the birdcage. Her legs were demurely draped across his lap, her dress rearranged to cover them.

"We're home," he said quietly, leaning in to brush his fingers through her hair, which she was pretty sure was a tangled mess by now, no longer pinned in the lovely swept-up twist she'd fought so hard to get right only hours before.

With his help, she sat up, struggling to get her bearings and stop her cheeks from flushing bright red with awkwardness. It didn't help that the front of Alex's pants were noticeably tented by the bulge of his erection.

Spotting the direction of her gaze, he chuckled, shifting

slightly to alleviate the pressure behind his zipper. Then he reached down and plucked a scrap of sheer blue fabric from the car floor.

She held out her hand, expecting him to return the lost article of clothing. Instead, he dangled it from one finger, continuing to grin.

"Alex, those are my underwear," she said on a harsh whisper. Not that anyone else was around to hear. "Give them back."

"Nope."

She made a grab for them, but he slipped them into the pocket of his tuxedo jacket before she even got close. Sliding across the seat, he opened the door and stepped out, reaching a hand back to help her out.

"Come on. Let's go inside before Javier asks what all that screaming was about."

Fifteen

"Oh, no," Jessica groaned in utter mortification.

Taking his hand, she followed him to the house as fast as she could, making a concerted effort not to look around for fear she'd make eye contact with Alex's driver and die of humiliation right there on the front drive.

Once inside, he slammed the door shut, then spun her around to press her back flat to the thick wooden panel. His body boxed her in, arms braced on either side of her head, chest and hips and upper thighs pressing against her like a big, warm, heavy blanket.

His mouth crashed down on hers, stealing her breath and reviving every sensual, red-blooded nerve ending in her body, even the ones she'd thought had gotten their fair dose of pleasure for the night. She gripped the lapels of his jacket, hanging on for dear life while their tongues mated and their lips clashed hard enough to bruise.

One minute she was standing upright, pressed to the front

door. The next she was biting off a yelp of surprise as he swept an arm behind her knees, placed another at her back and yanked her off her feet.

Reluctantly, he pulled his mouth from hers and turned to march up the stairs. He carried her as though she weighed no more than Henry, but still she could feel his heart pounding beneath the layers of tuxedo jacket and dress shirt.

She kept one hand flattened there on his chest, the other toying with the short strands of hair at his nape. All the while she pressed light butterfly kisses to his cheek, his jawline, his ear, the corner of his eye, the pulse at his neck.

He growled low in his throat. She gave a long purr in response.

Stopping in the middle of the hallway, he gave a sigh that had her lifting her head. They were standing only a few feet away from the nursery door, which was slightly ajar.

"As much as it pains me," he said, "I don't want you to blame me later for not letting you see Henry before we go to bed. Especially since I intend to keep you there for a very long time. Do you want to run in and check on him?"

Her body might be humming, her blood so hot it was close to boiling her alive, but she was still a mother, and she really did want to see the baby one last time before Alex made her forget her own name.

"Would you mind?" she asked, lips twisted in apology.

He made a face. One that told her he didn't want to waste even a second on anything but getting her naked and between the sheets. But just as she'd always known, he was a good man. A kind, generous, sometimes selfless man.

Without a word, he slowly lowered her to the floor until she was standing none too steadily on her own two, three-inch-heeled feet. Keeping a hand at the small of her back, he walked with her to the nursery door.

Pushing it open, she tiptoed inside. Wendy was sitting

in the rocking chair in one corner, reading beneath the low
wattage of the only lamp in the room. She lifted her head
and smiled when she saw them.

"How was he tonight?" Jessica whispered, continuing over
to the crib. Henry was on his back on the zoo animal sheets,
covered almost to his chin by a lightweight baby blanket.

"He was an absolute angel," the nanny said, moving to
Jessica's side. "We played most of the evening. I read him a
story and gave him a bottle around eight. He's been sleeping ever since."

"That's great," Jessica replied, even though she was a little disappointed he wasn't still awake so she could wish him
good-night. Doing the next best thing, she kissed the tips of
two fingers then touched them to his tiny cheek. His mouth
moved as though starting to smile—or more likely to give an
extra suck of his pacifier—and warmth washed through her.

Straightening away from the side of the crib, Jessica
thanked Wendy. "You can go to bed now," she told her. "I'm
sure he'll be fine for a few more hours, at least."

The nanny nodded and moved back to the rocker to gather
her things.

Standing close, having looked into the crib at Henry himself, Alex said, "Keep the monitor with you, if you would,
please. We'll be available if you need us for anything, of
course, but we'd prefer not to be disturbed tonight, if at all
possible."

Jessica was sure that his hand at her waist and the high
color riding her cheekbones left nothing to the nanny's imagination.

But she nodded without blinking an eye. "Of course. Not
a problem, sir."

"Thank you," Alex murmured, applying pressure to Jessica's waist to get her moving toward the door.

"Thank you," Jessica said again, casting one last glance

over her shoulder at both the nanny and what she could see of the baby through the slats of the crib. "Good night."

And then she was back in the hall, being hustled next door to Alex's bedroom. She laughed at his speed and single-minded determination as he shoved her inside, catching a quick glimpse of dark wood, a masculine color palette and sprawling space before he closed the door, shutting out the light from the hall and locking them in near darkness.

As soon as they were alone, he was on her like a bird of prey, holding her face in both of his hands while he kissed her and kissed her and kissed her, turning her round and round and round as he walked her in circles farther into the room.

"Wait," she breathed between tiny nips and full-bodied thrusts of his tongue. "Turn on the lights. I want to see your room."

"Later."

"But..."

"Later," he growled.

She started to smile in amusement, but then his hands skimmed up the length of her spine, found the miniscule tab of the gown's zipper and slid it all the way down. The billowy, strapless blue material fell away from her breasts and dropped to the floor in a soft whoosh.

Since the dress didn't allow for a bra, and her panties were currently tucked in the pocket of Alex's jacket, the action left her completely naked but for her strappy stilettos and all four pieces of priceless Bajoran jewelry. Cool air washed over her, cooling the diamonds against her skin, raising gooseflesh and pebbling her nipples.

Or maybe it was the anticipation of making love with Alex again after what seemed like forever.

He stepped back, his eagle eyes roaming over her nude-but-bejeweled form from head to toe. Though how he could see much of anything in the dark, she didn't know. Only the faint glow of moonlight shone through the sheer curtains at the windows.

Not that the lack of illumination seemed to bother him. Not letting it slow him down one tiny bit, he shrugged out of his tuxedo jacket and started to undo his tie, collar and cuff links.

One by one, items were discarded, the buttons at the front of his starched white shirt slipped through their holes. Slowly, the hard planes of his chest came into view. Shadows of them, at any rate.

Heart rapping, she closed the scrap of distance between them, covering his hands at the waist of his slacks. His movements stilled and she pushed his hands away entirely.

He let them fall to his sides, giving up so easily. Yet she could feel the tension emanating from his body, in the steel-cable rigidness of his stance and every tightly held muscle.

His chest rose and fell in sharp cadence as she tugged the tails of his shirt out of the waistband of his pants. Pushing the fabric open and off over his shoulders, she let her palms run the full expanse of his wide masculine chest.

Just as she remembered from so long ago, it was broad and smooth, throwing off heat like a furnace. A light sprinkling of hair tickled her fingertips while she explored his flat abdomen; the rise of his pectorals with their rough, peaked centers; the hard jut of his collarbones and the curve of his strong shoulders.

The white material floated to the floor, and she returned her hands to the front of his pants. Sliding them open, she lowered the zipper past his straining erection while he sucked in a harsh breath and held it. She let her knuckles brush along his length through his black silk boxers.

Muttering a curse, he kicked out of his shoes, stripped the slacks and underwear down his muscular legs, and dragged her away from the entire pile of their shed clothing. He walked them over to the large four-poster bed, lifting her onto the end of the high mattress.

He moved in for a kiss, tipping her chin up and cupping her face in both hands. His thumbs gently brushed the line of her jaw while he drank from her mouth. She parted her knees, making room for him in the cradle of her thighs, and he pressed close, brushing every part of her with every part of him.

Her nails dug into the meat at the sides of his waist, then she brought her legs up to hitch her knees over his hips. He groaned, the sound filling her mouth as he leaned into her even more.

A second later she found herself lifted by her buttocks and tossed several inches closer to the center of the bed. Alex came with her, landing on top of her even as she bounced lightly, the glossy satin coverlet cool at her back.

While she wrapped her legs more firmly around him, he buried his face in her neck and began trailing kisses down her throat, tracing the lines of the necklace until it gave way to the bare flesh of her chest and one plump breast. He pressed his mouth dead center, then started to lick and nip all around.

Beneath him, Jessica arched, moaned, writhed. And Alex reveled in every ripple, every soft whimper of sound.

He'd wanted to drape her in his jewels, and now he had. And she was just as glorious as he'd known she would be in nothing but what he'd borrowed from the company safe.

He could hardly believe he actually had her in his bed again.

Different bed. Different city and state. Different year. Maybe even two different people…different than they'd been the first time around, anyway.

But so much was the same. The instant spark between them that quickly turned into a five-alarm fire. The uncontrollable desire he felt for her almost every minute of every day. Her hot, liquid response to his touch.

She humbled him and made him feel like a superhero all at once. And it was quite possible she'd given him a son. An heir. Another Bajoran to someday take over the family business.

That thought made him want to put her up on a pedestal and treat her like a queen. Surround her in swaths of cotton and bubble wrap, and keep her safe for the rest of their lives.

But for now, with her warm and willing beneath him, he most wanted to drive her to the brink and then straight over the edge into mind-bending bliss.

If only he could hold back his own climax long enough to get her there. And the way her legs were wrapped around his hips, her damp heat brushing him in all the right places, was making that more and more impossible.

Her stiff nipple abraded his tongue as he swiped at it over and over again. Around it, her dusky rose flesh puckered and tightened.

With a groan, he moved to her other breast and did the same. Her hands stroked his bare back, his shoulders, through his hair and along his scalp. Her nails scraped and dug and clawed.

Between her legs her warmth beckoned. He burrowed closer, locking his jaw to keep from moaning aloud. Continuing to toy with her nipples and the sensitive area surrounding them, he trailed his hands down her sides, over her hips and the mound of her femininity. She gasped as his fingers found her, and he captured the sound with his mouth.

For long languorous minutes, he explored her feminine core. The soft folds, swollen channel and tight, sensitive bud, all slick with tantalizing moisture.

"Alex, please," she whimpered against his lips, her pelvis rising upward, straining for the pleasure he was so cruelly withholding.

As much as he wanted to keep playing, keep touching and stroking and teasing her for hours on end, he didn't have all that much restraint left, either. Not after a year of celibacy since their last time together and the torturous session in the limousine.

Sliding more closely against her, he let her wet heat engulf him as he slowly pressed forward. He gritted his teeth while she took him inch by inch, her chest hitching beneath him in an effort to continue taking in oxygen. His own lungs burned just like hers, every muscle bunching tight.

"I remember this, you know," he grated, nostrils flaring and mind racing while he tried desperately to distract himself from the incredible sensations threatening to make him come apart at the seams.

She made a sound low in her throat. Part agreement, part desperation.

"I never forgot," he told her, "even though I tried hard to do just that."

Jessica's breath blew out on a shuddering sigh. "Alex?"

"Hmm?"

"Let's talk later, okay?"

She panted the words, her nails curling into his shoulder blades and making him shudder from the top of his scalp to the soles of his feet.

He chuckled. "Okay."

Grasping her about the waist, he yanked her toward him as he thrust, driving himself to the hilt. She gasped, and Alex ground his teeth to keep from doing the same.

Rolling them both to their sides, he held her there, moving inside of her, kissing her while temperatures rose, sensations built and the air filled with the sounds of heavy breathing and needy mewls. Jessica's hands on his body licked like flames. Tiny flicks of pleasure that shot straight to his center.

They rocked together on the soft, wide mattress. Side to side. Forward and back. Tongues mingled while bodies meshed, slowly becoming one. Her hips rose to meet his every thrust, her breasts rubbing his chest.

"Alex," she whispered, pulling her mouth from his to suck in a heartfelt breath. "Please."

She didn't need to beg. He was right there with her, desperate and so close to going over, his bones ached.

Clasping her smooth, bare buttocks, he tugged her closer, then rolled them again so that she was on her back and he was above her, covering her like a blanket. Faster and faster they moved until she was clenching around him and he was straining not to explode.

Which would have been a lot easier if she weren't grabbing at his hair and murmuring, "Yes, yes, please, yes," over and over again in his ear.

"Jessica," he bit out, not sure how much longer he could hold out.

"Alex," she returned with equal urgency. "Alex, please. Now."

"Yes," he agreed, forcing the word past his locked jaw. "Now."

And then he was breaking apart with Jessica spasming around him, her cries of delight filling the room and echoing in his ears.

Sixteen

Jessica stretched and rolled to her opposite side, surprised to find herself alone in the wide king-size bed. All through the night, Alex hadn't let her get more than half an inch from him except to run to the bathroom or peek in on Henry.

He'd wrapped his arms around her, tugged her snug against his long solid frame and held her while they slept. Then he'd woken her with kisses and the light caress of his hands on her skin to make love to her again. And once she'd awakened him the same way.

As nights went, it had been just about perfect.

Finding herself alone with the midmorning sunlight shining through the curtains put a bit of a damper on that perfection, though. It made her wonder if the entire evening had been as wonderful as she remembered. If the feelings she'd felt for Alex and *thought* he might return were real.

Insecurities flooding her, she slipped from the bed, pulling the rumpled coverlet along to tuck over her breasts, letting it trail behind her like a long train. She gathered her dress and shoes and other personal items from the seat of a chair where Alex had apparently collected them from the floor. Checking the hall, she tiptoed to her room and dressed in something other than an evening gown and three-inch heels.

With her hair pulled back in a loose ponytail and her body encased in comfortable cotton and denim, she headed for Henry's nursery only to find the crib empty. Far from being worried, she simply assumed he was with the nanny.

Making her way downstairs, Jessica checked Alex's office first, wanting to see him again, even though she wasn't entirely sure how he would respond to her in the bright light of day. But the room was empty, the door standing wide open and Alex's chair pushed back from his desk.

Turning toward the other side of the house, she trailed along to the kitchen, deciding that even if she didn't find Alex or Wendy and Henry there, she could at least grab a bite of breakfast.

As soon as she stepped into the deluxe gargantuan room, she heard the sounds of her son's giggles over the gentle din of pots and pans, spoons and spatulas. Alex sat in the breakfast nook before the wide bank of tall windows with Henry balanced on one strong thigh.

He was dressed more casually than she'd ever seen him in a pair of simple tan slacks and a white dress shirt open at the collar. Henry had a bib tucked under his chin, and there were small dishes of assorted baby foods on the table in front of them. Alex was obviously attempting to feed him, but he must have been teasing too much because Henry couldn't stop laughing and wiggling around.

Slipping her fingers into the front pockets of her jeans, Jessica strolled to the table. She was a little nervous after what she and Alex had shared last night, but happy, too, to see him so friendly and comfortable with the baby.

"What are you two up to?" she asked in a near singsong voice, sliding onto the bench seat across the table from them.

Raising his head, Alex shot her a wide grin, a spoonful of orange goop—peaches, she assumed—hanging from his free hand.

"Just letting you sleep a little longer," he replied. "And getting to know my son a bit better."

He said it so easily, so casually that she almost didn't catch his meaning. Then the words sank in and her eyes snapped to his.

Her sharp gaze must have been questioning enough, because he gave an almost imperceptible nod. "The doctor called this morning. The test results are positive—Henry is most definitely mine."

Jessica almost couldn't hear for the sound of her heart pounding in her ears. She'd never doubted Henry's paternity, of course—she *knew* Alex was the father for the simple fact that there'd been no other men in her life at the time of his conception…as well as long before and after. But she'd nearly forgotten Alex's doubts, and that DNA results were what they'd both been waiting around for.

Taking a moment to mentally slow her rampant pulse, she swallowed and then cocked both her head and a single brow. "Am I allowed to say *I told you so?* Because I *did* tell you so."

To her surprise, he chuckled, a genuine smile breaking out across his normally stern features. "Yes, you did." His smile slipping a couple of notches, he added, "I hope you know I wanted to believe you. I wanted it to be true, I just… I had to be sure."

His heavy-lidded eyes were storm-cloud blue and almost— she could have sworn—apologetic. She did understand. Alex alone was worth millions of dollars, his family as a group likely worth hundreds of millions. For all she knew, dozens of women had shown up on his doorstep claiming he was the father of their children.

Her own father had run off many a young man he suspected was more interested in the Taylor fortune than in her. It had made dating in high school an adolescent nightmare.

"So what do we do now?" she asked quietly.

Before Alex could answer, Mrs. Sheppard appeared at her elbow, sliding a plate of scrambled eggs and toast in front of her. She added a glass of orange juice and then disappeared again to the other side of the room, well out of earshot.

"Are you going to eat?" Alex asked after she'd sat there a few long minutes staring at the meal but making no move to touch it.

Taking a deep breath, she picked up her fork and stabbed at the eggs but turned her true attention to him instead.

"I'm a little distracted right now," she told him.

"For good reason, I suppose," he said, inclining his head and taking a moment to feed Henry another spoonful of pureed baby breakfast.

"I need to run into the office for a while this morning, but was hoping you'd meet me there later. Do you think you could do that—and bring Henry with you?"

"A-all right," she stuttered, confused by his nonchalance and focus on a topic unrelated to the recent discovery that he was, indeed, Henry's father. "But what about—"

Pushing to his feet, he carried Henry over to her and deposited the baby into her arms instead. Henry giggled, kicked and wiggled until she got him arranged on her own lap. Alex moved the jars of baby food to her side of the table and handed her the tiny peach-caked spoon.

"Just meet me at my office in a couple of hours, okay? Around one o'clock."

He leaned down and pressed a kiss to the crown of her head, ruffling the top of Henry's at the same time.

"Trust me," he added.

Calmly, competently, completely at ease while her insides were jumping around like seltzer water.

Two hours later, almost on the dot, Jessica walked into the Bajoran Designs office building. She wasn't sneaking around this time, hoping to get in and out without being spotted by security. Instead, Alex had made sure a car and driver were available to bring her into the city and drop her off at the front door.

She'd also changed from jeans and casual top to a short burgundy wraparound dress, and put Henry into a long-sleeve shirt covered in cute yellow ducks with a pair of brown corduroy overalls. She didn't know what Alex's intentions were for asking her to come to his office with the baby, but she wanted to be prepared. And knowing she looked good helped to boost her self-confidence.

At least that's what she told herself as she made her way up to the twelfth floor in the main elevator. The doors slid open and she stepped out.

She was a little surprised to find the reception desk and hallway completely empty on a Wednesday afternoon. Not even a receptionist behind the main desk. If the place had been this deserted when she'd left Henry on Alex's boardroom table, she wouldn't have had nearly as much trouble sneaking in and out or been half as nervous about getting caught.

Since Henry's carrier—with Henry strapped safely inside—was getting heavy, she set him on the low coffee table in the waiting area, wondering if she should stay here or go in search of Alex.

Before she could decide for sure, a door opened at the end of the long hallway and voices filtered out. A minute later Alex stepped into view, standing aside while several other men, also dressed in expensive, conservative suits, filed out. The last man exited the room, flanked by two security officers.

He wasn't handcuffed. In fact, they weren't touching him at all. But it was clear they were escorting him, and he looked none too happy about it.

Jessica stayed where she was, watching as the group of men made their way to the elevators, waited for the car to arrive and stepped on. The second elevator carried the angry man and the two security guards to the lobby.

After both sets of doors slid closed, she turned her head to find Alex striding toward her, a warm smile softening the strong lines of his face. From the moment he'd issued the invitation, she hadn't known what to expect. That look encouraged her, made her think they might be here for something other than bad news.

"You came," he said, leaning in to press a light kiss to her mouth. He stroked a hand down her bare arm to thread his fingers with hers at the same time he patted Henry's leg and sent the carrier rocking back and forth.

"You asked us to," Jessica replied carefully, not quite sure what else to say.

"And you trusted me enough to do it, even though I didn't tell you why I wanted you here."

He seemed infinitely pleased by that fact, and she found herself returning his near grin.

"I have a surprise for you," he said. "But first we need to talk."

"All right."

He gestured for her to take a seat on the low leather sofa, then sat down beside her. Their knees brushed, and he reached for her other hand so that he held both of hers in both of his, resting on his upper thigh.

Inside her chest, her heart bounced against her ribs, her

diaphragm tightening with nerves. She had no idea what he was going to say, but she felt like a teenager about to be reprimanded for missing curfew.

"I looked into the problem you mentioned about your family," he told her. When her brows came together in a frown, he clarified. "The belief that Taylor Fine Jewels was forced out of partnership with Bajoran Designs."

She understood what he was talking about, but was no less confused.

"It turns out you were right. For the record," he was quick to point out, "I knew nothing about it. All of that was over and done with before I took over the position of CEO, and behind my father's back. But my cousin George apparently decided he could rise higher and bring in more money for the Bajorans if our two families were no longer in business together."

Jessica's eyes widened. She wasn't all that stunned by Alex's pronouncement, considering she'd known the truth all along. Maybe not the details—about his cousin being the impetus for her family's ruin—but she'd certainly known the rest.

What surprised her was that Alex had listened to her and looked into her claims rather than automatically taking his family's side and dismissing her as crazy or scorned.

"Thank you," she said with a small hitch in her voice.

Knowing what Alex had done—that he'd discovered the truth and was man enough to admit it—suddenly meant the world to her.

It was so much more than she would have expected of anyone...but especially Alex.

"Don't thank me," he said with a shake of his head. "Not when I owe you an apology. What my cousin did was wrong and is what started all the bad blood."

Jessica gave a watery chuckle. "It seems we both have evil cousins hiding in the branches of our family trees. What I

did to you back in Portland thanks to *my* cousin was wrong
and unfair to you, as well. If you can forgive me for that, I
think I can forgive you for something you had absolutely
nothing to do with."

Lifting a hand to his lips, he kissed her fingers. "I forgive
you," he murmured in a tone so resolved she could never
doubt his sincerity.

"I forgave you long ago," he continued, "though I'm not
sure I realized it until recently. But I owe you—and your
family—more than that."

She started to shake her head. "You don't owe me—" she
began, but he cut her off with a smile and the pad of one
index finger pressed to her lips.

"It's already done, so just sit there for a minute and let me
tell you how I'm making this right."

She swallowed hard, taken aback by his determination on
the subject. But she did as he asked, sitting back and giving
a short nod to let him finish.

"The man you saw being led out by security…that was my
cousin George. The others were board members who came
in for an emergency shareholders meeting. Once I explained
to them what George had done and showed them definitive
proof, they agreed to his immediate termination."

His lips twisted at her shocked gasp. "He only went quietly
under threat of having criminal charges leveled against him."

"I can't believe you would fire your own cousin," she
whispered.

Alex scowled. "He's lucky I didn't throttle him. I might
yet. But that doesn't do much to help your family, so I want
you to know that I intend to approach them about going into
business with us once again."

Jessica's lungs hitched, her pulse skipping a beat. "Oh,
Alex," she breathed.

"Do you think it's something they'll go for?"

"There may be hard feelings at first," she said with a laugh. "The Taylors can certainly be stubborn at times. But once they've had a chance to consider your offer and realize it's genuine, I think they'll be delighted."

On a burst of pure gladness she bounced off the sofa cushion and threw herself against Alex's chest, hugging him tight. "You really are a wonderful man, Alexander Bajoran. Thank you."

His arms wrapped around her, squeezing her back. He cleared his throat before speaking, but even then his voice was rough.

"You're welcome. There's more, though," he said, giving her one last embrace before setting her away from him and taking her hands again.

His chest swelled as he took a deep breath. This next part was delicate. She was either going to be thrilled with him and throw herself into his arms again, or she was going to be furious and possibly slap him a good one.

"Your parents are here," he announced quickly—almost too quickly, like tearing off a bandage. He saw the question in her eyes, the incomprehension on her face.

"What? Why are they... What?"

Mouth dry and pulse racing, Alex tightened his grip on her fingers. "I'm hoping you'll consider sticking around Seattle for a while longer, preferably staying with me so that we can see if this...*thing* between us is as real and as strong as it feels. And in order to do that, your parents need to know where you are—and that they have a grandson."

He'd crossed the line in contacting Jessica's parents behind her back and without her permission, but he hadn't known how else to get all of their problems ironed out and taken care of in one fell swoop. And for some reason it was important to him to get everything out in the open and dealt with *right now*.

There had been too many secrets, too many lies already. Starting years ago with his cousin's slimy, despicable actions toward her family on behalf of his, to as early as this morning when the doctor had called and announced that he *was* indeed Henry's biological father.

That phone call had both elated and disgraced him.

Elated him because he couldn't imagine anything that would make him happier than knowing Henry was his. Especially after last night when he'd pretty much decided he didn't care one way or the other.

Being with Jessica again, in and out of bed, had reignited the same powerful feelings he'd felt for her a year ago, and he'd known he wanted to keep her in his life. Jessica and Henry both, regardless of DNA.

But the test results had shamed him, too, because they reminded him that he'd doubted Jessica to begin with. Doubted her word, doubted her integrity, let pride and suspicions cloud what his heart and gut had been trying to tell him.

Hadn't he known as soon as he'd seen her again that he was in love with her? Hadn't he known the minute she'd told him Henry was his son that she'd been telling the truth?

She'd made some bad decisions, but he had some making up to do, that was for sure. And today's business was a step in that direction.

Still clutching Jessica's hands in his lap, he stroked her long slim fingers distractedly.

"I told them everything. Explained how we met last year, how you tried to steal company secrets to avenge the wrong that had been done to your family. And I told them about Henry."

With each word he uttered, Jessica's eyes grew wider, her expression panicked while the color leeched from her skin. On his lap her hands started to quiver.

"I'm sorry," he told her quickly. "I know it was probably

your place to tell them about the baby and why you disappeared on them, but I didn't want them to feel ambushed once they arrived. And I sort of hoped that having time to think during the flight—" he'd sent his own jet to pick them up "—would help them absorb the turn of events more easily."

"Oh, God," Jessica groaned, dropping her head to rest on their clasped hands. She was breathing fast and shallow... he hoped *not* on the verge of hyperventilating.

"Oh, God, oh, God. What did they say?" she asked in a muffled voice. "Were they angry? Do they hate me? Did my mother cry? I can't handle it when my mother cries. Oh, they must be *so* upset and disappointed in me."

Her hysterics were enough to make him chuckle, but he very wisely held back. Instead, he freed a hand to rub his wide palm up and down the line of her spine.

"Your mother did cry," he said, remembering his meeting with them in his office before he'd crossed the hall to deal with his cousin and the board.

"But I'm pretty sure they were happy tears. She's delighted to have a grandson, and can't wait to see him. They're eager to see you again, too, though your father did admit that if you'd shown up pregnant with my child, they probably would have been none too pleased. Realizing how they likely would have reacted to the news helped them to understand why you've stayed away these past months, I think."

Taking a deep, shuddering breath, Jessica raised her head and met his gaze. Her eyes were damp and worried.

"Do you really think so?"

He gave her a reassuring smile. "I do. Your parents are very nice people," he added. "I liked them, and am looking forward to working with them if they agree to partner with Bajoran Designs again."

The anxiety in her features seemed to fade as she reached

up to stroke his cheek. "You're something else, you know that?"

Alex quirked a brow. "In a good way or a bad way?"

"Oh, a very good way. I might even go so far as to say amazing, but I don't want you to get an inflated opinion of yourself. Or more of one, at any rate," she teased.

Then she sobered again. "I mean it, Alex. What you've done, all of it, it's…wonderful. And you didn't have to. You didn't have to do any of it. I'd have told my parents everything eventually. And what happened between our families, with the company… It was so long ago, and you had nothing to do with it. You could have let it all go on just as it has been."

"No," he said with a sharp shake of his head and the beginning of a scowl, "I couldn't. I don't want either of us to go into this relationship with baggage."

Jessica licked her lips, eyes darting to the side before returning to his.

"Relationship?" she asked in little more than a whisper.

"Yes." His tone was low, serious. Because this was possibly the most serious, important conversation of his life.

"I meant what I said," he continued, being sure to hold her gaze. "I want you to stay. Move in with me officially, as more than just a temporary guest. I'd really like to see if we can make this work. As a couple. As a family."

For several tense seconds she didn't respond. Except to blink, her thick lashes fluttering over wide eyes.

She was silent for so long, Alex nearly squirmed. Maybe this had been a bad idea. Maybe he was pushing for too much too soon.

As usual he'd forged ahead with his own plans, his own desires, expecting everyone and everything to fall into place just as he wanted it. After all, wasn't that how it had been his entire life?

This was so much more important than anything else

had ever been, though. And it wasn't only about what he wanted—it was about what Jessica wanted, and what was best for both her and Henry.

His ideal would be for them to stay with him. He didn't know if they were ready for forever just yet, but he certainly wouldn't mind if they moved in that direction.

If Jessica wanted something different, however, if her ideal was something else entirely, then he would have to accept that. He would still be in Henry's life, there was no doubt about that. And he didn't think Jessica would ever try to keep him out of it.

When the near-static buzz of intense silence became oddly uncomfortable, Alex cleared his throat and made a concerted effort to loosen his grip on Jessica's fingers. As romantic and sweeping as he'd hoped his actions and this gesture would be, it was a lot to digest. He couldn't blame her for being wary and needing time to consider her options.

"It's all right if you're not ready for something like that," he told her. He kept his tone even, devoid of the disappointment churning in his gut. "I shouldn't have sprung everything on you quite so quickly. I understand if you need time to think it through. And maybe last night was just one of those things. It didn't have to mean anything—"

The pads of two fingers pressed to his lips stopped him midsentence.

"It meant something," she said, barely above a whisper. "And I don't need time to decide anything. Yes—Henry and I would love to move in with you. Your house—mausoleum that it is—" she added with a grin "—is starting to feel like home already. I'm just…surprised you're asking. I'm shocked by all of this," she admitted, leaning slightly away from him and sweeping her arms out to encompass the waiting area and beyond.

Turning back to him, her eyes were warm, her expression

open and inviting. It made his heart swell and his own blood heat to a healthy temperature as it pumped through his veins.

"But, Alex," she began, her voice quietly controlled, "are you sure about this? You were so unconvinced of Henry's paternity, so suspicious of me. I didn't think you felt…*that way* about me."

She wasn't trying to make him feel like a heel, but he did. And if he'd ever needed confirmation that she was one of the most honest, genuine women he'd ever met—*not* a gold digger after his or his family's fortune—her cautious protests would have done it.

With a grin he felt straight to his bones, he brought her knuckles to his lips and kissed them gently. "Maybe I wasn't convincing enough last night."

"Oh, you were plenty convincing. But that's just sex, Alex. What you're talking about is…more. At least if you're saying what I think you're saying."

"I am," he told her. No hesitation, no mincing words. "It was definitely more than just sex between us. Last night and a year ago—I think you know that. From the moment we met," he murmured, alternately brushing the tops of her fingers and the underside of her wrists, "there was something between us. I'm just asking now for a chance to make it work. To see if we have a future together."

A short, shaky laugh rolled up from her throat. "I'd like that. More than you can imagine."

Yanking her to her feet, he held her close and kissed her until they were both gasping for breath.

"I'd like to take you home right now and celebrate properly," he told her, hands tangled in the hair at either side of her head while he cradled her face. "But your parents are still waiting in my office, no doubt growing more agitated by the minute. I know they're eager to see you…not to mention meet their grandson for the first time."

She inhaled deeply, then let the air slip from her lungs in a quavering sigh. "Will you come with us? I don't want to do this alone."

Rubbing his thumb along the full swell of her lower lip, he smiled gently. "You don't ever have to be alone again."

Epilogue

One Year Later...

The ballroom was brimming with guests dressed in tuxedos and designer gowns. Their voices were a loud din, interspersed by laughter and the clinking of glasses.

Beside her, Alex smiled and nodded as an associate droned on about his recent vacation in Milan, while the butterflies in Jessica's stomach fluttered violently enough to break through and fly away.

She tried to pay attention, really she did. And her cheeks hurt from trying to keep such a pleasant smile on her face. Inside, though, she was shaking, her fingers cold and stiff around her flute of champagne.

Apparently noticing her silent distress, Alex wrapped up his conversation with the couple before them and took her elbow to lead her several feet away. There weren't many quiet corners in the overflowing ballroom, but he managed to find one.

"You look like you're going to pass out," he remarked, clearly amused. His hands moved up and down her bare arms, rubbing warmth back into them along with a semblance of normalcy.

"Take a deep breath," he commanded. "Now slow and easy. Relax. You're the guest of honor tonight...you should be walking on air."

She followed his instructions, *tried* to relax and was relieved to feel her pulse slow by at least a couple of beats per minute.

"What if they hate it? What if you lose money? What if they hate *me* and start hating Bajoran Designs? You know the rumor is that I trapped you for revenge, and blackmailed you into bringing my family back into the company."

He had the nerve to chuckle, which earned him a less-than-ladylike scowl.

"Only a few very shallow, catty and jealous people think that. Everyone else—everyone who counts, at any rate— thinks you're delightful and knows how lucky I am that you and your family gave me a second chance."

Continuing in her downward spiral of unladylike behavior, she snorted with disbelief.

Alex lifted a hand to her face, brushing his knuckles lightly along one cheek and into her hair, which was currently loose around her shoulders, streaks of cotton-candy-pink spiraling through the otherwise blond curls.

Another bit of ammunition the gossips relished using against her, but she liked it and Alex claimed it was "hot."

"It's true," he told her. "Just as it's true that you're magnificently talented, and your True Love Line is going to be hugely successful."

Dropping her head to his chest, she inhaled the spicy masculine scent of his cologne and fought not to cry. "I just don't want to embarrass you or make anyone at your company mad for taking a chance on me."

Thumbs beneath her jawline, he raised her gaze to his. "First, you could never embarrass me. And second, it's not *my* company. Not anymore. It's *our* company, which means you have just as much say in what takes place there as I do. Besides, everyone at Bajoran Designs knows incredible natural talent when they see it. Giving you your own line was, as they say, a no-brainer."

That brought a smile to her face, the first honest one of the evening.

"Your family is here," Alex continued. "My family is here. Even Henry is here."

He cast a glance over his shoulder to where their fifteen-month-old son—the only child in attendance—was perched on his grandmother's hip in his adorable miniature tuxedo. He was starting to pull himself up and toddle around now, eager to learn to walk so he could become even more independent and keep up with the adults in his life. Until he managed that, however, he spent his time alternately napping, charming the world or getting into trouble as only a rambunctious toddler could.

But she and Alex both adored him more each day. Even the days they fell into bed utterly exhausted from chasing him around Alex's sprawling estate.

She'd been surprised, actually, when Alex had insisted they bring the baby along tonight, despite the fact that it was well past Henry's bedtime and they were inviting public crankiness by keeping him awake. But Alex had wanted—in his words—his "entire family" there for the debut of Jessica's True Love Line. A gesture that had both touched her and filled her with added anxiety.

"All to show how proud they are and how much they support you."

Chest finally beginning to loosen, she gave a peaceful sigh. "You're better than a full body massage, do you know that?"

Alex made a low, contented sound at the back of his throat. "I'll remind you that you said that—later, when we get home."

Leaning into him, she let his warmth and love surround her, calm her, remind her why she'd been inspired to name her debut jewelry line True Love to begin with. The wisdom of that decision was only underscored when he pressed a kiss to her brow.

"At the risk of sending you into a near faint again," he murmured against her skin, "I have one more thing I need to discuss with you before we unveil your designs."

A shimmer of tension rolled through her, but nowhere near the level of moments before.

Reaching into his pocket, Alex drew out a small velvet jewelry box with the Bajoran Designs logo stamped on the outside.

"We've been together a year now. Living together, raising Henry, loving each other like a real family. And I, at least, think it's working."

Popping open the lid of the box, he held it out to her. Inside was the most beautiful, sparkling diamond engagement ring she'd ever seen. Her heart lurched and the air stuck in her lungs.

"So how about we make it official?" he asked. "I love you, Jessica. I have almost since the moment we met, even if I didn't quite realize it. You getting pregnant with Henry that first night together was the greatest miracle of my life, because it brought you back to me when I might have lost you otherwise."

Moisture prickled Jessica's eyes as emotion filled her with a wave of unadulterated joy, tightening her chest.

"Oh, Alex," she breathed. "I love you, too. And I'm so glad you saw Henry and me as a blessing rather than a burden."

He tugged her close once again, framing her face with both hands, placing a hard kiss on her lips this time. When he spoke, he had to clear his throat, and even then his voice was rough and deeper than normal.

"The only burden you or Henry could ever cause me is making me hold this ring much longer. Will you marry me, Jessica? Be my wife, my lover, my partner both at home and at the office, and the mother of not just the child we already have, but any others who might come along?"

It was the easiest question she'd ever had to answer.

"Oh, yes." A tear slipped down her cheek, and she couldn't have cared less that it might mar her perfectly applied makeup.

He took the ring from its nest of velvet and slipped it on her left hand. The stone, roughly the size of a dime, glittered in the light of the room. She turned her hand one way, then another, taking pleasure in every facet and detail that caught her eye.

"It's beautiful, Alex, thank you."

It was also huge and quite heavy. She would need a little red wagon to cart it around with her all day, every day.

"I designed it myself," he told her, chuckling when she shot him a surprised look. "I may not be as talented as you, but I knew what I wanted. I also know what you like."

Taking her hand, he slid the ring back off her finger. "I know you think it's too big, too ostentatious, even though secretly, you adore how large and showy it is."

Well, he had her there. Didn't every woman want an engagement ring the size of a compact car to show off and use to impress their friends?

"Which is why it's actually two rings that come together to form one."

He wiggled things around with a little click, and suddenly he held a piece in each hand. They were both gorgeous and still quite remarkable, while also being a bit more manageable.

"You can choose which to wear on a regular basis, or switch back and forth, if you like. And when you want to flaunt your wealth or show off just how much your husband adores you, you can put them together and cause temporary blind spells everywhere you go."

She laughed, amazed at his ingenuity and how much thought he'd put into it when he could have pulled any ring from the Bajoran Designs collection instead, and she wouldn't have known the difference.

"I'm *very* impressed," she admitted as he clicked the two bands into place and slipped all umpteen carats back on her finger.

Going on tiptoe, she wrapped her arms around his neck and pressed a soft kiss to his waiting lips. "I also love it. And I love you. Coming to Seattle was the best decision I ever made, even if we got off to a slightly rocky start."

His own arms came up to circle her waist, holding her close while he nibbled lightly at the corners of her mouth and jaw.

"Ah, but don't you know that the rockiest paths sometimes lead to the very best destinations?"

With a perfectly contented sigh, she leaned back to stare deep into his crystal-clear sapphire eyes.

"Yes, I guess I do," she whispered as everything else faded away, leaving them the only two people in the world, let alone the crowded ballroom. "Because my rocky path led me to you."

* * * * *

HER IMPOSSIBLE BOSS

CATHY WILLIAMS

CHAPTER ONE

WIDE, sensual mouth compressed, Matt stared down at the makeshift CV sitting in front of him. It was difficult to know where to begin. The colourful list of jobs complemented by the even more impressive lack of duration at each one of them told their own story. As did the brief, uninspiring academic profile. In the normal course of events he would have tossed this application into the bin without even bothering to read the sketchy handwritten personal profile at the end. Unfortunately, this was *not* the normal course of events.

He finally looked across his highly polished mahogany desk at the girl perched nervously on the chair facing him.

'Eight jobs.' He pushed himself away from the desk and allowed the lengthening silence to fill in the blanks of what he wanted to say.

Tess Kelly had come to him via a reference from her sister, and, in no position to be choosy, here he now was, interviewing for a nanny for his daughter. From what he could see, not only was Tess Kelly resoundingly lacking in any relevant experience, she was also flighty and academically challenged.

Huge green eyes looked back at him and he followed

her nervous gesture as she chewed her bottom lip. He might have his hands tied, but that didn't mean that he was going to make this process easy for her.

'I know it sounds like a lot...'

'You're twenty-three years old and you've held down eight jobs. I think it's fair to say that it is a lot.'

Tess looked away from the cool dark eyes resting on her. Under his unflinching, assessing gaze, she was finding it impossible to keep still. Why on earth was she here? She had arrived in New York three weeks previously to stay with her sister, with the proviso that she take some time out to consider her options and get her act together. At least those had been the parting words of her parents as they had waved her off at the airport before she'd disappeared across the Atlantic.

'You're twenty-three years old, Tess,' her mother had said firmly, offering her a plate of homemade biscuits to soften the blow, 'and you still don't seem to have any idea what you want to do with your life. Your dad and I would just like to see you settle down. Find something that you enjoy doing—something you might want to stick with for longer than five minutes... Claire knows all the ins and outs of the business world. She'll be able to give you some helpful advice. It would do you good to spend your summer somewhere else...'

No one had mentioned that part of the process would involve getting a job as a nanny. She had never worked with any child in her life before. She couldn't remember having ever expressed the slightest curiosity about working with one. And yet here she was, sitting in front of a man who chilled her to the bone. The very second she had spun round at the sound of his velvety voice, to see him lounging against the doorframe, inspecting her, she had felt a shiver of apprehension skim down her spine. She had prepared herself for someone portly and middle-aged. He was, after all, her sister's boss. He owned the company, he ran it, and according to Claire he took no prisoners. How could he do all that and still be in his early thirties? But he was—and, contrary to all expectations, not only was he young, he also had killer looks. Drop-dead, truly sensational killer looks.

But his emotional detachment was terrifying, and his perfect bone structure proclaimed a face that never cracked a smile. Tess wondered how her sister could work for him without having a nervous breakdown.

'And your academic history… I'm finding it hard to tally your lack of qualifications with your sister's achievements. Claire has a first class degree and is head of my corporate law department. You have…let's count them…six mediocre GCSE grades and a certificate in Foundation Art…'

'Yes, well, I'm not Claire, Mr Strickland.' Two patches of colour appeared on her cheeks. 'Claire and Mary both excelled at school…'

'Mary being…?'

'My other sister. She's a doctor. They were both high-achievers. Not everyone is built along the same lines.' Cheerful by nature, Tess was finding that she *loathed* this man. From his opening words to her— *'You're half an hour late and I don't tolerate lateness.'* —to his sweeping assumption that she was a failure. He hadn't said it in so many words, but it was there, lurking in the cold, disdainful expression behind those bitter chocolate eyes.

'Okay. Let's do away with the formalities and cut to the chase, shall we?' Matt leaned forward and rested his elbows on the desk. 'You're here because I am not in a position of choice. I don't know what, precisely, Claire has told you, but let me clarify. My ex-wife died some months ago and since than I have had full custody of my ten-year-old daughter. In that period she has seen off almost as many nannies as you have seen off jobs. Consequently, the agency I deal with have effectively closed their doors to me. I have three housekeepers, but they are not suitable for the demands of the job. I could look further afield, but frankly this is a three-month posting—and finding a career nanny who is willing to offer herself for such a short period of time will not be easy. Time, Miss Kelly, is of the essence as far as I am concerned. I work huge hours. I have neither the time nor the ability to cover. Your name cropped up. Your sister sings your praises when it comes to your sociability. Ergo, you are here now—despite your glaring shortcomings.'

Not for the first time, Matt considered the train of events that had led to where he was now.

Divorced for eight years, he had been an infrequent spectator to his daughter's life. Catrina, his ex-wife, had removed her to Connecticut a year after their divorce had become final, and had played so many games when it came to making arrangements for him to visit that the years had elapsed without him ever really feeling connected to Samantha. And then, six months ago, Catrina had died in a car accident, and the daughter he had never really known had landed on his doorstep—resentful, grieving, and silently, wilfully hostile.

Nannies, a necessity for him, had come and gone, and he now found himself between a rock and a hard place.

'I'm sorry. I'm *so* sorry. Claire didn't mention details... Your poor, poor daughter...' Tears of sympathy were gathering in the corners of Tess's eyes and she blinked them away. 'I'm not surprised she's finding it difficult to settle down.'

Taken aback by such an emotional response, Matt reached into a drawer in his desk and pulled out a box of tissues, which he handed to her.

'So, whilst you're not my idea of the ideal candidate...' He carried on over the subsiding threat of her tears.

'I guess you're worried because I've had so many jobs over the years...' Tess was prepared to give him the benefit of the doubt. He might be harsh and forbidding, but he was in a difficult position and no doubt justifiably anxious that he take on someone who wouldn't let him down.

'Correct. Samantha would not benefit from someone who decides to stick around for a few days and then walks out because she's bored. Even though there have been a lot of nannies, they have all endeavoured to give it their best shot. Are you capable of that?'

'Yes. Yes, I am.' She looked at him. Despite the unforgiving nature of his expression, a little voice whispered, he really was very good-looking—beautiful, almost. Suddenly hot and bothered, she looked away, twisting the tissue between her fingers.

'Convince me.'

'I beg your pardon?'

'I may not be in a position to pick and choose, Miss

Kelly, but I would still like you to persuade me that I am not about to make a mistake with you. Your sister may well sing your praises, and I trust Claire, but...' He shrugged and relaxed back. 'Persuade me...'

'I wouldn't leave anyone in the lurch. I really wouldn't, Mr Strickland.' She leaned forward, her face flushed and sincere. 'I know you think that I'm probably not very good at sticking to anything. Well, actually,' she confessed, 'my family would all probably agree with you. But I've actually been indispensable in many of my past jobs. I've never let anyone *down*—not really. No, not at all, come to think of it. Even when I quit the receptionist's job at Barney and Son, Gillian was there to take over. To be honest, I think they were all a little relieved when I decided to leave. I was forever transferring people to the wrong department...'

'Let's try and stick to the theme.'

'Yes. Well, what I'm trying to say is that you can trust me with your daughter. I won't let you down.'

'Even though you have no experience in the field and might get bored with the company of a ten-year-old child?'

'I don't think kids are boring! Do you?'

Matt flushed darkly. *Was* he bored in Samantha's company? He had precious little experience in that area to provide a qualified answer. His relationship with his daughter was fraught at best. They conversed intermittently, and across a seemingly unbreachable chasm. She was sulky and uncommunicative, and he knew that he was not a feelings person.

Matt dismissed that brief moment of intense introspection.

'So how would you plan on looking after her?' He pushed the conversation forward and focused on her.

She had a fascinatingly transparent face. Right now, giving his question some thought, she was lost in a slight frown, her lips parted, her apple-green eyes distant. Tess Kelly wasn't the sort of woman he had been expecting. Claire was tall, brisk, efficient, and permanently attired in a suit. The girl sitting opposite him was a living, breathing testimony to the power of misconception. She looked as though she had never been anywhere near a suit and her hair...

No fashionably tailored bob, but really, *really* long. Several times he had been tempted to angle himself so that he could see just how long for himself.

'Well...I guess there are the usual sights. Museums, art galleries. And then there's the cinema, the zoo... I love Central Park. We could go there. I'm sure she'll be missing the familiarity of her home and all her friends, so I'll make sure to keep her busy and occupied.'

'And then there's the matter of schoolwork.'

Tess blinked and looked at him in confusion. 'What schoolwork?' she asked, perplexed. 'It's the holidays.'

'Samantha's education was severely disrupted because of Catrina's death, as you can imagine. More so when she came to New York. There seemed little point in registering her for a school here, which she wouldn't be attending on a permanent basis, and the tutors I employed for her came and went as regularly as the nannies. Consequently there are gaps in her learning which will have to be addressed before she sits exams at the beginning of September for her new school.'

'Okaayyy…and where do I fit in?'

Tess continued to look at him blankly and he clicked his tongue with impatience. *'You're* going to have to take charge there.'

'Me?' Tess squeaked in consternation. *'I* can't become a tutor! You've seen my application form! You've *made fun* of my lack of qualifications!'

The thought of trying to teach anything to someone else horrified her. She wasn't academic. She became nervous just thinking about textbooks. The youngest of three girls, she had grown up in the shadow of her clever sisters, and from an early age had dealt with the problem by simply opting out. No one could accuse her of being thick if she simply refused to compete, could they? And she had known that there was no way that she could ever have competed with either Claire or Mary. How on earth could he expect her to suddenly become a *tutor*?

'I'm sorry to have wasted your time, Mr Strickland,' she said, standing up abruptly. 'If teaching is part of the job, then I'm going to have to turn down the position. I…I can't. Claire and Mary are the brainy ones. I'm not. I've never been to university. I never even wanted to go. I did a foundation course in Art when I was sixteen, and that's the extent of my qualifications. You need someone else.'

Matt looked at her narrowly and allowed her to ramble on. Then, very calmly, he told her to sit.

'I'm getting the picture about your academic qualifications or lack of them. You hated school.'

'I didn't *hate* school.' Having not wanted the job to start with, Tess now realised that she did. His daughter's plight had touched her. The thought of her being so young, and dependent on a father who was obviously a workaholic, tugged at her heartstrings. For the first time she really wanted to get involved. 'I'm just no good when it comes to textbooks.'

'I have no time for people who wave a white flag and concede defeat before they've even given something a fair chance,' Matt said bracingly. 'I'm not asking you to teach to degree level. I'm asking you to tutor Samantha in some of the basics—maths, english, sciences. If you want to persuade me that you're interested in taking on this job, then you're going about it the wrong way.'

'I'm just being honest! If...if you don't want to employ any more tutors for your daughter, then why don't *you* help her with her schoolwork?' She faltered. 'You run a business, so you must be qualified...or maybe you don't need maths and English in what you do...? Some children don't cope well with home-tutoring. Perhaps your daughter is one of those...'

'Samantha could cope very well with home-tutoring,' Matt said shortly, 'if she was prepared to put effort into it. But she's not. She might benefit more from teaching in a less structured manner. And, no, there is no way that I can help out. I barely have time to sleep. I leave this apartment at seven-thirty in the morning, which is an hour later than I used to before Samantha arrived, and I try and make it back by eight in the evening when I'm not away. Which is a push at the best of times.'

Tess was distracted sufficiently from her own agonising to shoot him a look of frank horror. 'You work from seven-thirty in the morning to eight at night? Every day?'

'I cut myself some slack on the weekends.' Matt shrugged. He could think of no one who would find anything out of the ordinary about those working hours. The high-fliers in his company—and there were a lot of them—routinely had punishing schedules and thought nothing of it. They were paid fabulous sums of money and quid pro quo, after all.

'What does that mean?'

'Where are you going with this?' Matt asked irritably. 'You're straying from the topic.'

'I'm sorry,' Tess breathed. 'I just feel so sorry for you.'

'Come again?' Matt could hardly credit what he was hearing. If they haven't been discussing something so important, he would have laughed. Never, but *never*, had anyone *felt sorry* for him. Quite the opposite. Being born into a legacy of wealth, power and influence had opened a thousand doors. Without siblings, the task of taking hold of the family fortunes had fallen onto his shoulders, and not only had he looked after the billions but he had gone several steps further and dramatically increased their worth. He had diversified and invested in areas his father would never have dreamed of, and in so doing had attained a position of impenetrable power. He was virtually untouchable. The economic and financial crises that had seen off so many of his rivals had skirted harmlessly around him. It was a situation he had engineered, and one he enjoyed.

'I can't think of anything more horrible than being slave to a job, but you're right. I'm getting off the subject.

I was just wondering why you didn't cover the school-work with Samantha yourself if you think that the home-tutoring doesn't work, but I can see that you don't have the time.'

Was it his imagination or was there a hint of gentle criticism there?

'Good. I'm glad we agree.'

'Would you mind me asking you something?' Tess ventured, clearing her throat. When he tilted his head to one side she said, tentatively, 'When do you have time for your daughter, if you work such long hours?'

Matt stared at her in disbelief. The directness of the question put him soundly on the back foot—as did the fact that he was seldom in a position of having to field direct questions of a personal nature. Women just *didn't* go there. But she was waiting for an answer.

'I fail to see what this has to do with the job,' he said stiffly.

'Oh, but it has lots to do with the job! I mean, I'm sure you have special times set aside, and I would want to know that so that I didn't intrude. I just don't see where those special times would fit in if you're working from seven-thirty to eight every day, and only taking a bit of time off over the weekends.'

'I don't have a structure for the time I spend with Samantha.' His voice was cold and uninviting. 'We very often go to The Hamptons so that she can see her grandparents on the weekend.'

'That's lovely.' Tess was unconvinced.

'And now that we've covered that, let's move on to your hours.' He tapped his pen absently on the desk, beating a staccato rhythm that made her feel as though she was being cross-examined rather than interviewed. 'I'll expect you to be here every morning no later than seven-thirty.'

'Seven-thirty?'

'Does that pose a problem?'

Torn between truth and tact, Tess remained silent until he prompted, with raised eyebrows, 'I'm taking that as a *no*. It's a requirement of the job. I could occasionally request one of my housekeepers to cover for you in an emergency, but I would hope that the occasion doesn't arise.'

Tess had always been punctual at all her jobs—the very many she had had over the years—but it had to be said that none of them had required her to wake up at the crack of dawn. She wasn't an early-morning person. Somehow she knew that was a concept he would never be able to understand. She wondered whether he ever slept.

'Do all your employees work long hours?' she asked faintly, and for some reason Matt had the strongest inclination to burst out laughing. Her appalled look said it all.

'They don't get paid the earth to clock-watch,' he said seriously. 'Are you telling me that you've never worked overtime in your life before?'

'I've never had to,' Tess told him earnestly. 'But then again, I've never been paid the earth for anything I've done. Not that I mind. I've never been that interested in money.'

Matt was intrigued, against his will. Was this woman from the same planet as he was? He should stick to the programme, but he found himself strangely willing to digress.

'Really?' he said with scepticism. 'In that case, I applaud you. You're one of a kind.'

Tess wondered whether he was being sarcastic, but then, looking around her at the luxurious surroundings of his penthouse, where the old sat comfortably with the new and every hanging on the walls and rug strewn on the floor screamed wealth, she realised that he would be genuinely mystified at her indifference to money.

It had very quickly struck her, the second she had walked through the front door of his apartment, that Matt Strickland was a man who moved in circles so far removed from her own that they barely occupied the same stratosphere. The people he mixed with would share the same exalted lifestyle, and it was a lifestyle that could not be achieved without an unswerving dedication to the art of making money.

But Tess had been telling the absolute truth when she had told him that money didn't interest her. If it had, she might have been a little more driven when it came to a career.

Nor did she have a great deal of respect for someone who put money at the top of their list. Someone, in short, like Matt Strickland. Even though she could appreciate that he was clever and ambitious, there was a hard, cutting edge to him that left her cold.

She sneaked a quick look at that striking face, and her heart beat a little faster and a little harder in her chest.

'You're not saying anything. I take it that you disapprove of all of this?' He gestured sweepingly with one hand. This was a woman, he realised, whose silences were as revealing as the things she said. It was a refreshing trait.

'It's all very comfortable.' Tess tiptoed around telling him the absolute truth—which was that expensive furnishings and investment paintings all came at a price.

'But…?'

'I prefer small and cosy,' she admitted. 'My parents' house is small and cosy. Obviously, not *that* small. There were five of us growing up. But I think that their entire house would fit into just a bit of this apartment.'

'You still live at home with them?' His sharp ears had picked up on the intonation in her voice and his curiosity was instantly roused. What was a twenty-three-year-old woman still doing living at home? And, he noted distractedly, a strikingly pretty twenty-three-year-old girl? Huge green eyes dominated a heart-shaped face that even in moments of thought carried an air of animation. Her long hair was the colour of caramel, and…

His eyes drifted lazily downwards to the full breasts pushing lushly against a small cropped vest, the silver of flat stomach just visible between the vest and the faded jeans that moulded slim legs.

Annoyed at being distracted, Matt stood up and began to prowl through his office. Originally a library, it was still dominated by the hand-made wooden bookcase that stretched along the entire length of the back wall. A rich Oriental rug, handed down through the generations, covered most of the wooden floor. The only modern introductions were the paintings on the walls and, of course, the high-tech paraphernalia essential to his work.

'I…at the moment I do,' Tess mumbled, with sudden awkward embarrassment.

'And you've *never* lived on your own?'

The incredulity in his voice made her spin round to glare at him defensively. She decided that he really was truly hateful. Hateful and judgemental.

'There was never a need for me to live on my own!' she said in a high pitched voice. 'I didn't go to university, and there was no point looking for somewhere to rent when it was just as convenient for me to carry on living at home.' As if it were spelt out in bold neon lettering, she was appalled to hear with her own ears just how hopeless that made her sound. Twenty-three and still living with Mum and Dad. Angry tears threatened to push their way to the surface and she blinked rapidly, forcing them back.

'Remarkable.'

'Most of my friends still live at home. It's not that remarkable.'

'And you never felt the need to spread your wings and do something different? Or did you give up and wave the white flag before you could get around to challenging yourself?'

Tess was shocked at the strength of her reaction. She had never shown any inclination towards violence before, but she could easily have leapt out of her chair and thrown something at him. Instead, she subsided into angry silence. Her entire nervous system picked up pace as he circled her and then leant down, arms on either side of her chair, effectively caging her in.

'I don't see what my home life has to do with this

job,' she breathed jerkily, looking anywhere but at the brown muscular forearms on either side of her.

'I'm trying to get a measure of you as a person. You're going to be responsible for the welfare of my daughter. You come with no references from a professional agency. I need to find out that you're not going to prove a liability. Shall I tell you what I've concluded so far?'

Tess wondered whether she had a choice. Had her tongue been able to unglue itself from the roof of her mouth, she might have summoned up the courage to say something along those lines, but sarcastic rejoinders weren't her forte and his proximity was wreaking havoc with her composure. Her skin was tingling, and she felt as though she was having to drag the oxygen into her lungs in order to breathe.

It was a relief when he pushed himself away from her chair and resumed his place behind the desk.

'You're lazy. You're unfocused. You're lacking in self-confidence and you've been perfectly happy to carry on being that way.' He enunciated each derogatory bullet point with the cold precision of a judge passing sentence on a criminal. 'You still live at home and it doesn't seem to have occurred to you somewhere along the way that your parents might not be as happy with that situation as you are. You pick jobs up and you put them down again because you don't want to be stretched. I'm no psychologist, but I'm guessing that it's because you think you can't fail at anything if you never bother to give your all to it.'

'That's horrible.' Unfortunately there were elements of truth in some of what he had said, and for that she hated him. 'Why are you interviewing me for this job if you have such a low opinion of me?' she asked on a whisper. 'Or has the interview ended? Is this your way of telling me that I haven't got the job? Yes, it is. And, that being the case—' Tess inhaled one deep breath that steadied her fraying nerves '—then I can tell you what I think of you too!' She looked at him with stormy green eyes and drew herself upright in her chair. 'I think that you're arrogant and rude. You think that just because you...you make a lot of money and grew up with a lot of money you can treat people any way you want to and be as offensive as you want to be. I think that it's awful that you obviously work so hard that you have no time left over to give your daughter—who *needs* you! Or maybe you just don't know *how* to give yourself to anyone else!'

Her breathing was jerky from the effort of pouring emotions she'd never known she possessed into what was, for her, an all-out shouting match. The worst of it was that she didn't feel good about herself—even though she had spoken her mind, and even though speaking her mind should have achieved some sort of healthy cleansing.

'And I'm *not* lazy,' she concluded, deflating like a balloon with its air suddenly released. 'If that's all.' She stood up and tried to gather some shreds of dignity. 'I'll be on my way.'

Matt smiled, and Tess was so flustered by that smile that she remained rooted to the spot, dithering as though her legs had forgotten how to work.

'You have fire. I like that. You're going to need some of it when it comes to handling my daughter.'

'Wha—at?'

He waved her down into the chair and leaned back. 'It's healthy to hear a little criticism now and again. I can't remember the last time anyone raised their voice in my presence.' Particularly, he could have added, when it came to women. As if a switch had been turned on in his head, he suddenly keenly noted the fading pinkness in her cheeks. Her hair had fallen forward and was now spread over her shoulders, falling like spun silk over her breasts, almost down to her waist. She was regaining some of her lost composure but her breasts were still heaving.

He was shocked by the sudden responsive stirring in his loins. God, he had a girlfriend! An extremely clever, very high-powered girlfriend. One who understood completely the constraints of his job because they mirrored her own! They were on the same wavelength. She was diametrically, radically and dramatically the opposite to the elfin creature with the big green eyes sitting opposite him. Vicky Burns was focused, driven, and university-educated to the highest possible level.

So why the hell was he wondering what Tess Kelly looked like with her clothes off and only her long, long hair to cover her modesty?

He wrote a figure on a piece of paper and slid it across the desk to her.

Tess leant forward, and of their own accord his eyes strayed to the cleavage she revealed as she reached for the paper.

With a sigh of pure frustration Matt rubbed his eyes and half swivelled his chair, so that he was facing the vast windows of the library, framed with their heavy velvet curtains. It was a safer sight than the one his rebellious eyes had been absorbing.

'This is too much, Mr Strickland. I couldn't possibly accept.'

'Don't be ridiculous!' Annoyed with himself for his uncustomary lapse of self-control, Matt made his voice sharper than intended. He reluctantly turned to look at her. 'It's perfectly reasonable. You're being asked to do a hugely important job, and for that money...well, consider yourself on a learning curve as far as over-time goes. There's just one more thing. You'll have to dress the part.' He flushed darkly at the confusion on her face. 'Looser clothing. It's more practical in this heat. Particularly if you intend on doing...er...outdoor activities...'

'But I don't have any loose clothing.'

'Then you'll have to buy some. It's not an insur-mountable problem, Tess. You will have access to an account for all expenses to do with the job. Make use of it.' He stood up, back in control of his wayward body, and waited as she scrambled to her feet, gathering her satchel which she slung over her shoulder.

'Now it's time for you to meet my daughter. She's upstairs in her bedroom. I'll show you to the kitchen. You can familiarise yourself with it. Make yourself a cup of coffee. I'll bring her down.'

Tess nodded. After her gruelling interview, from which she was still reeling, the prospect of meeting Samantha wasn't as daunting as she would have ex-pected. What could be more full-on than her father had been?

The apartment, sprawling in all directions, occupied

the entire top two floors of the building. Matt showed her into a kitchen which was as stunningly modern as the rest of the apartment was shamelessly and opulently old. Granite surfaces positively gleamed, and were completely bare of any of the normal clutter associated with day-to-day life. Tess foresaw problems should she attempt to do any cooking with her charge. She would be terrified of ruining the show home look.

'Make yourself at home,' he insisted, while she continued to look around her with the lost expression of someone suddenly transported to foreign territory.

For a few seconds Matt watched her with rare amusement. 'It doesn't bite,' he said, and Tess flushed. 'There's tea and coffee in one of the cupboards, and in the fridge...' he indicated something sleek that was camouflaged to look like the rest of the kitchen '...there should be milk. My housekeepers make sure that the kitchen is stocked, especially now that Samantha's around. If you're lucky, you might even locate some biscuits somewhere.'

'You mean you don't *know* where things are in your own kitchen?'

Matt grinned, and Tess had a disconcerting window into what this man would look like shorn of his arrogance. Not just beautiful, but dangerously, horribly sexy.

She lowered her eyes as a new, prickly feeling undermined her still shaky composure.

'Terrible, isn't it?' He was still grinning and moving towards the door. He raised his eyebrows. 'Maybe you could work that one into the next speech you give me about my shortcomings.'

Tess smiled weakly back, but somewhere in a part of her she hardly recognised warning bells were beginning to ring—although what that meant she had no idea.

CHAPTER TWO

'WELL? *Well?* What did you think? Have you got the job?'

Claire was waiting for her. Tess had barely had time to insert her key into the front door and there she was, pulling open the door, her face alight with curiosity.

What did she think of Matt Strickland? Tess tried her best to sum up a guy who represented everything she so studiously avoided. Too rich, too arrogant, too stuffy. When her mind strayed to the peculiar way he had made her feel, she reined it back in.

'Can you believe he didn't want me showing up in tight clothing?'

'He's your boss. He can dictate your wardrobe. Do you think *we're* allowed to show up to work in ripped jeans?' Claire pointed out reasonably. 'Move on. Impressions of the apartment?'

'Barely had time to notice.' Tess sighed. 'I've never had such a long interview. I could tell you all about his office, but that's about it. Oh—and the kitchen. I *did* notice that his apartment is the size of a ship, though, and I'm not sure about his taste in art. There were lots of paintings of landscapes and random strangers.'

'That would be his family,' Claire surmised thoughtfully. 'Classy.'

'Really? You think?'

'And finally impressions of the daughter?'

No one had known that he even *had* a daughter, so private was Matt Strickland, and so far he hadn't brought her into the office once!

Tess wondered what there was to tell—considering she hadn't actually met the child. She had waited in the kitchen for what had seemed an unreasonable length of time, and Matt had finally returned in a foul temper and informed her that Samantha had locked herself in her bedroom and was refusing to leave it.

Tess had sipped her tea, distractedly helped herself to her fifth biscuit, absentmindedly gazed at her feet, which had been propped up on a kitchen chair in front of her and pondered the fact that, however powerful, self-assured and downright arrogant Matt Strickland was, there was still at least one person on the face of the earth who was willing to ignore him completely.

'You shouldn't have locks on the doors,' she had informed him thoughtfully. 'We were never allowed to when we were growing up. Mum was always petrified that there would be a fire and she would have no way of getting in.'

He had looked at her as though she had been speaking another language, and only later had she realised that he would have had no real experience of all the small details involved in raising a child.

'So, Monday looks as though it's going to be fun,' she finally concluded now. 'Samantha doesn't want to know, plus I have to be there by seven-thirty. You know how hopeless I am at waking up early...'

Which earned her a look of such filthy warning from Claire that she decided to back off from further complaints on the subject. Of course she would do her very best to wake at the crack of dawn. She would set her alarm, and she would set her phone—but she knew that she might easily sleep through both. What if she did?

She still remembered all the choice words he had used to describe her, and her fact was still worrying at the problem when, the following evening, she answered the landline to hear Matt's dark, smooth voice at the other end of the phone.

Immediately Tess was hurled back to his apartment and that first sight of him, lounging against the doorframe, looking at her.

'You've probably got the wrong sister,' Tess said as soon as he had identified himself—as though there had been *any* chance of her not recognising that voice of his. 'Claire's having a bath, but I'll tell her you called.'

'I called to speak to you,' Matt informed her smoothly. 'Just to remind you that I'll be expecting you at seven-thirty sharp tomorrow morning.'

'Of course I'm going to be there! You can count on me. I'm going to be setting a number of gadgets to make sure I don't oversleep.'

At the other end of the line Matt felt his lips twitch, but he wasn't about to humour her. He got the distinct impression that most people humoured Tess Kelly. There was something infectious about her warmth. However, when it came to his daughter, a stern angle was essential.

'Hello? Are you still there?'

'I am, and to help ease you into punctuality I'll be sending a car for you. It'll be there at seven. You forgot to leave me your mobile number.'

'My mobile number?'

'I need to be able to contact you at all times. Remember, you'll be in charge of my daughter.'

Unaccustomed to being reined in, Tess immediately softened. Of *course* he would want to have her mobile number! He might not be demonstrative when it came to his daughter—not in the way that her parents had always been demonstrative with *her*—but keeping tabs on the nanny showed just how important it was for him to know the whereabouts of Samantha at all times.

She rattled it off, and turned to find Claire looking at her with a grin.

'Step one in being a responsible adult! Be prepared to be answerable to someone else! Matt's a fair guy. He expects a lot from the people who work for him, but he gives a lot back in return.'

'I don't like bossy people,' Tess objected automatically.

'You mean you like people who don't lay down any rules to speak of and just allow you to do whatever you want. The joys of being the baby of the family!'

Tess had always been perfectly happy with that description in the past. Now she frowned. Wasn't the unspoken rider to that description *irresponsible*? Her parents had shipped her out to New York so that she could learn some lessons about growing up from her sister. Was it their way of easing her out of the family nest? Had Matt been unknowingly right with his observations? Taking on the job of looking after someone else's child—a child who had already been through a lot and clearly had issues with her father—was not the job for someone who refused to be responsible. Matt Strickland was prepared to give her a chance in the face of some pretty strong evidence that she wasn't up to the task. Being labelled *the baby of the family* no longer seemed to sit quite right.

She had half expected to arrive the following morning and find herself taking orders from one of those mysterious people he had mentioned who would be there to pick up the slack, but in fact, after her luxurious chauffeured drive, during which she'd taken the opportunity to play tourist and really look at some of the sights from air-conditioned comfort, she found herself being greeted by Matt himself.

The weekend had done nothing to diminish his impact. This time he was dressed for work. A dark suit, white shirt and some hand-tailored shoes—a combination that should have been a complete turn off, but which instead just seemed to elevate his sexiness to ridiculous levels.

'I wasn't expecting you to be here,' Tess said, immediately taken aback.

'I live here—or had you forgotten?' He stood aside and she scuttled past him, weirdly conscious of her body in a way that was alien to her.

Under slightly less pressure now, she had her first opportunity to really appreciate her surroundings. It was much more impressive than she could ever have dreamt. Yes, the place was vast, and, yes, the paintings were uniformly drab—even if the portraits *were* of his family members—but the décor was exquisite. Where she might have expected him to err in favour of minimalism, with maybe just the odd leather sofa here and there and lots of chrome, his apartment was opulent. The patina of the wooden floor was rich and deep, and the rugs were old and elaborate. A galleried landing looked down on the immense space below, and stretching the full height of the walls were two windows which, she could now see, offered a tantalising view of Manhattan. The sort of view to which most normal mortals could only aspire via the tourist route.

'Wow! I didn't really take much notice of your apartment the last time I was here. Well, office and kitchen aside.' She stood in one spot, circling slowly. 'Sorry,' she offered to no one in particular, 'I know it's rude to stare, but I can't help myself.' Her eyes were round like saucers, and for the first time in a long time he fully appreciated the privileges to which he had been born.

'Most of the things in here have been handed down to me,' he said, when she had eventually completed her visual tour and was looking at him. 'In fact, I could trace the provenance of nearly everything here. How was the drive over?'

'Brilliant. Thank you.'

'And you're ready to meet Samantha?'

'I'm sorry I didn't get to meet her last time,' Tess said with a rush of sympathy.

Matt, eager to get the day under way, because he had back-to-back meetings, paused. 'Like I said, she's been through a very rough time. It can be difficult to get through to her sometimes.'

'How awful for you. I would have thought that she would have clung to you after her mother's death.'

'Some situations are not always straightforward,' Matt informed her stiffly. 'I don't see you with any books.'

'Books?' Tess was still trying to figure out what *not always straightforward* might mean.

'Schoolbooks,' he said patiently. 'I hope you haven't forgotten that teaching is going to be part of your duties with Samantha?'

'Not on day one, surely?'

'I'm not a believer in putting off for tomorrow what can be done today.'

'Yes, well... I thought that I would get to know her first, before I start trying to teach her the importance of fractions and decimals...'

'Ah. I'm glad to see that you've dropped your defeatist approach and got with the programme!'

'I don't have a defeatist approach! Really I don't.' She had thought a lot about what he had said to her, about her waving a white flag, and decided that he had been way off target. She had always firmly believed herself capable of doing anything. Why else would she have attempted so many varied jobs in the past?

Matt held up his hand to silence her. 'No matter. Samantha's collection of tutors have left a number of books over the course of the past few months. You'll find them in the study. Most are untouched,' he added, his mouth tightening. 'I'm hoping that you prove the exception to the rule.'

'I *did* warn you that I'm not academic...'

'I've tried the academics,' Matt pointed out. 'None

of them worked out. Why do you keep running yourself down?'

'I don't.'

'If you insist on labelling yourself as stupid then don't be surprised when the world decides to agree with you.'

'Wait just a minute!'

He had spun around to lead the way, but now he turned slowly on his heels and looked at her with mild curiosity.

'I'm not *stupid*.' Tess had had time to realise that she couldn't cave in to his much stronger, more dominant personality. It wasn't in her nature to make a fuss, but she would have to stand firm on what she believed or let him ride roughshod over her. 'I could have got very good grades, as it happens.'

'Then why didn't you? Was it easier to fail for lack of trying rather than risk trying to compete with your brilliant sisters and not do quite as well? Okay, I withdraw my remark about your being lazy, but if you want to prove your abilities to me then you've got to step up to the plate. Stop apologising for your lack of academic success and start realising the only thing I care about is that you drop the assumption that you can't teach my daughter. She's in the kitchen, by the way.'

Behind him, Tess quietly bristled. While he explained the working hours of his various housekeepers, who took it in turns to come in during the week to ensure that his apartment was never allowed to accumulate a speck of dust, Tess mulled over what he had said like a dog with a bone. She had blithely gone through life doing as she liked, only half listening to her parents' urgings that she settle down and focus. Claire and Mary were focused. In her own good-natured way she had stubbornly refused to be pushed into a way of life which she thought she couldn't handle. No one had ever bluntly said the things that Matt had said to her, or implied that she was a coward, scared of looking like a failure next to her sisters. She told herself that he knew nothing about her—but his words reverberated in her head like a nest of angry wasps.

She nearly bumped into him when he stopped at the kitchen door. She stepped past him to see her charge sitting at the kitchen table, hunched over a bowl of cereal which she was playing with—filling the spoon with milk, raising it high above the bowl and then slowly tilting the milk back in, unconcerned that half of it was splashing onto the fine grainy wood of the table.

Tess didn't know what she had expected. One thing she really *hadn't* expected was, glancing sideways, to see the shuttered look of pained confusion on Matt's face, and for a few powerful seconds she was taken aback by the burst of sympathy she felt for him.

He was tough and uncompromising and, yes, judgemental of her in a way that left her trembling with anger—yet in the face of his daughter he literally didn't know what to do.

Frankly, nor did she. Stubborn, sulky ten year olds had never featured even on her horizon.

'Samantha. Look at me!' He shoved his hands in his pockets and frowned. 'This is Tess. I told you about her. She's going to be your new nanny.'

Samantha greeted this by propping her chin in her hands and yawning widely. She was probably wearing the most expensive clothes money could buy, but Tess had never seen a child dressed with such old-fashioned lack of taste. Clumpy brown sandals and a flowered sleeveless frock. Silk, from the look of it. What ten-year-old ever wore silk? Her long hair was braided into two plaits with, of all things, ribbons neatly tied into bows at the ends. She was dark-haired, like her father, with the same stubborn, aristocratic set to her features. She would doubtless be a beauty in time, but just at the moment her face was sullen and set.

Tess cleared her throat and took a couple of steps forward. 'Samantha! Hi! Okay, you really don't have to look at me if you don't want to...' She giggled nervously, which earned her a sneaky glance, although the spoon and milk routine was still in full force. 'But I'm new to this place so...' She frantically thought of the one thing she and a ten-year-old girl might have in common. 'Do you fancy exploring the shops with me? My sister doesn't wear the same stuff that I do, and I'm far too scared to venture into some of those department stores without someone to hold my hand...'

'Well, it went okay.'

This was the debriefing. When Matt had called her on her mobile, to tell her that he would expect daily reports of progress, she had been at a loss for words. But expect it he did. In his office. Six sharp, after she had handed over her charge to Betsy, the girl who came in to prepare the evening meal.

The very same car that had collected her in the morning had duly collected her from his apartment and delivered her, like a parcel, to his offices, which occupied some prime real estate in downtown Manhattan.

Having seen where he lived, Tess had been more blasé about where he worked. She'd been swept up twenty-eight storeys and hadn't been surprised to find that his office occupied half of the entire floor, with its own sitting room, meeting room, and a massive outer office with chairs and plants, where a middle-aged woman had been busy packing up to go home.

'Define *okay*.' He leaned back into his leather chair and folded his hands behind his head. 'Take a seat.'

He could hardly believe how easily and effortlessly she had managed to break the ice with Samantha. Compared to the other nannies he had hired, who had smiled stiffly and tried to shake hands and had thereby seemed to seal their fate.

Tess shrugged. 'We're still a long way from being pals, but at least she didn't give me my marching orders.'

'She spoke to you?'

'I asked her questions. She answered some of them.' His low opinion of her still rankled, but she would rise above that if only to prove to herself that she could. 'She hates her wardrobe. I think we bonded there. I'm sorry but I'm going to have to turn down your request to purchase "loose" clothing. I can't take your daughter shopping for young, trendy stuff and then buy drab, tired stuff for myself...'

'Young, trendy stuff?'

'Do you know that she's never owned a pair of ripped jeans?'

'Ripped jeans?'

'Or trainers. I mean proper trainers—not the sort you get for school sports.'

'What *are* proper trainers?'

Matt looked at her. She was flushed, her skin rosy and dewy from walking in the heat, and her hair was up in a high ponytail with long caramel strands escaping around her face. In every conceivable way she was the complete antithesis of any woman he had ever gone out with—including his ex-wife. Vicky, his girlfriend, was striking, but in a controlled, intelligent, vaguely *handsome* way, with short brown hair and high cheekbones, and a dress code that consisted almost entirely of smart suits and high heels. And Catrina, while not a career woman, had descended from old money and had always dressed with subtle, refined, understated glamour. Cashmere and pearls, and elegant knee-length skirts.

He could easily believe that Samantha had never owned a pair of ripped jeans, or faded jeans, or possibly even *any* jeans. As far as he could remember neither had his ex-wife.

He felt his imagination do the unthinkable and begin to break its leash once more, throwing up all sorts of crazy images of the fresh faced girl in front of him.

She was telling him about *'proper trainers'* and he was appalled to discover that he was barely taking in a word she was saying. Instead, he was fighting to dismiss thoughts of what she looked like out of those tight jeans and that small green vest with its indistinct logo of a rock band. It was a primitive urge that had no place in his rigidly controlled world.

'Anyway, I hope you don't mind, but I bought her

one or two things. Trainers, jeans, a few tops from the market...'

'You bought her stuff *from a market*?'

'A lot trendier. Oh, gosh, I can tell from your expression that you don't approve. Don't you ever go to a market to shop?' It was an innocuous question, but for some reason it shifted the atmosphere between them. Just a small, barely noticeable shift, but she was suddenly and uncomfortably aware of his almost black eyes resting on her, and the way her body was responding to his stare.

'I've never been to a market in my life.'

'Well, you don't know what you're missing. One of my friends used to work at a market on the weekends, before she went to college to do a course in jewellery-making. I know a lot about them. Quite a bit of what gets sold is imported rubbish, but some of it's really, really good. Handmade. In fact, I thought at one point that *I* could go into that line of business...' Her cheeks were bright with enthusiasm.

'Never mind. You're here now,' Matt said briskly. 'Tell me what your plans are for the rest of the week. Have you had a chance to discuss the business of schoolwork with her?'

'Not yet...it's only been one day! I *did* glance at those books you mentioned, though...when we got back to the apartment and Samantha was having a bath...'

'And?'

Tess opened her mouth to let him know in advance that she had never been that good at the sciences, and then thought better of it. 'And I suppose I can handle some of it.'

'That's the spirit! Now all we have to do is devise a curriculum...'

'She's nervous about going to school here,' Tess blurted out. 'Has she told you that?'

Matt shifted uncomfortably in his chair. 'I hope you reassured her that there is nothing to worry about.' He papered over the fact that he and Samantha had barely had *any* meaningful conversations since she had arrived in Manhattan.

'It's *your* job to reassure her of that.' Tess looked at him squarely in the eyes. Confrontation had always been something she had studiously avoided. She could remember many an argument between her sisters, both intent on emerging the winner, and had long ago reached the conclusion that nothing was worth the raised voices and the heated exchanges—except she wasn't going to duck under the radar now and assume responsibility for something she knew wasn't hers.

'I've been thinking...' she ventured tentatively.

'Should I be alarmed?'

'You have all these rules that I'm supposed to follow...'

Matt threw back his head and laughed, and then, when he had sobered up, directed a grim look at her. 'That's what normally happens when you do a job for someone else. I've taken a big risk on you, and you're being richly rewarded, so don't imagine for a second that you can start trying to negotiate on some of the things you're supposed to do.'

'I'm not trying to negotiate anything!' Tess said heatedly. 'I just think that if there are all these rules for me, then there should be some rules for you.'

Matt looked at her incredulously, and then he burst out laughing again.

'What's so funny?'

'What *you* seem to consider rules most people would consider their job description. Is that how you approached all those jobs you had? With the attitude that you weren't prepared to work for anyone unless they were prepared to bend their rules to accommodate *you*?'

'Of course not.' When things had become too tedious she had simply given up, she thought uncomfortably. 'And I'm not trying to bend any rules.' What *was* it about this man that fired her up and made her argumentative?

'Okay. Spit it out, then.'

'I made a little list.' She had scribbled it in the car on the way over. Several times she had ever asked Stanton, the driver, what he remembered about his childhood—what stood out in his head about the things he had done with his parents that he had really enjoyed.

Matt took the list and read it through. Then he read it again, his expression of disbelief growing by the minute.

'"Monday night,"' he read aloud. '"Monopoly or Scrabble or some sort of board game as agreed upon. Tuesday night, cookery night."' He looked at her flushed, defiant face. '"Cookery night"? What the hell is *cookery night*?'

'Cookery night is an evening when you and Samantha prepare something together. It could be anything. A cake, perhaps, or some cookies. Or you could be even more adventurous and go for something hot. A casserole.'

'Cakes? Cookies? Casseroles?' His voice implied that she had asked him to fly to the moon and back. 'Isn't that *your* job?' he asked with heavy sarcasm. 'Correction. It shouldn't be a question. It's a statement of fact. Everything on this list consists of things *you* should be doing. In case you'd forgotten, my work keeps me out of the house for long periods of time.'

'I understand that you're a workaholic—'

'I'm not a workaholic.' He considered crumpling the list and chucking it into the bin, but was tempted to carry on reading. 'I run a company. Various companies. Believe it or not, it all takes time.'

'DVD night' was scheduled for Wednesday. He couldn't remember the last time he had watched a DVD. Who had time to sit in front of the television for hours on end? How productive was *that*?

'You have to make time for Samantha,' Tess told him stubbornly. 'I don't think you even know how scared she is of joining a new school. All her friends were at her school in Connecticut. She's terrified of making new ones!'

'Understandable, but kids adapt easily. It's a known fact.'

'That's easy for you to say,' Tess retorted, digging her heels in and refusing to budge. 'I can remember how scary it was going to secondary school! And I *knew* people who would be going with me. Just the thought of new teachers and new schoolbooks...'

'You didn't see it as a challenge you could rise to? No, maybe not, if you refused to settle down and do the work. But this isn't about you, and you're not Samantha. Granted, things haven't been easy for her, but being surrounded by new kids her own age will be a good thing. I'm *not*,' he said heavily, 'asking her to forget all the people she knew in Connecticut…'

'Maybe it feels that way to her.' Tess despaired of getting through to him. Where she had always seen the world in shades of grey, he seemed to see it entirely in black and white. Which, she wondered, was worse? The shades of grey that had prevented her from ever focusing on any one thing, or the black and white that seemed to prevent *him* from letting go of the reins for a second?

'What,' he asked, looking down at the list, 'is a "talking evening…"?'

'Ah. That one. I *was* going to slot in a games night…'

'I thought we had a Games night—where we play "Monopoly or Scrabble or some sort of other board game as agreed upon…"'

'I mean perhaps, take her to a rugby game. Maybe not rugby. Not in America, anyway. A soccer game. Or basketball. Or baseball. But then I really can't see you getting into any of that stuff.'

'Ah, *those* games. For guys who aren't workaholics…'

'You're not taking any of this seriously, are you?'

Matt looked at her speculatively. *Was* he taking any of it seriously? None of the previous nannies had presented him with lists before. He didn't think that any of them would have had the nerve. In fact he couldn't think, offhand, of anyone working for him who would have had the nerve to tell him what he should and shouldn't do.

On the other hand, none of the other nannies had had the success rate that she had—even after one day.

'Okay—here's the deal.' He sat back and folded his hands behind his head, the very picture of the dominant male. 'I'll consider some of your suggestions, but you'll have to be present.'

'Sorry?'

'Baking cookies and cakes... What do I know about that? My housekeeper looks after that side of things, or else I ensure food of the highest standard is delivered.'

'You just have to follow a recipe,' Tess pointed out. Did he even possess a recipe book? She hadn't seen any in the kitchen. Maybe he had a stash of them in his library—although she doubted that.

Matt stood up abruptly and walked towards the window, looking down at the matchstick figures scurrying along the pavements and the small yellow taxis like a toddler's play-cars.

'Have you shown this list to my daughter?' he asked, turning around to look at her.

In return she frowned at him. 'Not yet. I did it in the car on the way over. I mean, I *would* have had it typed out, but I...I didn't have time.'

'Then how do you know that she's going to go along with any of these schemes?'

'They're not *schemes*.'

'Okay. Ideas. Suggestions. Brainwaves. Call them what you want. How do you know that she's going to be keen to...let's say...play a board game for two hours?'

'Oh. Right. I see what you mean.'

'I very much doubt that,' Matt said irritably. 'Kids

these days prefer to sit in front of their computers. It's how they connect with their friends. Samantha has a very advanced computer. It was one of the first things I bought for her when she came here to live with me.'

'I'll do it,' Tess decided. 'If you need me around, then I'll do it.'

Need was a word that didn't feature heavily in his vocabulary—not insofar as it applied to him, at any rate. He opened his mouth to point that out, and then realised that, like it or not, the prospect of trying to coax a positive reaction from his daughter whilst trying to appear relaxed in front of a game of Scrabble was the equivalent of looking up at an insurmountable precipice and trying to work out how to scale it in a pair of flip-flops.

'It's hardly a question of need,' he stated, frowning.

'Some men find it difficult to take time out for quality family time...'

'Spare me the psychobabble, Tess.'

He met her eyes and for a split second she felt almost dizzy. She wondered whether it was because she was just so unused to any of this. Standing up for something and refusing to back down. Telling a man like Matt Strickland—who was her sister's *boss*, for goodness' sake—that he *should* be doing stuff, when it was obvious that no one *ever* told him what he should be doing. Getting involved enough to go beyond the call of duty for a job she had been reluctant to accept in the first place.

Her mouth went dry and she found that she was sitting on her hands, leaning forward in her chair. Crazy!

'It's not psychobabble,' she said faintly. 'It's the

truth! What activity would you...would you like to start with?'

'Ah. A choice?' Matt looked at the list. 'You do realise that choosing to participate in these activities will curtail your free time in the evenings?'

'That's okay.'

'I'll make sure that you're paid overtime, of course.'

'I don't care about the money,' Tess muttered, looking in fascination at his downbent head as he continued to frown over the list, as though trying to work out which was the most acceptable of the options on the table.

'But you might,' he murmured, not looking at her, 'regret committing to something that's going to involve time you might otherwise spend seeing New York...going out and having fun. Isn't that going to be a problem?'

Quite suddenly he raised his eyes to hers, and there it was again—that giddy feeling as though she was free-falling through space.

'Why should it be a problem?' she asked breathlessly.

'Because,' Matt murmured, 'you're young, and I've gathered that you came here to have fun. Since when has your definition of *fun* been spending time with your employer and his daughter, playing a game of Scrabble?'

Never, Tess thought, confused.

'Right.' He stood up, and she hastily followed suit. Her allotted time was over. 'First of all, you will be reimbursed—whether you like it or not. And as for which activity takes my fancy...having done none of them for longer than I can remember...'

He grinned. A smile of genuine amusement. And

for a few heart-stopping seconds he ceased to be Matt Strickland, the man who was employing her, the man who represented just the sort of staid workaholic that she privately abhorred, and was just a man. A suffocatingly sexy man who made her head spin.

'Your choice. I'll be home tomorrow by six.'

CHAPTER THREE

'OKAY. So let me get this straight. You've now got your-self a clothes allowance, no limits, and *you're going on a date with my boss.*'

'It's not a date,' Tess said irritably, but she was only half concentrating on Claire who was lounging fully clothed in a tight green dress with high heels—also green. Claire was killing time before going out with the guy she had been seeing for the past eighteen months—an investment banker whom Tess had met several times and liked very much, despite the fact that the second he left the room she could never seem to quite remember what he looked like.

'No? What is it, then? Cosy restaurant? Bottle of Chablis? Candlelight? No one's ever had a clue as to what Matt Strickland does in his private life, and here you are, less than three weeks in, and *you're on a date.*'

Small and black or small and red? Tess was thinking, looking at the selection of outfits she had bought earlier that day. Five seconds of tussling with her moral con-science and she had shamelessly capitulated once inside the fashionable department store to which she had been directed—because, he had told her, he would be taking her to dinner to get her feedback, and she would need something fairly dressy to wear. Were it not for him, she'd reasoned to herself, she wouldn't have to spend money on clothes for restaurants she wouldn't be going to. So if he wanted to foot the bill, then why not?

Besides, Samantha had been having fun. They had made a deal. Tess would pretend to yawn inside the toy shops and Samantha would tap the over-sized face of her newly acquired Disney watch in boredom inside the grown-up clothes shops, and then they would break for lunch at a place upon which they had both agreed, and which was based on a menu of pizzas and burgers. Good, fortifying food before they dutifully visited some place of culture in the name of education.

Tess had discovered that in New York there was a cultural destination for every day of the week for at least a year. Having always considered places of culture as unutterably boring, she was slowly discovering that they weren't half bad—especially when being explored with someone with an equal lack of knowledge. Even if that particular someone happened to be a ten-and-nine tenths-of-a-year-old child. They would learn together along the way, and it had to be said that Samantha was as sharp as a tack. Indeed, Tess had delegated most of the guidebooks to her, and her job was to describe what they were looking at, including its history.

'I think I'll go red.'

'Why do you care if it's not a date?' Claire smirked, easing herself off the bed and dusting herself down. 'And please don't tell me again that it's not a date. For the past three weeks I've hardly seen you, and now you're off to a restaurant with him. Surely you've said everything there is to say over your games of Monopoly and your cinema evenings?'

'Has it been three weeks?' Yes. Yes, it had. Time seemed to be moving at the speed of sound. After her initial hesitation about getting involved with Matt and the tense relationship he had with his daughter, she seemed to have dived in—headlong. Games night—their first night—had been a muted success, and since then things had picked up because he had been making an effort. He was getting back to the apartment before seven without fail, and throwing himself into every activity with such enthusiasm that it was difficult not to be swept away along with him. Samantha, wary at first, was slowly beginning to thaw, beginning to really enjoy herself, and it was hard not to be caught up in the changing tide.

'It's a *debriefing*,' Tess concluded. 'And I only wish I didn't have to go. I'd much rather be living it up in Manhattan on a Friday night out with you and Tom. Okay, maybe not you and Tom, but with other people. Young, exciting people. Artists and writers and poets.' The sort of people she thought she *should* be thrilled to hang out with, in other words. 'I haven't really had a chance to report back to Matt on how things are going with Samantha. This is purely about my job. I think I've put on weight. Have I put on weight? This dress feels a bit snug.'

'Tess…' Claire said hesitantly. 'You're not going to do anything stupid, are you?'

'Anything stupid? Like what?'

'I don't know what Matt Strickland gets up to in his

personal life, but there's a reason why he is where he is today. He's tough and he's pretty ruthless…'

'What are you trying to say?'

'Don't fall for the guy.'

'I wouldn't!' Tess turned to her sister. 'My dream guy isn't a high-flier who wants to make money. You know that. My dream guy is down to earth and sensitive, and when I find him I'll recognise him.'

'That's not how life works.'

'I'm just doing my job, and for the first time in my life I'm actually enjoying what I'm doing. You have no idea what it's like to see Matt and Samantha together. Okay, it's not perfect, but it's beginning to work, and I'd like to think that I've had something to do with that. It seems to me that the whole world wants me to settle down and find something I wants to stick with. I think I've found it. I like children and I like working with them. It's something positive that I'm going to take away from this whole experience and please don't confuse that with anything else!'

It was the first time she had come even close to being at odds with her sister, and she relented as soon as she saw Claire's shocked expression.

'I can take care of myself, so don't worry about me. I'm not falling for Matt Strickland! I'm getting to know him. And the only reason I'm getting to know him is because I need to for the sake of his daughter.'

She could have added that Matt Strickland had become three-dimensional, and that her head was slowly becoming crowded with images of him. Matt frowning in concentration in front of a recipe book for beginners she and Samantha had bought three days ago. Matt exultant when he managed to buy a hotel and charge exorbitant rent in a game of Monopoly. Matt teasing but tentative as his daughter brought him hesitantly into her life in Connecticut over the images of her friends on her computer.

This dinner, she knew, was purely about business. He would point out any areas of concern he had with her. He would see room for improvement. No need for nerves, and no need to be unsettled by anything Claire had said.

For the first time Tess was beginning to get a handle on just how much she had been protected through the years by her parents and by her sisters. They had allowed her to retreat from the competitive race academically. Claire and Mary had indulged her when she had turned her back on schoolwork. Had they felt sorry for her because they'd known how impossible it would be to live up to the standards they had set? Or had they enjoyed vicariously living a different kind of life through her? A life without responsibilities? And her parents had been almost as bad. No wonder Claire now thought that she was incapable of protecting herself when it came to the big, bad world! The fact was that she was finally growing up. She was taking on responsibilities. She was more equipped now that she had ever been to deal with whatever life threw at her.

Self-confidence restored, she slipped on the red dress, stuck on high, wedge-heeled sandals with delicate straps, and then stood back and examined her reflection in the mirror.

She didn't often do this—stare critically at herself in the mirror—but doing it now, really taking time to see how she looked, she wasn't disappointed. She would never be tall and spindly, but she looked okay. Her hair was loose and it shone, and she was already acquiring a healthy glow from the baking summer sun. Claire and Mary both had a typically Irish complexion: dark hair, pale skin with a hint of freckles, and of course the family trademark—bright green eyes. Tess, however, was warmer in colour, and it showed. The sun had also lightened her hair. She wasn't blonde, but lighter, with more varied shades of caramel.

With Claire loitering somewhere outside, ready to resume their conversation, Tess waited until Matt's driver paged her on her cell phone and then hurried out of the apartment, stopping to peep into the kitchen only to announce that she was off.

After three weeks she had become accustomed to being driven around New York. She no longer felt like royalty inside the limo, and she was hardly aware of the streets slipping by until the car finally stopped outside an elegant restaurant—just the sort of restaurant that would have chucked her out had she turned up in her normal gear of jeans and a tee shirt.

Stanton, Matt's driver, swooped round to open the car door for her.

Inside, a small foyer opened to an expanse of gleaming wooden floors and circular tables with starched white linen tablecloths and comfortable brown leather chairs. Every table seemed to be full of people chattering and, frankly, looking unashamedly glamorous. It was almost as though a Hollywood director had decided to film a movie inside a restaurant and supplied his own cast.

CATHY WILLIAMS 55

Two impressive wooden tables were home to the most towering vases of flowers Tess had ever seen. White lilies intricately laced around a honeycomb of twisted driftwood neatly partitioned the restaurant, so that there was at once an atmosphere of pleasant busyness that was yet strangely intimate.

Even by the impossibly high standards of opulence to which she had been exposed, this was in a league of its own, and Matt, sipping a drink and waiting for her in the most private corner of the restaurant, looked perfectly at ease in the surroundings.

Nervous tension beaded her upper lip, and suddenly, unexpectedly, her body was doing strange things. For a few seconds her breathing seemed to stop, and—perversely—her heart began beating so fast that it felt as though it would burst out of her chest. Her mind had shut down. There was not a thought in her head. Even the sound of the diners and the clatter of cutlery faded to a background blur.

He was wearing a black jacket that fitted him like a glove, and the white of his shirt threw the aristocratic harsh angles of his face into stunning prominence. He looked vibrant and drop-dead gorgeous, and she almost faltered in her high heels as she walked towards him.

In the act of lifting his glass to his lips, he seemed to still too.

Suddenly self-conscious, and embarrassed at being caught red-handed in the act of staring, Tess plastered a brilliant smile on her lips as she weaved her way towards him.

'I didn't realise that we would be having a meeting in such grand surroundings,' she carolled gaily, making sure to get the conversation onto neutral work-orientated territory as soon as possible. If nothing else, it did wonders to distract her from the glimpse of hard-muscled chest just visible where the top two buttons of his shirt were undone, and the way his fine dark hair curled alluringly around the dull silver strap of his watch.

Matt tore his eyes away from her and glanced round at the sumptuous décor which he casually took for granted. 'The food's good. It's the reason I keep coming back here. French food always makes a change from steak.'

'Not nearly as good as the spaghetti Bolognese your daughter cooked for you a few days ago, though. You have no idea how long it took us to stockpile all the ingredients. Everything had to be just right. The mushrooms. The shallots. The quality of the mince.'

Tess was babbling. Where had this sudden attack of nerves come from, she wondered. She had seen enough of Matt Strickland in the past few weeks to have killed any nerves she might have around him, surely? But her pulses were still racing and her mouth still felt dry, even after the two hefty sips of wine she'd gulped down from the crystal wine glass in front of her.

'And let's not go into the length of time it took us to find just the right recipe book,' she confided. 'I think Samantha looked at every single one at three separate bookshops. I had to stop her from trying to wheedle me into buying her a pasta machine. Can you believe it? I told her that it might be better to start simple and then move on to the complicated stuff. You...er...have an incredibly well-equipped kitchen. Everything new and shiny...' She trailed off in the face of his unnerving silence. 'Why aren't you saying anything?' she asked awkwardly. 'I thought you wanted me here to talk about how things were coming along with Samantha.'

'You have a way of running away with the conversation,' Matt murmured. 'It's always interesting to see where it's going to lead.'

Tess tried and failed to take that as a compliment. The smile she directed at him was a little wobbly at the edges. 'You make me sound like a kid,' she said in a forced voice, and he tilted his head to one side, as though giving that observation some thought.

'Maybe that's why you've worked out so well as her nanny.' He flashed her a veiled amused look, but for some reason Tess was finding it hard to see the funny side. 'The other nannies the agency supplied were nothing like you. They were far more regimented. Samantha refused to be told what to do, ran circles around them, and they eventually ended up handing in their notice. The more she had, the more I gave instructions to the agency that the next one should be stricter. I can see now that it was completely the wrong ploy. I should have been trying to find someone who was more on her level.'

'How many did she have?'

'Five—although one only lasted three days. They did their best to discipline her. In nine times out of ten they might have had success with that approach...'

'*I* discipline her,' Tess interrupted defensively.

'Do you? How?'

'If you don't like the way I do things...'

'Don't be ridiculous, Tess. Haven't I just told you how well I think you're doing? You've achieved wonders in a matter of weeks!'

'But I don't want you to think that the only reason

I've succeeded is because I let her do exactly what she wants! You gave me permission to get her a new wardrobe of clothes. Do you remember I discussed this with you? Do you remember I told you to look around at the other kids her age in New York and see what they were wearing? When she goes to her new school she might find it easier if she shows up in the same sort of clothes as everyone else. I said all this to you and you agreed! So we went shopping and, yes, some of her things *did* come from markets, but she'd never been to a market before. She enjoyed the experience!'

'How have we landed up here?'

'We've landed up here because…because…' What should have been a cool, businesslike conversation in relaxed surroundings was falling apart at the seams— and it was *her* fault. Was it any wonder that he was staring at her as though she had taken leave of her senses? He had complimented her on her progress and she had responded by snapping. She was miserably aware that she had snapped because she didn't want him implying that she was somehow immature, and she wasn't sure why she cared.

'Because it hasn't all been about Samantha having fun. I've had to really coax her out of her shell, and I admit it's easier to coax a child when you dangle something in front of her that she wants. But I've also been doing schoolwork with her…'

'Yes. I know.'

'You do?'

'She's told me.'

Tess didn't miss the flash of quiet satisfaction that crossed his face, and she made a big effort to remind herself that *this* was why she so enjoyed the job. Because she had been instrumental in helping to heal some of the rifts between Matt and his daughter. And if Matt patted her on the back and patronisingly complimented her on getting the job done because she was immature enough to win over her charge, then so be it.

'You've proved yourself wrong.' He leaned back in the chair as menus were placed in front of them and more wine was poured into glasses. 'How does that feel?'

'I've only gone through the basic stuff with her,' Tess mumbled, blushing.

'It's a mountain when your starting point was insisting that you were incapable of doing simple maths and science.'

A slow, palpable sense of pleasure radiated through her, made her feel hot and flustered, and although she knew that his dark, lazy eyes were on her, she couldn't bring herself to meet them.

'Well, I won't be taking a degree course in them any time soon.' Tess laughed breathlessly.

Claire might have given her long lectures about his ruthlessness, but this was a side of him to which she had been not privy. Claire hadn't seen the complete human being. She had just seen the guy who issued orders and expected obedience.

'But doing something of which you didn't think yourself capable must have gone some distance to bolstering your self-confidence...'

Her eyes flew to his, and she had a few giddy seconds of imagining that those dark, deep, brooding eyes of his could see right down to the very heart of her. Her voice was shaky as she gave her order to the waiter, and when she thought that the conversation might move on she was greeted with a mildly expectant silence.

'I've always had bags of self-confidence,' she muttered eventually. 'You can ask either of my sisters. While they were buried under heaps of books, I was always out having a great time with my friends.' Why did she get the feeling that he didn't believe her? And his disbelief had to be infectious, because she was almost failing to believe herself. 'I may not be going out a great deal in the evenings now, because of my working hours,' she said, relentlessly pursuing the point even though he hadn't contradicted a word she had said, 'but I'm normally the kind of girl who always had lots of invitations.'

'And you miss that?'

'We're not here to talk about me.'

'But in a way we are,' Matt pointed out smoothly. 'You spend more time with my daughter than I do. It's important for me to know your frame of mind. I wouldn't want to think that you might be storing up resentments. So…you've spent most of your evenings over the past few weeks at my apartment. Does that bother you? When you're accustomed to spending your time going out with friends?'

He watched her fiddle with the stem of her wine glass. Her cheeks were flushed. Her thick, straight, toffee-coloured hair hung like a silky curtain over her shoulders, halfway down her back. Amidst the plush, formal surroundings she looked very, very young, and suddenly he felt very, very old. A quick glance around him confirmed that there was almost no one in the restaurant under the age of fifty. The fabulously high prices excluded all but the very rich, and he was an exception when it came to being very rich and the right side of forty. He had grown up in an ivory tower and had never had cause to leave it. It discomfited him to think that curiosity, if nothing else, should have driven him out at least for a brief period of time.

Annoyed to find himself succumbing, even temporarily, to an unusual bout of passing introspection, Matt frowned, and Tess, seeing the change of expression, was instantly on her guard.

Was he going to tell her that she needed to stop spending her evenings at his home? Did he *disapprove*? Maybe he hankered after more one-to-one time with Samantha and she, blithely unconcerned, was in the process of just *getting in the way*.

Maybe she should suggest reverting to normal working hours...

Dismayed, Tess realised that she didn't want to do that. How had that happened? How had Matt Strickland and his daughter and their complicated family life suddenly become so integral to her day-to-day existence?

Her thoughts were in a whirl as food was placed in front of them—exquisite arrangements of shellfish and potatoes that Tess would have dived into with gusto were it not for the feverish whirring of her mind.

'I'll curtail my hours if you want me to,' she heard herself say in a small voice.

'I don't believe that's what I was asking you,' Matt told her impatiently. He had become accustomed to her never ending cheerfulness, and the despondent droop of her shoulders made him feel like the Grinch who stole

Christmas. 'You're my employee,' he said tightly. 'And I have certain obligations as your employer.'

Tess hated that professional appraisal. She realised that she didn't *want* him to have any obligations as the guy who had hired her, but when she started to think about what she *did* want her thoughts did that crazy thing again and became tangled and confusing.

'I wouldn't want you to turn around at some later date and accuse me of taking advantage of you.'

'I would never do that!' Tess was horrified and offended.

'You've insisted on forgoing any overtime payments...'

'You pay me enough as it is! I *like* sticking around in the evenings and helping out with Samantha.'

'Doesn't do much good for a social life for you, though, does it?'

'I didn't come over here to cultivate a social life,' Tess said firmly. Well, she admitted to herself, that *was* a bit of an exaggeration, thinking back to the dismay with which she had greeted the suggestion of a job, but that was in the past so it didn't count. 'I came here to try and get my act together and I have.' Her natural warmth was returning and she smiled at him. 'I feel like I've finally found something I really enjoy doing. I mean, I think I have an affinity with kids. I don't get bored with them. You'd be surprised how clever and insightful Samantha can be without even realising it. I can get all the socialising that I want when I get back home.' Which was something she wasn't going to start thinking about just yet.

'And do you socialise with anyone in particular there?'

'What do you mean?'

'You're an attractive young woman.' Matt shrugged and pushed aside his plate, which was swept up by a waiter seconds later. 'Left any broken hearts behind?'

'Oh, hundreds!' Tess said gaily. If he thought that she was immature and green around the ears, how much more cemented would that impression be if he knew that being 'one of the lads' and having loads of friends who happened to be boys was a far cry from having a solid relationship with one in particular.

'So was that part of the reason you came over here?'

'No!' Tess protested uncomfortably.

'Because no boy is worth it. Not at your age.'

'I'm twenty-three. Not thirteen.' Just in case he had missed that, which she suspected he had. Because she had never, not once, caught him looking at her with male interest. While she…Tess flushed and felt something scary and powerful stir in her, as though finally being allowed to take shape. *She* had looked at *him*. Released from their Pandora's Box, little snapshots of him began swirling in her head. The way he looked when he was laughing, the way he raised his eyebrows in lazy amusement, that half-smile that could send shivers down her spine—except it hadn't. Not until now.

Uncomfortable in her own skin, Tess struggled to get her thoughts in order while her innocuous remark hovered in the air between them, challenging him to assess her in a different way altogether.

As though the reins of his rigid self-control had

suddenly been snapped, Matt was assailed by a series of powerful, destabilising images. She might look young, with the stunning attraction of dewy skin and an open, expressive face that was a rare commodity in the hard-bitten world in which he lived, but she wasn't thirteen. She especially didn't look like a teenager in that dress she was wearing, which left just enough to get the imagination doing all sorts of interesting things. It took massive will-power to pull himself back from the brink of plunging headlong into the tempting notion of taking her to his bed.

She was his daughter's nanny! What the hell was going on in his head? It grated on him to know that this wasn't the first time he had played with the idea. He should know better. Work and play mixed as successfully as oil and water. He had never brought his private life to work and he wasn't about to start now. Tess Kelly might not hold down a job within the physical walls of his offices, but she was as much his employee as any one of the hundreds who worked for him.

And, even taking that small but vital technicality out of the equation, Tess Kelly didn't conform to anything he required from a woman. Having lived through the horror that had been his marriage, wedded in unhappy matrimony to a woman who had fulfilled all the requirements on paper and none in practice, as it turned out, his checklist when it came to women was stringent.

It was essential that they were as focused as he was. Focused and independent, with careers that were demanding enough to stave off any need for them to rely on him to define their lives. Like him, Catrina had come from old money, and her life had consisted of

fundraisers and charity balls and lunches and all those
other little things that had left her with plenty of time to
decide that his duty was to provide a never-ending diet
of excitement. There had been no need for her to work,
and she had, in any case, never been programmed for it.
And into the void of all those empty hours when he had
been working had crept the seeds of bitterness and dis-
enchantment. She had wanted a rich partner who wanted
to play, and he had failed to fulfil the specification. In
the aftermath of that experience, and the consequences
it came to entail, Matt was diligent in never straying
beyond his own self-imposed boundaries.

Belatedly, because she had been away and contact
between them had been sporadic and via e-mail, he
remembered Vicky. She was in Hong Kong, getting a
taste for the Eastern markets. She was due back in a
couple of days' time. He tried to pull up a memory of
what she looked like, but the second he thought of her
dark tailored bob and the neat precision of her personality another image of a bubbly, golden-haired girl with
a dusting of freckles on her nose and a personality that
was all over the place superimposed itself on the woman
who claimed to be dying to catch up with him.

Irritated, he frowned. Then his face cleared and that
vague feeling of being out of sorts began to ebb away.

'Tell me your plans for the next few days.' He pushed
himself away from the table and signalled to the waiter
for some coffees.

'Plans?' Still fretting over her tumultuous thoughts,
it took Tess a few seconds to register that he had completely changed the subject. 'A museum, and then a quiet
day just relaxing with Samantha tomorrow. Maybe I'll

grab an early evening and catch up with my social life, now that you've put that idea into my head.'

'And then on Friday perhaps we might visit the zoo...' said Matt.

This was a breakthrough. Instead of just following the tide, he was actually generating an idea of his own! Pure delight was all over her face as she nodded approvingly. She would take a back seat, watch father and daughter together, remind herself that her involvement with them both began and ended as a job.

And Matt, watching her carefully from under lowered lashes, calculated on Vicky's presence. The two of them, side by side, would squash uninvited rebellious thoughts for which he had no use. He and Vicky might not be destined for the long haul, but she would be a timely reminder of what he was looking for in the opposite sex.

Matters sorted satisfactorily, and feeling back in control, he signalled for the bill.

CHAPTER FOUR

OVER the next two days Tess had ample opportunity to think about herself. Matt had asked some very relevant questions, and had kick-started a chain of thoughts that made her uneasily aware that the things about herself she had always taken for granted might just be built on a certain amount of delusion.

She had always considered herself a free spirit. Her sisters had been the unfortunate recipients of their parents' ambitions. Neither of their parents had gone to university. Their mother had worked as a dinner lady at the local school, and their father had held down a job in the accounts department at an electrical company. But, they were both really clever, and in another time and another place would have gone to university and fulfilled all sorts of dreams. They hadn't, though, and consequently had taken an inordinate interest and delight in Claire and Mary's superhuman academic achievements.

Tess had set her own agenda from an early age and had never deviated. Just in case her parents got it into their heads that she was destined to follow the same path, she had firmly set her own benchmark.

She had always thought that she loved *living* too much to waste time hiding away in a room in front of a pile of books. She liked *sampling* things, getting a taste for different experiences. She refused to be tied down and she had always been proud of her thirst for freedom.

Matt's take on things had badly damaged that glib acceptance. She wondered whether her happy-go-lucky attitude stemmed from a deep-rooted fear of competition. If you didn't try, then you weren't going to fail—as he had said to her on day one—and she had never tried and so had never set herself up for a fall. She had been offended and resentful at his implication that she lacked self-confidence, and yet she knew that she had never made the most of her talents. Underneath the pretty, popular, happy-go-lucky girl, had there always been an anxious, scared one, covering up her insecurities by wanting to be seen as the antidote to her sisters? Had she cultivated her social life—always being there for other people, always willing to lend a hand and always in demand—because that had helped her prove to herself that she was every bit as valuable as her two clever sisters?

Tess didn't like this train of thought, but, having started, she was finding it impossible to stop. One thought seemed to generate another. It was as though a locked door had suddenly been flung open and out had spilled all manner of lost, forgotten and deliberately misplaced things from her childhood.

For the first time she had no inclination to share her thoughts with her sister, indeed, was relieved that Claire had taken herself off for a week's break with Tom and wouldn't be returning until the middle of the following week.

As she was getting ready on Friday morning for their

expedition to the zoo, Tess made herself address the other discomforting issue that had been nagging the back of her mind—the other loaded pistol that Matt had pointed at her head and forced her to acknowledge. *Why* had she suddenly jettisoned her social life? Why? She had arrived in Manhattan a carefree, fun-loving girl, with no thoughts beyond enjoying a lovely break from Ireland and perhaps trying to figure out what job to apply for when she returned. So how had she suddenly found herself in the position of willingly sacrificing her social life for the sake of a job? Why did the thought of going out and having a good time with young people her own age leave her cold? Of course she enjoyed Samantha, and loved the small changes in her personality she could detect as the days passed. It was rewarding to watch the person emerge from the protective, wary shell—like watching a butterfly emerge from its cocoon—but beyond that she just really liked being in Matt's company because she fancied him.

Tess hadn't recognised that for what it was because she didn't think she had ever truly fancied anyone before. She had never questioned all those stolen glances and the way her body responded when he was around. Even now, as she wriggled into a navy and white striped vest and brushed out her hair before tying it up into a ponytail, she could feel her body tingling at the thought of seeing him. *That* was why she had thought nothing of putting her social life on hold. *That* was why she was happy to spend evenings at his apartment, sometimes just sitting cross-legged on the sofa with Samantha, watching something on the telly, while on the chair close by Matt pretended to watch with the newspaper in front of him and a drink at his side.

Tess felt a little thrill of excitement race through her. She was in lust, and it felt good even if nothing would come of it. Because she certainly hadn't caught him stealing any glances at *her*, and she couldn't imagine him thinking about her in some way—not the way she realised she thought about him.

Tess could only assume that the very sheltered life she had led was the reason why she was only now feeling things that most women her age would have felt long ago. Where her sisters had flown the nest and pursued university degrees, then moved to new, exciting cities to begin their illustrious careers, she had remained at home, circulating with more or less the same crowd she had grown up with—a protective little circle that had, she could see now, been comforting and restrictive in equal measure. She felt as though she was finally emerging from cold storage. It was exciting. And who knew what lay round the corner? she thought, with the optimism with which she had always greeted most situations.

The journey to Pelham Parkway was baking hot, but she had dressed for the heat in a pair of cool linen trousers and flip-flops. It was going to be a long day. The zoo was enormous—one of the largest urban zoos. She had agreed with Matt that she would contact him by text as soon as she arrived, so that they could agree a meeting point, but with this new awareness of him burning a hole in her she found herself texting Samantha instead, and then making her way to a convenient spot where she could wait for them to finish their animal sightseeing on the monorail.

On the way, her stomach rumbling, she bought herself a giant hot dog, and was sinking her teeth gratefully into the eight-inch sausage, onion, ketchup and mustard indulgence when she spotted Samantha running towards her.

Samantha was no longer the primly dressed ten-year-old of a few weeks ago. She was in a pair of trendy cut-off denims, some flat espadrilles and a tee shirt that advertised a teenage musical.

'Have a bite.' Tess offered the hot dog to her and stood up. 'I'm never going to finish this.' She was driven to search out Matt, but resisted the impulse.

'I thought you were giving up junk food.' Samantha took the hot dog and smiled up at her. 'Because you were piling on the pounds.'

'Next Monday. I have it pencilled in my diary.'

'Anyway, they're waiting for us, so we'd better go.'

'They...?'

'Vicky was tired and had to rest, even though she's been sitting on the monorail for twenty minutes.' Samantha made a face while Tess confusedly tried to compute a name that meant nothing to her and had never been mentioned before. Was Vicky a relative?

She hurried after Samantha, and after a few minutes came to a shuddering halt by a café—one of the many that were dotted around the zoo. It was packed. Kids were eating ice cream, infants with more common sense than the adults were howling in pushchairs because they were hot and sticky and wanted to leave. She could easily have missed the couple sitting at the back, because they were surrounded by families trying to find somewhere to sit and children being called back to tables by anxious parents. But her eyes were automatically drawn to Matt and she grinned, because he looked just as she would have expected him to look away from the comforts to which he was accustomed. He was a man who took for granted the bliss of air-conditioning in summer and the luxury of personal shoppers who did everything for him and spared him the inconvenience of having to do battle with crowds. It was a real indication of how determined he was to involve himself with his daughter that he would ever have suggested a zoo expedition and accepted this less than luxurious experience as a necessary consequence.

For a few seconds she found it hard to tear her eyes away from him. In a pair of light tan trousers and a navy blue polo shirt, he looked dark and sexy and dangerous. He was wearing dark sunglasses, which he proceeded to remove, and the thought of his eyes on her as she tried to manoeuvre a path through the crowds sent a little shiver down her spine.

She could fully understand how he had managed to turn her notion of sexual attraction on its head. She had foolishly assumed that because he represented the sort of man she didn't find attractive personality wise her body would just fall in line and likewise fail to respond. She hadn't bargained on the fact that her body would have a will of its own and would go haring off in the opposite direction.

Samantha had made it to him, and it was only when they were both looking at her that Tess took in the woman sitting next to him at the small, circular metal table. For a few seconds her steps faltered, because if this was a relative then she certainly wasn't a relative of the comfortable variety.

Holding a cup primly between her fingers, and with dark shades concealing all expression, was a strikingly attractive woman with an expertly tailored bob that was sharply cut to chin level. A pale lemon silk cardigan was casually draped over her shoulders.

Matt half stood as she reached the table but his companion remained seated, although she pushed the shades onto her head revealing cool brown eyes.

'Tess...I'd like you to meet Vicky.'

The expected return of his common sense was failing to materialise. It had been a trying morning. Samantha had been disappointed that their cosy party of three had expanded to include Vicky, and although Matt told himself that it was healthy for her to deal with the fact that Tess was not a member of the family he had still felt as though some of the progress he had made with his daughter had been somehow undermined by the inclusion of Vicky in their day out.

And then had come his disappointing reaction to seeing Vicky. His interest had not been re-ignited, and indeed he had been irritated by her.

She had had precious little contact with Samantha before her three week visit to Hong Kong, but had immediately seen fit to try and establish a relationship. He had been all too aware that his daughter had retreated into herself and had blamed him for this unwelcome development.

All in all, a bit of a nightmare, and now, seeing Tess

next to Vicky, he was already beginning to draw unwelcome comparisons.

'You're the nanny!' Vicky offered a cool smile. 'Matt's told me about you in his e-mails. What a blessing that you turned up when you did! This little thing has been super-naughty with her nannies—haven't you, sweetie? You're very young, aren't you?'

E-mails? Tess didn't like the thought of being discussed behind her back, and it was dawning on her that this was Matt's girlfriend. The fact that he even had one came as a shock, but as the reality of it began to sink in she wondered how on earth she could ever have expected otherwise. Men like Matt Stickland were never short of women throwing themselves at him. He was as rich as Croesus and sinfully good-looking. Now, in light of this, her silly infatuation with him—if it could even be called that—struck her as tellingly naïve.

This woman was far more the type he would go for, even if his body language was saying otherwise. She was clever and accomplished, and, as the day progressed, Tess was left in very little doubt that there was absolutely nothing the woman hadn't already achieved or else was about to.

Vicky talked non-stop. She tried to make jokes with Matt, who smiled stiffly and contributed very little to the conversation. She gave long, educational lectures to Samantha about every animal they passed and was undeterred by the silent, faintly hostile response. She confided in Tess every qualification she had ever gained and her progress in her career step by step, starting with when she was a lowly junior manager and culminating in her exalted position now, as CEO of one of the largest listed companies in America. She was smart and she was self-confident, and she had scaled heights in her career that most women might only ever dream of.

Matt wouldn't raise his eyebrows and make some dry, amused remark about *her* taste in television programmes. He would have informed discussions with her and talk about everything from the state of the economy to world politics.

Tess waited two and a half hours before she felt it polite to tell them that she would be on her way. Samantha, like her, was drooping, and had been for a while. A small, quiet bundle, shorn of the tentative beginnings of exuberance that had marked the past week or so.

What a hellish disaster, Matt thought in raging frustration. What the *hell* was Vicky's agenda? She had monopolised the conversation, glorified herself, done her level best to ingratiate herself with Samantha.

'You've hardly been here two minutes.' He frowned at Tess, who was fidgeting apologetically, playing with the clasp on the leather satchel slung over her shoulder. 'What do you mean *you're going*?'

'I have some stuff to do.'

'Your working day hasn't come to an end. It's not yet five-thirty.'

He felt, with considerable irritation, Vicky's arm link through his and the weight of her as she leant against him.

'We could go off and do something,' Samantha interjected in a cool, childish voice. 'Tess could drop me home. Couldn't you, Tess? We could even stop off and have something to eat on the way. Burgers and fries,' she added, because somewhere along the line there had been a long lecture from Vicky on the dangers of the wrong diet. At the time she had been focusing on the last of the hot dog disappearing into Samantha's mouth.

'You'll leave with us,' Matt rasped, sliding his eyes down to where his daughter was staring at him, sullen and tight-lipped. 'And I don't want any arguments, Samantha. I'm your father and you'll do as I say.'

In the sweltering heat, tempers were frayed. Tess miserably wondered whether Matt would rather have stayed at home with his girlfriend. Did his foul mood stem from the fact that he could think of better things to be doing with his time? Didn't he know that his relationship with Samantha was still so fragile that coming down heavy on her now was going to jeopardise everything they had begun building together?

She felt as though she had failed them both. She told herself stoutly that their relationship wasn't her concern, that she was just a ship in the night, passing through their lives, but right here, with people bustling around them and Samantha looking to be on the verge of tears, Tess suddenly felt miserable and depressed.

'I'll be at work bright and early on Monday morning,' Tess said brightly. 'Or we could even do something tomorrow, if you like…?' This was to Samantha, but Vicky was quick to step in, smiling and giving Matt's arm a gentle squeeze.

'We'll be fine.' Her voice was hard as nails. 'I just got back from the Far East. I'd quite like to have my little unit to myself over the weekend. Besides, don't you have anything better to do than spend your Saturday with a ten-year-old child?'

Those ringing words were a timely reminder to Tess that she needed to get her act together. Hadn't Matt mentioned something along those lines to her himself? Had he and his girlfriend been exchanging jokey e-mails about her? The sad little nanny with no life to speak of in one of the most exciting cities in the world?

The journey back to her sister's apartment was long and hot and tedious. The upside was that there would be no one around to question her tearful mood. The downside was that she did, actually, feel as though she needed a sympathetic shoulder to cry on.

Nothing could distract her from the sobering realisation that she had made a complete fool of herself by lusting after a man who wasn't interested in her. It was a sign of her own vanity—which was something she had never even known she *possessed*—that she hadn't once stopped to ask herself whether he was involved with a woman. There had seemed to be none on the scene, and he had mentioned no names, and so she had made her own incorrect conclusions.

It was a little after eight when the buzzer sounded. Claire had an intercom system in her flat. It was an excellent way of avoiding unwanted visitors. You could see them on the little television-style screen and then just duck low until they got the message and disappeared.

Her heart flipped when she made out Matt's face. He looked impatient and at the end of his tether, and she was determined to ignore him, but instead found herself picking up the phone to ask him what he wanted.

'You. I need to talk to you.'

'What about? I thought you were going to be spending

the weekend playing house with your girlfriend.' She clapped her hand to her mouth. 'I'm sorry I said that. I'm tired. Can it wait until Monday?'

'No. It can't. Buzz me up.'

'What's so important?' Tess persisted. 'I'm about ready to go to bed.'

'It's not even nine. It's a Friday evening. You're not ready to go to bed. Buzz me up.'

'What do you want!' was the first thing she asked when he was standing in the doorway, filling it out and sending her nervous system into frantic disarray. He was still in the clothes he had worn to the zoo. She, however, had changed, and was now wearing a pair of black pyjama bottoms and a small vest. No bra. She folded her arms and backed away, following him with her eyes as he strode into the apartment and headed directly to the kitchen.

'I think,' he said, opening the fridge and extracting a bottle of beer, which he proceeded to flick open after he had hunted down a bottle opener in one of the drawers, 'I need a drink.'

'Look, you can't just barge in here—'

'Your sister's away, isn't she? Visiting the boyfriend's parents, if I remember correctly?'

'Who is with Samantha? Is…is your girlfriend with her?'

Matt drained a quarter of the bottle in one long, thirsty gulp while looking at her as she hovered to the side, ill at ease and wary. Tension was climbing its way up her spine. What did he want? When she thought about the excitement that had infused her at the start of the day, when she had dressed with thoughts of him in her head, she felt humiliation washing over her all over again.

'Today didn't go as planned.' Matt finished the beer, wondered whether to have another. But he had already drunk too much for his own good—had had to get his driver to ferry him across to Tess's apartment. Hell, what else was alcohol for, if not to smooth away the rough edges of uncomfortable situations? He had made an appalling mistake in asking Vicky to accompany them. It had been a massive error of judgement. And for a man who could count his errors of judgement on the fingers of one hand, it tasted like poison. He helped himself to another beer and angled her a challenging look as she mutely stared at him, her mouth half open in surprise.

'No,' Tess agreed stiffly. Now that she was looking at the detail, she could see that his hair was rumpled and he looked a bit *askew*—a bit like a guy who wasn't completely in control of everything around him. Vulnerable, it struck her. 'If you'd wanted to spend time with your girlfriend, then a group outing might not have been the best idea. Or did you think that I would be a good buffer between your girlfriend and your daughter?'

Matt tilted his head back to swallow some beer and continued to stare at her.

Held reluctant captive by those dark, brooding eyes, Tess felt her skin begin to tingle—and she hated the feeling. It reminded her of how weak she had been to allow this man to climb under her skin. She hated the intensity of his silence. It felt as if he was sifting through her thoughts, turning her inside out and exposing all her doubts and weaknesses. He already seemed too capable of forcing her to face up to failings she hadn't known existed.

'Well?' She angled away from him and sank into one of the kitchen chairs. 'I got the impression that Vicky hadn't had a lot of contact with Samantha.'

'Almost none,' Matt agreed.

'So what was the grand plan, Matt? To get the nanny to pave the way for a happy family unit? Take some of the heat off your girlfriend?'

'Vicky was never a contender for a happy family unit.' He had been leaning against the wall. Now he pushed himself away, dumping the empty beer bottle on the counter *en route* to a chair, which he sat on, his big body indolent and relaxed under the influence of drink. Not too much, but certainly enough to paper over the sharp edges of his mood.

'Well, that's none of my business,' Tess muttered. Of their own volition, her eyes flicked towards him, taking in all the details of his body, and she realised that there was a familiarity to what she was seeing that was scary.

'Turns out—' he laughed shortly, stretched out his legs and stuck his hand in his trouser pocket '—that I was on my own when it came to that misconception.'

'I don't know what you're talking about. Have you been drinking?'

'Now, what would give you that idea?' His eyes locked with hers and there was a lazy amusement there that made her go hot and cold. Even when she hurriedly looked away, she could feel him *looking* at her in a way that he hadn't looked at her before—looking at her in a slow, leisurely way that made her want to fidget. 'I let that relationship get out of hand,' Matt mused. 'I took my eye off the ball. While I was under the impression that we were having a casual fling, it turns out that Vicky was making all sorts of plans.'

'What sort of plans?' Tess was fascinated to hear more. Matt had never breathed a word about his personal life, but she wasn't looking at the Matt she knew. She was tiptoeing on the very edge of seeing a side to him that hadn't been in evidence before, and she was eaten up with curiosity.

'Are you having fun?' He laughed softly under his breath and Tess flushed.

'Of course not! *You* came here, don't forget! And if you want to talk, then that's fine by me.'

'I actually didn't come here to talk about Vicky,' he murmured. He shifted in the chair, leaned back into it. 'You distract me.' He enjoyed the way she blushed madly when he said that, and leaned forward as though not quite believing her ears. 'You make me lose track of what I want to say.'

'*I'm* not making you lose track of anything,' Tess said briskly, but there was slow burn inside her that felt good.

'Oh, right. It's the demon drink. I'll stick to the agenda, in that case. My daughter has reverted to her old ways.' He leaned forward abruptly, elbows on thighs, and pressed his thumbs against his eyes.

His body language spoke a thousand words and Tess automatically moved towards him, hovered for a while, not quite knowing what to do, and eventually pulled her chair so that she was sitting right alongside him. Should she reach out and try to comfort him? Confused and addled, she opted for sitting on her hands.

'What do you mean?'

'I mean...' Matt looked directly at her and raked his hand through his hair. 'We got back to the apartment and she promptly proceeded to shut herself in the bedroom.'

'But didn't you go in to try and talk to her?'

'Of course I went in! She lay there with her back to me and her headphones stuck in her ears—and, *hell*, I can't *force* her to have a conversation with me, can I?'

'So what did you do?'

'I had a couple of whiskies in rapid succession. It seemed like a good idea at the time.'

'And Vicky...?'

'Dispatched. The point is, I'm back to square one.' His smile was tight and bitter. 'It seems that the ground I believed I'd covered was just a bit of wishful thinking.'

'That's not true!'

'No? Then perhaps you'd like to explain my daughter's lack of response?'

'She's ten years old! She's not capable of thinking things through in an adult way. She's had a disappointing day. I suppose she thought that she would have you to herself...'

'You mean have *both of us*...'

'No,' Tess said firmly. '*You*. She didn't bank on your girlfriend showing up, and she really didn't bank on her—I don't know—being so proprietorial...'

'Nor did I,' Matt muttered under his breath. Vicky had made *plans*! A stint in the Far East together, his daughter conveniently dispatched to a boarding school somewhere... She had even checked out possible acquisitions he could make once they were living in Hong Kong! He had been furious and appalled, and then had turned his wrath against himself—because, as he had told Tess, he had taken his eye off the ball and had reaped his just rewards. But his relationship with his daughter was the biggest casualty of his slip-up, and damn if he knew how he was going to rescue the situation.

'Samantha's not...'

'Not *what*?' he gritted into the developing silence. 'No need to tread on eggshells, Tess. I've already blown it. I think it's fair to say I can withstand whatever you have to say.'

'You haven't blown it! It's just that Samantha... Well, I don't think she ever really understood why she saw so little of you over the years.'

'She's told you this?'

'In bits and pieces. I mean, please don't think that we sat down one day and had a heart-to-heart, because we didn't. I don't think children of that age ever do. I don't think they know *how to*. But I've gleaned it over time.'

'You've *gleaned* it? And how did you respond?'

'What could I say? You've never spoken to me about your marriage...and, anyway, it wouldn't be my place to have that conversation with your daughter. That's something you would have to do. I thought, I guess, that you would. In time.'

'God. What an unholy mess.'

He looked wiped out, and she reached out and tentatively put her hand on his shoulder. When he responded by taking hold of it, she assumed it would be to politely dismiss her gesture of sympathy, but instead he kept hold of it, playing idly with her fingers with frowning concentration.

'Catrina and I were the perfect couple on paper.' Matt glanced at her, but Tess wasn't sure that he was seeing *her*. 'Our families knew each other. We moved in the same circles and came from the same background. I suppose you could say that there was an understanding—and the understanding was hastened along when Catrina fell pregnant. I wasn't gutted. Yes, I was young, but I was content to marry, and marry we did. With all the pomp and ceremony that vast wealth can buy. The cracks opened up almost immediately. Catrina was a socialite. I was an ingrained workaholic. She saw no reason why I should put time and effort into making money. As far as she was concerned my job should have been to lead the life of a playboy. Go skiing in winter for a couple of months. Take long summer holidays at her parents' house in the Bahamas. Take up golf. Lead a life that would complement hers.'

Tess tried and failed to picture Matt taking up golf and having long holidays. He was still playing with her hand, and it was doing all sorts of strange things to her body. Whilst she was desperate to concentrate one hundred percent on what he was saying, part of her was wrapped up with the tingling in her breasts, the dampness spreading between her thighs, the warm feeling in her belly that made her want to sigh and close her eyes.

'The more she nagged, the faster I withdrew into the

safety of work. We were a divorce waiting to happen, but I'm not sure it would have if I hadn't found out that my best man at the wedding had stepped in to carry out the duties she felt I was failing to do.'

Tess couldn't imagine what that would have done to a man as proud as Matt.

'My divorce was what dictated the relationship I developed with my daughter, and so here we are.' He gave her a crooked smile. 'Any thoughts?'

CHAPTER FIVE

'I DON'T understand. Surely the court would have awarded you joint custody, Matt?'

'A vengeful wife has a lot of tools at her disposal when it comes to making free and easy with court judgements,' Matt told her drily. 'Weekends were cancelled on a whim. I lost count of the number of times I travelled to Connecticut only to find that Catrina had taken Samantha off on a trip, destination unknown, leaving a bewildered maid to try and explain in broken English that there would be no visit that weekend. Toys were routinely left at an empty house. I never knew whether Samantha got them or not.'

Matt's eyes glittered with open pain and bitter regret. This was a man who opened up to no one, and Tess wasn't sure whether this flood of confidence and self-recrimination was something he would live to rue, but she stroked his face with a trembling hand while her mind frantically spun off at another devastating angle.

While she had been busily telling herself that what she felt for Matt was an understandable case of lust, she had failed to recognise that it ran much deeper than that. She had long stopped being a concerned spectator to someone else's problems. She hadn't forsaken her social life because she lusted after Matt Strickland and was driven to spend as much time in his company as she could, like a lovelorn teenager. She had forsaken her life because she had unwittingly become sucked into his. It had been easy, at first, to dismiss him as the sort of man who took advantage of everything and everyone around him, but slowly but surely she had begun glimpsing other sides of his complex, absorbing personality.

She had watched him subdue his natural inclination to dominate so that he could make strides in getting to know his daughter. She had been ensnared by a wit and intelligence that was far greater than she had originally imagined. She had been seduced by those snatches of humanity she saw in his less guarded moments.

She had fallen in love with the whole man, and the time she had spent ignoring that reality hadn't served to protect her—it had just rendered her horribly defenceless.

Looking back now, Tess could see that love had just been waiting round the corner, ready to ambush her and turn her world on its head. Matt Strickland had overwhelmed her. She had been waiting for something gentle and careful, and had been unprepared for the chaos and power of real love, gutsy and demanding, when it finally came. She had expected that the guy who won her heart would be kind and sensitive. She had been utterly unprotected against a man who'd broken through to her heart like a battering ram and grabbed it when she hadn't even been looking—when she hadn't even taken the time to steel herself.

Her heart was racing. Inexperience left her unsure as to what to do. She had never considered herself extraordinary because she hadn't fallen into bed with any man. It just had never happened, and she had accepted that with a shrug of her shoulders.

'My relationship with Samantha became distant,' he said heavily. 'Stilted. Nothing I did, when I *did* manage to see her, could reverse the effects of the separation, and God only knows what Catrina had been telling her when I wasn't around. And just when I thought that some progress was being made...*this*...!'

'You came here,' Tess murmured.

'Where else? You know the situation better than anyone.'

He gazed at her with those stunning eyes and her breathing became laboured. Without warning, the atmosphere shifted. She could sense him grow still. It was impossible to think straight and nor could she tear her eyes away from his dark, outrageously sexy face. She wanted him so badly that it was a physical pain inside her, and her craving was made all the more irresistible because of the intensity of the emotion underlying it. She leaned forward and kissed him very chastely on his cheek, and the shock of contact almost had her reeling back.

'It'll be all right,' she whispered huskily. 'Samantha may have been disappointed at the way today turned out, but you've already started building the blocks of a relationship with her and she'll have that to fall back on.'

She was losing herself in the intensity of his gaze, and with a soft moan she did the unthinkable. She placed the palm of her hand on his chest and leaned into him once again. This time her kiss—not on his cheek, but daringly, recklessly, on his lips—was sweetly lingering, and an exquisite rush of pleasure crowded her mind, driving coherent thought away, taking away the ability to analyse what she was doing. She felt that if she stopped breathing just for a second she would be able to hear the frantic beating of her heart.

It didn't occur to her that she might be making a complete fool of herself. She had acted on impulse and she didn't regret it.

When he curved his hand at the nape of her neck and pulled her towards him she melted into the embrace as though this was the moment she had been born to savour.

This wasn't why he had come. Was it? He knew that she had been the first person he thought of in his frustration. He had called his housekeeper and had been waiting by the door for her to arrive so that he could come here and do...*what*?

What had he been expecting? At the back of his mind, had he already succumbed to the desire to take her to bed? From every angle, seeing Vicky had been a disaster. Not just from the point of view of his daughter. He had looked at her standing next to Tess and suddenly he hadn't been able to remember what he had ever seen in the woman.

Her statuesque beauty now seemed angular and unappealing. Where Tess was soft, her face open and transparent, Vicky was a hard-bitten career woman. He had been bored by her monotonous monologues about the Hong Kong market, impatient with her informed conversation.

Had he come here because he had been driven by something more than just an urge to offload?

The fact that he had even felt the need to offload was, in itself, cause for wonder.

The honeyed moistness of Tess's mouth was driving him crazy, but he still managed a final last-ditch attempt to control the situation.

'What's happening here?' He pushed her away and his resolution was immediately floored when he felt her tremble against him. 'We...shouldn't be doing this.' His voice was rough and uneven.

'Why not?'

'Hell, I can think of a hundred reasons!'

'You're not attracted to me...?'

'That's not one of them.' His mouth hit hers with a hunger that detonated an explosive pleasure inside her that she had never known existed. Her whole body was suddenly on fire and she could hardly sit still. She needed to wriggle just to try and assuage the burning restlessness blazing a trail through her.

'I'm not about to make love to you in a kitchen!' Matt growled, and Tess whimpered, her eyes fluttering closed, as he lifted her off the chair and began heading towards a bedroom—mistakenly kicking open the door to Claire's room first and then, two seconds later, getting it right.

He deposited her on the bed and she lay there in a state of heightened excitement, watching as he closed the curtains and then fumbled with his belt, finally whipping it off in one swift pull.

Released from the mindless intoxication of his body

being in contact with hers, she felt the reality of her virginity penetrate through to her fuddled brain.

This was a situation she had never envisaged, and there was no ready process she could think of for dealing with it. She just knew that she was beyond the point of walking away. And it felt *right*, she told herself fiercely. She was in love with him! She wasn't going to listen to any little voices in her head trying to push their way to the surface and preach to her about consequences. She wasn't—because there were always consequences to everything. If she didn't do this—if she turned her back on this one moment in time—then she would forever live with the consequence of that. Would forever wonder what it would have been like to surrender to this big, powerful man who had stolen her heart.

Optimistic by nature, she pleasurably played with the thought that this could lead anywhere. Who was to say?

He had stripped off his shirt. Her breath caught in her throat and she drank in the muscular beauty of his body. When he moved, she could see the rippling of sinew and the raw definition of his torso. He reached for his zip and she nearly fainted in anticipation. Her clothes were an irritating encumbrance, but she lacked the courage to divest herself of them.

He walked slowly towards her and she squirmed. Her eyes flickered away as he tugged down the zip and she heard the soft drop of his trousers, the sound of him stepping out of them, and then she was looking at him, shyly at first, and then mesmerised by the massive surge of his powerful erection.

With small, squirming movements, she edged up

into a sitting position and hooked her fingers under her vest.

'I've thought about this,' Matt muttered in a driven undertone, and her eyes widened in surprise.

'You have?'

'Why so shocked? You're sexy as hell. You must know the effect you have on a man... No, don't lift a finger. I want to take off your clothes piece by gradual piece.' He gave her a slow, curling smile that made her bones melt, and then he straddled her.

She fascinated him, and suddenly he could barely wait a second longer. Like a horny teenager, he covered her body with his own and kissed her with bruising ruthlessness, his hand moving along her thigh and easily slipping underneath the silky trousers. She was as soft and as smooth as satin. Just the feel of her was enough to wreak havoc with his control, and he had to slam the door shut on his raging libido or else risk making a fool of himself.

She wasn't wearing a bra. He had spotted that the second he had walked through the door. He caressed her full breasts through the thin, stretchy fabric of her vest, felt the way they moulded into his big hands and the way her nipples were tight and stiff under his fingers. He wanted to do this slowly, to take his time, and was disconcerted to realise that he had been fantasising about this for weeks. It had never risen to the surface of his consciousness but it must have been nagging at the back of his mind, and touching her now had released the nebulous, intangible notion. His hand shook as he heaved himself up so that he could pull off the vest with one hand.

'God, you're so damned beautiful,' he rasped, bending to nuzzle one breast, teasing her nipple with the tip of his tongue while she panted and moaned.

Having thought that he had barely noticed her as belonging to the female sex, Tess allowed herself to fully occupy Cloud Nine. He wanted her. He thought that she was beautiful. For the moment it was enough, and as she squirmed underneath him, desperate to get rid of her clothes, she felt herself letting go.

She pushed her fingers into his hair and urged his head down so that he could fiercely suckle her pouting nipple. He grappled with her trousers, levering himself up so that she could wriggle herself free of them.

His effect on her was electrifying. She felt as though this was what her body had been designed for—to be touched by this man. She arched upwards and cried out helplessly as he continued to move his mouth over her breasts. She ran her hands across his shoulders and felt the bunched muscles. She couldn't seem to remain still. When she angled her body up her nakedness touched his, and his stiff erection against her was explosive.

Tess had had boyfriends in the past, but none of them had ever affected her like this. Indeed, she'd had no desire to submit her body to theirs the way she wanted to submit her body to this man. She had enjoyed kissing, and there had been a bit of amateurish fondling, but this was in a league of its own, and her body sang under his expert touch.

He parted her legs with one hand, and as he continued to lavish attention on her breasts he began to move his hardness between her thighs, driving her into a frenzy.

'Talk to me,' he commanded hungrily, and Tess looked at him, confused.

'About what?'

'About how much you want me. I want you to tell me...' He laughed softly, and then demonstrated exactly what he meant by talking to *her*, telling her how much he wanted her and what he wanted to do to her. All the time his hard, pulsing erection pushed between her parted legs. Tess was going out of her mind.

'I want you...*now*...' she groaned, when she thought that she wouldn't be able to take any more.

'I'm not finished enjoying you yet.' He gradually began trailing an erotic path down the length of her body, relishing the salty taste of her perspiration on his tongue. Her uncontrolled passion matched his own and he liked it. As with everything she did, she was generous in her lovemaking. He realised that it was what he had expected. She didn't hold back. Her personality was forthright, open, giving. Her lovemaking was the same, and it unlocked a barrage of mindless desire he hadn't been aware he possessed.

He paused as he neared her thighs, and reared up to support himself on his hands so that he was looking down at her, appreciating her soft, feminine mound which was slick with moisture. The sweet, honeyed, musky smell of her threatened to tip him over the edge— and that was before he even touched her. Which he fully intended to do. With his hands, with his fingers, with his mouth, until she was begging for release.

He blew softly against her and Tess gasped. She was discovering a whole new side to herself, and she wouldn't have been able to stop herself now even if she had wanted to. She didn't think that she had ever known what it was like to have a man turn her on—but then she had never *met* a man like Matt.

She froze as he gently parted the delicate folds of her femininity, and sank back with a soft sigh of pleasure as he darted his tongue between and tasted her. She covered her face with one arm and her mouth fell open. The sensation was so exquisite that she could hardly breathe. All the muscles in her body seemed to go limp and she gave herself over to his gentle, persistent mouth which continued savouring her.

His dark head between her legs was the most erotic thing she had ever seen in her whole life. His exploring mouth became more demanding, and she could no longer keep still. Her body was spiralling out of control.

But before she could climax right there, Matt heaved himself up.

'I need,' he muttered shakily, 'to get some contraception.'

'Please,' Tess whimpered, digging her fingers into his shoulder, because he just couldn't leave her *now* to start fumbling for a condom. Her periods had always been as regular as clockwork. She was as safe as houses and she needed him inside her *right now*. Her body was screaming out for it.

'I'm safe,' she gasped.

Matt needed no further encouragement. He really wasn't sure whether he had any contraception on him anyway. He was ultra-careful, always made sure to carry his own protection, but his sex-life with Vicky had been sporadic, and she had, anyway, been on the pill. He was uneasily aware that even if he hadn't had any, if she hadn't given him the green light, he might just have chanced it—because his body was on fire and the only way he could douse it was by taking her. He had never been so out of control in his entire life. For someone who had imposed stringent discipline in all areas of his life, because there was no such thing as a happy surprise, it was weirdly exhilarating to be suddenly and temporarily freed from the shackles.

He thrust into her with an intensity that made her wince and cry out in pain. Confused, Matt eased himself back. He was big. He knew that. And she felt tight—so tight that he might almost think...

'Are you a *virgin*?' he asked with dumbstruck incredulity, and Tess turned her head away.

After the initial discomfort the pain was receding fast, being replaced by a driving, burning need to feel him push into her again.

'Just carry on, Matt...please...I need you...'

'Look at me,' he growled. 'I'll be gentle...' His eyes held hers as he moved slowly and surely, building into a rhythm that took her breath away. However much he had teased her and touched her, in unimaginable places, to have him inside her was the greatest intimacy of all. Tess wrapped her arms around his waist and her body bucked as he moved faster and deeper. She felt his physical release just as her own body spiralled out of control, causing her to cry out and dig her fingernails into his back. His spasms as he ejaculated into her were the most wonderful things she had ever experienced.

She loved this man, and she had to resist the urge to tell him. She held that warm knowledge to herself, and there was a smile of pleasure and fulfilment on her lips when she finally shuddered one last time and then lay, spent.

Matt rolled off her and propped himself on his side to look at her.

'So...tell me about that...'

'Tell you about what?' Tess murmured sleepily. 'That was amazing. Was it...' She looked at him, suddenly anxious. 'Was it okay for you?'

'It was...pretty amazing. I was your first.'

'I'm sorry.'

'Don't apologise.' He smiled and stroked the side of her face. A *virgin*. A twenty-three-year-old virgin. He hadn't known they existed. 'I liked it. Why me?'

Tess drew her breath in sharply. 'I guess,' she said, reaching to hook her hand around his neck and nuzzle the dewy moisture there with her lips, 'you just really turn me on. I don't understand it, because you're not the type of guy I ever imagined myself going for, but when I'm near you I just seem to fall apart.'

'You might have guessed that it's the same with me,' Matt confessed a little unsteadily. He could feel his body confirming that admission, hardening again in record time. 'I should have been able to restrain myself, but...'

Tess felt him stir against her naked thigh and a heady sense of power filled her. But nudging its way through to her fuddled brain were snatches of uneasy recollection of how, exactly, they had ended up in bed together. He had come to talk about Samantha. Had he been drinking? He certainly hadn't been as composed as he usually was. It had been the first time she had seen him with all his barriers down, and his unexpected vulnerability combined with her fledging acknowledgement of how she felt about him had been an intoxicating mix. From being the girl who had stayed on the sidelines as her friends had all fallen into bed with guys they'd later avoided, or succumbed to languishing by telephones waiting for calls, she had gone to being a girl who had flung herself at a man because she just hadn't been able *not* to.

'Why should you have been able to restrain yourself?' she asked anxiously. 'Did I take advantage of you?'

Matt shot her a gleaming look of surprise. 'When you say things like that I feel about a hundred years old.' He laughed softly. 'Don't worry. I'm wonderfully adept when it comes to women cruelly trying to take advantage of me. I find it pays to just relax and go along for the ride.'

'You're teasing me.'

'I'm enjoying your lack of cynicism. When I came here, I was at the end of my tether. You relax me, and I like that.'

Tess wasn't sure if that was strictly accurate. It could be said that simply lovemaking had relaxed him. But she wasn't going to analyse the finer points of his remark. She was going to take it at face value because she had never felt so wonderfully, gloriously *complete* in her whole life.

She guided his hand to her breast, and he grinned wickedly and pushed her back against the bed, slung his thigh over hers. She felt the weight of it with a feeling of bliss.

'You're a fast learner.' His voice was thick with satisfaction.

This time their lovemaking was fast and hard. Matt liked giving pleasure. He knew just where to touch her and how to make her body respond. Shorn of inhibitions, Tess was his willing student. She wanted to be guided. She wanted to give him as much pleasure as he gave her. She was guiltily, horribly aware that she wanted a great deal more than he probably suspected, but for the moment she was greedy enough to take what was on offer.

Their bodies were slick when they were sated. In a minute Matt would have to leave. He would talk to Samantha in the morning. He told her this as she lay against him, her body naturally curving against his as though it had been fashioned just for that purpose. His admission that it would be an uphill task made her smile.

'Talking's not that difficult,' she breathed with drowsy contentment. 'Communication is the key thing when it comes to all relationships. I know that sounds like a cliché, but I think it happens to be true. Maybe...' she tested the water '...that's why your relationship with Vicky didn't work out...'

Matt shrugged. 'It doesn't matter why my relationship with Vicky didn't work out.'

Tess thought that it mattered to *her*. He had married the perfect person and it hadn't worked out. He had gone out with the perfect replacement and that hadn't worked out. Amongst her tangled thoughts she figured that if only she could pinpoint *why* the perfect exes hadn't worked out, then maybe—just maybe—she could avoid the mistakes her predecessors had unwittingly made.

She refused to accept that the most wonderful physical and emotional connection she had ever made with another human being was destined to be short-lived.

'She seemed very nice...' Tess persisted. 'And you must have had a lot in common.'

'Look.' Matt propped himself up and turned on his side to face her. 'Drop it, Tess. It's of no importance. Like I told you, I took my eye off the ball with Vicky. She started getting ideas.'

His face was shuttered. He was locking her out of this conversation.

'I guess it's understandable.' Tess tried to laugh. She was no good when it came to playing underhand games. She would have been hopeless at persuading a confession out of anyone, and it showed in the shaky tremor of her voice when she spoke.

Matt looked at her narrowly. Her upturned face was sweetly, delectably soft and vulnerable, and a prickle of unease curled in him. But the touch of her was so heady, and the feel of her was like a shot of adrenaline to his jaded palate...

In short, she was irresistible. But just in case...

'Vicky wanted a happy ending,' he said bluntly. 'It wasn't going to happen. I've been married once and I lived to rue the day. The only good thing to emerge from that disaster was my daughter. I'm not a candidate for a repeat performance. I'm telling you this because I don't want *you* to get any ideas.'

'You mean crazy ideas like Vicky got?' It was like being sliced in two. The path was forked and she was being given a choice. Follow the road he indicated or else walk the other way. If she had thought that a fleeting glimpse of his vulnerability indicated hint of softness, then she had been mistaken. The dark, fathomless eyes locked onto hers were deadly serious, and Tess very quickly made her decision.

Take what he was offering. She had fallen in love with him and she couldn't walk away. When had she ever been able to do anything by halves? She had given herself to him completely, and if it made no sense then that was something she would have to learn to deal with.

'I guess…well…she's in her thirties. Maybe she could hear her biological clock ticking away. But not me! At twenty-three, life is still a grand adventure, and I don't want you to think that I'm going to start demanding anything of you—because I'm not.'

It would be a disaster if he found out what she felt about him. One night of passion and a woman confessing undying love would be his nightmare. He would run a mile and he wouldn't look back. She would cease being the girl who could make him relax and would turn into a needy, clinging harridan who wanted more out of him than he was willing to give. Having never had much of a head for numbers, Tess could do the maths pretty quickly when it came to *this* particular scenario.

'In fact, like I said, you're not the type of man I would ever fall for,' she confided.

'I'm not…?'

'No! I may not be experienced, but I'm not foolish enough to think that lust has anything to do with love.'

'You just gave your virginity to me because…?'

'Because I wanted to. No one's really ever turned me on like…'

'Like me?' Matt interjected smoothly. 'I believe you. Lust can be powerful. Overwhelming. And maybe you came to New York looking for an adventure. Why else would you be using contraception? You're young, you're beautiful… Did you get bored where you lived?'

Tess was still lagging behind, wondering whether she should own up to the fact that she wasn't actually using any contraception at all but was perfectly safe anyway. Matt's low, seductive murmur seemed to be coming from a long way away. His clever mind was leapfrogging through what she had said and making its own deductions. She had come to Manhattan seeking adventure. She had been bored and restless. She had taken the necessary precautions not because she was desperate to lose her virginity but because she wanted to be prepared in case the situation arose. Perhaps she had been dazzled at the thought of Manhattan and everything and every*one* it could offer. That would make perfect sense to him. He was a man with a healthy sexual appetite. He would fully understand how, at the age of twenty-three, her virginity might have become an albatross around her neck rather than a treasure to be hugged until the perfect man came along. Hell, there was no such thing as a perfect soul mate anyway!

Tess half listened and made vague appropriate noises. For a man with a brilliant mind he seemed very good at arriving at all the wrong conclusions, but she knew that he had to. He had to make sense of her and slot her into a category that didn't threaten the pattern of his orderly life because he wanted her. He wasn't at all surprised that she had chosen to lose her virginity with *him*. He was supremely confident of his own sexual magnetism. His misguided conclusions and freewheeling assumptions even made sense in a weird, convoluted way.

She wasn't sure she recognised herself as this woman who knew what she wanted, was in search of sexual adventure, and had the good sense to go on the pill, throwing caution to the winds so that she could have a no-strings-attached relationship with him.

It would have been so much easier if she *had* been that person, she thought ruefully. Instead, here she was—not too sure what she was doing or what she had got herself mixed up in.

'So on Monday...' He kissed her with such leisurely, thorough expertise that she forgot how precarious her life had suddenly become. 'I'll make sure that I'm back by six. We'll take Samantha out for a meal somewhere. I'm hoping conversation might be back on the agenda with her. And afterwards...'

Tess felt the thrill of excitement. It flooded her veins like a toxin. It closed her mind to any question that she might be doing the wrong thing.

CHAPTER SIX

TESS stared in the mirror at the woman she had become in the space of four glorious weeks. The changes were slight, but *she* had no difficulty in noticing them. Matt Strickland had turned her into a woman. In a series of barely recognisable stages she had grown up. She dressed differently now. The trainers had been replaced with flats. The vests were a little less clinging.

'I don't want other men looking at you,' he had told her, with a possessiveness that had thrilled her to the bone. 'Is that a crime? When you wear those tight vests men look, and when they look I want to kill them. And don't even *think* of going anywhere without a bra. That is a sight to be afforded only to me.'

The vests had been replaced with looser silk tops that made her look sophisticated and glamorous, and she liked her new image. He claimed not to have an ounce of jealousy in his body, but when she had idly watched a man walk past a week ago, her mind a thousand miles away, he had tilted her face to his and told her, with a forced laugh, that he wanted her to only have eyes for *him*.

Tess stored and treasured all those passing moments. They had to mean *something*! He made no effort to conceal the fact that he wanted her. Sometimes, with Samantha between them as they ate dinner, she would glance up and find his eyes on her, and she would see naked hunger there. Her breasts might ache just at the sight of him, and she might feel that telltale dampness between her thighs, but she knew that her effect on him was just as powerful. He had told her that business meetings had become a minefield because just the thought of her could give him an instant erection.

Tess loved hearing things like that, because they seemed to indicate that something would come of their relationship—although she was smart enough never to let any mention of that leave her lips.

She had also made sure not to breathe a word to Claire. Nor had she mentioned it to her parents or any of her friends, whose lives seemed so distant now anyway.

At first she had worried that keeping it secret might be difficult. Claire had always been able to read her like a book, and she would have been able to chivvy it out of her without any trouble at all if she had smelled a rat, but in all events it had been much easier than expected. Tom had proposed, and Claire was residing in a parallel universe. She spent most of her time at his place, and disappeared on weekends to his parents' house in Boston, where a wedding planner was feverishly working to produce a magical wedding in six months' time. Even her parents skirted over what was happening in her life because they, too, were wrapped up in their contribution to the Big Day.

Menus were discussed and seating plans were debated and bridal magazines were pored over until Tess wanted to scream—because where was *she* going with her clandestine relationship with Matt?

Time was moving on. Her ticket to return to Ireland was booked for the beginning of September. But she could easily alter that. Her parents had lived for years in America before they'd moved back to Ireland. All three children had been born in America. Tess had dual nationality and she could have produced that, like a rabbit from a hat, at any given moment in time—but that moment had not arrived. Matt didn't talk about the future and nor did she.

But she would *have* to talk about it. She had spent weeks ducking below the radar and enjoying each day as it came. She could hardly believe that once she had been a girl who *had* lived her life like that, content never to dip her toes in the water.

Hence she was dressing with particular care tonight. Samantha was with her grandparents in the Hamptons for the weekend, and she and Matt would have the apartment all to themselves. It would be the perfect opportunity to discuss this *thing* they had, which had no name. She would use all the feminine wiles at her disposal. Wasn't all fair in love and war?

Her dress was a wonderful long affair in shimmering pale yellow. It fell softly to the ground and left her brown shoulders bare. Her shoes were delicate sandals with yellow straps.

The drive over gave her twenty-five minutes to plan what she was going to say and when. Just thinking about it made her nervous. She wondered whether he was still as allergic to commitment as he had once said he was, then told herself that that wasn't the most important thing, because she could stay on in Manhattan with him, looking after Samantha. She wouldn't actually be demanding anything. The words *a stay of execution* uncomfortably sprang to mind, but as quickly as they had taken shape they were dismissed, because she couldn't afford to let herself start being pessimistic.

Scrape the surface, though, and she was a bag of nerves by the time they reached his block of apartments and the elevator was silently transporting her to the top floor.

Matt had had a key to his penthouse cut for her, and occasionally she used it, but it had never felt right. She had been given a key to facilitate her job as Samantha's nanny. She wanted a key because Matt saw her as the other half of a couple and trusted her enough to come and go as she pleased. So now, as always, she rang the doorbell and waited in restless tension, clutching her little handbag in front of her.

When he pulled open the door her heart flipped over, as it always did, and for a few seconds she was completely lost for words.

He never failed to render her speechless. She saw him almost every day, had made love to him countless times, had watched, fascinated, the lithe suppleness and latent power of his naked body, and yet every time she laid eyes on him it was as if she were seeing him for the first time. He took her breath away, and however much he assured her that she had the same devastating effect on him she didn't believe him. Compared to the women he could have at the click of his fingers, she was just an averagely pretty face.

But she wasn't going to think like that. Not tonight, when she wanted to think positive.

The long look he gave her thrilled her from the crown of her head to the tips of her toes and she smiled shyly.

'Do you like it?' She stepped into his luxurious apartment and gave a little twirl. The dress followed her, as soft and tantalising as a whisper.

He caught his fingers in her hair and pulled her towards him.

'You look like a goddess,' he murmured. 'Some kind of exquisite, ethereal creature.' His finger was now tracing her bare shoulder and her body reacted with mindless excitement. She could already feel her nipples tightening, and her breasts were heavy and sensitive, in expectation of being touched by him. She felt faint thinking about his mouth circling her nipples and licking them until she could scarcely breathe.

But she pushed him gently away and walked towards the kitchen, from which was wafting a delicious smell.

'Have you surprised me by cooking?' she teased, putting some necessary distance between them because she didn't want the evening to start with them in bed.

'You know I don't do that.' She looked so damned edible standing there, delicate and fragile and breathtakingly pretty—an exotic counterpoint to the hard masculinity of his kitchen. He would have pinned her against the wall and taken her without preamble, but she had dressed to impress and he would savour the anticipation of getting her out of her clothes. 'My dependable caterers have done justice to some fillet steak and...' he came close, close enough for her to breathe him in, and lifted the lid of a saucepan '...some kind of sauce.' He remained where he was, dipped his finger into the sauce and held it to her mouth. 'Taste it and enlighten me,' he murmured, already so hot for her that it was beginning to get painful.

He lounged against the counter, his feet loosely crossed at the ankles, and gave her a look of burning satisfaction as the pink tip of her tongue licked the sauce from his upheld finger. Like a cat finishing the last remains of the cream.

'Brandy and peppercorn, I think. And I don't see why you *can't* cook for me now and again.' She gave a mock sigh of wistfulness. 'You're a perfectly good cook. I know. You've done lots of wonderful things with Samantha. Remember that risotto?'

'Correction,' Matt told her wryly, 'Samantha has done lots of wonderful things with me. My role is solely to do as I'm told.'

'Since when do you *ever* do as you're told?' She relaxed enough to smile, but tension was still blazing inside her.

'You can always put that to the test.' He leant against the counter, hemming her in. 'Command me, my beautiful little witch,' he breathed into her ear, before nibbling the side of her neck and sending a flurry of piercing, pleasurable sensations rippling through her. 'Would you like me to get down on my knees and push that sexy dress up so that I can drive you wild with my mouth? Hmm? Or we can always go for something a little more kinky.... It would appear that dessert comes with custard...'

'Stop it!' Tess laughed, hot and flustered, and feebly pushed him away—but he had set up a very evocative image in her head that she was finding difficult to dispel. 'We're not going to do any such thing.'

'Sure? Because I saw a flash of temptation in your eyes just then… Now, let me just see how much you dislike the idea…' To hell with not moving too fast and giving the dress time to have its moment of glory. Still supporting himself with one hand flat against the edge of the granite counter, he reached down and inched the silky fabric upwards. His eyes didn't leave her face.

'You have no self-control, Matt Strickland,' Tess protested weakly.

'Tell me about it. And what about you? I'd say we're even on that score.' He felt the softness of her thighs. The cloth was bunched around his hand and he shrugged it away as he dipped his fingers beneath the lacy band of her thong and slipped them into her.

Tess melted. Her eyelids fluttered shut. This wasn't playing fair! She blindly searched for his mouth with hers, but after just a fleeting kiss he pulled back and whispered, in a sexy, velvety voice, 'No chance. I want to see your face when you come…'

'Okay. You win,' she groaned jerkily. 'But let's go to the bedroom…make love…ah…' She couldn't finish the sentence. Her body was moving of its own accord. Her head was flung back and her eyes were shut as his fingers continued to plunder her, moving fast and hard, then slowly and gently, teasing every ounce of sensation out of a body that felt as limp as a rag doll.

Colour climbed into her cheeks and her breathing became laboured, and then she was falling over the edge, shuddering with the power of her orgasm and crying out, at which point Matt brought his mouth against her so that he could breathe in the wildness of her groaning.

'That,' he murmured when she had climbed down from the mindless heights of pleasure, 'is an excellent way to start any evening.'

Under normal circumstances Tess would have been in enthusiastic agreement with that statement. Matt knew just how to excite her in unimaginable ways. But to-night she had another purpose, and as soon as she had smoothed down her dress she was back to feeling as nervous as a kitten.

Without looking for ways to be critical, she realised that he was utterly oblivious to her mood—but then thoughts of her leaving would probably not have crossed his mind. For weeks Tess had nurtured the hope that what they had would leave him wanting more. They shared a lot together. He might be ruthless and driven in the work place, but with her he had been tender and thoughtful, and with Samantha he had shown boundless patience and a resilient ability to take the knocks and somehow find a way of turning them around. Would he be able to give her up without a backward glance? She had subconsciously chosen to think that he wouldn't, but now, as he whistled softly and made a great show of doing things with the pots and pans, she wasn't sure.

If he was that tuned in to her feelings then surely he would have picked up on the fact that she was more subdued than usual?

Now he was chatting to her about work. He sometimes did that, even though he had once commented wryly that he really didn't know why he bothered, because the second he started he could see her eyes glazing over.

She accepted the drink that was proffered and settled on one of the leather dining chairs at the kitchen table. He was fairly useless in the kitchen. A tea towel was slung over one shoulder and every cooking utensil seemed to be out, even though he was really just heating up a variety of dishes. In between stirring things and peering under lids he chatted and sipped his wine, occasionally glancing round at her, and even in the midst of her anxious thoughts she still warmed at the hot possessiveness in his eyes.

'But do you miss it?' Tess asked abruptly, as a plate of food was placed in front of her with exaggerated flourish. 'The long hours, I mean? For weeks you've managed to be pretty sensible about getting back here in time, to see something of Samantha, so do you miss the work you would have been putting in otherwise at the office?'

In the middle of topping up their glasses, Matt paused and looked at her. Something uneasy stirred in him, but he quickly put that to rest by telling himself that nothing was amiss. She might be a little quieter than she normally was, but she had melted at his touch the way she always did. He never seemed to tire of her helpless excitement whenever he touched her. It turned him on in ways that he no longer bothered to question.

'That's a strange question. I work for several hours after Samantha has gone to sleep. It's satisfactory.'

'So...does that mean that you've restructured your life?'

'Where are we going with this conversation?' Matt

tried to keep the irritation out of his voice. He had become accustomed to her undemanding nature. It suited him. She was always happy to fall in with whatever he wanted, and over the weeks he had discovered that her lack of complication suited him in ways nothing else seemed to have suited him in the past, but there was something insistent about her at the moment that seriously threatened to ruin the atmosphere.

'It doesn't have to go anywhere,' Tess told him, picking at her fillet steak. Her appetite was fading fast. 'I'm just asking.'

Matt pushed back his chair and tossed his napkin on a plate of food that was only half eaten. 'I haven't restructured my life.' He linked his fingers behind his head and looked steadily at her flushed face. 'I'm in the process of trying to find a balance.'

'Does that mean you thought it was out of sync before?'

'It means that Samantha is a reality I have to deal with. Originally I thought that I would more or less be able to carry on as normal, with a great deal of help to cover for my absences. It wasn't a viable option. It's a necessary sacrifice and it's been worth it. Whether I'll be able to carry on being consistent remains to be seen. There will be instances when I have to go abroad, and I'll have to get overnight cover when that arises. My mother would be happy enough to come here for a few days, so I don't foresee any problems that won't be surmountable. Now, does that satisfy your curiosity?'

'I wish you wouldn't act as though I'm being a nuisance just by trying to have a conversation with you!' Tess heard herself snap, shocking herself by daring to rock a boat which she had steadfastly tried to keep level for the past two months. But she could no longer help the build-up of anxiety inside her. Once upon a time she had never had a problem in saying what she thought. This was like walking on eggshells. One false move and she sensed that the structure she had built around herself, the little fortress in which she had placed Matt and Samantha, would be shown for the house of cards that it really was.

She was finding it hard to hold on to her sunny optimism.

'What's going on, Tess?'

'Sometimes I like to think that there's a little more to us than just sex...'

The silence stretched endlessly between them, straining until it was so close to breaking point that she could hardly breathe. She certainly couldn't look at him. Instead she fiddled with the fork on her plate, making swirly patterns into the fast cooling brandy sauce which she had hardly tasted.

She looked up when he began clearing the table, and had to resist the temptation to fling herself at him and tell him that she was just kidding. She knew that she had embarked on this relationship with the understanding that she would demand nothing, and she had been good to her word, but she had fallen deeper and deeper and deeper in love with him. She realised now that she had vaguely assumed that time would sort them both out and provide a way forward for their relationship.

When she stood up to help him, her legs felt wobbly. She was relieved when he told her to wait for him in the living room.

She was so absorbed in her thoughts that she wasn't aware of him framed in the doorway until he spoke. She twisted round to look at him.

'You were saying…?' Matt prompted, strolling into the living room to join her on the sofa.

Tess was finding it difficult to reconcile the man looking at her now with a closed, shuttered expression with the man earlier, who had laughed into her mouth and caressed her with such gentleness that she had felt as though they were two halves of the same person.

'I was saying that I'd like to think that what we have is more than just sex.' She smoothed her hands nervously along her dress. 'Do you care about me at all? I guess that's what I'm asking.'

'What kind of a question is that? If I didn't care about you I wouldn't be having a relationship with you.'

'So I'm on a par with Vicky? Is that what you're saying? You care about me the way you cared about her?'

'I prefer not to make comparisons between the women that I sleep with.'

'What's the difference between us?' Tess persisted doggedly.

Matt glared at her. He didn't like being hemmed in, and as someone who had never made a habit of giving an account for his actions he was infuriated that she was persisting with this line of questioning.

'For a start, Vicky never had a relationship with my daughter.'

'But if you take Samantha out of the equation…'

'How *can* I take her out of the equation? She's part of my life.'

'You know what I'm saying,' Tess insisted stubbornly. Having come this far, she was committed to this course of action whatever the outcome.

'No. I don't.' Matt couldn't believe that the evening to which he had been looking forward with impatience and anticipation was collapsing into a mess of awkward questions and unreasonable demands. They should have eaten a very good dinner, drunk some excellent wine, chatted with the ease with which they always chatted, and then progressed into bed where he would have lost himself in her. The fact that she had seen fit to scupper his plans ratcheted up his foul temper by a couple of notches.

'Okay, then I guess I'd better spell it out for you. I know you don't like the thought of planning ahead. *I know that.* The only stuff you ever seem to think about long-term is stuff to do with your work. You can think fifty years in advance when it comes to arranging your work life!'

'There's nothing wrong with that,' Matt gritted, avoiding the unwelcome topic of conversation that was staring him in the face. 'Businesses don't function on a let's-see-what-happens-next basis! Foundations have to be laid and plans have to be followed through.'

'I understand that. But I just want to know where your personal life features in all that foundation-laying and following through. Where do *we* feature in all that? I need to know, Matt, because I'm due to leave America in a couple of weeks...'

Pinned to the spot, Matt refused to be told which direction he should take. He had embarked on a fling with her and had spared little thought for the temporary nature of what they had. She was due to leave the country and, since he wasn't into long term situations, the nebulous matter of her departure didn't impinge at all on his conscience.

He had been clear as to what he wanted and she had readily agreed.

Hell, hadn't she come to America to sort herself out? Hadn't she gone on the pill because she had been willing for an adventure?

He uneasily cast his mind back to her shyness—that tentative, easygoing, sunny disposition that he still found endearing. His notions of her being a wild girl let loose in a big city had been crazily misplaced. Suddenly, like a jigsaw puzzle coming together with the final piece, Matt faced the truth that he had effectively spent the past few weeks subconsciously dodging, and he blanched at it. He had wanted her, and he had therefore talked himself into getting what he wanted by closing his eyes to the obvious.

'What do you want me to say?'

'I…I can stay on if you want me to. I've been giving it a bit of thought. It's not as though I have a job to go back for, and I love working here—working with Samantha. I know when she starts school she won't need me to be around during the day, but that doesn't matter. I could look around for something to do here. You see, I have dual nationality, so that wouldn't be a problem…' Her voice trailed off and she sifted her fingers through her hair and looked at him. 'It's not as though I would *live* here or anything…' The sound of her pride being washed down the drain was as loud as a fog horn in her ears. 'Claire would be happy to have me continue to stay with her. She's hardly ever around, anyway…she spends so much time with Tom. In fact, I would probably be doing her a favour…looking after her place when she's not there…'

'This isn't what we signed up for, Tess.'

The gentleness of his voice brought a lump to the back of her throat. He was letting her down and making sure not to be brutal about it. But at the end of the day being let down remained the same, whether it was done brutally or not. She sat on her hands, not trusting herself to speak for a few fraught seconds.

'I know. I never wanted to get involved with you…'

'Because I'm not the type of guy you ever saw yourself getting involved with.'

'Right. But…' She lifted her eyes bravely to his face and swallowed hard. 'I did. I let myself get involved with you and I just need to know if there's any chance for us.' She couldn't bring herself to tell him that she had fallen in love with him. He didn't want to hear anything she was saying. It was written all over his face. 'Even though,' she qualified gamely, 'it isn't what either of us signed up for.'

Matt was still. A series of flashbacks was playing in his head like a very rapid slideshow. His wife, his marriage, his resolve never to put himself in such a position again. The women he had dated since then had been ships in the night, and he had enjoyed having it that way. He had determined not to take on commitments he knew he would eventually dislike and resent. However ideal the woman in question might seem, it would only be a matter of time before she was shorn of her halo and revealed to have all the needs and expectations that would be guaranteed to drag him under.

And was Tess the ideal woman anyway?

She had never held down a job aside from this one. She had spent her life cheerfully drifting, content to live in the shadow of her sisters. She wasn't independent. She was hopeless when it came to most things of a practical nature. Her personality was so diametrically the opposite of his that he sometimes had to take a step back and marvel.

Yes, those differences were charming at the moment, but they would irritate him on a long-term basis. He was sure of it. Nor, he admitted to himself, did he care for the fact that she was, in effect, offering him an ultimatum. Ask her to stay or else watch her walk away. Matt didn't like ultimatums. He especially didn't like them insofar as they applied to his private life.

'You have some time remaining here,' he heard himself say brusquely. 'Why start asking about the future? Why not just enjoy what we have?' In his way, it was as close as he could come to expressing his feelings. He could promise her nothing.

'What would be the point?' Tess cried out with anguished feeling.

'So in other words,' Matt filled in, his voice unyielding, 'unless I can promise you marriage, you see no reason to stick around?'

'I told you…I don't *want* marriage…'

'Come off it, Tess! Are you going to tell me that you would be happy to get a part-time job over here and shack up in your sister's apartment just so that you could be at my beck and call?'

'I wouldn't see it that way,' she muttered inaudibly.

'I'm honest enough to tell you that you would be making a big mistake.' Feeling suddenly restricted, Matt stood up and paced through the room. She had effected small changes in the time she had been coming to the apartment. There was a little frame of some pressed flowers she had done with Samantha. Some of her CDs had found their way over and were sitting on his antique sideboard. A handful of pictures had been developed, and she had framed those and arranged them on the windowsill. He glared at all those intimate touches, which he had never asked for but to which, he thought bad-temperedly, he had become accustomed.

'We've had fun together. I would like us to continue having fun together until you leave. But if you don't want to then that's your choice.'

He hardened himself to the sound of her silence. He wasn't ending this because he was cruel. He was ending this because he was a hell of a lot more experienced than she was and he could foretell the mistake it would be even if she was wilfully choosing to close her eyes to it.

He needed to lead by example, and he would. It was what he had always done. It didn't feel good, but he couldn't allow himself to give her false hope. *More* false hope. Because it was obvious that she had been mulling over their situation longer than she had let on.

Mind made up, he turned to look at her. He brushed aside a momentary feeling of panic and clenched his jaw.

'You're going to have to be strong to take what I'm going to say now, Tess. We're not suited for one another.

You're right when you say that your choice of ideal man would be the opposite of someone like me. I have a hell of a lot more experience than you, and trust me when I say that I would drive you round the bend.'

'What you're saying is that *I* would drive *you* round the bend.' She breathed in deeply, angry with herself for having revealed so much, and angry with him for his patronising tone of voice. 'You don't mind sleeping with me, but I'm just not good enough for you to have a proper relationship with!'

Dark colour accented his high cheekbones. 'This has nothing to do with whether you're *good enough* for me or not!' he roared, losing control.

She was searching around for her bag, which she located in the kitchen. 'I still have a couple of weeks left working for you.' She held her head up high. 'I'd really appreciate it if I could see as little of you as possible.'

'That,' Matt said tightly, 'can be arranged. Consider yourself relieved of your duties.' Angry frustration ripped through him. He could barely look at her, and yet at the same time was driven to watch in glowering, hostile outrage as she headed towards the door, only pausing when her fingers were curled around the doorknob.

'Would you mind if I at least said goodbye to Samantha?' she asked jerkily, and Matt nodded an affirmation.

Which meant that there was nothing left to be said. It had all gone horribly, catastrophically wrong, but indecision pinned her to the spot until she told herself that it was pointless.

She closed the door quietly and firmly behind her.

CHAPTER SEVEN

DESPERATE to convince Claire that she was on the mend, Tess lay in bed trying to think happy thoughts.

For the first time in two months, she was rudderless. She literally felt like one of the walking wounded. She had told Claire that she felt she might be coming down with something. Actually, she *did* feel she might be coming down with something. She had woken up every morning—every morning for five interminable days, during which time she had heard nothing from him, not a text, not a phone call—with a vague feeling of nausea.

She no longer knew how to plan her days, and no longer had any interest in doing anything, anyway. She would be leaving the country in just over a week, and all she really wanted to do was hibernate. She wanted to scuttle somewhere dark and safe and warm, like a mole, and sleep until the memory of Matt had faded from her consciousness, allowing her to pick herself up and carry on.

She finally understood how much she had allowed him to become the axis of her entire universe. In a matter of just a couple of months she had given away all of her carefree independence, and now that the umbilical cord had been slashed she was floundering like some-one deprived of oxygen. She missed him. She missed Samantha, with whom she spoke daily. She had seen her two days previously, and had obviously looked so dreadful that her mumbling something about *being a bit under the weather* had been one hundred percent convincing.

Claire had been sympathetic to start with, and had made a production of keeping her distance.

'I can't afford to catch anything,' she had apologised. 'Life's too hectic at the moment for me to take time out with an infection.'

Tess was beginning to think that she might actually be *willing* herself into a state of ill health. She could barely keep a thing down. If things continued in this manner she would have to be ferried back to Ireland in an air ambulance.

However, now, after five days, Claire was running out of patience.

Tess still lay with her eyes closed, telling herself that her nausea was all in her mind, when the bedroom door was flung open.

'It's nearly ten-thirty!' Claire was dressed to go shop-ping in one of her signature summer outfits—a silky short dress which would have cost the earth and a pair of complicated gladiator-style sandals—and was munching on a sandwich the size of a brick.

Tess tried to duck under the duvet.

'You can't *still* be under the weather, Tess!'

'You know I've never been a morning person.' She averted her eyes from the sandwich because it was making her stomach lurch.

'Well, it's Saturday, and you're coming shopping with me. You can't spend the rest of your time here feeling sorry for yourself because you have a bit of a stomach bug! You'll get back to Ireland and you'll kick yourself because you wasted your last week and a half. Might I remind you that there's *nothing to do* back home?'

'I'm going to do that teaching course. I told you!' After years of never settling down to anything, one good thing, at least, had come of her stay in Manhattan. She had been pushed into coming to New York so that she could find direction, and she had.

'Well, whatever,' Claire dismissed bracingly, 'you're still going to get out of that bed and come shopping with me—because tonight you're coming to a party! And I've already got a ticket for you so don't even *think* of telling me that you can't go because your tummy hurts! We're going to get you something glamorous and wonderful and you're going to *have a brilliant time*!'

That was Claire-speak for *do-as-you're-told-or-you-won't-hear-the-end-of-it*.

'I'll give you half an hour, Tess, and then I'll expect to see you up and ready to take on Manhattan!'

Tess had no idea where they would be going that night. She obediently spent the day traipsing behind Claire, making a heroic effort to show enthusiasm over the clothes that were paraded in front of her and being compelled to try on. At five-thirty they returned to the apartment and she was instructed to 'get your act together and change as quickly as possible because the taxi's booked for seven.' She was also instructed to *look happy*, because there was nothing worse than a party-pooper.

Tess did as she was told because she knew that her sister had a point. She really would have to start moving on. She couldn't continue to feel sorry for herself indefinitely. Matt had never promised her anything. He had never, ever given any indication that what they had would extend beyond her stay in America. *She* had been the one guilty of misinterpreting their relationship. She had flung herself headlong into something that defied all common sense and had started building castles in the air because she had been naïve.

When she thought logically about it, she and Matt stood on opposite sides of a great divide. He was the sophisticated, accomplished and confident product of a birthright of wealth and power. Not only had he grown up within the cocoon of a privileged background, but he had expanded a thousandfold on his fabulous inheritance. He had taken over his father's massive business concerns and diversified and branched out because it was in his nature. He was too clever to stand still and so he hadn't.

Compared to him, she was the equivalent of a minnow swimming next to a Great White. In her calmer moments she grudgingly conceded that there had never been a chance for them—not in any real sense of the word. Even if he had loved her madly—which he hadn't—it would still have been a big deal for him to have committed to someone so far removed from his own social background.

So moving on was her only option.

When she was fully dressed she could almost feel confident that she was beginning to. At least she *looked* the part—which was some of the battle won, if nothing else.

Claire rapped on the bedroom door at six-thirty and after twenty minutes of clinical inspection pronounced herself satisfied.

She had ended up buying an off-the-shoulder long dress, deep green in colour, which was gathered at the bust and then fell to the ground. It should have made her look shapeless, but it didn't.

'You have the boobs for it,' Claire had said approvingly, when Tess had emerged from the changing room. 'And the colour goes with you complexion.'

It was a style that couldn't be worn with a bra, and Tess found herself thinking back to Matt's possessive reaction to any thought of her going braless in public. She had found it so intoxicating at the time, and had read too much into it.

Now, she felt a welcome spurt of rebellion as she followed Claire out to the taxi.

It was a forty minute drive to a building which, she was told, was actually a very well known art gallery that rented out its premises for a select few. Outside a crowd of people, dressed to kill, were entering in an orderly line, showing tickets to two doormen.

Inside, the party was in full swing. The art gallery was über-modern. A large, brilliantly white reception area branched out on either side to two massive rooms. In one, a quartet played melodious jazz music. In the other, people networked. There was the feel of a very expensive warehouse about the place. The walls in both the rooms adjoining the reception area were painted a pale slate-grey and adorned with large modernistic works of art. The lighting comprised thousands of spotlights which, to Tess' relief, were dimmed to a mellow glow. It was like nothing she had ever seen before, and for a while she actually forgot her misery.

Tom was waiting for them, and he and Claire both made a big effort to introduce her to people, but after fifteen minutes Tess could see that her sister was becoming bored with playing babysitter. She shooed her away because, actually, she was quite happy to wander around looking at the art work, and after a while she slunk into the room with the jazz band, so that she could sit and listen to the music.

She had tucked herself at a table at the back of the room, with a glass of champagne in front of her, and was listening to a very perceptive song about unrequited love when a low, familiar voice behind her made her freeze in the act of raising the glass to her lips.

She spun round and half stood. Just one look, one second, told her that she had not even begun to put Matt behind her. He was formally dressed and was wearing a red bow tie—the only splash of colour against the blackness of his suit and the crisp whiteness of his shirt.

'What are you doing here?' Tess asked, in a daze.

'I could ask *you* the same question.' He had seen her from behind, walking into the room with the jazz musicians. There must be at least three hundred people at the do. Not only were the rooms on the ground floor crowded, but upstairs several more rooms were filled with employees and important clients. It had been pure coincidence that he had seen her, because he had spent most of his time upstairs, preferring the arrangement of comfortable leather sofas and chairs to the cocktail party atmosphere of the rooms on the ground floor. However, there had been no mistaking that caramel hair falling down her slender back as she weaved a path through the crowds. For a second he had been shocked enough to lose track of what was being said to him by one of the directors at his Boston office. Then he had made his excuses and followed her.

It irked him that he had not been able to get her out of his head. Everything he had said to her had made perfect sense, and yet she was still managing to infiltrate his waking moments with irritating consistency—like a high-frequency noise that had managed to lodge itself in his head, disrupting his thought patterns and making him lose concentration at inconvenient times.

Of course it had only been a few days, and her absence had been made doubly worse by the fact that Samantha was constantly talking about her. She had accepted the fact that Tess had left. She had known that her stay in America would come to a close, and it was a source of unending relief to Matt that his daughter was in a much better place than she had been a few months ago and so had found it easier to adapt to the young student who had replaced Tess for a few weeks. But she still mentioned Tess daily. Matt had been forced to make noises about plans for Tess returning for a visit, perhaps the following Easter. Maybe sooner! He had been obliged to grit his teeth as he was shown all the photographs they had taken together. He had listened, nodding in agreement, as he was told how much Grandma and Grandpa would have loved her.

He hadn't been allowed to forget the woman! Little wonder that he had found himself following her into

this room, standing for a while to watch as she leant
forward at a table, one hand idly curled around the stem
of a champagne flute, the other cupping her chin as she
tapped her feet to the quartet.

If he had been stupid enough to worry about her,
he now scowled as any questions on that front were
answered. She looked on top of the world. In fact she
looked a knockout. And it was clear that she had come
to pick up a guy. Why else would she be wearing something that left her shoulders bare and moulded the fullness of her breasts with such loving perfection?

Tess was completely and utterly thrown by the sudden
appearance of Matt. It was as if her feverish mind had
summoned him up.

'I...I came with Claire,' she stammered, before remembering that she was in the process of *moving on*
and therefore letting herself go weak at the knees at the
sight of him just wasn't going to do. But he looked so
sexy. Had he come with someone? Even if he hadn't, he
would surely be *leaving* with someone. All eyes were
on him, sidelong glances, but then he *was* head and
shoulders above every other man at the party.

He was also in a bad mood, and her spirits deflated
because she knew why. He had come to a party and the
last person he wanted to bump into would be *her*, when
he thought that he was well and truly rid of her.

'I never expected to see *you*!' Tess forced herself to
laugh. 'What a coincidence! But I guess Manhattan is
smaller than you think! Mary says that London is like
that! She'll be out having a drink somewhere, and before
she knows it she recognises someone!'

'Pull the other one, Tess. You must have known that

I was going to be here.' Matt swallowed the contents of his whisky in one, and dumped the empty glass on the table at which she was sitting. He shoved his hands in his pockets. Did she think that he was going to stand here and make nice with a lot of polite conversation? Well, he wasn't in the mood.

'Why would I know that?'

'Because this is a company do. *My* company do, not to put too fine a point on it. So telling me that you had no idea that I might possibly attend my own party doesn't really wash.'

'*Your* party...' Claire hadn't mentioned it. She didn't know the circumstances of her departure from Matt's employment. Tess had told her that she had contracted a bug, and that with only a short period of time left had been given leave to get well and then enjoy some time out by herself rather than spend her remaining days working once she recovered. Claire would have expected her to have known about the party, and as Tess had asked no questions Claire had offered no information beyond the fact that it was a very dressy affair.

Matt's lips curled as he looked down at her generous breasts, pushing against the soft dark green fabric. 'Is that why you made a point of coming?' he rasped. 'You knew that I was going to be here and you thought that it would be a good opportunity to show me what I was missing? Well, it won't work.' All of a sudden he needed another drink. He glanced around, frowning, and like magic a waiter bearing drinks on a large circular tray appeared. Matt took a glass of wine, though he would rather have had a whisky, and drank half.

Tess had got lost trying to work out what he was attempting to say to her.

'I *didn't* know you were going to be here,' she protested truthfully. 'Claire never mentioned that it was a company do!' She was adding up the implications behind his remark, which had been delivered in a derisive tone of voice targeted to offend, and she was suddenly shaking with anger. 'And even if I *had* known that you were going to be here—*which I didn't*—I would *never* have come here to…to show you what you were missing!'

'No? Then why the over-the-top sexy dress? Not to mention the fact that you're not wearing a bra!'

The mere mention of that did horrible things to her body, reminding her of how easy it was to respond to him even when he wasn't touching her. Even, it would seem, when he was being rude and arrogant and insulting.

'This isn't for *your* benefit!' Her nipples were throbbing and she was mortified at her reaction. She felt that he must be able to see what he was doing to her with those laser-sharp, all-seeing black eyes of his.

'No? Because, like I said, it won't work. I've seen that ploy too many times. It's lost its effect over the years. We're no longer involved, and the best thing you could do for yourself is to move on.'

'I can't believe how arrogant you are, Matt Strickland! I…I can't believe what I ever saw in you!'

'I would bet that it wouldn't take much to remind you.'

The look in his eyes had changed suddenly. Tess's breath caught sharply in her throat. That simmering, *hot* gaze was not what she needed—not now! Did it give him a kick to put her meagre will-power to the test? To prove how much of a hold he still had over her? She wanted to weep in frustration.

Perversely, Matt was relishing this hostile clash of words. He had been chatting and socialising like a man on a tour of duty—looking covertly at his watch, mentally bemoaning the fact that the party still had hours to run. Now he was having fun, in a grim, highly charged sort of way. And he couldn't peel his eyes away from her delectable body. If there hadn't been a roomful of people watching, he would have been sorely tempted to remind her of just what she had seen in him! He pictured himself yanking down that flimsy piece of nothing shielding her glorious breasts, cupping their fullness in his big hands, teasing her nipples with the abrasive pads of his fingers.

From where the memory had been lying, close to the surface, he recalled their last evening together, when he had brought her to a shuddering orgasm in the kitchen of his apartment. He had a graphic flashback to the feel of her body writhing against his fingers. He could even recall the soft fall of that yellow dress she had been wearing.

'Has it occurred to you that I *am* moving on?' Tess lied, tossing her head and trying hard to remember the name of the guy who had badgered her for a while and slipped her his business card.

No. Quite frankly, it hadn't. Nor was he having a good time assimilating the concept.

'Maybe,' she threw at him defiantly, 'you're really not the reason I wore this dress—considering I didn't know that you were going to be here anyway! In fact, for your information, I've already been asked out on a date!'

That was a red rag to a bull. Having just told her that she should move on with her life, Matt underwent a rapid turnaround and was outraged that she should be out on the prowl within *seconds* of their split.

'Who by?' he demanded, keeping his voice well modulated, although inside he was seething with what could only be termed *jealousy*. His weakness infuriated him.

'Tony!' The name came back to her in the nick of time. 'Tony Grayson.'

Sales manager. His career now looked perilously short-lived. Matt drained his glass, flicked back the sleeve of his shirt to look at his watch. 'Well,' he drawled with lazy indifference, 'good luck with that one. I should be careful if I were you, though. New York isn't a small village in Ireland. Give off too many obvious signals and you'll have to be prepared to take the consequences. In other words, don't go near the fire unless you're happy to get burnt.'

He turned on his heel and walked away. Like a punctured balloon, Tess felt herself deflate. She could no longer put on a show of having fun. She just wanted to leave, to get back to the apartment. Like a patient suffering a severe relapse, she needed immediate time and space to recover, because seeing Matt again had knocked her for six.

Knowing that Claire would feel obliged to try and persuade her to stay, she didn't bother to look for her. Instead, she took the coward's way out and texted her a message. By the time she checked her mobile phone Tess would be at the apartment, in her pyjamas.

Three days later, Tess emerged from the doctor's surgery on wobbly legs. At Claire's insistence, she had finally gone.

'You can't climb on a plane feeling under the weather!' Claire had announced, in that voice of hers that permitted no argument. 'The flight back is a nightmare—it's so long, and if you start feeling really poorly on the plane it's going to be awful. You obviously have some kind of persistent stomach bug and you *have* to go to my doctor and get it sorted. If you like, I can come with you.'

Now Tess was weak with relief that she had turned down her sister's offer to accompany her. What would she have said if she had been confronted with the news that Tess was pregnant?

In a daze, she went to the nearest coffee shop and sat down, unseeing, in front of a cappuccino which, having ordered, she no longer wanted.

Her initial reaction—one of sickening disbelief— had ebbed. Now it was replaced by a recognition that all the signs had been there. She had just missed them. After their first time together, when she had been so convinced that there had been no danger of her falling pregnant because she was as regular as clockwork, she had gone to Claire's doctor—the very same doctor who had broken the news to her twenty minutes ago—to have a contraceptive device inserted. The pill would have been easier, but Tess had an aversion to tablets.

'You must be very fertile,' the doctor had said, while Tess had sat here like a statue, trying to absorb what had just been said to her. She had been thinking that it certainly explained her dodgy stomach. A quick look in her diary had confirmed that her period had been late—something she hadn't even noticed because between being on Cloud Nine and then catapulted back down to Planet Earth she just hadn't been thinking straight. In fact, she hadn't been thinking at all.

Across from her, a woman leaned over and asked if she was all right and Tess returned a wan smile.

'I've just had a bit of a shock,' she said politely. 'I'll be fine once I drink this cup of coffee.'

Of course she would have to tell Matt. He deserved to know. But just thinking about that brought her out in a cold sweat of nervous perspiration.

Their last bruising encounter had left her in no doubt that he was over her. He had given her her walking papers and instructed her to move on—because he had. He had spoken to her in the patronising tone of someone dealing with a nuisance who showed promise of becoming a stalker. He had accused her of dressing to attract him, and she knew, deep down, that he hadn't believed a word she had said about not knowing that he would be at the party. He wanted nothing further to do with her and what was he about to get? A lifelong connection that he hadn't engineered. He had trusted her because she had told him that she had taken care of contraception, and in return for his trust he would find himself a father in a few months' time.

But to keep the truth from him would be immoral.

Without giving herself the opportunity to dwell on what she knew she had to do, Tess stood up and hailed the first cab to his offices. If she thought too much about it she would think herself into a change of mind. She was having his baby.

The traffic, as usual, was gridlocked, and Tess was a bag of nerves by the time she paid the cab driver and looked up at the offices that commanded one of New York's prime locations in the heart of the financial sector.

She had been to his office several times before—little visits with Samantha—so she was recognised at the vast reception desk and waved across to the bank of elevators, one of which would take her to the top floor of the thirty-four-storeyed building.

His offices were the working equivalent of his apartment. Luxurious, plush, silent, industrious. His own office, perched at the end of the thickly carpeted corridor, was as big as some people's flats, with one section partitioned for his personal assistant and another, larger one, comprising a comfortable sitting area with leather chairs and plants and little tables. She knew that there was even a bathroom adjoining his office, for those times when he came in very early or was obliged to leave very late.

It struck her forcibly that the size and the opulence of it was a glaring reminder of just one of the many differences between them.

Thinking like that made her feel even more nervous, and she tried to project a composed demeanour as she stopped to chat to his secretary.

He wouldn't be aware that she was even there, and Tess was tempted to give him just a little bit longer to enjoy his carefree life before she blew it to smithereens.

Matt, buzzed eventually by his secretary, felt a kick

of satisfaction knowing that Tess was waiting to see him. She had been on his mind even more, having seen her at that party. He didn't know what she wanted, but when he thought that she might actually be reconsidering her options he felt like a predator in full and final control of its elusive prey. Maybe she had gone to the party to meet a man, but he had thought about that and eventually dismissed the notion. It really didn't tally with what he had come to know about her. At any rate, he liked to think that seeing him had made her realise what she really missed. She would only be around for a few more days, but he was more than willing to reluctantly set aside his pride and take her back to his bed. In fact—and he barely acknowledged this—it was a shame that she had made the fatal mistake of trying to tie him down, because who knew what might have been the next natural step for them...? He might just have offered her the very thing she had so obviously craved...

He didn't immediately look up when she quietly entered, although his senses went on sudden red alert. When she cleared her throat he finally raised his eyes, and then sat back in his chair without saying a word.

'I'm sorry if I'm disturbing you...' she began, painfully aware of his lack of welcome. He might just as well have set a timer on his desk and told her that she had one minute to state her case.

'You're lucky to find me here,' Matt told her politely. 'I have a meeting in a matter of minutes, so whatever you've come to say, you need to say it quickly.'

Faced with such bluntness, Tess dithered in an agony of uncertainty. She had vaguely rehearsed what she might say, but now she was looking at him every single thought vanished from her head. She felt possessed of roughly the same amount of confidence as a rabbit staring at two headlights bearing down on it at great speed.

'Well?' Matt said impatiently. 'What is it? I haven't got all day.'

'Even if you had, I still don't think I'd find this easy to say,' Tess told him shakily.

Something in the tone of her voice infused him with ominous foreboding. He went completely still and waited.

'You're going to be mad, but…I'm pregnant…'

CHAPTER EIGHT

MATT froze. He wondered if he had misheard her, but then immediately revised that notion as he looked at her face. She was white as a sheet and leaning forward in the chair, body as rigid as a piece of wood. *Mad?* She thought that he might be *mad*? That seemed to be the understatement of the century.

'You can't be,' he asserted bluntly, and Tess flinched.

'You mean you don't want me to be—but I am. I did a test this morning. In fact, I did more than one test.'

His usually sharp brain seemed to have shut down. Nothing had prepared him for this.

'You were protected,' he told her flatly.

With an abrupt movement that took her by surprise, he propelled himself out of his chair and walked towards the window. For once, his natural grace had deserted him.

'If this is some kind of ruse to get money out of me, then you can forget it!' He leant against the window and then restlessly began to prowl the office. He couldn't keep still. Running through his head was the thought that this just couldn't be happening.

'Why would I be using a ruse to get money out of you?'

'You can't accept that we're finished. You want to walk away with more than just a few memories. You *know* how much I'm worth!'

'I don't know how you can say that!' Tess exclaimed, dismayed. 'Since when do you know me to *ever* think about money? And I wouldn't make something like this up!'

No, she wouldn't. Painful sincerity was etched on her face. Whether he liked it or not, she wasn't lying. She was carrying his baby, and that was a fact with which he would have to deal whether he liked it or not. While he tried to scramble for some other explanation, he was already accepting the truth that had been forced upon him.

But beyond that there were still a lot of questions to be answered, a lot of perfectly reasonable suspicions to be dispelled—if, indeed, they could be. Surfacing through the fog of his confused thoughts, a line of pure logic crystallised, and in the face of that every natural instinct he possessed took second place.

She had bewitched him, made him behave in all sorts of ways that had been alien to him. Yes, he had had a good time with her. She had known how to make him laugh and she had relaxed him in a way no other woman had. But in the bigger picture how much did that really count for?

He had known her for a couple of months! And lo and behold, having assured him that she was fully protected, here she was—pregnant and knowing full well that her future would now be a gold-plated one. Did that make sense? Wasn't there something strangely suspicious about the circumstances?

Matt slammed the door shut on any shady areas in this scenario. He was conditioned to be suspicious. It was his protection. He wasn't about to abandon it now, even if he could see the glisten of tears in her eyes. He reached for the box of tissues he kept in his drawer and handed them to her, but there was a cold cast to his features that sent a chill to her heart.

'So. Explain.'

'That first time…'

Matt cast his mind back with a frown. 'If I recall, you assured me that—'

'Yes, I know what I said!' Tess interrupted fiercely. 'Okay. I lied.' Her eyes skittered helplessly from his dark, incredulous face.

She was aware of him picking up his phone, talking in low tones to his secretary, knew that he was telling her that he didn't wish to be disturbed. While he spoke, she did her best to get her tangled thoughts in order.

'That didn't come out right,' she said, as soon as he was off the line. Nervously, she plucked a tissue from the box on her lap and began shredding it with shaking fingers. 'It wasn't so much a lie as…I economised a bit with the truth. When you asked me whether I was taking any contraception, I was so…so turned on that I didn't want us to stop…'

Without warning Matt's mind did an abrupt detour and swerved off back to that night when they had made love for the first time. He had never been so turned on in his life before. Even thinking about it now… But, no, there was no way that he was going to let his body dictate his handling of this situation. He didn't care how turned on she had been. She had deliberately lied—taken a chance with life-altering consequences attached.

'So you decided to let me go ahead. You *risked a pregnancy* for a moment of passion. You threw away your virginity and played fast and loose with both our lives because you *just couldn't help yourself...*'

'I didn't *throw away* my virginity. I gave it away. I gave it to you because I wanted to—because you were the first man to make me feel like that. I've always had a very regular cycle. I honestly thought that there would be no consequences.'

'I'm flattered that you were so overwhelmed by me that you just couldn't help yourself, but excuse me for thinking of a more prosaic reason that you hopped into bed with me.'

Tess looked at him in confusion. Everything about him was designed to threaten, and she didn't know whether he was aware of that. She had to twist in the chair to follow his movements, and her neck was beginning to ache from having to look up as he towered over her—a cold, distant stranger who had sliced through the fragile bridge that had once connected them. Her heart was breaking in two.

'Yes, I concede that you were turned on. But maybe it occurred to you that if you had to lose your virginity with anyone, why not lose it to someone who was a damn good financial bet? If I recall, I gave you every opportunity to take a step back, but maybe you didn't want to lose the chance. Maybe, subconsciously, you didn't mind playing with fate, because if you did get pregnant then it would be a very profitable venture for you...'

Anger brought a rush of colour to her cheeks. 'A

profitable venture? You think I *wanted* to get pregnant? You think I *want* to have a child at the age of twenty-three, when I'm just finally beginning to see a way ahead for myself? I was actually thinking about going into teaching! I was going to work with children because I got so much pleasure from working with Sam. I was going to go back to school and try and get the qualifications I should have got years ago! Do you really think that I *want* to ditch all of that?'

She stood up, trembling. She shouldn't have come. She had messed up his wonderful life. She should have just returned to Ireland. He would never have known about the pregnancy. In fact, she should never have got involved with him in the first place. She should have taken one look at the fabulous trappings surrounding him and realised that he was not in her league and never would be.

'I'm going to leave now,' she mumbled, frantically trying to hold on to her composure. 'I just thought that you needed to know...and now you do.'

She began walking towards the door. She didn't get very far. In fact two steps. Then Matt was standing in front of her—six feet two inches of menacing male.

'*Going to leave?* Tell me that was a joke.'

'What else is there to say?'

Matt stared at her as though she had taken leave of her senses—maybe started speaking in tongues.

'You've dropped a bomb on me and you *don't think that there's anything more to say?* Am I dealing with someone from the same planet?'

'There's no need to be cruel and sarcastic. It's...I'm dealing with the same shock as you...'

Matt raked his fingers through his hair and shook his head, as though trying to will himself into greater self control.

He was shaken to his very foundations. Had he felt the same way when Catrina had declared herself pregnant with Samantha? He had been so much younger then, and willing to drift into doing the right thing. Since those youthful days a lot of lessons had been learnt. He had erected barriers around himself and they had served him well.

Now he was staring at a problem, and whether he liked it or not it was a problem that would have to be dealt with. But all problems had solutions, and flinging accusations at the woman who was going to be the mother of his child would get neither of them anywhere.

And how clever had he been to accuse her of ulterior motives? Now she was staring at him with big, tear-filled green eyes, as if he had morphed into a monster, when in fact he had just reacted in the way every single man in his position would have reacted under similar circumstances.

That didn't alleviate the niggle of guilt, but he firmly squashed that momentary weakness.

'I don't feel comfortable having this conversation here,' he told her shortly.

'What difference does it make where we have the conversation?' Tess looked down at her feet, stubbornly digging her heels in. She didn't want to go to his apartment. Nor did she want to go to Claire's apartment. For starters, Claire knew nothing of what was going on. Right now she was on a job in Brooklyn, but what if she and Matt went to the apartment to continue their conversation and Claire unexpectedly showed up?

Tess knew that sooner or later everything would have to come out in the wash, but right now she felt equipped to deal with only one horrendous situation at a time. Her mind just wouldn't stretch further ahead.

In truth, she wanted to be somewhere as public and as impersonal as possible. It seemed to make things easier to handle.

'This is my place of work,' Matt intoned, already taking it as a foregone conclusion that she would follow his lead by heading towards the jacket which was slung over the back of one of the leather chairs. 'I've instructed my secretary not to disturb me, but a lot of meetings will be cancelled. Sooner or later she will come in and expect some kind of explanation from me, and when she doesn't get a satisfactory one she'll be curious. Frankly, I would rather not generate public curiosity in my private life.'

'What will you tell her?' Tess reluctantly conceded his point. He was an intensely private man. 'I'm not going to Claire's apartment and I won't go to yours.'

'Why not?' Matt paused and looked at her through narrowed eyes.

Heat shimmered through her. Alone with him... She didn't want her strength to be put to the test. She knew how weak she could be when she was around him. She had to build up an immunity, and enclosed spaces would be the worst possible start to doing that. If he could be considered an illness, and falling in love with him some kind of terrible virus that had flooded her entire system, then detachment was the first step to a possible cure.

'Are you suddenly scared of me?' he asked softly. 'What do you think I'm going to do?'

Tess shamefully thought that the danger would be *wanting* him to do things that he shouldn't do and she definitely shouldn't want. Given a lifebelt, she clutched it with both hands. Hadn't he accused her of the most horrible things? That being the case, why shouldn't she accuse *him* of a few?

'I don't know!' she flung back in a shaky voice. 'You've insulted me. You've as good as told me that I set everything up—that I took risks because I wanted to trap you. You've been a bully. Of course I don't want to be anywhere with you, unless there are lots of people around.'

'Are you saying that you're afraid that I might be physically threatening?'

'No, of course I'm not...'

A dark flush had accentuated his high cheekbones. 'I have never laid a finger on a woman before, whatever the provocation. The thought of it alone is anathema to me!'

'I'm tired,' Tess muttered wearily. 'I don't want to be badgered. Maybe you should just think about things overnight and then we can speak tomorrow. Or the day after, even.'

Matt didn't bother to dignify such delaying tactics with a response. He had never been a believer in putting off for tomorrow what could be done today. Problems not faced head-on, he had discovered to his personal cost, never went away—they just got out of hand.

'Wait for me by the lift,' he instructed her, 'I will need to discuss rearranging my schedule.'

'Really, Matt. There's no need to put your entire day on hold! Just let me go home and we can both discuss this when it's sunk in and…and we're both calmer.'

'I'm perfectly calm. In fact, given the situation, I couldn't be calmer.' Nor was he lying. The fog was beginning to clear and a solution was presenting itself. It was the inevitable solution, but already he was coming to terms with it. He was rising to the occasion and that, for him, was something of which to be proud. She would discover soon enough that he was a man who shouldered his responsibility—even when, as in this instance, it was occasioned by something out of his control.

Strangely, he didn't feel as cornered as he might have expected.

Tess regarded him helplessly. He could be as immovable as a block of granite. This was one such occasion. 'Then we'll go to a café. Or a coffee shop. Or even just find a bench somewhere.' When he nodded, she gave a little sigh of resignation and left him slipping on his jacket, shutting down his computer, getting ready to face one of the most important conversations of his life.

It was pointless pushing the button. He was with her in less than five minutes. He had told her that he was calm and he looked calm. Cool, calm and composed. If nothing else, he was brilliant when it came to hiding his feelings. In fact, he could have been nominated for an award, judging from the performance he was putting on as he depressed the button and they took the lift down.

There was a coffee shop two blocks away, he was

telling her. It would be relatively quiet at this time of day.

When she asked him, stiff and staring straight ahead like a mannequin, what he had told his secretary, he shrugged and said that he had intimated some sort of situation with his new nanny. Nothing new there, he had implied to her. It had been a thirty-second conversation. His secretary wasn't paid to ask intrusive questions.

As the lift door purred open, Tess thought that anyone listening to their impersonal, polite conversation would have been forgiven for thinking that there was absolutely nothing amiss.

Matt continued to talk to her as they walked towards the coffee shop.

He certainly didn't think he had overreacted to a word she had said, but he had still managed to scare her—and that didn't sit right with him. To think that she had looked at him with those wide green eyes and effectively informed him that she didn't want to be in his company without the safety of an anonymous public around her had shocked him to the core.

It was essential to put her at ease. Talking about nothing in particular as they covered the short distance to the coffee shop was step one in that procedure.

Once there, he installed her at a table away from the window and any possible distractions and ordered them both something to drink and eat—although when he appeared with two lattes and a selection of pastries Tess glanced at him and blushed.

'To be honest, I've gone off coffee,' she confessed. 'And food in general. I have morning sickness that lasts all day, pretty much.'

Which made it all so real that his eyes were drawn to her still flat stomach. His baby! Unlike the Matt of ten years ago, this Matt was finding it strangely pleasurable to contemplate impending fatherhood—even with the dilemmas involved. There was much to be said for maturity.

'I can get you something else. Name it. Whatever you want.'

'You're suddenly being nice. Why?'

Matt sat down and helped himself to a cinnamon roll. 'If you think that I reacted too strongly, then I apologise, but this has come as a shock. I've been very careful when it comes to making sure that…accidents never happen…'

Tess hung her head in guilty shame. And, as luck would have it, this 'accident' had occurred with a woman who had never been destined to be a permanent fixture in his life. He might not have lasted the course with Vicky, but Tess couldn't imagine that he would ever have accused *her* of staging a pregnancy for his money.

'However,' Matt continued, interrupting her train of thought before it had time to take hold and plunge her into further depths of misery, 'there's no point dwelling on that. We're both facing a problem and there are always solutions to problems. Have you told anyone about…this situation?'

'I've only just found out myself!' Claire didn't have a clue as to what was going on. She would be in for a double shock. Tess shuddered just thinking about it. When she paused to consider her parents, her mind went blank. Beyond that, there were so many practical concerns that she hardly knew where to begin—and here he was, cool as a cucumber, working it out as though it was a maths question with an easy answer.

'Well, sooner rather than later, that's going to have to change. Your parents are going to have to know, for a start.'

'Yes, I *realise* that…'

'How do you think they're going to react?'

'I…I haven't thought about it. Yet.'

'And then there's the question of money.' He watched her carefully, but she was obviously still mulling over the thought of breaking the news to her parents. He knew that she was very close to them. He could see where her thoughts were going. 'Fortunately for you, I am prepared to take full responsibility for this. I think you know where this is leading.'

Cinnamon roll finished, Matt looked at her over the rim of his mug and said nothing until he had her full and undivided attention.

'We will be married. There is no other option.'

He waited for signs of relief and gratitude. Now that his proposal had been made, he decided that things might have been considerably worse. Their relationship might have come to an end, but that end had been prematurely engendered by the fact that she had given him an ultimatum—by the fact that time had not been on their side. Yes, he had certainly concluded that she was not his ideal match, at least on paper, but his thinking had had to change and change it had. Never let it be said that he wasn't blessed with an ability to get the best out of a thorny situation.

Relief and gratitude were taking their time, and Matt frowned at her. 'Well? We're going to have to proceed quickly. I will break it to my parents, and then arrangements can be made for a wedding. Something small would be appropriate, I think you'll agree.'

'Are you *proposing* to me?'

'Can you think of a better solution?' Matt was prey to a one-off, very peculiar feeling. He was a knight in shining armour, she the damsel in distress. He had never been given to fanciful notions of this nature, but he was now, and a sensation of general wellbeing spread through him with a warm glow.

Her eyes glistened and he whipped out his handkerchief—pristine white.

'This is everything I ever dreamed of,' Tess said bitterly. 'And I'm not going to embarrass you by bursting into tears in the middle of a coffee shop, so you can have your handkerchief back.'

'I guess it is,' Matt concurred.

'All my life,' Tess continued in a driven undertone that finally caught his attention, 'I've dreamt of a man proposing to me because he has no choice. What girl wouldn't want that? To know that a guy who doesn't love her, and in fact was glad to see the back of her, is big enough to marry her because she's pregnant!'

For a few seconds Matt was stunned into speechlessness. Twice in one day so far he had been lost for words! Tess wondered whether a world record had been set.

'Furthermore,' she carried on, 'haven't you learnt *any* lessons from your past?'

'You're losing me. Correction. You've *lost* me.' Having leant forward, he now flung himself back in the chair and gave her a scorching look from under his lashes. 'I can't think of a single woman who wouldn't be jumping up and down with joy at this juncture! Not only am I *not* walking away, I'm positively offering a solution. You are having my baby. You will therefore be protected—as will our child. With my ring on your finger you will never need or want for anything in your life again. And what *lessons*,' he added belatedly, 'are you talking about?'

'I'm talking about your ex-wife, Matt! Catrina?'

'What about her?'

'You married her because she fell pregnant. You married her out of a misguided sense of responsibility.'

'I married her because I was young and foolish. Her pregnancy had very little to do with it.'

'Look…' She took a few deep, calming breaths. 'I understand that you want to do the right thing but the right thing, isn't for us to get married.'

'You're telling me that a stable home life for a child is unimportant?'

'You *know* that's not what I'm saying,' Tess cried in frustration. 'Of *course* a stable home life is very important for a child! But two people living under the same roof for the wrong reasons doesn't make for a stable home life. It makes for…for bitterness and resentment. It wouldn't be right for both of us to sacrifice our lives and a shot at real happiness because I happen to have fallen pregnant.'

Matt was finding it hard to credit that she was turning him down, but turning him down she was. Only days ago she had been desperate to prolong their relationship, and now, when he was offering her the chance to do so, she was throwing it back in his face as though he had insulted her in the worst possible way! On some very basic level, it defied understanding.

'You're not being logical.'

'I'm being incredibly logical. I won't marry you, Matt. I know I wanted us to carry on seeing one |another—I know I would have stayed here a while longer if you had wanted me to—but I've had time to think about that, and you were right. It would never have worked out. We just aren't suited, and we're not going to become magically suited just because I made a mistake and fell pregnant.'

Matt felt the ground shifting awkwardly under his feet.

'You won't be returning to Ireland.' He delivered this with brutal certainty. 'If you think that you're going to make your bid for happiness across the Atlantic, then you're going to have to think again.'

A shot at real happiness? He pictured her having her shot at real happiness with one of those sappy guys she claimed to be attracted to and it was a picture that made him see red. He wasn't going to get embroiled in a long debate about it, however. Reluctantly he admitted that he was in a very vulnerable place. The second he had arrived at his solution to their problem, the very minute he had understood what would have to be done and had reconciled himself to the inevitable with a great deal of largesse, he had expected her to follow suit.

'Then I guess we'll have to talk about arrangements,' she said heavily.

Matt shook his head in the impatient gesture of a man trying to rid himself of something irritating but persistent.

'I would never deprive you of having a bond with

your child,' she continued gently. 'I know what you went through with Samantha.'

'So what are your suggestions?' When it came to the art of compromise, his skills were remarkably under-developed, but now Matt understood that compromise was precisely what he would have to do. Until he could persuade her round to his point of view. Legitimising their relationship made perfect sense to him, but he knew that he would have a lot of ground to cover. He had sidelined her, and she wasn't going to let him forget that—even though circumstances had now irrevocably changed.

Like a dog with a bone, he chewed over her assumptions that they were better off apart, that they were ill suited to one another. She seemed to have forgotten very quickly just how compatible they had been—and not just in bed. This about-turn in his thinking was perfectly acceptable to Matt. Things were different now. Instead of trying to spot the possible downsides, she should be trying to see the definite upsides. As he was! He was prepared to make any necessary sacrifices. Why shouldn't she?

'I could stay on in Manhattan…'

'That's non-negotiable.'

'Maybe live with Claire until I find myself a flat and a job.'

'Have you heard a word I said?' Matt looked at her incredulously. 'You won't be working. There will be no need. Nor will you be rooming with your sister.' His face registered distaste. 'If you're hell-bent on not accepting my proposal, then a suitable place will be found. Somewhere close. *Very* close.' He scowled, still disgruntled with the way his plans had been derailed. 'With regards to my work, I know that you want to contribute financially, but there will be no need for you to think that I come as part of the package.'

'Why are you so determined to put obstacles in my way!'

'I'm not putting obstacles in your way, Matt. You accused me of having ulterior motives in going to bed with you...' Tess felt her voice wobble, just thinking back to that hurtful accusation.

'I apologise,' he inserted quickly. 'You have to understand that it's my nature to be suspicious. I was just taking a step back and voicing possibilities.'

'There's no point trying to backtrack now,' Tess told him stiffly. 'You said what you said in the heat of the moment but you meant every word. I'm not happy about the thought of living off you, and I won't do it.'

'Most women would kill for what you're being offered,' Matt intoned with intense irritation.

'I'm not *most women*, so don't you go bundling me up in the same parcel as everyone else!'

'What job are you going to get?'

'I want to go into teaching. I told you. I'll investigate the process.'

Matt instantly determined that, whatever the process was, he would make sure that he decided it. He would not envisage a life with his child being raised separately while Tess vanished off to teach other people's children. She should be with her own, keeping the home fires burning for him, looking after Samantha...

It was a comfortable image. Seductive even.

'Now—' Tess stood up '—I feel really drained. It's

been stressful for me too, believe it or not, and I have a lot of things to be thinking about. So if you don't mind I'm going to head back to the apartment. I'll be in touch with you tomorrow.'

He was being dismissed! Control had been completely wrested from his possession, and for once he was in the position of having to grit his teeth and take it.

'What time? I could send Stanton for you. We can have lunch. Dinner, if you prefer. There's still a lot to discuss...'

'I'll...I'll let you know...' Tess said vaguely. She had so much to think about. Was she doing the right thing? He had offered marriage. Was it fair to the baby growing inside her that she turned him down? Her head felt as though it would burst.

They both needed space to think, and she wouldn't let him call the shots. That was a dangerous road which she had already travelled. Matt Strickland didn't love her. He never had and he never would, and the arrival of a baby wouldn't change that. And without love how could she marry him? That thought infused her with strength.

'Perhaps the day after tomorrow,' she amended. 'And then we can meet up and talk this over like two adults. Once we've done that, we can start sorting out the practicalities. This sort of thing happens to loads of people. We're not unique. We can both deal with it and move on.'

CHAPTER NINE

TESS returned to her sister's apartment to find that nothing in life ever went according to plan. The answer-machine was blinking furiously and there were five messages. Four were from her sister and one was from her mum. Her mother's message, delivered in an awkward, stilted voice—her *I'm-leaving-a-message* voice—informed her that her father had been rushed to hospital with a suspected heart attack. 'Everything will be fine, we're sure,' her mother had added as an afterthought. 'No need for you to come back home early. Our Mary is on top of things. It's wonderful to have a doctor in the family.'

The remaining messages were from Claire, repeating what their mother had communicated and adding that she was at the airport and would be in the air by the time Tess got the message. Then she demanded, 'Don't you ever answer your cell phone?'

There were eight missed calls and several text messages. Her cell phone had been innocently forgotten and was still in the kitchen, on charge.

The thoughts that had been driving her crazy on the trip back to the apartment now flew out of her head, replaced by panic. Her father was *never* ill. In fact, Tess

didn't think that he had ever registered with a doctor—
or if he had he had been a once-in-a-lifetime patient. If
her mother had seen fit to call, then it must be serious.
That was the path her logic took. It also advised her to
get on the next flight out.

She flung some things in a hand luggage bag, and
on the way to the airport reflected that getting out of
the country for a while was probably the best thing that
could have happened. Away from Manhattan, she would
have time to think in peace. She would phone Matt in a
few days and arrange to meet with him just as soon as
she judged that her father was fit and fine.

Not seeing him would be the biggest act of kindness
she could give herself, because seeing him earlier on
had just reconfirmed what she had already known. He
wreaked havoc with her peace of mind. The second she
laid eyes on him it was as if an electric charge had been
plunged into her, and it didn't matter how much she tried
to think herself out of feeling that way, she was helpless
against his impact.

Some time away from him—even a few days—would
allow her to build up some defences. She would have to
face the unappealing reality that her life was going to
change for ever. Not only would she have a permanent
tie with Matt, but she would be condemned to follow
the outcome of his choices through the years. She would
have to watch from the outside as he became involved
with other women, shared his life with them, introduced
them to Samantha and to their own child. However much
he wanted to take on responsibility, she'd had to release
him from a sacrifice that would have destroyed them

both, and it wouldn't be long before his relationship with her became purely functional.

She would have to learn to deal with that. She would get a job when the baby was born. Not immediately. First she would check out colleges and see what might be required of her. Those weeks of teaching Samantha had bolstered her confidence. She would start her academic climb with a positive outcome in sight. In time, she would get a job and meet someone else. Someone more suitable.

When she began to think about this mystery man, waiting just around a mythical corner, her thoughts became vague, and she had to stop herself from making the sweeping assumption that no one could ever possibly compete with Matt.

As soon as she landed in Ireland she phoned her mother who, like her, had a habit of forgetting her mobile phone—leaving it on counters, in the bedroom, sometimes on top of the television. Because, 'If it's important, whoever it is will call the proper phone.' There was no reply.

Exhausted after her long flight over, and greeted with a damp, unappealing Ireland which seemed so much quieter and so much less vibrant after the excitement of New York, Tess took a cab back to her home.

The buzz of the city was well and truly left behind as the taxi meandered along the highway and then trundled along narrow streets surrounded by great stretches of countryside, as though the cab driver had all the time in the world.

He talked incessantly, and Tess made a few agreeable

noises while allowing her thoughts to wander like flot-
sam and jetsam on an ocean current. She pictured her
father lying grey-faced and vulnerable on a hospital
bed. Mary would know exactly what was going on, and
would give her a more realistic assessment than either
her mother or Claire. When she thought of her father
being seriously ill she began to perspire, and switched
her thoughts to her own problem. Although she would
be seeing her entire family, she would not be able to
breathe a word about her condition. She would have to
wait until things calmed down a bit—then she would
break the news. The very last thing either of her parents needed was yet more stress. Maybe she would wait
until she returned to Manhattan. She hoped her mother
wouldn't expect her to stay on.

It was yet another possible complication that she once
again shied away from facing. Life as she once knew it
now seemed simple in comparison, but looking around
her as the taxi drew into the small village where she had,
until recently, lived with her parents, Tess wondered how
she hadn't itched to fly the coop long ago. Everything
was so *small* and so *static*. They drove past the village
hall, the shops, the cinema. Several miles away there
was a bigger town, where she had always gone with
her friends, but even that seemed rural and placid in
comparison to the vigour of Manhattan.

The house was empty when she arrived, but signs of
occupation were everywhere to be seen. Mary's jacket
hung on the banister. Claire's bag had been dumped in
the hall and lay half open, with items of clothing spilling
out.

The immediacy of the situation grabbed Tess by

the throat, and all thoughts of Matt were temporarily jettisoned.

The next few hours were a blur of activity. She was deeply, deeply exhausted, but her body continued operating on autopilot. She contacted Claire, then drove her mother's car to the hospital—and that felt very strange after a diet of public transport, taxis and Matt's private chauffeur.

'He just complained of feeling a bit out of breath,' her mother whispered, drawing her to one to whisper. 'The old fool.' Her eyes had begun watering but she soldiered on and blinked her tears away. 'Never had a day's illness in his life, so he didn't want me to call the doctor. Thank the Lord I did! They say it's just a scare. He's going to be fine. But he'll have to give up some of his favourite foods. He's not going to like that. You know your dad.'

It was late by the time Tess's body finally caught up with. One minute she was chatting with her sisters and her mother in the kitchen, then she was having her shower, slipping into a nightie, and then her head hit the pillow and she disappeared into sleep as though tranquillised.

And that continued to be the case for the next three days. She settled into a routine of sorts—back in her old bedroom, sharing the bathroom with Mary and Claire and bickering with them about the length of time they took whenever they ran a bath. Her father was improving steadily and had begun to complain about the hospital food, which seemed a good sign.

Lurking at the back of the gentle chaos and the cosiness of the familiar was Matt's dark, brooding presence, and the pressing situation with which they had yet to deal. But every time Tess reached for the phone to call him her hand faltered and she began sweating, and then she'd postpone the conversation which she knew would inevitably have to be made. After the second day he began to leave messages on her mobile, and missed calls were registered. Tess decided to give it until the weekend to get in touch. The weekend would mark five days out of contact.

Mary would be returning to London and Claire would be going with her, taking a few days off to remain in the country and using the opportunity to import Tom, so that they could do some shopping and also meet the parents if she deemed that her father was up to it. She had already e-mailed her resignation and seemed to have no regrets about losing her high-flying job in Manhattan because Tom would be transferring to London. Between her father's improving health and Claire's exciting news Tess was happy to sideline herself in the background, where she could nurse her own worries in peace.

Which was precisely what she was doing in her room, with her tiny, very old television turned on very low, telling her about unexpected flooding in Cornwall, when her mobile went and an unknown number was displayed.

At the very height of his frustration Matt had invested in a new phone, with a new number, because after days of trying without success he could think of no other way of getting in contact with her.

He'd hesitated to telephone her sister. What excuse could he possibly give? Tess had been adamant that she would break the news to her family in her own time.

Already dealing with having his perfectly formulated plan to marry her turned on its head, the last thing he needed would be to arm her with more grounds for grievance.

Over a period of three days his mood had travelled on a one-way road from poor to appalling. He couldn't get her out of his mind. Then he'd begun to worry. What if she had been taken ill? Been in an accident? Was lying somewhere in a hospital, unable to get in touch? The surge of sickening emotion that had filled him at the thought of that had been shocking—although, as he had shakily reminded himself, perfectly understandable given her condition. He was a man of honour. He *would* be shaken to the core at the thought of the mother of his child falling ill and being unable to get in touch with him.

But before he began ringing round the hospitals in the area he'd had the last-minute brainwave of buying a new phone   one with a new and unrecognisable number— just in case she simply wasn't answering his calls.

The second he heard her voice at the other end of the line he felt a spasm of red-hot anger envelop him like a mist. He realised that he had been *worried sick* about her.

'So you *are* alive,' were his opening words.

On the other side of the Atlantic, Tess sat up in bed. The sound of his voice was like a shot of adrenaline, delivered intravenously.

'Matt…I've been meaning to give you a call.'

'Really? When?' It was just as well that she wasn't within strangling distance, he thought with barely suppressed fury. 'In case you haven't noticed, I've made several hundred calls to you over the past few days. *Where the hell are you?* I've been to the apartment four times and no one has been there!'

'I needed to have a little time to myself.' She glanced around her furtively, half expecting to see him materialise out of thin air, so forceful was his personality even over a telephone thousands of miles away.

'I'm sick to death of hearing what *you* need!' He had to stop himself from roaring down the line. There was no place for anything less than civilised behaviour in their situation, but the woman brought out a side to him that he hadn't known existed and one which he found difficult to control. Not even with Catrina, at the very height of their dysfunctional marriage, when revelations had been pouring out from the woodwork like termites, had he felt so uncontrollably responsive. Where with Catrina he had taken refuge from his problems by burying himself in his work, with Tess that was no solution. However hard he tried, it was impossible to focus. 'Running away isn't the solution! Where *are* you?'

'I'm...' Two things stopped her from telling him the truth. The first was the knowledge that to confess that she was on the other side of the Atlantic, having taken off without bothering to let him know, would make him even angrier than he already sounded. The second was the fact that she *couldn't* let him know where she was. He was her problem in America, and with her father still recuperating there was no way that she wanted him to intrude and possibly risk jeopardising her father's recovery. How would her parents react if he phoned the house and gave the game away? Let slip that she was pregnant? Single and pregnant by a man who wasn't going to be her husband? Her parents would have to be gently eased into that, and this was not the right time.

'I'm out of New York. Just for…for a few days. I know we have stuff to talk about, and I'll give you a call just as soon as I return.'

'Where. Are. You?'

'I'm…'

'If you don't tell me where you are,' he said in a calmer voice, 'then I'll do some investigative work and find out for myself. You would be surprised how fast I can get information when I want it.'

'I told you—'

'Yes, I know what you told me, and I'm choosing to ignore it.'

'I'm back home,' Tess confessed, 'in Ireland. My dad got rushed into hospital and I just had to get to the airport and fly over.'

Matt paused. 'Rushed into hospital with what?'

'A heart attack scare. Look, I'm sorry—'

'And is he all right?' Matt interrupted tersely.

'On the mend. We're all very relieved.'

'Why didn't you say so in the first place? No. Better question. Why didn't you answer one of my five hundred calls and *tell* me that?'

'I had a lot on my mind…and I wanted to have some space to think…'

Across the water, alarm bells started ringing.

Matt was in no doubt that her initial reaction to hearing about her father would have been to hop on the first flight out. Although he was close enough to his parents, they had always been highly social and very much involved in their own lives. Tess, on the other hand, was fiercely attached to her parents and her sisters. He assumed that she would not have broken the news about her pregnancy to them—not given the circumstances.

But *why* hadn't she picked up any of his phone calls? Or returned any of them?

Space to think amongst her tightly knit family unit, back on her home turf, allied itself, in his head, with her desire to find happiness with someone else. It was not a happy alliance. With the comforting familiarity of her village around her, how long before she started contemplating the prospect of foregoing the stress of the unknown in New York? He was certain that her parents would react kindly to her pregnancy. Perhaps a small moral lecture, but they would weather the news and immediately provide support.

New York would fast become a distant memory. She might nurse some scruples about running away, but how long before she recalled the adverse way in which he had reacted to news of the pregnancy? How long before she started thinking of his insinuations about the financial benefits of having his baby—his implication that she might have engineered an agreeable financial nest egg for herself? Would she take time to step back and consider *his* side of the story? See where *his* perfectly understandable concerns stemmed from?

Not for the first time, Matt wondered why she couldn't have been one of the scores of willing women who would have been *overjoyed* at a marriage proposal from him and the financial security for life it entailed. But then the thought of Tess falling into line with one of those women was laughable.

She was telling him now about how much it was helping, being back in Ireland.

'So when exactly do you expect to be back here?' he cut in. Now that his brain had taken off on another tangent, like a runaway horse, he was alert to that shade of hesitation before she answered, and was composed and understanding when she mumbled something about as soon as she could—though she couldn't very well leave her mum on her own immediately. Not with Mary and Claire both gone.

He rang off shortly after.

There was a considerable amount of work for him to do. Meetings with important clients, bankers, lawyers. It only took a few phone calls to rearrange that situation.

His next call was to his mother, who would cover for him at home in his absence, ensuring that Samantha had a familiar face when he wasn't around. She had only just started at her new school and, whilst everything seemed to be progressing with startling ease, he still felt better knowing that she would return to the apartment and someone who actually had a vested interest in whether she did her homework or not.

Then he called Samantha, who had to be fetched out of her class and was breathless when she picked up. Amidst the turmoil, her moment of disappointment when he broke the news that he would be out of town for a couple of nights was a light on the horizon.

His calls completed, Matt informed his secretary to get him on the first flight out to Ireland.

He was thinking on his feet—something he was excellent at. He left his office with instructions for his flight details to be texted to him within the hour, and then he was heading back to his apartment, packing the minimum of things, fired up by an urgency to *act*.

He didn't know whether Tess would have run away to find her space to think had she not been called on an emergency, but now that she *had* left the country he wasn't going to hang around to find out whether her return was on the cards.

Tess Kelly was unpredictable in the extreme. There were also hormones rushing through her body. He wasn't completely clueless about pregnancy. Under the influence of her hormones, she was capable of pretty much *any* rash decision!

As fresh thoughts superimposed themselves on already existing ones, his decision to go to Ireland seemed better and better by the second.

Having checked out the paperwork which she had dutifully filled in at her time of employment, he had easily ascertained her parents' address. The only question was whether he would show up unannounced on the doorstep, or get to see her via a more roundabout route.

Respecting the situation concerning her father, Matt arrived in Ireland intending to settle himself into a local hotel and then consider his next step forward. His intention was blocked when he discovered that there was no hotel in the village, which was much smaller than he might have expected.

'Where *is* the nearest hotel?' He impatiently directed his question to the taxi driver, who seemed quite pleased to have delivered his fare to the middle of nowhere.

'Depends on what sort of hotel you're looking for.'

Fed up, Matt decided to take his chances on going directly to her parents' house, and he handed the driver a slip of paper on which he had scribbled the address. He would deal with whatever problem arose from his decision with his customary aplomb.

It was a matter of fifteen minutes before the taxi was pulling up in front of a Victorian house with a pristine front garden and enough acreage to just about avoid being overlooked by the neighbours.

The flight had been long and tiresome, even in first class, but Matt was raring to go. He felt as though he had spent the past few days sitting on his hands, and that just wasn't his style. He was confrontational by nature.

He was prepared for anything and anyone as he pressed the doorbell and waited.

Not for a moment did it occur to him that no one would be home, and the sound of hurrying footsteps rewarded him for his confidence.

Tess had been looking forward to a bit of peace and quiet. Claire had left not an hour ago, and shortly after that her mother had gone to the hospital, leaving Tess to tidy up the house, which hadn't been touched properly since her father had been taken into hospital.

She had no idea who could be at the door. She debated not answering and hoping that the caller would eventually get the message and disappear, but she couldn't do it.

Pulling open the door, dressed in old clothes which she had worn as a teenager—faded track pants and an old tee shirt that should have been thrown out a long time ago—Tess half wished that she *had* ignored the bell, although for a few heart-stopping seconds, she didn't quite believe her eyes.

Matt was larger than life—dramatic against the crisp Irish scenery and the quietness of the rural backdrop.

'You look surprised to see me.'

He remained on the doorstep and looked at her. Her caramel-coloured hair was pulled up into a scruffy ponytail, and her clothes looked as though they had seen better days, but even so he still found it a strain to keep his hands to himself. He always knew when she wasn't wearing a bra, and she wasn't wearing one now. He could make out the slight hang of her breasts, and the tiny peaks where her nipples were jutting against the soft jersey of her tee shirt.

'Are you here on your own?' he asked, when she made no attempt to break the silence. 'I didn't want to crash land on you, Tess, but I felt that it might be better all round if I came here instead of waiting for you to return to America.'

'I haven't told anyone about us!' she breathed. 'There's no one at home now, but it would have been a disaster if you'd come two hours ago!'

'Oh, I don't think so,' Matt drawled, running out of patience. 'Sooner or later everyone is going to have to know, and ducking and pretending that that time isn't going to come won't solve anything. Are you going to invite me in?' He held out his hand and gave her a duty-free carrier bag from the airport. 'A book for your father—it's the latest one by that guy you told me that he likes—and a scarf for your mother.'

Tess stepped aside and watched warily as he entered the hallway. As happened everywhere he went, he dominated his surroundings and she couldn't wrest her eyes away from him. The sight of one of his designer holdalls in his hand broke the spell.

'How long are you planning on staying?' she asked, dismayed.

'I'm staying until you're ready to come back to America with me.'

'You mean you came all the way here to escort me back to New York? Like a kid who has run away from home?' Annoyed with herself, because her excitement levels had rocketed the second she had clapped eyes on him, thereby proving that all her hard work over the past few days had been for nothing, Tess was ready to pick a fight. Did he think that he could do just as he pleased? What did that herald for their future? Would she be relegated to being told what to do at a moment's notice, just because he could? Rich, beautiful Catrina from another powerful family had been able to assert her own terms, even if they had been unfair. *She*, on the other hand, had no such power behind her, so where exactly would she stand?

'Well, you may be here longer than you think.' Tess folded her arms. 'Claire and Mary have both left for London, and someone has to stay with Mum until Dad's back home. Maybe even longer. Who knows? She's going to need lots of help.'

'And you're going to volunteer for the post without breathing a word to either of them about your condition? I can't allow that.'

'You can't *allow* it?' Tess looked at him incredulously. 'Since when do you have a say in what I do and don't do?'

'We've been over this.' So he *had* been right to get on a plane and pursue her. She had no intention of hurrying back to New York. 'And I can't allow it because you're in no kind of condition to start doing heavy manual chores around the house. I will ensure that there is someone here to take the strain off your mother—'

'You'll do nothing of the kind!' Tess cried. 'She won't even know that you've been here!'

'And how do you figure on keeping me a secret?' Matt grated. 'Are you going to lock me away in a room somewhere and feed me scraps of food through a hole in the door? Because I'm telling you right now that's the only way you're going to be able to keep me out of sight. I didn't come here to have a fight with you!'

'No, you came to cart me away!' *You don't care about me*, she thought, as furious resentment rose to the surface and threatened to spill over. *You would have happily turned your back and never seen me again, but now here you are, suddenly concerned for my welfare because I happen to be pregnant with your child!*

'If needs be,' Matt confirmed with implacable steel. 'In the process, I intend to stay until I meet your parents and tell them what's going on.'

Tess blanched. 'You can't. Dad's not well.'

'What do you think will happen if you break the news to him? I'm tired of playing games with you over this, Tess. You're twenty-three years old. You're sexually active. You got pregnant. Which bit of that do you imagine would affect them most?'

Tess chewed her lip and looked away.

'Well?' Matt pressed. 'Do you think that they will

collapse on the spot if they find out that you've had a relationship.'

'It wasn't a relationship.' She knew exactly where the sticking point was with her parents—her charming, old-fashioned parents, with their old-fashioned ways and gentle moral code. 'They won't like the fact that I'm pregnant...they won't like it that I'm going to be a single mother. Neither of them can deal with that shock right now. You have to trust me.'

'I'm staying, Tess—and you can always spare them the shock of your being an unmarried mother, can't you? Think about it. Think about how happy they would be if they knew that their daughter was pregnant but was going to *marry* the father of her child...'

CHAPTER TEN

TESS looked at Matt in disbelief. 'I need to sit down,' she said shakily. She walked on legs that felt like wood into the comfortable sitting room and sank onto a squashy sofa, tucking her feet under her.

For a few moments Matt strolled through the room, barely noticing the pictures in the frames, the ornaments, all the reminders of a life greatly enhanced by children. His attention was focused on Tess. She looked small and vulnerable, huddled on the sofa, but Matt wasn't going to allow himself to feel sorry for her.

She had fled to Ireland without bothering to call him, she had ignored every phone call and message he had left for her, and she had as good as admitted that she had no intention of hurrying back to New York.

'That's blackmail.' She raised huge, accusing eyes to his and his mouth tightened.

'It's problem-solving. You're terrified that your parents are going to be disappointed in you, and I'm showing you that there's no need for that.'

'I've spent ages telling you why it would be a bad idea.'

'Yes. I heard all the reasons you churned out.' He sat heavily on the sofa, depressing it with his weight, and

Tess shifted awkwardly to avoid physical contact. 'You don't see the need to marry me just because we made a mistake. Life's too short to be trapped in a marriage for the wrong reasons. You want to spread your wings and find your soul mate.'

'You're twisting everything I said.'

'Tell me which bit you think I've got wrong. The trapped bit? The soul mate bit? Were you *ever* going to return to Manhattan? Or did you come back here with good intentions only to decide that you would erase me out of your life?'

'Of *course* I was going to return to New York! I'm not irresponsible! I want you to have a real bond with this child.'

'You're one hundred percent irresponsible!' Matt snapped. He looked at her with glowering, scowling intensity. 'You refuse to marry me. You refuse to acknowledge that a child needs both parents. You witnessed first-hand the hell I went through gaining Samantha's trust—trust that should have been mine by right but was destroyed by a vengeful ex-wife.'

'I can't bear to think of you putting up with me for the sake of a child.' Tess defied the suffocating force of his personality to put across her point of view. She thought of her parents and how they would react to the thought of her living a single, unsupported life in New York. Based on their experience, children should be born into a united home. How would they ever understand that love and marriage didn't necessarily go together? They were savvy enough when it came to the rest of the world, but she had a sinking feeling that they would be a lot less savvy when it came to their own offspring.

The fact that Claire was excitedly due to be married to the man of her dreams would make it all the harder for them to understand how she, Tess, had managed to become embroiled in the situation that she had.

Matt was offering her a way out, and for a split second she desperately wanted to take it. It wouldn't be ideal—no one could say that—but it would solve a lot of problems.

She pulled herself up short when she remembered how her cotton-candy daydreams and pointless, optimistic fantasising had landed her where she was now. She had fallen in love with him and dared to hope that time would work it's magic and miraculously *make* him love her. It hadn't, and she would be a complete fool to forget that. Marry him, she told herself sternly, and she would witness the slow build-up of his indifference. He would have affairs, even if he kept them under wraps for the sake of maintaining a phoney front, and she would never, ever be able to give herself a chance at finding someone who could care for her.

'Don't try and get into my head, Tess.'

'I know you.'

'I'm willing to make the sacrifice. Why aren't you? You were happy with me once,' he said brusquely. 'We got along. It's ridiculous for you to assume that we can't make a go of it.'

'If we could have made a go of it—if you had *wanted* to make a go of it—you would have asked me to stay. You would have been prepared to make a go of it then.'

Matt hesitated. 'This is too big for wounded pride

to come into the equation. Anyway, maybe I made a mistake.'

'Mistake? What kind of mistake?' She looked at him suspiciously. She had dared to hope so many times that the prospect of daring to hope again was literally exhausting. 'Since when does Matt Strickland *ever* make mistakes?' she muttered, and he gave her a crooked smile that made her heart flip over. 'I don't say that as a compliment,' she qualified quickly, before that smile made her start to lose ground. 'It's important to make mistakes. People learn from their mistakes. I made mistakes growing up. I've learnt from them.'

'Did you make a mistake with me?'

Tess flushed. 'If I could turn back time, I—'

'That's not what I'm asking. I'm asking if you think you made a mistake with me. I don't want an answer based on hypothesis.'

He was no closer to her now. In fact, he was leaning back, looking at her with brooding, narrowed eyes, and still she felt as though she was being touched.

'Because I don't think *I* made a mistake with *you*. I think the mistake I made was to let you go.'

Suddenly the air seemed close and the room too small. The breath caught in her throat and her skin was on fire.

'Don't you dare!' She stood up, trembling, and walked towards the window. Outside, the scene was peaceful. The carefully tended garden was ablaze with flowers. However, Tess was oblivious to the colourful summer landscape. Her heart was beating so hard that if she held her breath she was sure she would be able to hear it.

When she turned around it was to find him standing so close to her that she pressed herself against the
window-ledge. His proximity brought her close to a state
of panic. She trusted *him*. She just didn't trust *herself*.

'Don't dare...*what*? Come close to you? Why not?'
He shoved his hands into his pockets. If he didn't, he
knew what he would do. He would reach out and touch
her, maybe just tuck that stray strand of hair behind
her ear. Hell, her eyes were wide and panicked, and
he hated seeing her like this. He clenched his jaw and
kept his hands firmly tucked away. 'Why fight me?' he
muttered, and dark colour slashed his cheekbones. 'Why
fight *this*?'

'I don't know what you're talking about, and I don't
need you to try and undermine me. I know what you're
doing.'

'Tell me. What *am* I doing?'

'Everything it takes to get what you want,' Tess heard
herself say with unaccustomed bitterness. 'You've come
here so that you can take me back to New York because
you don't trust me. I'm sorry I didn't phone you, and I'm
sorry I didn't answer your messages, but I've needed to
take a little time out and I've been worried sick with
Dad being in hospital. Not that you care. The only thing
you care about is making sure that I'm in place, and
you'll do whatever it takes to get me there—even if it
means blackmailing me into doing what you want. You
know what it could do to my parents in the situation
they're in if you dump this news on them, but you'd go
right ahead and do it if you thought it would get you
what you want! And you expect me to *want* to commit
myself to you? When everything you do just confirms

that you're arrogant and ruthless and only care about what you want?' She drew in a deep breath and braced herself to continue. 'Don't even think of telling me that you made a mistake throwing away what we had!' Her voice was shrill and unforgiving. 'It's easy to say that now. Do you really think that I'd believe you?'

'You're upsetting yourself.'

'I'm not upsetting myself! *You're* upsetting *me*.'

'I don't want to do that. I…I never want to do that.' With an effort, Matt pushed himself away from her and returned to sit on the sofa. Like a slow motion sequence in a film, every mistake he had made with her rose up with reproving clarity.

He had been attracted to her, and without a second thought he had seduced her into his bed. He had accepted the gift of her virginity without bothering to question the devil in the detail, and then, when she had suggested remaining in New York, he had run a mile. Conditioned to identify himself through his work, and accustomed to always ensuring that it was placed at the top of the agenda, he had reacted to her reasonable requests about where their relationship was heading by backing away.

To compound his sins he had greeted news of her pregnancy with suspicion—only to further raise her guard and drive her away by insisting on trying to determine what she should do and what she shouldn't.

Had he even *once* thought about stepping back and taking stock of how he actually felt?

Not in the habit of doubting his ability to manage situations, Matt was shaken to the core at the realisation that he had blown it. She might tremble the second he got near her, but a physical response wasn't enough. It had never been enough. And yet he knew that if he told her that now she wouldn't believe a word he said, and he couldn't blame her.

Tess looked at him uneasily. For once his deepening silence didn't seem to indicate anything ulterior. He wasn't even looking at her. He was staring into space and his expression was unreadable.

She took a hesitant step away from the window, but it was only when she was standing in front of him that he raised his eyes to hers.

'I've screwed up,' he said bluntly. He raked his fingers into his hair and lowered his eyes. 'Of course I'm not going to blackmail you into anything.'

'You're not?'

'Sit. Please? And that's not a command. It's a request.'

Tess, caught off guard by this strangely unsettling and subdued side to him, perched primly on the edge of the sofa, ready and willing to take flight at a moment's notice—although her hands wanted to reach out, and she wanted to lace her fingers through his. Frankly, she had to resist the powerful urge to do anything necessary to bring a smile to his lips, even if that smile was laced with cynicism. This was not a Matt she was accustomed to seeing, and it disconcerted her.

'You think I'm trying to take advantage of you? I'm not.' Matt felt as though he was standing on the edge of a precipice, arms outstretched, about to fling himself over the side in the wild hope that he would be caught by a safety net. He also felt very, very calm. 'I've done so many things wrong that I don't even know where to begin to try and explain myself, and I fully understand that you probably won't believe a word I say to you. Frankly, I wouldn't blame you. I entered into a relationship with you for the sex—pure and simple. I've been bitten once, and I've lived my life since then making damn sure that I wouldn't be bitten again. Every woman I've ever been with since Catrina has been like Vicky. It was easy never to become involved. My personal relationships were effectively, just extensions of my working life, with sex thrown in.'

Tess, all ears, found that she was holding her breath. With his walls breaking down, this was a vulnerable Matt laying his soul bare. She knew that instinctively, and she wasn't going to break the spell. Every word wrenched out of him was like manna to her ears. If she wasn't being hopelessly enthralled, she would be slightly ashamed.

'I should have questioned what it was I saw in you when you came along, but I didn't. I've always had absolute, unwavering control in my personal life. How could I expect that what I had with you would be any different?'

'And it was? Really? How different?' Tess cleared her throat and blushed sheepishly. 'It's important, you know—to…um…let it all out…'

'In that case, it's very kind of you to let me talk,' Matt murmured wryly. '*Very* different, in answer to your question. You made me a very different person. I did things with you that were all firsts—although at the time I hardly recognised it. I stopped work for you. Yes, I went to meetings—I organised deals, I met with the usual lawyers and bankers and hedge fund directors—but for the first time in my life I couldn't wait to get back to the apartment. I managed to persuade myself that that was because my relationship with my daughter was finally beginning to take shape. Of course that was part of the reason. You were the other part. You made leaving work behind easy.'

Tess allowed herself a little smile of pure joy, because whatever came out in the wash, nothing would ever erase the warm pleasure that his admission was giving her, and like a kid in a toy shop she didn't want the experience to end. When would she have the opportunity to visit that place again?

'When you asked to prolong our relationship, I reacted out of habit and instinct. Both told me to walk away. I didn't bother to question it, and once it had been done pride entered the equation. But you never left my head. It was as though you had become stuck there. No matter what I did, you followed me everywhere I went—a silent, nagging reminder of what I'd thrown away.'

'But you would never have said a word if I hadn't shown up in your office and told you that I was pregnant,' Tess said ruefully.

'Wouldn't I?' Matt caught her eyes and held her gaze. 'I'm inclined to think that I would have. I'm inclined to think that I would have been right here, in this place, doing what I'm doing now, even if you hadn't made life so much easier for me by falling pregnant.'

'But it was unplanned. You were furious. You *blamed* me!'

'I've never had any lessons in being in love. How was I to know what to say and how to react?'

'Being in love?' Her voice trembled, and her hands trembled too as he took them in his.

He stroked her fingers with his thumb. Sincerity blazed from his eyes. 'If I'd ever known true love,' he admitted gruffly, 'I might have recognised the symptoms. But nothing prepared me for you, Tess. Looking back, I can see that Catrina was just an expectation I fulfilled without thinking too hard about it. You were the unexpected. You crash-landed into my life and everything changed overnight. I didn't come here to take you away against your will, and I'm sorry that that was the impression I ended up giving.'

'You love me?' She repeated it with wonder, trying it out on her tongue for size and liking the way it felt. Too good to be true. But when she looked at him she knew that he meant every word of what he had said. 'I love *you*,' she whispered. 'I slept with you because I loved you. You were everything my head told me I shouldn't want, but you crash-landed into my life as well…'

'I want to marry you, Tess. I don't want to marry you because you're having our baby. I want to marry you because my life isn't complete unless you're in it. I want to go to sleep with you beside me every night, and I want to wake up in the morning with you right next to me.'

With a sigh of contentment, Tess crawled onto his lap and closed her eyes, happy to be enfolded in his warmth and to feel his fingers gently stroke her hair.

'I've never been so happy in my entire life,' she confessed. 'I think I might cry, given half a chance.'

'Will you marry me as soon as possible?' he breathed. 'I know you probably don't want to take the attention away from your sister, but I don't know how long I can wait. I want you to flash my ring on your finger so that every man out there knows that he's not to come within ten feet of you unless specifically given permission.'

Tess laughed into his shoulder, and then wriggled so that she could look up at him.

'That's ultra-possessive…'

'I'm an ultra-possessive man,' he growled, 'and don't ever forget it.' At last he felt free to touch her, to feel the wonder of her body that was slowly going to be transformed with his baby in it. He pushed his hands up under her tee shirt and groaned as the rounded curves of her breasts filled them. He stroked her nipples, and the familiar feel of them hardening under his touch was beyond erotic.

'Is there any chance that a family member might surprise me in the middle of making love to you?' he questioned in a shaky undertone. 'Because if there is, then we're going to have to get to your bedroom quickly. I love you and I want you and I need you. It feels like it's been years…'

Upstairs, on her small double bed, they made love with sweet, lingering slowness. To Matt it really did feel as though it had been years since he had touched her, even though it had been only a matter of a couple of weeks.

He touched her everywhere. He kissed and nuzzled the breasts that would enlarge over the months, and suckled on nipples that would darken and distend. When he came into her, her slippery sheath brought him to an almost immediate orgasm. Never had making love been such a liberating experience—but, then again, never had a woman unlocked him in the way she had…

They were married less than two months later. It was a quiet and very romantic ceremony, at the local church where her parents had been members of the congregation for ever. Matt's parents and a handful of close friends made the journey, and of course Samantha was the centre of attention and as excitable as it was possible to be.

Tess had never doubted that her parents would embrace Matt as a member of their family, and they did. She was more surprised and thrilled that his parents were just as warm and welcoming towards her. Maybe it was because they could see the devotion on their son's face whenever he looked at her, and the love on his daughter's face at the prospect of Tess becoming her stepmother.

Small but subtle changes took place over the ensuing months. They continued to live in Matt's vast penthouse apartment, which was convenient for Samantha's school, but they also bought a country house of their own, and spent most weekends there. Tess hadn't abandoned the prospect of a career in teaching, although she was now going to wait until the baby was born and then take everything slowly and in her stride. The fact that both Matt and Samantha had one hundred percent belief in her was a huge encouragement.

Tess had never thought that such happiness was possible, and her feelings of contentment must have transmitted themselves to her baby, for little Isobel was born without drama. Eight and a half pounds of apple-cheeked, green-eyed, black-haired, good-natured little girl.

She could only smile and agree when Matt, as he was fond of doing, told them that at long last he was where he had always wanted to be—surrounded by beautiful females who had finally succeeded in domesticating him.

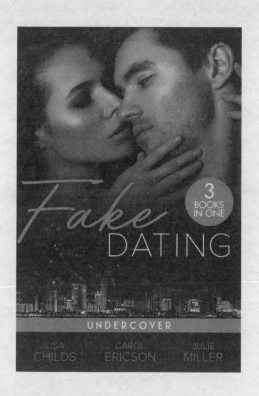

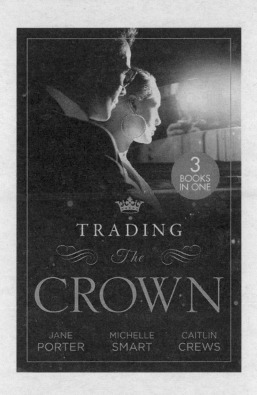

MILLS & BOON

MODERN

Power and Passion

Prepare to be swept off your feet by
sophisticated, sexy and seductive heroes, in some of
the world's most glamourous and romantic
locations, where power and passion collide.

Eight Modern stories published every month, find them all at:

millsandboon.co.uk

MILLS & BOON
True Love
Romance from the Heart

Celebrate true love with tender stories of heartfelt romance, from the rush of falling in love to the joy a new baby can bring, and a focus on the emotional heart of a relationship.

Four True Love stories published every month, find them all at:

millsandboon.co.uk/TrueLove

MILLS & BOON

HEROES

At Your Service

Experience all the excitement of a
gripping thriller, with an intense romance
at its heart. Resourceful, true-to-life
women and strong, fearless men face
danger and desire – a killer combination!

Eight Heroes stories published every month, find them all at:

millsandboon.co.uk

MILLS & BOON

Desire

Indulge in secrets and scandal, intense drama and plenty of sizzling hot action with powerful and passionate heroes who have it all: wealth, status, good looks…everything but the right woman.

Six Desire stories published every month, find them all at:

millsandboon.co.uk